A LEAP

✴

$\mathcal{J}$OANNA WAITED, scarcely breathing, her back pressed against the warehouse wall. Time trickled by. She was distantly aware of the lap of water against the pilings, the creak of rigging. The air smelled of salt mingling with the aroma of the tidal flats beginning slowly to be revealed as the current shifted. At any moment she feared to hear the clank of the anchor chain being raised.

A sudden shrill whistle pierced the night. Her moment had come. Heart in throat, Joanna darted from the shadows and ran swiftly down the lane toward the pier. Ahead of her was the bow of the bull's-head vessel. It rushed toward her as she ran, eclipsing all else in her sight. For the space of a heartbeat she thought of Hawkforte, of home and safety, of the peaceful routine of the days, of all that could be hers again if she only stopped, was sensible, went back.

Then she thought of her brother. And she discovered there was no decision to make.

A single breath, drawn deep. An instant to gird the soul . . .

Leaping high, hands stretching for the line, Joanna felt the dock, the land, the world she knew falling away beneath her in a great rush as exhilarating as it was terrifying. For a moment she hung suspended between one reality and the next.

Then the rope was in her hands, and she was pulling herself along without pause until her head bumped against the hull of the ship. She strained to see the nearby porthole. It was open and just large enough for her to squeeze through. She dragged herself toward it, clinging to the rope with her knees. Her head was through, her shoulders following. Something sharp scraped down her arm, but she scarcely felt it. The rope fell away behind her as she slid the remaining distance into the darkness. . . .

Also by

JOSIE LITTON

Dream of Me

Believe in Me

Come Back to Me

DREAM ISLAND

JOSIE LITTON

Bantam Books

NEW YORK · TORONTO · LONDON · SYDNEY · AUCKLAND

DREAM ISLAND

A Bantam Book
PUBLISHING HISTORY
Bantam paperback edition / March 2002

ISBN 0-553-58389-1

PUBLISHED SIMULTANEOUSLY IN THE UNITED STATES AND CANADA

Bantam Books are published by Bantam Books, a division of
Random House, Inc. Its trademark, consisting of the words "Bantam
Books" and the portrayal of a rooster, is Registered in U.S. Patent and
Trademark Office and in other countries. Marca Registrada. Bantam
Books, 1540 Broadway, New York, New York 10036.

PRINTED IN THE UNITED STATES OF AMERICA
OPM   10 9 8 7 6 5 4 3 2 1

For readers, who have been so kind and encouraging. For those who have written to tell me about sitting up all night to finish one of my books, about meals skipped and laundry undone, and even about unanticipated vacation days. Thank you! You make me smile, you make me laugh and you guarantee that I'll keep writing.

DREAM ISLAND

chapter
ONE

✴

June 19, 1811
London

$\mathcal{D}$AMN, IT WAS HOT. Not that Alex minded heat ordinarily. Indeed, he liked few things better than shucking off his clothes on a sun-drenched beach and letting the golden warmth touch every inch of his body. But that was a thought for a different time, so far removed from his present circumstances that it might have belonged to a world entirely apart from benighted England.

Worse yet, the heat stank. The combined smells of two thousand bodies, all liberally perfumed, were bad enough but the candles set in silver sconces and crystal chandeliers throughout the ballroom added the weight of melting wax to the already stultifying air. The odor clung to the heavy blue silk draperies festooned with the white fleur-de-lis in honor of the evening's exalted guests, the exiled French royals whose presence provided a fragile excuse for the Prince Regent to show off his latest extravagance.

The tall windows stood open, admitting not the relief of a freshening breeze but the stench of the London streets beyond and the crowds that still thronged them. Only the select few, if two thousand could be called that, had received the coveted invitation to the unveiling of the newly redecorated Carlton House. For weeks, the sound of teeth gnashing had competed with the frantic drumbeat of entreaties as the neglected jockeyed to avoid social catastrophe. How gladly he would have yielded his entrée to anyone who would have it, but that had never been a choice. He was, for better or worse, compelled to be precisely where he was, if only for a few more hours.

It was truly a challenge to decide which was worse, the heat, the smell, or the ever-mounting noise as the chattering guests struggled to be heard over each other and the combined efforts of the musicians playing manfully despite the total absence of any room in which to dance. Briefly, he sought distraction of a minor sort with the charming brunette who had attached herself to him shortly after his arrival. Lady Eleanor Lampert was the well-endowed widow of a wealthy lord who had married her when she had scarcely seventeen summers and he had solidly seventy. Presumably, he understood the risk. Dead six months later, it was widely rumored that he departed this world with his banner at an impressive full mast.

So now did Lady Lampert keep herself well amused. She shunned remarriage, being sensible about maintaining her independence, and chose her pleasures with care. Alex found her a skilled and worldly bedmate, which suited him perfectly. A woman clinging to his arm was acceptable in the short term; one clinging to his life was another matter entirely. When that happened, not if but when, for there was no question that he would wed, it would be in that entirely other world for which he found himself so unexpectedly yearning. Duty intervened, keeping him in England longer than he would have liked. But duty was life, life duty. He could hardly complain of the course he himself had set.

All the same, he had to leave soon. Not only this damnable ball but the country itself. His responsibilities were fulfilled, for a time at any rate, and he had been away too long. Just a few more days and he would be free...

𝒜 FEW DAYS. Hard to believe she had been searching for him only that long. It seemed a lifetime. Tromping about London, calling at his residence, leaving her card, ever ignored, slowly realizing he must have given orders after the first day that she was not to be admitted or given any information as to his whereabouts. Her cheeks still flamed at such treatment but she was determined. Embarrassment and frustration mattered no more than did discomfort. Even anger counted very little. She would find him. He would hear her out. He would help her. She would succeed. To fail was incomprehensible.

Perhaps it had not occurred to the exalted Lord Alex Haverston Darcourt, Marquess of Boswick, Earl of Letham, Baron Dedham that Lady Joanna Hawkforte was not without resources apart from her stubbornness. She might be lacking in allies among the *ton,* preferring as she did to keep the greatest possible distance apart from them, but she had money enough to acquire the season's most coveted invitation through the simple expediency of bribery and to hire a clever little man who skulked near her quarry's residence long enough to confirm his movements. Alerted to his departure for the Carlton House fête, Joanna had proceeded there in all haste.

Haste she strove mightily to conceal as she continued her search. Long ago, in what seemed another life, her beloved mother had taught her the language of the fan. Supposedly created by a clever Spanish lady, the coded messages allowed for a world of communication safe from eager ears. But not from discerning eyes, Joanna thought as she opened the exquisite fan of embroidered ivory silk that had been her mother's. It suited her unmodish gown of pale green silk well enough and that, in turn, complemented her hazel eyes and honey-hued hair sufficiently, but no such fashionable considerations had compelled her to bring the fan along. Rather had she brought it on impulse, for moral support. Her mother was long gone, her father as well. What family she might have left was lost on a distant shore. The fan, clutched tightly, gave her courage. She closed her eyes for just a moment and opened them to find herself staring over the ribboned silk at a man of such shocking beauty as to make her breath catch.

He appeared to her first in profile, the stark planes and angles of his face recalling the Greek statues she had admired five years ago during a visit to Athens with Royce. The high forehead beneath a sweep of midnight black hair, the forceful nose, full mouth, and firm chin aroused irresistible memories of the gods immortalized in marble.

Not that any stone could do justice to him. He radiated vitality and a kind of raw male strength that riveted her. When he turned slightly, she saw that his skin was bronzed by the sun. His brows appeared as dark wings set above eyes that even at a distance gave him the look of a hunter. Against the gaudy court fashion of the day, he wore black unrelieved but for a shower of white lace at his wrists and throat. Lace that served only to emphasize his unrelenting masculinity. Taller than any other man present, he held his head with a natural regality perfectly suited to the power of his body that no amount of tailoring could conceal. There was royalty in the room, all right, but it was of altogether a different sort from that of the plump Prince and his exiled French friends.

Different. Alien. And if the legends were to be believed, ancient.

Yet he was also English and just then she was glad to remind herself of that.

He smiled suddenly and she noticed the woman at his

side, the object of his amusement. A very beautiful woman with gleaming brunette hair and a magnificent figure draped in a gown of scarlet sarcenet cut in the tunic style with a low neckline and flowing lines that showed the lady to good advantage. Joanna required but a moment to put a name to that exquisite face: Lady Eleanor Lampert. The *notorious* Lady Lampert whose reward for kicking up her heels at propriety was the adoration of society. Capricious society, to be sure, and wounding when it chose. Best she concentrate on the man.

Or better yet, reach him. But that proved a daunting task for he was surrounded by a horde of hangers-on and sycophants that surpassed even those dancing attendance on the evening's host. Prinny might have resented that but he was said to admire Darcourt above all men, even fierce Wellington and fastidious Brummell. No wonder the elusive Marquess was present this evening. He must have known his absence at so august an occasion would leave the Prince Regent desolate. Mindful of his responsibilities, whatever exactly those were, he would set aside his well-known aversion for such events.

No doubt Prinny was pleased, but so, it seemed, was the entire *ton*, men and women alike, each and every one of whom appeared set on speaking with Darcourt. Joanna tried so long as she could manage to get even a small degree closer to him, only to find herself hurled back by a solid wall of people that proved to be impenetrable.

By midnight, exhaustion threatened to overcome her. It was all well and good for polite society to linger in bed until noon but she could never manage it, and most especially not since worry had become the constant goad to wakefulness. Coming to London had been her last resort, so she thought. But when no help was forthcoming from the Ministry, not even the acknowledgment that Royce could be in danger, she had conceived her admittedly desperate plan. To achieve it, she needed Darcourt's assistance. The unavailable Darcourt who even within sight remained beyond her reach.

REALLY, MY LORD, aside from managing to maintain himself in Lisbon, I fail to see what Wellington has accomplished to make him worthy of such praise as one hears these days. It's all bluster, if you ask me."

Alex had never had nor did he now have any particular desire to discuss military matters, a supremely sensitive subject upon which he was loath to reveal his particular expertise. But neither could he ignore the tall, slender man who had approached him through the press of the crowd. Charles, Second Earl of Grey and a power among the Whigs, was a close confidante of the Prince Regent's and thought likely to take the mantle as Foreign Minister when Parliament finally removed restrictions on the Regent's powers as it was expected to do within the year. Assuming, of course, that the stricken George III did not recover his sanity sufficiently to resume his rule.

"Wellington wears down the French," Alex said quietly. "Napoleon will tire of the drain on his men and matériel. He will turn elsewhere."

Grey shot him an assessing look quickly masked behind a smile of gentility. "Toward Britain, my lord? Is that what you expect?"

Alex hesitated. He was tempted to shrug off the question, yet he respected Grey. Besides, the well-placed aristocrat might be a convenient way to send a message. The Whigs assumed they would form a new government when Prinny came into his own and booted out his father's Tories. Alex privately thought they were wrong. Still, it didn't hurt to put a bee in more than one bonnet.

"Toward Russia," he said quietly. "Nothing else will salve his loss against the Turks."

Grey made a surprised sound he quickly sought to conceal, the result being that he seemed to bark. "My lord, Russia is Bonaparte's ally."

"An uneasy partnership, wouldn't you say? Rather like yoking two bulls together."

"Perhaps... Is this the Akoran view then? Is that what is expected beyond the Pillars of Hercules?"

Alex raised an eyebrow but did not reply directly. "I do not speak for Akora, my lord. Recall, I hold no diplomatic brief. My presence at court is purely unofficial."

"That is not the prevailing opinion, sir. It is believed you do indeed speak for your half brother, the Vanax. But perhaps even more importantly, you listen. If I may say, you do both very effectively."

"I appreciate the sentiment, my lord, but as you know, Akora maintains its sovereignty by maintaining its neutrality. Whatever thoughts may be held there about the current European situation are not spoken of beyond the confines of Akora itself."

"I defer to your wisdom in such matters, my lord." Grey inclined his head courteously. Yet the faint smile he allowed himself suggested he had in no way altered his opinion of Alex's true mission in England.

Nor, in all fairness, was there any reason why he should.

Grey turned his attention to Lady Lampert who exerted her usual effortless charm. They chatted amicably, Alex only half listening. He acknowledged the eager smiles and greetings of those clustered about him with a barely perceptible nod but did not let his attention linger long enough to invite conversation with any. Time had inured him to the changeless litany of gambits thrown out by those seeking to cultivate him. It was always the same: men of greed and ambition eager to boast of knowing him, dangling hints of political connections, claims of rare business opportunities, false camaraderie masking envy and sometimes even fear. And then there were the women. Between the eager mamas pushing forward their chicks in hopes of catching a title glittering with fortune and the blatant predators drawn by the exotic mystery he represented, he might have foresworn the ill-named gentler sex. Fortunately, there were also those like Eleanor, committed to enjoying life free of commitments.

It was all so unlike Akora, home of his heart. There women were . . . women, as they were meant to be. Understanding their place in life, they were content, never bold or intemperate as were so many English-women, including the one staring at him over the rim of her fan.

He had noticed her before in passing. For a scant moment, his eyes had fixed on her. She seemed distantly familiar in some way he could not place. Now, looking at her more directly, he felt a sudden shock of recognition. That honeyed hair, not quite blond or brunette, put him in mind of the beaches of Akora when they were damp from the lapping waves. And those eyes, slightly raised at the corners, staring at him with rare intelligence and determination.

She had come to see him several days before. A footman had brought her card, received his instructions that she was to be sent away. He had stood at the window of his library and watched her return to her carriage. That should have ended the matter but it seemed the lady was persistent. Despite himself, he could not deny a spurt of sympathy for her plight. If the rumors flying about London were to be believed, Royce Hawkforte had shown singularly bad sense or mayhap merely too great determination.

Alex's mouth tightened as he continued to contemplate her contemplating him. His own love and loyalty to his half brother made her concern understandable, yet there was nothing he could do for her. To involve himself in the disappearance of a British noble inevitably would involve Akora and that would be madness indeed. Besides, for all that he could understand her actions, he could also disapprove of them. The English were altogether too lax with their women. The lowest Akoran male would know better.

Deliberately, he held her gaze a moment longer before turning away. From the corner of his eye, he saw her frown and knew his point was taken. He had cut her quite directly, leaving no doubt of his unwillingness to acknowledge her. If a momentary twinge of guilt assailed him, he ignored it. For her sake, she should be left with no misapprehensions. Best she return to the countryside where she belonged. A few minutes later, when he glanced circumspectly in her direction, he expected to see that Lady Joanna Hawkforte was gone.

She was not. Incredibly, indeed astoundingly, she was headed straight for him. Unless he was very much mistaken—and at that moment, he was willing to question the evidence of his own eyes, so startling was it—she appeared to be *pushing* people out of her way in her determination, indeed by the look of it, her fury to reach him.

Damnable man. How dare he look at her as if she were something beneath his boot? After all the months of worry she had endured, the ever-growing dread, the fruitless effort to secure aid from those who should in all honor have stepped forward to help, and now this insufferably arrogant dismissal by a man obviously far too well accustomed to a life of privilege and indulgence. By God, it was not to be borne and neither was he.

"My lord—"

In the act of turning away, he stopped, turned back and looked at her. Really looked. She took the full impact of eyes so startlingly blue they seemed to hold within them the light of the noonday sun, and she just managed not to flinch. She would not give him that.

"My lord, I need to speak with you regarding—"

He held up a hand in a gesture of command so natural it could not have been other than inborn. His voice was steady and without expression. "I cannot accommodate you, Lady Joanna. I thought that had been made quite clear."

She was dimly aware of the people around them, listening avidly, and of Lady Lampert looking at her with unexpected sympathy, but none of that mattered. There was only Darcourt and the devastating blow he was dealing to the hope she had clung to all these months.

"My lord," she tried again, desperately, "I believe I understand your reluctance but—"

His tone turned cold as the wind of deep winter, cutting straight through to the bone. "It is not reluctance, it is refusal."

And with that, he did turn away, giving her his back. His very broad, elegantly garbed back. Short of pummeling it, there was nothing left for her to do.

Her head throbbed, probably because she was gritting her teeth. Disappointment churned within her sickeningly and with it terrible, clawing dread that she had failed. That all hope for Royce really was gone.

No!

Grappling for something, anything to hold on to, she stumbled away as the crowd closed behind her, a seething mass of hungry-tongued vipers delighting in the tidbit of gossip she had afforded them. Somehow, she reached the top of a curving staircase leading down to the lower level of the residence. Holding tight to the bannister lest in her sorry state she fall, Joanna descended into the midst of a vast army of servants scurrying frantically back and forth, all far too busy to take any notice of her.

The vise gripping her chest was easing slightly as she entered a room that proved to be a library, or so she assumed, given the vast quantity of exquisitely bound volumes arrayed along its walls in elaborately carved floor-to-ceiling cases set between golden columns. Whatever his failings, the Prince Regent was at least a man of letters with a genuine love of literature. Even so, she doubted the books would ever be so appreciated as were the volumes in Hawkforte's magnificent collection. Each and every one of those was lovingly cared for and enjoyed, including the precious illuminated manuscripts, among them works believed to have been created fully nine hundred years before, near the time of the family's founding.

Thought of home and all it meant settled over her, a balm of strength that brought slow but steady calm. Nine hundred years. Beside that, the present dynasty of Hanovers were parvenues. So, too, was virtually every man and woman in attendance at Carlton House. Except for Darcourt, she reminded herself, and found she had conjured his image in her weary mind. A shiver of revulsion moved through her as she relived the debacle. He assumed her defeated and no doubt had dismissed her from his mind with no more thought than he would accord a troublesome gnat. But between what insufferable Darcourt assumed and the reality of her determination was a gulf wider than any he could ever imagine.

She was Hawkforte, plainly, simply and defiantly. It was just as well she remember that.

Ignoring both the pounding of her temples and her weariness, Joanna continued on beyond the library. She found herself in a private dining room with walls and ceiling paneled in the heavily carved Gothic style. Bemused, and beginning to feel as though she drifted through a dream, she passed into a drawing room that at quick glance appeared done entirely in gold. Truly, were there no limits at all to the Prince's extravagance? Seemingly not, for next she arrived in an immense room, very long and narrow, walled in glass. A conservatory, then, but by far the largest she had ever seen. The light of a hundred or more Chinese lanterns shone on the immense table in the center of the room. Set with the most elaborate gold-and-silver service Joanna had ever seen, the table also boasted...

No, that couldn't possibly be. A stream meandered down the center of the table, twisting and turning between the platters and tureens. She moved closer, bending slightly to peer at what seemed a miniature world of moss-draped riverbanks, tiny bridges, flowering plants and there, swimming along the length of the stream, gold and silver fish gleaming in the glow of the hundreds of flambeaux illuminating the table.

Truly, Prinny had outdone himself. Considering the sybaritic excesses of his life to date, that was astounding.

The table awaited the Prince and his most select guests, Joanna definitely not among them. She and all the lesser mortals of the *ton* would be served outside in the garden where the efforts of the servants had now reached a fever pitch. Dozens of harried young men resplendent in the Prince's blue and white livery hurried back and forth, fetching a seemingly endless array of soups, roasts, cold meats, collations, fruits, pastries and the like along with bucket after bucket of iced champagne to a vast tent set up beneath the stars.

It was all very impressive for those who cared about such things. Joanna did not. While the night wore on and those all around her gorged greedily on the bounty of the Prince, she tasted only the growing bitterness of defeat. She could see Darcourt just beyond the conservatory windows, but he might have been miles away for all that availed her.

He was seated at the Prince's table, indeed very close to Prinny himself, who was rigged out for the event in the scarlet splendor of a field marshall's uniform, the honor of which had been long denied him by his father, who was no longer in any position to object. Nearby, the would-be King Louis XVIII, brother of the beheaded French monarch whose death it was said his actions had hastened, look flushed and ill-at-ease. He was rumored to suffer mightily from gout, believable enough given his massive girth that outdid even plump Prinny's?

His niece, the Duchesse d'Angoulême, was the ranking lady among the French, but her status and the attention Prinny was paying to her did nothing to relieve the quiet look of endurance imprinted on features that might otherwise have been appealing. She was said to be prey to headaches but Joanna rather thought her pain was of another sort. As a young girl, the Duchess had been imprisoned with her royal parents, aunt and brother. One by one, all of them had been taken away from her and beheaded. Only the capricious softening of the revolutionary tribunal's mood had saved her from joining them and propelled her instead into a life of exile.

Shattered family bonds seemed the theme of the evening. The Prince Regent's wife, the despised Caroline, was present in London but most definitely not among the invited. Indeed, it was whispered that Prinny had instructed the gloriously garbed Hussars who formed the night's guard of honor to go to any lengths necessary to stop the Princess of Wales should she be so ill-advised as to attempt entrance. Hers was not the only royal face among the missing. The Queen herself, disapproving of both her son's excesses and his disordered marriage, had declined to attend and kept her daughters from doing so as well.

And then there was the mad king, locked away yet again in the grip of the insanity that had come upon him four times before at intervals in his life but now showed no sign of abating, leaving no course but to make his eldest son and heir regent. In the past, that worthy and his brothers had amused themselves mimicking their father's deluded prattlings and frenzied gestures. It was not known if they similarly indulged themselves this time. Joanna could only hope not.

Despite all that, or perhaps because of it, most of the guests seemed almost feverishly gay. Darcourt was an exception. He looked . . . not bored exactly but resigned. Yes, that was it. He looked resigned. Although why he should appear that way she could not imagine. He was being courted by all, Prinny included, and Lady Lampert seemed intent on making herself most pleasant.

How very nice for him. How delightful that he could sit in such secure and privileged circumstances, fawned over and adored, while she dwelled in an agony of dread and Royce . . . She would not think of where her brother was just then, of what he might be suffering. Tears hovered far too close as it was. She could bear anything but to let them fall.

Pride rescued her. Eventually, the ugly, bloated, stupid fête would end. Darcourt would leave and so would she, right behind him. She would be his Nemesis, unrelenting and remorseless. He would not—could not—escape her.

THE FISH WERE DYING. Darcourt watched as yet another golden body floated up to the surface of the water, the gasping mouth stilled, the eyes rapidly clouding. There seemed to be no end to the Prince Regent's capacity for waste. The vast, extravagant mounds of food were beyond even the capacity of the crowd to devour and would likely spoil before being consumed even by the army of servants. The best efforts of the guests to drink themselves into insensibility would not exhaust the veritable sea of champagne being offered, much of which would end up flat and sour. The flowers, enough to fill a hundred gardens, were already wilting. And now the fish trapped in that ridiculous stream were dying. There went another.

Truly, the evening exceeded even his considerable expectation of tawdriness.

Across from him, Lady Lampert who for all her charms he would not describe as a sensitive soul, paled and pushed her plate away. "Oh, dear," she murmured, averting her gaze. The plight of the fish was drawing the attention of others up and down the table. An abrupt pall fell over the hitherto chattering guests. In the midst of a story about his own, utterly imaginary military prowess, the Prince Regent belatedly took note of the disturbance. He frowned, bunching loose ripples of flesh between his brows, and jerked a plump, beringed hand as though the gesture could erase that which displeased him.

Alas, it failed. Very quickly in the warmth of the conservatory, the fish began to smell. A certain greyish pallor began to make itself evident among the guests, particularly those most overfed, overwined, and overheated.

Alex's mood brightened for the first time in hours. It was almost five o'clock in the morning. Dawn would arrive soon, the traditional time at which brilliantly successful parties ended. Obviously, the Carlton House fête could be nothing less than a triumph, and would be, save for the stinking fish.

He leaned over slightly, catching Prinny's bloodshot eye. "Sire, I am certain those of your guests consigned to the garden could find no greater heightening of their pleasure in this event save for the delight of your company, now in its closing hours."

Prinny blinked once . . . twice. Through the haze of food, wine, and flattery, understanding dawned. He nodded, his head appearing loose on his stout neck. "Absolutely right, Darcourt. Very good of you to think of it. Much as I treasure the presence of all of you, my dear,

dear friends, we mustn't be selfish. I really should let myself be seen."

He rose so abruptly that the pair of footmen who raced to remove his chair only just managed to prevent it from being knocked over. The company stood with him and moved hastily away from the table now thickly littered with dead and dying fish.

"Thank God," Lady Lampert murmured as Alex came round the table to offer her his arm. "I could not have borne that another moment. What a canard! Truly, there do not seem to be any limits at all, do there?" This from a woman with her own keen appreciation for the unrestrained life. When even Lady Lampert was offended, things had come to a pretty pass indeed.

"I rather think not," Alex murmured. It was as close as he would come to criticizing their host. But privately his concerns about where the shallow, self-centered Prince Regent would take British policy were growing by the day. With Napoleon astride the continent of Europe, Britain looked for power and prestige wherever they could be found. Australia and India might not prove enough for them. They might, in due course, cast their gaze upon the small but strategically placed kingdom beyond the fabled Pillars of Hercules, perfectly situated to control entry to the Mediterranean.

Not, however, if he had anything to say about it. His words to Grey had been true, he held no official diplomatic brief from the Kingdom of Akora. But he was charged with a mission all the same, one with which he would allow absolutely nothing to interfere.

Outside in the garden, the nearest several hundred guests quickly clustered around the Prince Regent and his party, blocking off all others. Prinny no doubt believed them unable to contain their enthusiasm for their host, but to Alex's jaded eye, they looked mainly relieved by this signal that the fête was ending.

Nothing could compete with the dying fish, a tale

that would be repeated over and over, and likely be one of the very few details anyone actually remembered of the occasion. Still, the gardens would run a close second for they appeared to have taken a serious beating. Everywhere Alex glanced, bushes were trampled down, flowers destroyed, even several small trees appeared ready to fall. The guests themselves were in little better condition. Makeup on men and women alike was smeared, wigs askew, and lavish costumes stained from encounters with so much food and drink in such crowded circumstances.

The Prince Regent, having received the fawning gratitude of his guests, was preparing to retire. Alex restrained a surge of relief. He saw a momentary opening in the crowd and took it, Lady Lampert following with alacrity. They reached the edge of the garden even as Prinny turned, bestowed a last regal look upon his guests, and vanished back inside. Scarcely had he done so when Alex murmured, "Through here." A convenient break in the hedges led them out onto the lawn that gave way in turn to the gated wall surrounding Carlton House. Beyond that lay the city, the mob, and escape.

Alex spared a scant moment to observe that his strategy for a swift withdrawal had been well laid. His carriage awaited him precisely where expected, sufficiently removed from the press of the crowd to afford an easy exit. While less-farsighted guests remained caught in the crush of traffic until long after dawn, he and his congenial companion would find more comfortable surroundings for themselves.

With a nod to his driver, who was already in his perch, reins at the ready, Alex opened the carriage door, handed Lady Lampert inside, and followed swiftly. The wheels of the gleaming black landau were already rolling as he took his seat.

chapter

TWO

✴

JOANNA WATCHED THE LANDAU go with grim satisfaction. She had suspected Darcourt might make a swift exit and he had not disappointed her. How fortunate that she had taken the trouble earlier to note the location of his carriage, a task greatly simplified by the stunning perfection of his matched pair of greys. As Carlton House and the mass of people still surrounding it faded behind her, she allowed herself a small sigh of mingled relief and weariness.

Had she truly needed any reminder of why she did not enjoy society, the past few hours would have been more than adequate to that end. Although several people had stared at her outrightly and one or two had almost spoken to her, all had caught themselves in time to avoid the gaffe of affording a woman slighted by the illustrious Darcourt any real recognition. They were content to whisper behind their hands, cast speculative looks that sailed just slightly past her, and smile mockingly.

She could almost, for a flickering moment, be glad Royce was not there.

But then, had he been, the whole matter would never have arisen in the first place.

Or had Darcourt deigned to see her days ago, sparing

them both the unfortunate but ultimately meaningless scene in the Prince Regent's ballroom.

He would see her now, on that she was entirely resolved. Her carriage was close behind his own. Before he could reach the door of his town house, she intended to accost him and this time he would hear her out even if she had to shout the street down.

Except for one small problem. Glancing out the carriage window, she frowned. Darcourt was going away from, not toward his townhouse. Indeed, he appeared to be heading toward the river.

"Keep on him," she called to her driver. "Do not let him out of your sight."

The warning was timely for even as she spoke the fog that lingered so often near the Thames began to thicken around them. The grey light of early day should have been revealing the streets but instead they were slipping away into ghostly obscurity.

Joanna muttered a very unladylike remark under her breath and leaned farther out the carriage window. "What can you see?"

"Not much," Bolkum Harris returned. He was a short but well-set man with unkempt black hair and beard, and twinkling eyes. By trade he was a smithy, but when Joanna announced she would be journeying to London, he promptly announced his intent to accompany her. She allowed it both as the right of a man she considered an old friend and as a practical matter. London was, in her estimation, a nasty place. If she was to have a shadow, she preferred it have the spirit and strength of Bolkum.

"Where do you think he's headed?"

"Southwark, looks like. We're near the bridge."

Did the estimable Darcourt intend to top off a night of Prinny's hospitality by crawling through the stews of Southwark? And further, do it in the company of Lady Lampert? Joanna would have thought either unlikely, but she freely admitted she had no notion of what society found amusing.

"I can hardly see anything," she murmured.

"Ah, but listen," Bolkum advised, "we can hear them."

True enough, they could. The greys in their harnesses were not far ahead. There were very few other vehicles on the bridge at that hour and they were all lumbering wagons. Never could they be mistaken for so elegant and well-drawn an equipage as the landau.

"They're slowing," Joanna murmured a few minutes later. "Ease up a little."

Bolkum did so, bringing the carriage to a stop. They both heard the landau move on a little farther before it, too, came to a halt. One of the greys whinnied softly. Then there was only silence save for the nearby lapping of water against wooden piers.

"We shouldn't linger long, my lady," Bolkum said. "Elsewise we'll have trouble finding our way back."

"The sun will burn the fog off once it's up. But in the meanwhile . . ." Joanna alighted from the carriage. "Secure the horses, will you? Then come with me. I just want to get a look at where they went."

Bolkum did as she asked but grumbled all the same. "This is no place to be wandering about, my lady."

"It can't be far. We heard them stop." Joanna peered through the fog. She could still hear the water but also, she thought, the murmur of voices. With Bolkum close beside her, she started down the lane that ran between what looked like warehouses before ending in one of the innumerable docks that made Southwark the central port for London. Full day would reveal the proud masts of hundreds of merchant vessels, many heavily armed despite their peaceful purpose. The British navy still ruled the seas but the navy of the emperor Napoleon was closing the gap quickly. In such turbulent times, no sensible person set out beyond local waters unarmed.

A breeze cut slits through the fog. Joanna peered

through one, saw the shape suddenly revealed to her, and gasped. Her imagination must be playing tricks on her. For a moment, she thought she had seen—

Again, the fog parted. Through the wisps of spectral grey that twined around the dock and surrounding buildings, she could just make out the prow of a mighty vessel, rising far up above the waterline, curving like the throat of a mighty beast to its very peak where the horned head of a great, red-eyed bull glowed dully in the ghostly light. The vast, extended neck of the bull was deeply incised with elaborate carvings, as was the edge of the hull, so far as she could see it. Rigging on the powerful center mast clanked softly. Again, she heard voices and glimpsed several large men who appeared to be standing guard near the gangplank. They were speaking among themselves in a language she did not know yet, but which sounded hauntingly familiar.

Beside her, Bolkum stiffened and made to pull her back. She went unresistingly, all too well aware of the reasons for his concern. The vessel was unlike any other in the port. Indeed, it was different from any craft seen for several thousand years. Any, that was, save for the vessels of the legendary Kingdom of Akora, the fortress world wrapped in myth and mystery. The land beyond the Pillars of Hercules to which almost no foreigner had been admitted in uncounted centuries.

The land where Royce had gone and, although her heart cried out against it, quite possibly died.

"Akoran," Bolkum rasped between his teeth. He might as easily have said *danger*, so well known were the warriors of that land. Rumor had it that just within the last few years, a French expeditionary force had ventured into Akoran waters, never to be heard from again. Before that, there were other tales about eager Spanish, Portuguese and English explorers who thought to make their name penetrating the hidden kingdom. They, too, had vanished without a trace. Ancient though Akora might be, her weapons were of the most modern sort and her men apparently so adept at using them that they could stand against the strongest nations of the day.

"It is true then, what they say of the Earl?" Bolkum murmured as he continued towing her firmly back in the direction of her coach.

"That he is Akoran, or half so at any rate? So it seems."

A shiver moved through her as she spoke, part apprehension but the rest pure, unbridled astonishment that there truly was someone, however distant and remote, who personified the mystery of that faraway kingdom. For as long as she could remember, she and Royce had been fascinated by Akora. That was not so surprising, considering that Hawkforte boasted the only collection of Akoran artifacts known to exist anywhere beyond the kingdom itself. The jewelry and other items had been brought to England under rather mysterious circumstances in about the year 1100, at the time of the First Crusade. Family legend had it that a younger son had remained on Akora and that for some time thereafter, a connection of sorts had been maintained. That might or might not be true. What was certain was that the long, rainy afternoons spent in the library at Hawkforte with Royce, studying the exquisitely crafted pendants, arm rings, knives, statuettes and scrolls had instilled in both of them an insatiable desire to know more. For Joanna, there seemed to be no way of ever satisfying her curiosity but not so her brother. He sought a posting to the Foreign Ministry specifically because he knew interest in Akora was growing there daily.

"If they don't let in foreigners, as I've heard tell," Bolkum asked, "how come a fellow from there turns out to be an English lord?"

"Rumor has it the Marquess's father was shipwrecked on Akoran shores," Joanna replied absently even as she continued to mull over what she had just seen. "His life was spared because he was found by a beautiful girl who not only turned out, conveniently enough, to be a princess but also fell madly in love with him. It's a pretty story but there just might be something to it because about a dozen years ago, the then Marquess of Boswick who had long mourned his vanished son suddenly announced that he had a grandson."

"Turned up on his doorstep, did he?"

"I don't know the circumstances. I do know the Marquess promptly made the boy his heir. When his grandfather died five years ago, Darcourt became Marquess of Boswick as well as inheriting his other titles. That alone guaranteed he would be accepted in society, even without considering his fortune or the mystique that surrounds him. He is rumored to be the unofficial representative of the Akoran government. Royce met with him at least once."

Her words trailed away. Darcourt's presence on board an Akoran vessel hinted strongly that he was preparing to leave England. With him would go her last hopes of finding her brother.

"Up you go, miss," Bolkum said gently as he handed her into the coach.

Before he could close the door, she reached out a hand, catching his. "Do something for me?"

The smithy's hard face softened perceptibly. "Of course, my lady. You've no need to ask."

Breathing a silent prayer of gratitude for the unswerving loyalty of Hawkforte's people, Joanna said, "Take me home, then go by the Earl's townhouse. See if there is any indication that he is no longer in residence."

Bolkum nodded, stepped back, and closed the carriage door. A moment later, she felt the springs depress as he climbed into his seat. The wheels were turning when she leaned her head back against the tufted leather cushion and gave herself up, if only for some little time, to the fatigue of body and spirit that threatened to overwhelm her.

It was full morning by the time Bolkum deposited her in front of the gracious Mayfair establishment that had served as the Hawkfortes' London home for more than fifty years. But the fog was thicker than ever, requiring that the tall, wrought-iron lamps on each side of the entrance gate be left lit as they had been all night, awaiting her return. So, too, lamps burned in the spacious entry hall to which she was admitted by the stern-faced Mulridge, impeccably dressed as always despite the hour.

"Welcome home, my lady," the housekeeper intoned. "I trust the evening was satisfactory?"

"It was... enlightening," Joanna replied as she handed over her gloves and reticule. "I have an entirely new understanding of the word 'excess.'"

For several moments, she was silent as her mind conjured images of the past few hours, each more bizarre than the last, culminating in the sight of an Akoran vessel riding prosaically beside a London pier as though the veil of time itself had been rent. Aware that Mulridge was staring at her, she shook her head to clear it and met the housekeeper's sharp gaze. Mulridge was as usual and always ... Mulridge. Tall for a woman, she was about Joanna's height, with pale skin, deep-set eyes, and a blade of a nose perched above a tidy mouth.

Joanna had no idea how old Mulridge was but she had been precisely as she was now when she arrived at Hawkforte some fifteen years before and promptly made a place for herself. Her hair was black, her garb the same. She always stood ramrod straight and she seldom smiled. But she had a heart as good as any Joanna had ever known and could be fiercely protective when she chose.

"You could do with a bath," Mulridge said flatly.

Joanna wrinkled her nose and sighed. "I don't doubt it. It was quite a crush and dreadfully hot."

"Come along then. The water's heated."

Like the child she had been when Mulridge came, Joanna allowed herself to be prodded up the stairs. Then she had been nine years old, suddenly orphaned, and profoundly frightened. Royce had tried but he was only four years older and his own grief threatened to swallow him. The good folk of Hawkforte had done their utmost to help the children suddenly bereft of beloved parents swept away in a fierce summer gale. But it was Mulridge, stern and unbending, who had gathered both to her black-garbed breast, absorbed their tears, and helped them rebuild lives that for a time had seemed shattered beyond repair.

"I wasn't able to speak with Darcourt," Joanna said quietly. "I tried but he wouldn't listen."

They had reached the landing, where they paused. "I didn't think he would," Mulridge replied.

Joanna's throat tightened. "Damn man."

"Don't repeat yourself. Not that there aren't some good ones—Master Royce, for instance. But I knew the day you were turned away from the house of the fine Marquess that he would be no help."

Joanna stared up at the stained-glass window of the landing that on such a ghostly morning admitted very little light. Her eyes burned. "What would it cost him?"

"Who knows? Enough dawdling. You're too tired to be trying to think."

And so she must have been, for she was aware of very little more until she found herself stretched out in a steaming tub with a soothing cup of camomile tea close at hand. Mulridge moved quietly around the room, folding Joanna's clothes, laying out a nightrobe, turning down the bed.

"Don't stay in there too long. You'll get pruney."

From behind the floral modesty screen, Joanna managed a weak laugh. "Too late. At least I no longer smell like a rancid hothouse."

"Was it that bad then?"

"Worse. It was really quite incredible. No one looked . . . real. They were all so bewigged and bejeweled, their faces painted like masks, everything about them seemed artificial."

"All of them?"

No . . . not all. Not Darcourt. He had stood out, the unrelenting exception amid the crowd of popinjays, remorselessly himself. A small shiver ran through her as she remembered how he looked, and looked at her. "Pretty much all."

The water must be getting cold. She rose quickly, enveloped herself in the waiting towel, and held a hand out for the nightrobe Mulridge put into it. Moments later she emerged and glanced at the bed. "I don't think I can sleep. I never have been able to during the day."

"Perhaps not but you can lie down."

There was a knock at the bedroom door. Mulridge opened it to reveal one of the young maids, ever so excited to have been brought from Hawkforte. "Bolkum is back, my lady," the girl said. "He'd like a word with you."

"Tell him to wait," Mulridge instructed. "Her ladyship needs to rest."

"No, it's all right," Joanna said hastily. She pulled on a wrapper over her nightrobe. "I'll come down."

Bolkum was waiting in the entry hall. He ignored Mulridge's glare and inclined his head to Joanna. "Begging your pardon for disturbing you, my lady, but I thought you'd be wanting to know. It does look as though the townhouse has been closed up. I spoke to a tweenie from the residence next door and she said the Marquess has sent all his staff back to his country seat."

"Then he really is leaving," Joanna murmured.

Bolkum nodded. "It seems so." He and Mulridge exchanged a look. The housekeeper put her hands on Joanna's shoulders gently. "Back to bed with you then," she said.

Joanna went, mainly because at that moment she could think of nothing else to do. But later, staring up at the heavy silk canopy, a plan began to stir in her mind. At first she dismissed it as the far side of absurdity, but as the hours passed and no better option presented itself, it began to appear almost reasonable.

The PAPER HAD TO BE around somewhere. Faithful as the rising sun, *The Times* appeared each morning. Joanna considered that happy event to be one of the very few benefits of being resident in London. At Hawkforte, she had to wait for it to come down by post, which generally meant reading the news a day late.

In town, she expected to find the paper in the morning parlor where she breakfasted. But on this particular morning, or more correctly afternoon, *The Times* was not to be seen.

She had, despite all her expectations, slept if only a little and fitfully, too agitated by dreams to be rested. Rising was a relief, as was the temporary absence of Mulridge who had far too keen an eye. The housekeeper had gone out to market, leaving Joanna a solid hour or so to get herself in order.

But first she had to find the paper. It was not on the table or under it, nor was it tucked beneath any of the serving platters, the bounty of which expressed the staff's apparent belief that she had a plowman's appetite. A quick search of the floor revealed nothing, not even a missed speck of dust. Munching on a sweet roll, Joanna went into the hall and checked the table where mail was customarily left. There were several letters, none of any particular interest, but no paper.

Having exhausted the obvious possibilities, she sighed, swallowed the last of the roll, and stood very still. Her eyes half-closed, her breathing slow and deep, Joanna thought about the paper. She saw it inwardly, smelled the acidic scent of its ink, heard the rustling of its pages . . . reached out and . . .

Her eyes opened. She turned briskly on her heel and headed for the kitchens. Cook was in her parlor, taking a bit of well-deserved ease. The twin girls who served as tweenies, doing Cook's bidding, were in the garden behind the kitchens, having a fine time with a litter of kittens just old enough to be venturing out. Several footmen kept them company.

Joanna paused for a moment and cast an appreciative glance around the kitchens. They were her favorite part of the London townhouse, just as the kitchens at Hawkforte were her delight. She loved the high-ceilinged space bracketed at each end by a deep fireplace rigged with dripping pans, spits, and an intricate set of ropes and pulleys that allowed food to be positioned closer or farther away from the heat as needed. In between were stone sinks, marble-topped pastry counters, and cabinets holding the magnificent *batterie de cuisine* comprising dozens of gleaming copper pots and pans. In the center of the room was a wooden worktable some twenty feet long, its surface polished by a beach of sand applied over decades. The paper was on the end of the table nearest her.

Would that she could find Royce so easily.

The thought made her stiffen even as she pushed it aside firmly. There was no point dwelling on the vagaries of her strange gift. She could, when the circumstances were right, find things. Once she had even found a person. Pray God, she would do so again.

She plucked the paper up, leaned against the expanse of wood, and quickly found what she sought. *The Times* carried mainly commercial news, including the comings and goings of merchant vessels. In line with that, it also published the tide tables.

Apprehension trickled through her. What she contemplated was madness. At the least, she would be repeating the mistake Royce had made, the very one that might have led to his death. But what choice did she have really? To remain at Hawkforte, ignorant of his fate and tormented by it daily was unbearable. Any course was better than that.

Quickly, before she could think too much about it, Joanna went to the front parlor, took a seat at the spindle desk, and drew out paper, pen and ink. She wrote without pause, saying only what she must. When the letter was sanded and folded, she slipped it into the pocket of her high-waisted day dress and went back upstairs where she remained.

The rest of the day passed quietly. Joanna pleaded fatigue and kept to her chamber. She napped a little, then sat by the window, gazing out at the street but not seeing it. In her mind, she saw Hawkforte, the ancient gardens and majestic rolling lawns, the old stone walls of the original fortress that at this time of year blossomed with purple phlox, violets, pansies, bluebells, and primroses, and beyond all the sea, lapping gently at the shingle beach where she and Royce had played as children.

He had not returned to Eton after their parents' death but instead had stayed on at Hawkforte, the two of them clinging together as they slowly healed. His studies were continued with tutors who inevitably also found themselves teaching Joanna. By the time Royce was reading for Cambridge, she was fluent in several languages, adept at mathematics, and so well versed in the running of the manor that her brother didn't even hesitate before entrusting it to her rather than the expected steward.

It would be hay-making time at Hawkforte soon. She loved every season there, but especially the summers when the land so generously yielded its bounty. With very little effort, she could imagine the warmth of the sun on her face, the scent of newly mown fields, even the sweet tang of ice-chilled cider as the reward for labor well done.

Her heart cried out for the comfort of home with all its familiar rhythms. But she knew it to be a false hope. While yet Royce's fate remained unknown, there was no comfort to find anywhere.

Outside, the long summer twilight was settling over the city, softening the hard contours of buildings and bringing some relief from the warmth of the day. It was the hour when most people were in their homes, intending to stay there or busy preparing to go out for the evening. The street beyond was quiet, as was the house itself. Joanna rose and went over to the enameled wash basin painted with flowers and set in a teak cabinet. The water in the ewer was cool but that suited her perfectly. She splashed her face, struggling to banish fatigue, then burrowed in the back of her wardrobe to find the clothes she had chosen earlier in the day. Dressed except for boots, she gathered up the rest of what she had decided would be useful and secured it all in a small bundle she could carry easily. With all that done, there was nothing left save to wait for dark.

Glancing at the clock on the mantel to be sure she still had several hours before the tide turned, Joanna lay down on the bed again. She was certain that she was far too agitated to rest but decided she had best try anyway. Scarcely had her head touched the pillow than the exhaustion of a sleepless night overtook her and she fell into dreamless sleep.

Only to wake with a jolt sometime later. With a soft cry of surprise, she sat straight up in the bed and looked around. The room was illuminated by the flow of silvered moonlight through the thin summer curtains. Just then the clock chimed twelve times. Joanna groaned and grabbed for her bundle. Of all the damnable luck! There was real risk she would be too late.

Even so, she paused just long enough to place on her pillow the letter she had written earlier before easing open the bedroom door. Slowly and silently, she crept down the stairs. In the entry hall, a young footman sat with his head against his chest, sleeping peacefully. He was stationed there because London was prone to unrest, especially of late as the working poor feared the loss of what little security they had to the new factories sprouting across the land. Yet the footman's presence was only a gesture; no one truly expected Mayfair to come under attack.

Joanna did not begrudge him his rest. On the contrary, she breathed a small sigh of relief that he was not awake to see her slip past on her way to the kitchens. There she moved quickly, stuffing crackers, dried beef and a bottle of water into her small bundle. Though she was tempted to take much more, she knew she had to travel light. At the last moment, and purely on impulse, she snatched up a knife used for carving and added it to the rest. The kitchen door squeaked slightly as she eased it open. She froze for a moment, then breathed again when no sound came from the nearby rooms used by Cook. As silently as she could, she closed the door behind her and hurried along the brick path that led to a side gate.

Despite the warmth of the night air, she shivered. She had gone over the route in her mind again and again throughout the afternoon, but knowing which way to go and actually doing so were two quite different things. By night, familiar landmarks were erased. Before she walked more than a few dozen yards from her front door, she recognized almost nothing.

But then that was to be expected for she had spent little time in London, finding it tedious in the extreme. It would be foolish to imagine she would feel at home in such a place. She *knew* the route. All she had to do was keep her wits about her and follow it. By the time she reached the river and crossed over to Southwark, it was very late. Her heart beat frantically as she ran the last few streets to the pier where she had seen the Akoran vessel. If it was already gone . . .

Her relief at the sight of the bull-headed prow illuminated by torches gave way quickly to awareness of the enormity of what she was about to attempt. Instinctively, she stopped and pressed herself into the shadows of a warehouse. The sound of her heartbeat seemed very loud in her ears, so much so that she fancied it might give her away. Any moment, one of the guards on the dock would turn, see her, and her chance would be lost.

One man stood at either end of the pier, another at the central gangplank. More were visible on deck. In the fog of early morning, she had seen only that they were very large. Now she could also make out that they wore tunics ending above their knees with wide belts cinched at their waists. From those belts hung the glittering scabbards of short swords. They looked for all the world like beings from another time, perhaps from the frescoes of ancient Greece. Yet they were all too real.

A quick glance to either side revealed that no other ships were docked near the Akoran vessel. That hardly surprised her. So great was the mystery and mystique hanging over the Fortress Kingdom, and so entrenched were the superstitions of sailors, that she understood full well why no capitan would dare to drop anchor within hailing distance of them. The warehouses to either side of the quay also appeared deserted but that was likely because of the hour. Farther on, down the winding lanes and alleys of Southwark, she could hear faint laughter coming from the dens of iniquity that flourished there. She could wish that one such den were a good deal closer. As it was, she would have to go in search of what she needed.

She found it outside a dank tavern that looked half sunk into the ground, as though occupying premises old when the Romans knew London. The night being warm, the patrons had spilled outside where they sat downing gin and ale, playing at dice by moonlight, and fondling the amiable barmaids.

A pair of young boys lingered nearby. Joanna observed them for several minutes. In the healthful environment of Hawkforte, their size would make them about ten years of age. But here in the noisome city where growth was often stunted, they were likely to be somewhat older. Although on principle she disapproved of children being about at such an hour, and even more so of involving them in anything even slightly nefarious, she was not so blind to reality as to imagine her offer would be regarded as anything other than great good fortune.

Even so, she approached cautiously, waiting until she caught the eye of one of them to jerk her head to the side. As she stepped away from the crowd outside the tavern, she did not look back. The soft footfall behind her told her the pair was following.

She moved only a little distance off where she could speak to them privately. They stood, shoulders hunched, hands deep in the pockets of their tattered pants, and regarded her with a mixture of youthful excitement and too-old suspicion on their thin faces. Quickly, before she could think better of it, Joanna said, "I need a job done and I'll pay well. You two interested?"

"A jawb?" the bigger of the two, by an inch or so, repeated. He looked her up and down boldly and sneered. "Wha' sort o' jawb likes o' ye gawt? Ye tawk flash, right 'nuff, but yer no swell."

True enough, in the boy's clothes she had found in the attic of the London house, presumably left behind long ago by Royce, and with her hair tucked up under a cloth cap, she looked anything but the lady she was. At best, she might be taken for a stablehand. But one with coin to spend.

"A guinea now and a guinea after." When still they looked at her skeptically, she added, "For each of you."

She was taking a terrible chance and knew it. Realizing that she had money, the boys might simply decide to rob her. But poverty was no bar to honor, and they might also be drawn by a chance for adventure.

"Wha' ye be wantin'?" the second boy demanded. He had taken a step back and was already glancing over his shoulder toward the relative security of the tavern.

"I need help getting on board a ship docked near here. I want you to stage a diversion of some sort to draw the guards off." Quickly, she added, "But I don't want you to be hurt or endangered in any way."

The boys exchanged a glance. The taller one licked his lips thoughtfully. "Wha' ship?"

"Perhaps you know it? The Akoran vessel, the one with the bull's-head prow."

Two pairs of eyes opened wide and stared at her in dawning respect. "Ye aim t'board *her*?" the smaller boy asked on a note of awe.

The other clung to a thread of practicality. "Ye crazy, 'doff. Nobody with a brain in his head goes near them."

"You know who they are?" Joanna asked.

The boys nodded. "Aye," the smaller said. "That's their pier, they own it an' t'warehouses, too. Ships from there come in every few months or so. Lahk Noggin says, *nobody* goes near them an' they don' mix with anyone. Stay t'themselves, they do, an' seem t'want it that way."

Joanna's stomach tightened yet further but she ignored it and kept her voice steady. "Whether they do or not, I have to get on that ship. As I said, I'll pay well. Will you help me?"

Again, the boys looked at each other. Noggin spoke for them both. "Le's see yer money."

Gingerly, wondering if she was about to be coshed over the head and robbed, Joanna reached into the pouch under her felt jacket and carefully removed two guineas. They glinted in the light of the torches around the tavern. "And another two when it's done."

For a moment, the pair could do nothing but stare at the gold coins. Belatedly, Joanna realized it likely that they had never in their lives seen so much money at one time, much less thought to possess it. Again, she struggled with her guilt at involving them but whatever qualms they had vanished like ice in the sun. Grinning broadly, Noggin said, "Both now less after yer in no shape t'pay anyone."

Not a pleasant thought, to be sure, but a solid one all the same. With a quick nod, Joanna reached into her pouch again. "All right, but come with me to the pier first."

They trotted after her. At the top of the lane leading to the Akoran dock, she paused. Softly but with unmistakable firmness, she said, "I really don't want either of you hurt. You understand?"

"Aye, 'course we do," Noggin said, his gaze on the Akoran vessel riding at anchor. "Wha's yer plan then?"

"You stage a diversion, draw off the guards."

He rolled his eyes. "An' then wha'? Ye 'ave thought this through, 'aven't ye? Me an' Clapper can di-vert all ye wan' but how ye' plannin' t'get on board? Not gonna prance up the gangplank, are ye?"

Clapper snickered but silenced quickly when Noggin glared at him. Together, they waited for her reply.

"Is there... uh... something wrong with the gangplank?"

Noggin sighed deeply. "Look, we know these covs, least some ways. Lahk I said, they're here every few months or so. They don't take any chances. Their ships are guarded awl day long an' awl night, on deck an' on t'pier. We cause a commotion, some o'them are gonna wanna see wha's on but they aren't no fools. They're soldiers, see, real ones. Tough as they come, my old man says, an' he ought t'know bein' he did fifteen years at t'mast. Some of 'em'll stay on deck jus' in case someone's daft enough t'try wha' yer plannin'. Ye gotta find a way 'round them."

"There's portholes," Clapper said. "Bow an' stern. Warm tonight. Lahk t'be open."

"Go fer t'bow," Noggin instructed. "I seen 'em loadin' cargo down that end." Again, he looked at her narrowly. "Ye can swim, can't ye?"

"Of course I can and I do appreciate the advice." Quickly, before her nerve failed her, Joanna handed over the coins. "Remember, be careful."

The guineas vanished into grubby hands. A moment later, the boys disappeared into the darkness.

chapter

THREE

✳

$\mathcal{J}$OANNA WAITED, scarcely breathing, her back pressed against the warehouse wall. She had no idea if she had just been robbed or if she was about to attempt a leap across a precipice that, even if she made it, might prove deadly. A clammy warmth spread over her. She swallowed hard and forced herself to breathe deeply. Time trickled by. She was distantly aware of the lap of water against the pilings, the creak of rigging, the far-off sounds of the tavern and beyond all that the muted night murmurings of the great city itself. The air smelled of salt mingling with the aroma of the tidal flats beginning slowly to be revealed as the current shifted. At any moment, she feared to hear the clank of the anchor chain being raised.

What if the boys had gone? What would she do? Try to get on board unseen on her own? Or simply storm the vessel, demand to speak with Darcourt, and pray that somehow this time he would listen to her?

Neither seemed a good prospect, but she was just at the point of thinking she had to seriously consider doing one or the other when a sudden shrill whistle pierced the night. Following the sound, she stared up at the roof of the warehouse opposite her. To her astonishment, two figures danced there gleefully, silhouetted by the moonlight as they waved their arms, jumped up and down, and yelled for all to hear.

"Hey there! Fancy covs, ye on t'boat! We got yer warehouse. It's ours now! Wan' it back, come an' git it!"

Shock warred with laughter as Joanna beheld the pair. Even as she was terrified they might fall, she had to admire their ingenuity. They were visible enough to attract the attention of the guards but far enough away to elude immediate capture.

As she watched, several of the Akoran men looked toward the warehouse roof. She could hear them talking among themselves. Within moments, four of the guards were dispatched. They moved out in pairs, rapidly flanking the warehouse in what looked even to her relatively untutored eyes like a military maneuver.

The rest of the guards remained in place but their attention was directed toward the warehouse roof and the boys who continued to prance and shout there.

Her moment had come. Heart in throat, Joanna darted from the shadows and ran swiftly down the lane toward the pier. Behind her, Noggin's and Clapper's voices grew fainter. She guessed they had come down from the roof and were drawing the men farther off. But the Akorans were unlikely to follow wherever they happened to lead. Once they saw the warehouse was safe, they would return to the dock.

That left scant minutes. Ahead of her was the bow of the bull's-head vessel. It rushed toward her as she ran, eclipsing all else in her sight. For the space of a heartbeat she thought of Hawkforte, of home and safety, of the peaceful routine of the days, of all that could be hers again if she only stopped, was sensible, went back.

Then she thought of Royce.

And discovered there was no decision to make, for it had been made long ago in the quiet, raucous, happy, mourning moments of being brother and sister, being for each other. It had always been there, just waiting deep inside her for ... *now* ...

A single breath, drawn deep. An instant to gird the soul ...

Leaping high, hands stretching for the line, Joanna felt the dock, the land, the world she knew falling away beneath her in a great rush as exhilarating as it was terrifying. For a moment, she hung suspended between one reality and the next.

Then the rope was in her hands, hard as stone, and she was digging her fingers into it to hold on as she scrambled, twisting suddenly so that she was staring at the sky but pulling herself along without pause until her head bumped against the hull of the ship. She strained to see the nearby porthole. It was open and just large enough for her to squeeze through. Her hand grappled for the edge, caught. She dragged herself toward it, clinging to the rope with her knees. Her head was through, her shoulders following. Something sharp scraped down her arm but she scarcely felt it. The rope fell away behind her as she slid the remaining distance into darkness.

A matter of mere seconds. A lifetime.

She fell hard against wood and lay there panting. Despite the warmth of the night, she felt icily cold. Her limbs shook. Instinctively, she curled into herself, hugging her knees. While yet she trembled in reaction to what she had just done, she raised her head and looked around. No lights were visible but by the moonlight filtering through the portholes, she could make out rows of bunks with lockers built in beneath them for storage. There was a table bolted to the floor in the center of the room with benches ranked on the two long sides of it. Hooks on the walls held an array of shields and weapons.

Crew quarters. She had managed to land herself right in the midst of the quarters used by the very guards she was trying to avoid. Thankfully, no one was about but that could change at any moment.

Scrambling to her feet, Joanna ignored the stab of pain in her arm and darted for the door at the far side of the room. She flung herself through it without stopping to think someone might be on the other side and was hugely relieved to find the narrow corridor empty. About ten feet away in the floor of the deck was a trapdoor. She ran to it, pulled up on the metal handle, and as the trapdoor swung open, stared down into a dark abyss. Only after a moment did she realize that she must have found an entrance to the cargo hold. Her imagination raced ahead of her as though she had already been swallowed by the blackness below. For a moment she pulled back, looking frantically in all directions as she sought some other refuge. None appeared.

Footsteps sounded directly above her head. She heard voices that seemed to be coming closer. Stripped of choices, Joanna said a quick prayer, lowered herself into the darkness and pulled the trapdoor shut behind her.

At first, the utter black of the hold seemed impenetrable. Panic threatened but she forced herself to breathe slowly and deeply. When that proved insufficient, she thought of Royce. Focusing on her brother, and most particularly on her love for him, shored up courage that might otherwise have wavered. Gradually, her fear receded. She remained aware of it but as though from a distance where it could not hurt her. That was just as well since her circumstances presented danger enough.

Without sight, all her other senses seemed suddenly more acute. She was aware of every sound near and far, the creak of the hull, the muted voices still audible but no longer so immediately threatening, the bump of cargo moving very slightly. The hold smelled of wood, tar, salt and more. She could detect the faint but earthy aromas of olive oil and wine, hay and horses, leather and something else . . . sharp and oddly cold . . . iron.

Instinctively, Joanna reached out her hands. At first, she encountered nothing but when she took several steps forward, she walked straight into something very large and very hard. Her fingers felt the slightly rough contours of rounded metal that stretched out for several feet to either side of her, narrower to her left, widening to her right. Whatever it was seemed to be secured to the deck of the hold by strong chains. Cautiously, she felt toward the left, bending slightly. A new smell reached her, very faint but unmistakable. Gunpowder.

The metal tube she touched smelled of gunpowder.

Cannon. The Akorans had at least one cannon in their hold. Nor did she have any reason to think it was alone. As she continued to feel her way, Joanna encountered two more, also unusually large. There could well be others she hadn't found.

Years ago, Royce had conceived a fascination for weaponry common to young boys. No detail had been too arcane to enthrall him or to impart to the younger sister always happy to share his interests. Never had she imagined such knowledge would be of the remotest use. But now it allowed her to recognize that the cannons were much bigger than was common. Likely there were no more than a few foundaries in the world that could cast barrels of such size. The Akorans were reputed to be expert armorers yet apparently they were not adverse to acquiring even better weapons from beyond their borders. That surprised her for they were also said to reject all foreign influences.

Before she could wonder about the seeming contradiction, she was jolted back to awareness of her immediate circumstances by the sudden creak and clank of the anchor chain being raised. Quickly, Joanna stumbled until her hands found the nearest wall. She sank down against it, clutching the bundle strapped across her chest and taking deep breaths in an effort to calm herself. For better or worse, she was committed to a course that by any reasonable measure was lunacy. Yet the absolute certainty that she could not have done otherwise brought her a measure of comfort.

So, too, she had ever been an excellent sailor even after fate stole her pleasure in it. Despite the grim circumstances, the steady rocking of the vessel slowly eased the tension from her body. In its place came the fatigue of almost two full days with very little sleep. Her eyelids grew heavy and shortly her head drooped. Though she would not have thought it possible, Joanna slept.

And woke out of darkness into light. Faint light, to be sure, just the hint of day creeping through the planks of the deck above her head. But enough to make her surroundings far more visible than they had been the night before. She saw the cannons first and marveled at them anew, wondering what place she found herself in, until memory returned. With it came a shock that she had actually done as she set out. At least for the moment.

Before the full enormity of what she had done could sink in, Joanna began to stand up but stopped when she was struck by a wave of pain. She groaned and clutched her arm only to start in surprise when she felt the warm seep of blood against her palm.

"What—?"

Eyes widening, she stared down at the left sleeve of her shirt, seeing it darkly stained with old blood, against which the bright red of new bleeding shone brightly. Dimly, she remembered hurting her arm when she came through the porthole. Shock and exhaustion must have combined to render her oblivious to the seriousness of the wound. It had bled enough in the night to crust over but now she had reopened it.

Gritting her teeth against both the pain and this new source of worry, she eased the fabric away gingerly until she could slip her arm out of the sleeve. What she saw made her wince all the more. The cut was deep enough to account for the bleeding and was about six inches long, starting just below the curve of her shoulder. Were she at Hawkforte, she would waste no time making sure it was cleaned out thoroughly, stitched and bandaged to prevent further injury. In the hold, with only the small amount of water she had brought, the very rudimentary medical kit she had thought to pack, and no one to help her, she had very little chance of doing much of anything. Still, she had to try.

Used very sparingly, she had intended the water to last the better part of two days, by which time she expected to be far enough out to sea to risk sneaking out for fresh supplies. If she were caught, she reasoned, Darcourt would be disinclined to turn back. However angry he might be, and she assumed he would be very angry, she doubted that he would chuck her into the sea. At least she hoped not. But now it seemed the water would be gone much sooner. She would simply have to do without until such time as she thought it safe to seek more.

Long, painful minutes passed before the wound was finally cleaned and wrapped in linen torn from the extra shirt she had also brought along. The effort exhausted her and in its aftermath, Joanna sank back down onto the floor. There were crackers and dried meat in her pouch but she had no strength left to eat. Instead, she sat with her head against the wall of the hull, trying very hard to ignore the still burning pain of her arm.

Some unknown length of time passed. Above her, she heard the voices and movements of the crew. All around her, she felt the motion of the ship. By now, they would be somewhere off the coast of France. The French fleet would be on patrol but she doubted any French commander would be so foolish as to trouble an Akoran vessel, even one so obviously outward bound from England.

She dozed a little more and woke to a raging thirst. Though she tried to restrain herself, before she realized what was happening she had drained what was left in the canteen by more than half. With a heavy sigh, she forced herself to put the rest away for another time. Although she still had no appetite, she chewed and swallowed most of a cracker and several bites of dried beef. That would not sustain her for long, as she well knew, but she could not manage more.

Feeling stiff and sore in every bone, she stood and moved around the hold a little, trying to take advantage of the daylight while yet it remained. Besides the three cannons she had found by touch in the dark, there were three more, all of similar size. There were also dozens of wooden crates she suspected held shot for the weapons. Yet all that together did not fill the hold which could have accommodated far more. Akora's wealth was as legendary as the Fortress Kingdom itself. The cannons were proof that for once the stories were true. No lack of riches prompted the disinclination to fill the hold. The relative emptiness spoke to a rejection of anything foreign.

Anything except weapons that could strengthen the fierce Akoran defenses even more.

Had Royce considered that? When he embarked on his journey, had he given any thought at all to the immense risk he was taking?

Yes, in all likelihood he had for he was a sensible man, not given to selfish or impulsive behavior.

"I will be back by Christmas," he had assured her when he came to Hawkforte just before departing. She could still see his smile as he added, "Don't wear yourself out worrying. Everything will be fine."

But Christmas had come and gone six months before with no sign of Royce. Everything was not fine nor, she feared, would it ever be again.

Impatiently, she shook her head. This was no time to let fear overtake her. She had to keep her wits clear, the better to deal with whatever might be coming.

Yet that proved surprisingly difficult. As the hours wore on, the pain in her arm first increased, then drifted away from her, taking up residence some little distance off where she was still vividly aware of it yet seemed unable to mind. She found herself lying on the floor of the hold and did not remember getting there. At least it was warm. Indeed, very warm, unusually so for the time of year, what with being at sea. She had expected it to be chilly, had even brought along a thin blanket, all she could manage, in case it should prove needed. But far from wanting a blanket, she began to yearn for ice, imagining the ponds around Hawkforte in the winter when the ice would be thick enough for skating. How lovely it was, all cold and white, packed away in the icehouse where in summer it would provide precious shavings to cool fruits and run over the tongue in tantalizing relief from the heat.

So much heat. She moaned and pulled at the collar of her shirt, trying to ease her breathing. They must be much farther south than she had thought. Perhaps they had been traveling longer and she unaware. Akora would be very warm, would it not? Rather as Greece had been. Greece, from where it was said the Akorans had come originally.

Was that possible? Could anything so ancient have survived? Royce had thought the legend true. Part of his wish to travel to Akora had been founded on the conviction that he would find answers to many of his questions about ancient Greece.

Dear Royce, so good a brother. So good a man. How bitterly unfair if he had come to harm. The thought of him in distress was unbearable to her.

Unbearable . . . Rousing briefly from the daze of fever, Joanna gasped at the searing pain that radiated from her arm. She fumbled for her canteen, managed to find it, and drank what little water remained. Exhausted, she fell into a restless sleep. When she woke again, it was dark.

While yet it was night, and her movements more easily concealed, she really had to go in search of more water.

But when she tried to get to her feet, the vessel tipped alarmingly, making her wonder if they were caught in a sudden storm. Even so, she managed to stumble toward the ladder that led up to the trapdoor. She got her foot on the lowest rung, but just then her balance failed and she fell hard against a nearby crate. It skittered against the wall with a loud thump.

ALEX SET DOWN the tankard he had just drunk from and looked toward the door of the crew quarters. As was his custom on every voyage, he was taking supper with his men. It was the Akoran way for commanders to share the lot of their soldiers to a degree unknown in England or on the Continent. That suited Alex well. He liked the comradeship of his men. The bond forged between them on missions such as this could make the difference between life and death in battle. Officers who set themselves apart were, in his view, the cause of needlessly prolonged wars. Better the tight cohesion of the unit that could smash the enemy swiftly and ruthlessly, saving lives by quick victory.

In his spare time, what little there was of it, he was writing a treatise on the subject, contrasting the leadership styles of Akoran and British commanders. He just might manage to get some work done on it that evening.

Assuming he could identify the source of the odd thump he thought he had heard coming from below in the direction of the cargo hold.

"Is something wrong, *archos*?" the man seated beside him asked. He spoke quietly enough, but the use of Alex's title in these informal circumstances caught the ears of the twenty other men sharing the table. Instantly, all conversation ceased as they gave their commander their full attention.

"I heard a sound from the hold. The cargo may be shifting."

He was on his feet as he spoke, and the men with him. All knew the unlikelihood of such an event but appreciated its seriousness as well. With thousands of years of accumulated expertise in seamanship to draw upon, the average Akoran could secure cargo with his eyes closed. The men of the *Nestor* were anything but average and the cargo they carried had received the greatest care. Still, they were not in the habit of leaving anything to chance.

Neither was Alex. He was out the door before the last knife was set back down on the table, not hurrying but moving with fluid grace. While several of the other men stood by with oil lamps, he lifted the trapdoor to the hold. First down, he paused for a moment in the darkness until one of the lamps was handed to him. Holding it high, he looked around carefully.

None of the cannons appeared to have shifted, nor had the crates of ordnance. Yet he had no doubt of what he had heard. He moved away from the ladder, aware of several other men coming down behind him but his attention focused on his surroundings. He stood very still, only his eyes moving slowly, seeking anything out of place, anything unusual...

Such as the sudden flutter of movement toward the far wall. He was there in half a dozen strides, his arm lashing out to grasp the slender form that tried to melt into the bulkhead. Yanked into the light of the torches, the stowaway looked like a slim, disheveled boy. For just a moment, Darcourt assumed that was what he had found. But the illusion was fast fleeing. Too soon, he took in the fall of honey-hued hair tumbling around a face overwhelmed by large hazel eyes.

Shock filled him. This could not possibly be. It was out of keeping with everything he knew of the proper ordering of life. Yet with the keen edge of disbelief came a strange sense of inevitability. He was not a superstitious man; Akoran teaching did not hold with that. Yet he

was schooled to a philosophy that saw order and even inevitability to the pattern of life. Man controlled his own
destiny to an extraordinary degree, yet fate existed, it
was real. Only the fool believed otherwise.

Alex was very far from a fool. He was a warrior and a
leader. A man of iron control who had proven his worth
in the trials of combat and hardship that were expected
of anyone who aspired to the title of *archos*. He had
marched, swum, climbed, fought and endured without
water, without food, without sleep and without complaint. Never had he allowed his feelings to govern his
actions.

Until now. The expletive that broke from him caused
the men nearest to take several steps back. Oblivious to
their startled gazes, he strode from the hold, dragging the
girl along with him.

"Of all the harebrained, idiotic, insanely dangerous
schemes—" With every step down the corridor, Alex's
anger mounted. He'd been right to think Englishmen
were too loose with their women. Nothing else could
possibly explain how a well-born girl who should have
been living in comfort and safety on her family's manor
had instead taken it upon herself to stow away on a ship
bound for a kingdom everyone knew did not welcome
foreigners.

"What could your brother have been thinking? Bad
enough to go off in the first place, but to do so without
making proper provision to keep you out of trouble?"
The Akoran way was the right way. Women knew their
place and kept to it. However much change was coming
to Akora through the efforts of the Vanax and Alex himself, *that* at least would remain the same and damn glad
he was of it.

Reaching the door to his quarters, he thrust it open
and pushed the girl in ahead of him. She staggered
slightly and almost fell but righted herself. Holding on to
the edge of the table, she turned and glared at him. By

the glow of the lamp, she looked very young but also very determined.

"You left me no choice! The Foreign Ministry was useless and you refused to even speak with me. What else could I do?"

Her defiance stunned him. By all rights, she should be cowering, begging his pardon and his indulgence. Instead she faced him with unflinching determination.

They would see about that.

"You could have done what any proper woman would have, gone back to wherever it is you came from and let others handle this matter." He spoke with deceptive mildness hardened by a thread of steel.

"That's exactly what I did for six months! Just how long do you think I should wait, not knowing if my brother is dead or alive?" Before Alex could answer, she leaned against the table, clasping her left arm. The tumult of her hair concealed her expression but he was instantly suspicious.

"What's wrong with you?"

"Nothing, I'm fine. God, how I wish there had been some other way!" With each word, her voice grew thinner and fainter. She broke off on a deep sigh, as though struggling for breath.

"You are ill?"

She shook her head but Alex was having none of that. What else could he have expected? Of course it wasn't enough that she had stowed away, she would be hurt in the bargain. When the gods amused themselves at a man's expense, they had a tendency to overdo.

"What happened?" With a hunter's instinct, he spoke more gently even as he closed in on her.

She looked up, alarmed, and tried to back away but he was too quick. He had a chair under her and her in it before she knew what had happened. In the process, he brushed a hand along her cheek and felt the heat pouring from her.

She was still clasping her left arm. The sleeve around it was darkly stained.

"I got a cut coming through the porthole," she said weakly. "But it's all right. I've taken care of it." Looking up through the tangle of her hair, she said, "I don't need your help."

The claim alone was astonishing but even more so was the fact that she apparently believed it. He could blame the fever for that but he had the unmistakable feeling that it was due to her fiercely stubborn nature. Englishmen might tolerate that sort of behavior in a woman but it was inconceivable that he would do so. Most certainly, he would not be bothered to argue with her.

Her hand felt surprisingly soft and fine-boned as he lifted it away. Before she realized what he intended, Alex took hold of the fabric of her sleeve and ripped it neatly in two.

She did react then, trying to squirm away from him, but the chair and she in it were braced between his powerful legs. He could feel the warmth of her breath on his bare chest and the sudden, shocked stillness that froze her.

Even so, she did not keep silent. "What are you doing? Stop that!"

"Are you a child," he asked as he began to unwind the bloody bandage, "to fear what must be done for your well-being?"

"I told you, I've taken care of it."

He sucked in his breath when he saw the wound against the pale, delicate skin. It was ugly, jagged, and the area around it showed the hard redness of infection. That explained the fever. It also meant she had to be in considerable pain, yet she had said nothing. He did not know just then what made him angrier, her foolishness or her suffering. At the moment, it did not matter.

"You call this care?" he demanded. "The wound is infected and you are ill because of it." For the briefest moment, he allowed himself to regret not bringing a healer along. But the voyage was only a few days and his men were relentlessly healthy. It had never occurred to him that they might have need of such skill. Fortunately, he was not without medical training. Every Akoran warrior was taught to provide emergency care and each carried a pack of medicinals, bandages and the like.

Alex got his from the chest at the foot of the bed. He left her briefly to step into the bathing chamber adjacent to his cabin where he filled a basin with fresh water and cleansed his hands as ritual demanded. When he returned, she was watching him intently.

"The wound needs to be stitched," he said quietly. "But you need have no fear of that. I will give you a draught that will put you to sleep. When you awake, it will be done."

As he spoke, he began selecting the items he would need to prepare the sleep-giving medication. There was risk in using it; too great a dose and the patient might never wake. But he intended to give her only a very small amount, enough to last just long enough for what he must do.

"No."

He looked up, startled. Surely he had heard her wrong.

"At least four or five stitches are needed. That will be painful."

She flung her hair back out of her eyes and glared at him. "I've stitched wounds myself and when I was eight, my foot had to be stitched. I know what it will feel like."

"Then you will take the draught."

"No, I will not. There is no need. I will be fine."

Who was she reassuring, Alex wondered, him or herself? Not that it mattered. Before the first prick of the needle, she would change her mind.

"Very well," he said, and proceeded to clean out the

wound. Joanna turned her head away but not before he saw her wince. He worked as quickly and carefully as he could but knew he had to be hurting her.

"Now you will take the draught," he said when he had done. Fully expecting her to agree, he was unprepared when she shook her head yet again. Though her lips were tinged white around the edges, she said, "No, I told you, I'm fine. Just get it done."

He thought, briefly, about simply forcing the draught down her throat. But she would be hurt in the process, which would defeat his purpose. Thwarted by her stubbornness, he told himself yet again that she would relent. But through the long minutes that followed, as each stitch was put in place, she held perfectly still and made no sound at all save for a low whimper of relief when he was finally done.

Alex's forehead was beaded with sweat. As though from a distance, he observed that his hands shook slightly as he rebandaged her arm. With a deep sigh, he stepped back and looked at her. She was sagging in the chair, her face very pale, yet she managed a wan smile.

"That wasn't so bad," Joanna said, and fainted.

Damn stubborn, infuriating, frustrating . . . brave woman. Why couldn't she have fainted at the beginning rather than waiting until it was over? Just went to show how her thinking was addled, as though any more proof of that had been needed.

Well aware that his own thoughts were not entirely rational at the moment, Alex carried the girl over to the bed. He laid her down carefully so that no weight was on her left arm. She did not stir but her breathing was smooth and deep, reassuring him that she was slipping into a natural sleep. He removed her boots and would have left it at that had he not noticed the condition of her clothes. Besides the blood on her shirt, there was a variety of greasy, grimy stains, testament to her struggle through the porthole and her stay in the cargo hold. He had been taught that cleanliness was essential to good health and all the more vital to healing. He could not leave her as she was.

Gritting his teeth, he undid the laces of her shirt carefully and eased it up over her head. Her skin was very pale and smooth with a creamy, almost opalescent sheen. She was slender but not unduly so. Her breasts were small and perfectly shaped, the nipples a soft coral pink. He set the torn shirt aside, removed her boots, and decided he might as well make a clean sweep.

The pale perfection of her skin was marred along her left flank and thigh by dark purple bruises. Most likely she had fallen on that side when she got into the hold. Which raised the question of exactly how she had managed that feat. Belatedly, he remembered a report from his men shortly before sailing to the effect that a pair of local boys had climbed onto one of the warehouse roofs. Chased away, they had disappeared into the warren of alleys that crowded near the docks.

Was that when she came aboard? Probably, for he doubted she would have had any other chance. He made a mental note to speak with his men about the need for even greater caution when in the ports of people as given to lunatic adventuring as were the English.

His men would also want some explanation for her presence. Obviously, she had boarded his vessel without his knowledge, but that she had done so with every indication that her appearance would not be welcome would strike them as the far side of bizarre. Until he made up his mind what he was going to do about her, he would keep that information to himself.

About to pull the covers up over her, Alex remembered the English's odd preoccupation with nudity. With a sigh, he went back to the chest, selected a thin tunic, and maneuvered her into it. He was not catering to her sensibilities, definitely not. It was merely good sense to avoid the inevitable scene that would occur should she awaken to find herself naked in his bed.

For some time after that, Alex busied himself at his desk but concentration eluded him. He kept glancing over at the girl. More frequently than he intended, he got up to check on her. She was cooler than she had been and seemed to be sleeping peacefully. On impulse, he picked up the pouch she had carried and dumped out the contents onto the desk. He felt no hesitation in doing so for by boarding his vessel without the escort and protection of a man, she and everything with her had become his property. She didn't know that yet, of course, but she would soon enough.

A tin canteen—empty—a packet of dried beef, another of crackers, a thin blanket, a clean shirt torn at the bottom, a pouch containing twenty-six gold guineas, a bar of soap, a compass, a very small and utterly inadequate medical kit, a knife he promptly confiscated, and a book: *Speculations on the Nature of the Kingdom of Akora* by William, Earl of Hawkforte.

Alex had seen the volume before, had even read it, but that was in the library at Marsfield when he was fifteen years old, newly come to England and fascinated to find a book about his homeland. Authored by the grandfather of the present Earl of Hawkforte, the missing Royce, the book hinted at information gleaned from some ancient family connection with Akora. Darcourt thought that unlikely but not entirely impossible. He had personal reason to know that the Fortress Kingdom was not quite so inviolate as outsiders were encouraged to believe.

The contents of the bundle having been examined, he returned them to it and went yet again to check on the girl. She was cooler still and likely no longer in any danger, no thanks to her foolish behavior. It was very late and the coming day promised to be... challenging. He had no particular wish to be put out of his bed, yet neither had he ever shared it with a woman for other than the most obvious purpose. This did not appear an opportune time to try doing so. His anger was under control now but still very much present. Were the intruder a man, he would not hesitate to deal with him harshly. But she was a woman, despite her unwomanly actions, and as such she had to be treated differently.

Contemplating exactly how he would manage the unruly Englishwoman who had thrust herself into his hitherto well-ordered life, the Prince of Akora went up on deck to find his bed beneath the stars.

He slept little and restlessly. Waking in the cool grey light of early dawn, he lay on his back with his arms folded beneath his head and reflected on the situation he faced. On the surface, his latest mission to England was a success; the cannons in the hold attested to that. Their purchase had required the greatest discretion, occurring as it had without either the knowledge or approval of the British government. He was also reassured that no sense of the crisis looming on Akora had reached beyond the Fortress Kingdom. So far as the English knew, Akora remained as it had always been: a powerful monolith united against the world. If any hint to the contrary did emerge, he had no doubt the covetous eyes already focused on Akora would give way swiftly to unsheathed claws. It was more vital than ever that the internal problems be put to rest and quickly. At such a time, the intrusion of the Englishwoman was particularly ... unsettling.

Yes, that was the word, as well as the explanation for why he couldn't seem to get the chit out of his mind. Her courage disarmed him, sapping the anger that was only right and just, and to which he should have been able to hold on. Nothing in his life, certainly not on Akora and not even in England, had prepared him for dealing with the bewildering, infuriating creature inhabiting his quarters. He had to forcibly remind himself that she was a woman, a giver of life, and as such to be protected at all costs. Never mind that for just a moment he had been seized by a startling urge to put her over his knee.

The thought alone embarrassed him. It was unworthy of any Akoran warrior but most especially of a son of the royal house.

Damnation, what was he to do with her?

She was loyal to her brother—to a fault, to be sure—but loyalty was always to be respected. And she had courage. Of that, he had no doubt.

"*Archos*—?"

He looked up at the man who had approached him, a warrior well known to him, with whom he had shared many missions. The man's face was impassive, as was right, but the faintest hint of concern shone deep within his eyes.

"Ships have been sighted, Commander."

Alex turned in the direction the man indicated and looked out over the white-flecked water. It was a clear day and his eyesight was hunter keen. He had no difficulty picking out the billowing sails of three ships approaching from the east.

"French?"

The man nodded. He made a slight gesture with the spyglass he held. The glass was a product of Akora, the lens ground by Akoran craftsmen adept at such things, fitted into an intricately carved brass barrel about a foot long when closed but extending to twice that length. Such tools had existed on Akora for a very long time, longer by far than they had been known in the outside world. They were part of the reason why the kingdom had remained unmolested for so many centuries as battles for domination raged across nearby Europe, civilizations rose and fell, rulers appeared and vanished, progress occurred in tiny steps only to be hurled back time and again. And all the while Akora continuing. It was a source of pride and, on occasion, reassurance.

"They fly the French flag, *archos*."

Darcourt allowed himself a brief flicker of excitement but it died aborning. The French could be hotheaded but they were far from stupid. They would recognize the vessel as Akoran and give it wide berth despite the suspicion that it was outward bound from England.

Unless, of course, he chose to approach them himself. Any French captain would be delighted to make contact with an Akoran prince, and to be able to report such contact to his commander. Even more, any French captain would be more than happy to relieve said Akoran prince of an unwanted English female. The French were at war with the English but they were not uncivilized. On the contrary, in the aftermath of their bloody revolution and the ascension of their self-named emperor they were eager to prove themselves the epitome of all that was cultured and enlightened. She might be kept for a while, even displayed as an honored "guest" at Napoleon's court, but she would not be harmed. In time, she would be returned home. All in all, it might be a salutary experience for her. The thought would have been all too tempting were it not for the dishonor of putting her in the hands of her nation's enemy no matter how good the treatment she was likely to receive.

He scowled at the billowing sails a moment longer, then turned away. "Ignore them."

The man nodded and returned to his duties, and Alex was left alone with his original problem. What was he to do with her? Another few days would see them off the coast of Spain. He could leave her there, in British hands, assuming he could correctly identify Wellington's coastal positions. Those were proving very fluid and besides, he couldn't really see depositing her in the middle of a war zone.

Too much even for a woman of her astonishing strength and will.

Except that she wasn't only that. She was a frightened

but brave sister trying to do what was right for her brother. Alex himself was not without experience in the matter of love and loyalty within families.

He sat a while longer, looking out over the sea, thinking. The subtle changes in the color of the water and the quality of light toward the eastern horizon told him as much as the various instruments he had on board could do. He could judge the shifting of the deep currents whose paths had remained unchanged through all the centuries Akoran navigators had tracked them. So, too, could he judge how far they were from land by alterations in the light across the helmet of the sky. The touch of the wind in his hair and against his bare skin told him its speed and temperature. But above all was the smell. They were far enough offshore for him to smell only the sea. It was the smell of good wind and clear skies, a smell a sailor could count on. There were other smells—heavier and torpid—that were the warnings of danger. And twice, on especially long missions, he had smelled ice. That he did not particularly care to do again.

So he sat, his whole body attuned to the sea, and thought about what to do with the woman.

He could turn back, make for England, and deposit her right where she belonged. And so he might have considered doing were it not for the cannons.

There were people in England who did not know about the cannons. People who would not be pleased if they were to learn of them.

Returning to England with the cannons still in the hold would be a dereliction of his duty. He would face anything rather than that.

Lady Joanna Hawkforte would get her wish; she was going to Akora. The question was what would happen to her after she got there.

He was considering his options when his nostrils twitched. Alex looked toward the bow and grinned. Several of his men had a fire going on an iron grill. In a pot set above it, they were making fish stew. Not just any fish stew but *marinos,* the national dish of Akora, about which every Akoran had an opinion and which flourished in an infinity of variations lovingly handed down from one generation to another.

After three months of English food, Alex would have about killed for a taste of *marinos.* Fortunately, all he had to do was walk over and join the attentive crowd already gathering. He was accepting a bowl along with the usual piece of flatbread when his thoughts abruptly returned to his stowaway.

She was bound to be hungry.

Of course, she did have the crackers and dried meat she'd brought along.

For a brief moment, he indulged in the pleasantly vindictive possibility of allowing her to make do with such poor provisions. With a sigh, he put the thought aside and went back down to his cabin.

chapter

FOUR

✴

$\mathcal{B}$ LESSED COOLNESS. Borne on the memory of blistering heat, Joanna sighed and moved her cheek against cool, smooth...

Linen? She frowned slightly, recognizing the shape of a pillow beneath her head but uncertain why she should be surprised by anything so commonplace. Was she not at Hawkforte, in her bed? Maybe so, but the echoes of a strange dream lingered. A dream of...

No dream. She *had* come to London seeking Royce, had been turned away by the insufferable Darcourt, had stowed away on the Akoran vessel, had hurt her arm. And had been cared for by... him, who for all that he remained decidedly intimidating was perhaps not so insufferable after all. She remembered that now very clearly. Her eyes flew open even as her mind probed for pain, finding in its place only a dull ache.

She was lying in a large bed built into one wall of a spacious cabin. That much she could comprehend but the rest of what confronted her seemed out of a dream. The walls of the cabin were not the dark wood paneling she would have expected. Instead, they appeared to be whitewashed board painted from floor to ceiling with scenes of people, animals, birds and fish all so extraordinarily lifelike that she would not have been surprised to see them move. A tall, dark-eyed man stared at her even as his hand reached toward a blue-and-green parrot stretching its neck for the tidbit the man offered. Nearby, a slender woman sat at a loom, smiling as she wove. Beyond her, dolphins frolicked in an aqua sea that lapped gently along a golden beach.

She breathed in quickly, struck by the sudden thought that she might be getting her first glimpse of the hidden world she had come to find. For long moments, Joanna could not tear her gaze from the murals. Only with difficulty did she force herself to take note of the rest of the cabin. Along the wall opposite her, worked so cleverly into the painted scene that she almost missed them, were several portholes open to admit a fresh sea breeze. Through them, she caught glimpses of a clear blue sky swaying with the motion of the vessel.

Beneath the portholes a large desk was bolted to the floor. It would have appeared purely utilitarian but for the carvings of complex geometrical shapes along the edges and legs, the same shapes that formed the borders running all the way around the murals at both floor and ceiling. The desk held maps, with others rolled up and stored nearby in a wooden case fitted out with dozens of long, circular slots ideal for their purpose. The practical nature of the desk and case seemed at odds with the decorative beauty of the murals. They made her wonder further about the complex character of the Akorans.

She had done it; she truly was en route to Akora, the legendary kingdom shrouded in mystery. It was what she and Royce had talked of for years, and now it was actually happening—to her. She clasped her hands together tightly in an effort to contain her excitement but with no success.

The fever had left her weak but it did not stop her from tossing back the covers and slowly, with due care, standing up. Her legs felt shakier than she would have liked but after she had managed to take a few steps, she felt more confident. That was just as well for the inevitable demands of nature were making themselves felt.

There were two doors in the cabin. She chose the nearest one and opened it cautiously only to stare in amazement at what lay beyond.

"My heavens..."

A terra-cotta stall stood against one wall of the chamber. Painted in stark black and white with more of the geometric shapes she had seen on the desk, it was enclosed on three sides but open on the fourth facing her. Toward the top was the elaborately carved head of a bull. The bull's mouth was open, revealing a pipe pointed downward at such an angle as to shower whatever it carried on anyone standing in the stall. A drain on the floor seemed intended to carry away the excess. In between, set into the side of the stall, was a valve cast in the shape of a scalloped shell. Yielding to her intense curiosity, Joanna reached forward and turned the valve just a little way. Almost instantly, a trickle of water fell from the bull's head. Startled, she closed the valve at once and watched as the water vanished down the drain.

A stand-up bath! How astonishing. Only the previous year, she had seen a similar contraption, albeit one much plainer and far more awkwardly done, in a country house she and Royce had visited. The invention of an eccentric friend of the family, it amused everyone who encountered it. No one had seriously considered that it might replace the traditional bath.

Yet here was the same idea in a vastly more sophisticated form and on a ship no less, suggesting that the Akorans might be far more advanced in certain regards than she had ever imagined. Indeed, the stand-up bath looked undeniably appealing. After two days in the same clothes, she wouldn't mind giving it a try herself...

No, not the same clothes. Belatedly, she perceived

what had eluded her notice in the excitement of awakening under such extraordinary circumstances. She was no longer wearing the boots, trousers and shirt in which she had embarked. Indeed, she was wearing nothing whatsoever from the knees on down. The rest of her appeared more or less covered by a single, overly large garment of finely woven linen.

Shock stiffened every muscle. Surely he would not have... She remembered Darcourt's care of her wound, the pain he had tried to spare her, her limp relief when it was over. And then nothing, a void into which her overheated imagination rushed. That really would not do. The situation was far too serious and the stakes far too high to allow for missish sensibilities.

Yet she was still trembling inwardly as she stripped off the tunic and reached for the seashell valve.

Water falling on her head was a strange sensation but after a few minutes Joanna decided that she liked it. At least it distracted her from her unruly thoughts. With a sigh, she turned her face up to the water pouring from the bull's head and squinched her eyes shut. She felt a little silly with one arm stuck out of the stand-up bath but there was no other way to keep the bandage dry.

She turned around to let the water rinse the suds from her hair. She had found soap in a beautifully decorated wooden box attached to the wall beside a terracotta sink. There were bars scented with lemon and something else, a clean, tangy scent she could not recognize, and a stoppered stone bottle with liquid soap also with the unfamiliar but pleasant fragrance. She had used the latter on her hair and hoped it would rinse out before she used far more of the water than she should. It was fresh water, presumably from a supply stored on deck and piped into the bathing room. Even on a relatively short voyage, she was sure it should not be wasted.

Finishing quickly, she turned the flow off, stepped

from the stall and reached for the narrow length of finely woven cotton she had found on a low stool nearby. She dried herself, wrapped another length of cloth around her hair, wound one under her arms so that a corner tucked in between her breasts, and returned to the main cabin to look for her clothes.

They were not to be found but she did locate her pouch on the floor beside the bed. The contents were intact except for her knife, which was missing. She had only just discovered its loss and was contemplating what it meant when the other door suddenly opened.

The man who stepped into the cabin was not the Alex Darcourt she had seen at Prinny's fête. That austerely elegant lord was gone, replaced by the figure of barbaric splendor she had only glimpsed the night before through a haze of pain and fever. He wore a white linen kilt pleated and belted around his taut waist. Gold bands gleamed at his wrists and on his brow where a circlet of gold emblazoned in the center with a brilliant ruby barely tamed ebony hair that brushed the hard, rounded contours of his shoulders. His chest—astonishingly broad and ribbed with muscle—was also astonishingly bare. So for that matter were his legs—very long legs that looked chiseled from stone—exposed to above his knees. The considerable expanse of his skin thus revealed to her was bronzed except where thin, pale lines traced the path of old wounds, including one down the left side of his torso coming perilously close to his heart.

Something inside her did a long, slow flip that left her faintly giddy. She realized suddenly that she wasn't breathing and inhaled sharply but could not manage to look away.

He set a bowl down on the table and glanced at her. "You're awake, good. How are you feeling?"

His voice was as she remembered, deep and smooth, like water running over rock. He had a very slight accent, just enough to mark him as other than English-born. But his eyes were blue. Remarkably against that bronzed skin and midnight hair, they looked like the peak of the sky at full noon, deeply azure and brilliant.

For a horrible moment, Joanna could think of nothing save that she was standing almost nude in the cabin of a man who appeared to have stepped from the pages of Homer yet who was all too vividly real. Her sensible, well-ordered existence at Hawkforte might as well have been part of another life, so far away did it seem just then. Yet it was the virtues of courage and determination that life had instilled in her that came to her rescue.

She lifted her chin and, despite the vivid heat staining her cheeks, spoke with calm dignity. "Considerably better than I did last night, thank you. I apologize again for imposing on you. I hope you will understand that under the circumstances, I had no choice."

Hope, too, that he would not avail himself of any of the choices available to him. She truly did not want to be consigned to the brig, assuming there was one, but even that would be better than being abandoned on some convenient shore.

He took a deep breath. Joanna watched in unwilling fascination as that beautifully sculpted chest rose and fell. Indeed, so distracted was she that she almost missed his response.

"Your actions were impulsive, unwise and dangerous. Your presence raises serious difficulties."

"I am sorry about that, truly," she said earnestly even as she struggled to hide her surprise at his apparent lack of anger. "I will do anything I can to smooth over whatever problems I've caused."

He looked skeptical but did not reply directly. Gesturing to the table, he said, "The stew is hot. You should eat it before it cools."

She looked from him to the table and back again. He had brought her food. That had to be a good sign. He must not intend to starve her, and he had cared for her wound, even left her to rest in what she suspected were his quarters. But for the hardness of his eyes and the coiled stillness she felt within him she might have relaxed just a little.

Instead, she said hesitantly, "Thank you."

The smell was delectable; her stomach rumbled in response. But as scantily clad as she was, she could not bring herself to sit down at the table and eat, at least not in front of him.

A moment passed before he seemed to sense her difficulty. Still expressionless, he said, "Nudity is much more commonplace on Akora. That's probably because of our warm climate and our cultural traditions."

Her mouth was dangling open, partly because of how he looked, partly because of how she suspected she did, and just possibly because being thrown badly off stride by him was becoming a habit. She closed it with a snap and ignored the sudden drumbeat of her heart. "I am not nude." Not at all. In addition to the towel, she was wearing a very thorough blush.

"No, of course not."

She stared at a spot on the wall somewhere over his left shoulder. "Where are my clothes?"

"Those rags you came in? Gone. There are more tunics in that chest." He gestured toward the foot of the bed.

"They don't fit very well."

"There is nothing else." He went over to the chest and rummaged around in it until he found what he sought. He held out a garment very similar to the one she had awakened in but of heavier fabric.

"You won't be as comfortable in this."

"It will be fine, thank you." Quickly, she returned to the bathing room, unwound the cotton toweling, and dropped the tunic over her head. It came halfway down her calves and slipped off her shoulders but by hunching them slightly, she was able to keep the garment in place, if only barely.

Returning to the cabin, she found her host staring out one of the portholes. He spared her a glance before resuming his contemplation of the horizon.

Telling herself she was relieved, Joanna asked his back, "How far are we from Akora?"

"Ten days, if the wind holds." He nodded toward the table. "Sit down and eat."

This time she did as he said. One tentative taste was enough to make her eyes widen. Even granted that she was hungrier than she had thought, the stew was extraordinarily good. It was all she could do not to wolf it down. When she was done, she sighed softly and sat back. "That was delicious."

"It's just as well you think so. You will be eating Akoran food for the foreseeable future."

Her eyes met his. She tried to conceal a victorious smile but did not entirely succeed. Gravely, she said, "I am glad to hear that."

His response was a frown that made the nervous fluttering inside her return with a vengeance. "You may wish to temper your enthusiasm. As I said, your presence causes problems."

"What sort of problems?"

"You are *xenos*."

She spared a moment's gratitude for her study of Greek. "Foreign—"

He nodded. "Akora is closed to the *xenos*. We do not permit them to come to trade or for any other purpose. In this way, we have protected the purity of our culture and our sovereignty through more generations than there has been an England. Do you understand that?"

A cold current of panic moved through her but she ignored it staunchly. She had known the risk when she made the leap from the dock. "I've heard the rumors about what happens to foreigners who try to reach Akora. Just a few years ago when the French expeditionary force disappeared in Akoran waters, there was a great deal of talk about how even to approach Akora means death. But obviously that can't always be true."

His eyes were hooded, revealing nothing. "Why not?"

"Because of you. At least one person, your father, wasn't put to death. If he had been, you wouldn't exist."

For just a moment, she thought the corners of his mouth twitched but the impression was so fleeting she might have imagined it. Certainly, his voice held no hint of softening when he asked, "And that makes you think your brother may be alive?"

"Aside from the fact that all *xenos* obviously are not killed, my brother is a British peer. I cannot believe that the King of Akora would go out of his way just now to anger Great Britain."

Darcourt was silent for a moment before he said, "The correct title is Vanax. It does not mean king in the English sense. The translation is closer to Chosen."

"Oh . . . I didn't know that. But then I know almost nothing about Akora."

"Yet you trust your life to what you think its leaders will or will not do."

Her cheeks warmed. Put that way she sounded foolish, which she supposed was the point. "As I believe I've already said, I had no choice. It is impossible for me to simply accept my brother's disappearance. I have to do something to help him."

His eyes narrowed. He came closer to where she sat, his stance and manner reminding her that he was of the royal house, every inch a prince. Without warning, he asked, "Why do you say we would not want to anger Great Britain *just now*?"

She really should learn to keep her thoughts to herself. Even so, it was too late now to back down. The hard glint of his eyes made it very clear he would not allow her to do so. Just a little weakly, she said, "The cannons in your hold."

"It was dark. You were fevered."

"I felt them. Moreover, I smelled them. Iron and gun-
owder make a rather unmistakable mix. They'd been
red, of course, I suppose to test them."

He made no response, only continued to study her.

"Once it got light," she went on, gaining courage and
uriosity in equal measure for, after all, she had seen
hat she had seen and she wondered what it meant. "I
w them. They're very impressive. I don't suppose there
re many foundries that can cast such large barrels."

"What can you know of such things?"

She bristled just a little at that. He had a rather low
pinion of women, it seemed. But then so did most En-
lishmen she had met, at least among the aristocracy.
erhaps that went with the elevated notion they had of
emselves. "We still do much of our own metalwork at
awkforte, where I live. That means we still have our
wn forges. I have some sense of what is involved in cast-
g cannons of that size. Besides, anything to do with
kora is always of interest to people. If it were known
at you were acquiring such unusual weapons, I have
o doubt it would have been talked about."

"I see—" In truth, he did not seem to but she sensed
e was struggling to understand.

"Do Akoran women not concern themselves with
ch things?"

"Hardly, and that brings me to the matter at hand.
oy will have to alter your behavior." He looked down at
er sternly. "Considerably alter it, otherwise there will be
rave difficulties."

"Because I am *xenos*?"

Darcourt nodded. "Stand up."

"Why?"

"Your first lesson: Women are obedient. Do as you
re told."

Slowly, Joanna stood. She was extremely reluctant but
ardly in any position to refuse. To do so would seem
owardly and even churlish. He had taken her intrusion

with rather better grace than she could have hoped. At the very least, she should make a show of cooperating. Yet for all that, she was far too conscious of his height, she came just to his extremely broad shoulders, and of the vast expanse of his bare chest so very close that she would only have to reach out the smallest way to touch him—

His long fingers angled beneath the neckline of her tunic. Without warning, he slipped it off her left shoulder so far as to almost bare her breast.

She made a grab for the fabric. "What are you doing?"

He regarded her blandly. "Making sure your wound is healing properly."

"It's fine, couldn't be better. Let go."

She might as well have not spoken for all the impact it had, which was to say none at all.

"You didn't get it wet when you showered, did you?" he asked.

"No, of course not . . . Showered? Is that what I did? Like a rain shower?"

He nodded as he untied the bandage. "Just like that. Did you enjoy it?"

"Yes, it was wonderful. I saw something like it in England last year but nothing nearly as well done. Have you had them long in Akora? Are they commonplace?"

Belatedly, she realized that she was rattling on and that he had deliberately sought to distract her from his examination of her wound.

His fingers probed lightly around the injury. She had the fleeting thought that he was handling her very carefully, keeping his vast strength in check.

"The infection is healing well," he said.

Curiosity won out. She peered over his hand even as he tried to block her view.

"You don't need to see this."

Joanna regarded the red welt calmly. It ached but the pain of the previous day was gone. From what she recalled of how she had felt while in the hold, she was surprised the wound did not look worse. "It isn't so terrible. You did a good job of stitching." She continued to examine his work. "There will be a scar, of course, but not much of one I think."

"I regret there will be any," he said gruffly. With a fresh length of cloth, he rebandaged her arm.

By the time he was done, she felt oddly shaky yet unwilling to move away from him. He dropped his hands but continued standing very close to her, so near that she could feel the warmth of his body. She tried not to stare at his chest but that left her to focus on the powerful column of his throat and above to the chiseled line of his jaw, which appeared to be clenched.

"This may not have been a good idea," he murmured. Their eyes met.

Her toes curled, as though they clung to the very edge of a precipice. On a thread of sound, she said, "Which part? My coming to London, trying to see you, stowing away, getting hurt? Or perhaps we can say it was not a good idea for Royce to set out for Akora to begin with? We could lay all this at his door."

Alex tried very hard not to smile. She watched the struggle he waged and knew the moment he lost. His grin, for all that it was reluctant, was also quite devastating. She wondered if he knew it.

Quietly, he said, "It seems we will have to find your brother and tell him how badly he has behaved."

"Now that is a very good idea."

He sighed and moved away from her, leaving behind a stab of regret.

She took a deep breath, struggling to steady herself. "How well do you know my brother?"

Hands clasped behind his back, he regarded her from the other side of the cabin. "Not well. We met a few times in the ordinary course of events and he came to see me about going to Akora. I told him it was out of the question and to put aside all thought of doing so. Unfortunately, it seems he did not heed me."

"He did not go on a whim. I am certain he had good reason even if I do not know what it was. He told me he would be home in time for Christmas. That was six months past. There has not been a word from him."

"I left Akora just over three months ago. There was no word then of an Englishman nor has there been since."

Joanna's throat tightened. Face to face with the fear that had haunted her day and night, she said, "I do not believe my brother is dead."

"But you at least know that is possible?"

"He isn't. It's hard to explain but I know he's out there somewhere, just waiting to be found."

Alex said nothing for a moment. When he spoke finally, his tone was surprisingly gentle. "Then we must try to find him."

She nodded, blinking back tears. After the mounting worry of the past six months and the events of just the last few days, she was far too close to being undone. Exhaustion washed over her suddenly. Without knowing that she did so, she swayed. He was there at once, steadying her. His voice was still hard and distant but his touch on her uninjured arm was surprisingly gentle. "I think you've had about as much as you can take. It's just as well we have some time before we arrive."

"I'm fine, really. I'm not some weak-kneed little miss and I wouldn't have you thinking that. At home, I manage my family's manor. People actually think I'm quite capable and responsible." She laughed faintly, appalled by how close she still was to crying.

"Even so, you should get some rest."

She did not want to see the sense of what he said. She wanted to be strong and clearheaded, as she was so accustomed to being, to hear what problems she would face and what would be necessary to solve them.

But what she wanted just then and what was possible were very far apart. She hardly knew when he led her over to the bed nor did she feel the light stroke of his fingers on her cheek before he departed.

So DID THE BETTER PART of a week pass. Alex came three times each day with food for her but even so Joanna saw very little of him. They shared no more than snatches of polite conversation. He had accepted her assurances that she could assume responsibility for tending her wound, which filled her with an odd mixture of relief and regret. Being touched by him even so impersonally was strangely unsettling. But then so, too, was the frequency with which he drifted through her thoughts.

She knew that he slept on deck and occasionally she heard him in conversation with his men. Little by little, their language was becoming comprehensible to her. It was not the Greek she knew but there were enough similarities that she could begin to pick out words and even some phrases.

The deck was forbidden to her. She chafed at that even as she felt small for harboring any complaint under the circumstances. Alex had made it clear that no woman, *xenos* or otherwise, would be permitted to intrude into what was by tradition an exclusively male preserve. She thought that sounded rather like the men's clubs that were so popular not only among the *ton* but at all levels of society. Whether they gathered in lavishly appointed London townhouses or the corners of smoky country pubs, males seemed to harbor some irresistible need to draw themselves apart from females, which she thought was rather puzzling since at other times they made such a great deal out of pursuing them. No doubt there was some logic to it that escaped her.

Yet there were compensations for her solitude. The skies were clear, the wind brisk. She knew they were making good time. Soon enough, the world would intrude. Before it did, she turned her mind and, she hoped, her gift to finding Royce. Tentatively at first, then with increasing determination, she struggled to reach him. Moment to moment, hour after hour, she held him in her thoughts, straining for some glimpse, however small, of where he might be.

She found... a small hammer slipped down between two of the boards paneling the cabin... a silver stylus forgotten beneath the bed... a folded but blank sheet of paper caught behind the map case... and once she thought she caught a glimpse of a tiny island rising up out of the sea minutes before it actually came into sight.

Of Royce, there was nothing. Only a pounding headache and an aching sense of despair.

The fourth day out, Alex looked at her pale, strained face and said, "There are books in that chest." He gestured to one near the desk. "You may read them if you wish."

How often had she longed for time and books together? Now she opened the chest with nothing more than a desperate wish to escape the purgatory of seemingly endless, useless waiting.

She found weighty treatises on arcane details of mining, military tactics and ship construction as well as several volumes on up-to-date farming methods that might have interested her had she not been tempted by tastier fare. He read the poems of Coleridge, she discovered, for the pages of that book were already cut. So, too, were Keats and Wordsworth. A book she had read the previous year, and delighted in, was also in the chest—Sir Walter Scott's *The Lady of the Lake*. She was about to settle in for a happy second reading when she discovered, marvel of all marvels, a copy of the novel everyone seemed to be talking about even in quiet Hawkforte. Written by Anonymous, who was rumored to be a lady of the country gentry, *Sense and Sensibility* was attracting much attention.

Very shortly she knew why. Lost in the adventures of the Dashwood family, she stayed up far later than she would have otherwise and only fell asleep when the sisters' romantic adventures had been properly resolved.

She woke late the following morning to find breakfast on the table. Alex must have come in while she was asleep. Struck by self-consciousness, she reminded herself not to be foolish. Hadn't he cared for her injury, turned his cabin over to her, and treated her with every consideration? His behavior was everything she would expect of an English gentleman—even if he was also Akoran.

After she had eaten and enjoyed a quick shower, Joanna returned to the chest. Digging a little deeper, she exclaimed with delight. Beneath the English novels and poetry were several layers of scrolls.

Eagerly, she chose one and opened it with care. The scroll was of heavy vellum, familiar to her from some of the older books at Hawkforte. Inscribed by a careful and very clear hand, it was written in an alphabet she was surprised to discover she could understand, albeit it with some difficulty. Indeed, the first line of the scroll leapt out at her:

"Tell me, O Muse, of the hero who wandered far after sacking the sacred city of Troy."

The Odyssey. She held in her hands a copy of Homer's great epic about Odysseus, a work she knew very well. It was written in a language that had many similarities to the Greek she knew but also significant differences. Just as she could make out some of what she overheard being said on deck, so could she read some but not all of the scroll.

The remainder of the morning passed in a blur. She scarcely looked up from her study of the scroll. Slowly, one by one, she was becoming better able to pick out words previously unknown to her. She had no hope of remembering them all, and couldn't even be sure she was pronouncing them correctly, but she still felt she was making progress.

Odysseus had reached the land of the Lotus Eaters when Alex came down with lunch. Joanna did not hear the door open nor did she have any awareness of his presence until he asked, "What are you reading?"

She raised her head, stared at him, then abruptly recalled herself. She was seated cross-legged on the bed, a most unladylike position but undeniably comfortable, with the scroll unfurled on her lap. At least it was large enough to cover her legs, more or less. Even so, she tried to reposition it surreptitiously, hoping to conceal limbs and self-consciousness alike.

Would the shock of his appearance never lessen? Yes, he was far too handsome but surely by now that should no longer surprise her. Yes, he wore far less than any Englishman of her acquaintance but to his credit he was not garbed in skin-tight trousers that left nothing to the imagination and indeed were sometimes rumored to display not so much manly attributes as their artificial embellishment. He had not shaved in several days but the dark stubble of beard did little to soften the hard line of his jaw. On the contrary, it merely made him look rather more dangerous than he would have otherwise, which, all things considered, was saying quite a bit.

Indeed, she found it prudent to look away before responding. "*The Odyssey*. It's a favorite of mine."

He set the tray on the table. From the corner of her eye, she saw a quicksilver smile come and go across that mouth that held far too great fascination for her.

"It is a favorite on Akora as well."

"Is that because the Akorans were Greek originally?"

He hesitated as he always did before revealing any information about Akora. Overall, he had told her little but he had given her access to the chest and whenever she asked him a question directly, he answered it.

"That was your grandfather's theory, wasn't it?"

"How do you know that?"

"I've read his book, *Speculations on the Nature of the*

Kingdom of Akora, which I notice you brought with you. He had some interesting insights but overall don't expect the book to be of much help."

"So Akorans weren't Greek?"

He walked over to the desk and leaned against it, his arms folded over his broad chest. Sunlight pouring through the portholes glinted on the polished sheen of his shoulders and chest. "Yes and no. Some of my ancestors came from the Greek mainland but after they left there, Greece was invaded and overrun by others. That ushered in a dark age. The Greece that finally emerged centuries later, what you know as the Greece of Homer and ultimately of Athens and Sparta, was very different from that which my forebears had known."

Something about that bothered Joanna. Slowly, she said, "Yet for all that difference, you appear to use substantially the same alphabet."

He inclined his head slightly in acknowledgment of her reasoning. "That is because we both adapted it from the Phoenicians at about the same time. We had an earlier alphabet but it was very cumbersome and imprecise. The Phoenician alphabet was a major improvement. We were only one of many people who saw that and made use of it."

Joanna sighed. "I've learned more about Akora in the last three days than in a lifetime but I still know almost nothing. That rather worries me, as we are to arrive there soon." She dared a sidelong glance in his direction, hoping he might take the hint and indulge her.

His expression was not encouraging but then it never was. He was always aloof and guarded in his dealings with her. Yet a moment later that guard seemed to slip just a little as he began to speak.

chapter
FIVE

✴

$\mathcal{T}$HERE WERE GOOD REASONS for her to know more about Akora before they arrived, Alex thought. She was going to have a hard enough time adjusting without being burdened by complete ignorance.

Even so, the reticence of a lifetime was difficult to overcome. He had known from a tender age that he would be one of those chosen to go into the larger world but unlike most, he would go as an Akoran, his identity unconcealed. He would claim his English heritage but he would remain true to the love and loyalty instilled in him at birth. Most particularly, he would never reveal by word or deed anything that could be used to harm Akora.

His English grandfather had understood this, even perhaps appreciated it, for he was loath to speak of the place that had claimed his son. With others, it was an easy matter to deflect or ignore questions. Not so with Joanna. He was unaccustomed to a woman of such independent spirit, much less one capable of reasoning out for herself a matter of state security known only to the Vanax and his innermost circle.

That women were courageous he had never questioned. Their valor in childbirth merited any warrior's respect. But Joanna's stalwart consideration of her wound and her going so far as to compliment him on his stitching of it were utterly beyond his experience. That she was also not so much beautiful in the orthodox sense as oddly appealing was a further matter of concern. Not for the first time since discovering her in the hold, he reminded himself to be cautious in his dealing with her.

"Come and sit down," he said, gesturing to the table even as he remained standing some little distance away.

Half an hour later, Joanna finished the last of the delicately grilled fish lightly seasoned with olive oil and herbs, passed up the few crumbs left of the still warm flatbread, and popped the final handful of wild strawberries into her mouth. She swallowed, sighed, and leaned back in the chair.

"So we will put in at the main port, you said it is called Ilius?"

Alex nodded. While she had eaten, he had given her a very general description of what she could expect on their arrival.

"It is the royal city as well as the deepest harbor." He selected one of the maps from the case near the desk, brought it over to the table and unrolled it. Joanna pushed the dishes aside to give him room. He caught the scent of her hair, which in recent days had burst forth in a tangle of honeyed curls framing her face, defeating what he suspected were her increasingly frustrated efforts to tame it. She tried so hard to be calm and sensible but she had come away on a voyage to a far land without anything so reasonable as a comb. He rather liked that other side of her.

Reining in his wayward thoughts, he pointed a long, blunt-tipped finger toward the western coast of Europe. "Here is Spain and here the island you call Gibraltar. On the other side is Morocco and the place you call

Mount Hacho. Together, they form the Pillars of Hercules guarding the strait that is the only entrance to the Mediterranean."

Joanna indicated the group of islands about a hundred miles west of the Pillars. "This is Akora?"

When Alex nodded, she frowned. "I thought Akora was one island, but this shows two large islands with three small ones tucked in between them." She turned her head, looking at him. "How could we be so ignorant?"

Her eyes were a tantalizing green shot through with gold. They reminded him of a glen he knew where mossy banks were caressed by sunlight filtering through high branches.

He cleared his throat. "Your mapmakers can only observe the coastline from their ships, and then only at a considerable distance. They have mistaken the entrances to the Inland Sea for inlets."

Because the formidable Akoran navy patrolled the waters around the kingdom, turning back all foreigners— *xenos*—who tried to come near.

But she was not on a vessel that would be turned away. She was on the ship of an Akoran prince and within a matter of days, she would be setting foot on Akora itself. He saw the realization of that shimmer through her and felt some measure of her excitement.

"This is Kallimos," he said softly, pointing to the easternmost island.

"That means beautiful, doesn't it?"

"Yes, and it is. Can you read the others?"

She studied the map. "The western island is Leios. I have seen that word . . . something to do with a plain?"

"The interior of that island is very flat, excellent for raising crops and horses."

"These three," she said slowly, looking at the small islands, " . . . Phobos . . . Deimatos . . . Tarbos." She lifted her head, looking at him with eyes that were suddenly dark with apprehension. "I don't understand. All three of these names have to do with fear or terror. Are they bad in some way?"

"Not at all. They're quite pleasant."

"Then why such names for them?"

He took the map from her, rolling it up again and returning it to its place in the case. "They are the . . . memory, I suppose you could say, of something that happened a long time ago."

Returning to the table, he continued, "Akora was one island originally. Its inhabitants called the whole of it Kallimos and that name remains for the eastern island to this day."

"How could one island become several?"

"At the center of the island was a volcano that had been dormant for thousands of years, if not longer. One night it awakened. The explosion ripped the island in two. The sea rushed into the center, leaving nothing there except the trio of small islands that remain as testimony to the terror people experienced as their world was ripped apart."

"How horrible," Joanna murmured. "When did this happen?"

"More than three thousand years ago."

A moment passed before the significance of that sank in. "You have a history that goes back more than three thousand years?" When he nodded, she asked, "An oral history?"

"No, it is written. The original inhabitants of Akora were literate. Some of their records survived and those who came afterward had their own writings."

"But that is extraordinary! No one has a written history that goes back so far. Even the Egyptians, no one knows how old their hieroglyphics are but they can't be read anyway. There is that stone Napoleon's men discovered but it can't be deciphered . . ."

She gasped softly and he saw the moment her imagination leaped. "Atlantis!"

Alex's sigh was long and heartfelt. "Please, not Atlantis."

"But why not? Plato said it was west of the Pillars of Hercules. He said the Greek historian, Solon, had the story directly from Egyptian priests who had it in their ancient records. They said Atlantis was a mighty kingdom that was swallowed up by the sea—"

"As the result of earthquakes, according to Plato, not a volcano, and he claimed the Atlanteans had been conquered by the Greeks of Athens before Atlantis was destroyed."

"Details, nothing more. You would have to expect the story to be somewhat garbled. And, of course, Plato was Athenian so he would try to make his own people look good. Shakespeare did the same thing, you know. He was terribly flattering about the Tudors just to curry favor."

"You are unusually well-educated for a woman. There is a term for that . . ." He thought for a moment. "Bluestocking? Is that it? You are a bluestocking?"

The tunic was slipping off her shoulder. She tugged it back up again and avoided looking at him. Stiffly, she said, "I suppose there are those who would say so."

"I am sorry, I did not mean to offend you. I learned English as a child but there are certain words, slang especially, that I do not always understand, or at least not fully."

She forgot about the tunic and met his eyes. "There is something I don't understand. Actually, quite a few somethings, but one thing in particular."

"And what is that?"

"If men are supreme on Akora, as I have heard, and women are only supposed to serve, why are you willing to apologize to me?"

"It is not the act of a British gentleman?"

She attempted a casual shrug that did not quite come off. "It is contradictory."

"Not at all. No one would wish to give offense to a woman for that is hurtful to her. But if it happens, it is only right to make amends at once."

"That is the custom on Akora?"

He nodded and quickly turned away from any further discussion of that particular aspect of Akoran society. "It would be as well if we discussed some of the other customs there."

The simplest thing to do was to turn her over to the Akoran authorities. They would make what were always referred to as "appropriate arrangements." And therein lay the problem. He wanted no one making "appropriate arrangements" for Joanna Hawkforte. For days he had tried to convince himself otherwise and failed. Now he simply accepted what was.

"You are *xenos* and as I have told you, that will cause difficulties. There will be questions as to why I allowed you to come to Akora. Fortunately, you are a woman so there is a plausible explanation."

An explanation that would anger his brother's more conservative advisers who were already suspicious of the half-*xenos* Prince of Akora, but he saw no reason to tell her that.

"Aside from she who will be chosen to bear my sons, there is only one reason why I would permit a woman to accompany me on this voyage."

He was about to continue when the dull flush of color sweeping over her damask skin stopped him. This was not the becoming blush of modesty. It was, he quickly realized from the diamond-hard glitter of her eyes, inspired by anger, not to say outrage.

"'She-who-will-be-chosen-to-bear-my-sons'? Is that all one word? What an extraordinary way to refer to a wife, which is what I presume she would be."

Her ire distracted him from what he had intended to

say. "What is extraordinary about it?" he countered. "Englishmen put just as much emphasis on the getting of sons."

"They do not refer to their wives as though their sole purpose for existing is to breed!"

"How many couples, especially among the *ton,* endure each other only until there is an heir, then go their separate ways?"

He had trumped her easily and was rewarded with a look of chagrin but she regrouped quickly. "Are you saying Akorans subscribe to the same loose moral standards common among the British aristocracy? Once she-who-will-be-chosen-to-bear-your-sons has done her duty, she's free to amuse herself elsewhere?"

He felt his face darken and seemed unable to do anything about it. What was it about this woman that shredded his self-control and made him feel like an untried youth? Fortunately, there was a way to right the balance between them. An age-old way that the men of Akora had relied on for a very long time.

"No, I am not saying that." He took a step closer to her and another. Steadily, he closed the gap between them. She did not try to move back but she did stiffen. When he was standing so near that he could see the pale blue pulse of life in the slender column of her throat, he smiled. Gently, the back of his hand grazed her cheek. "Akoran women have no reason to stray. They are kept far too well satisfied. I understand Englishmen are rather lax about such things."

He was pleased to see her eyes widen. Indeed, he might even have dwelled on that a little had he not been so distracted by the melting softness of her skin. That was absurd, of course. Women had soft skin, it was a simple fact of nature. There was nothing in the least extraordinary about it. But her skin . . . He had a sudden, flashing memory of petals falling from peach blossoms, spilled by warm summer rain, and himself, a boy, trying to catch them. All in those long ago days, only dimly remembered, when he had not a care in the world.

Huskily, he said, "I have yet to explain how we are going to account for your presence."

She wanted to pull away from his touch, he could see that. But she did not. Was it pride that held her still, or susceptibility? He very much disliked the notion that only his blood heated, only his body yearned.

To right the balance...

"There is only one possible explanation anyone will believe. Only one reason why I would return with a *xenos* woman."

Her eyelashes were slightly darker than her hair but sun-tipped. They fell, concealing her gaze, but not before he saw the dawning of alarmed comprehension. When she looked up at him again, all expression was carefully concealed. "Because you decided out of the goodness of your heart to help her?"

"Alas, princes rarely have that luxury. We are servants of duty, yet allowed our little indulgences. You will have to seem to be just such a pleasant whim. A comely Englishwoman I chose to warm my bed and enjoyed sufficiently to bring back with me."

Her eyes flashed, not the gold of the sun but the cold of steel. Behind her softness and her youth he saw the sudden gleam of centuries of breeding, the proud tower that would hold her upright in the face of any storm.

Icily, she said, "You appear to have mistaken me for Lady Lampert."

No maidenly dismay here, no charming blushes or confusion, only the disdain of a woman for whom honor is not merely second nature but life itself.

He was torn, caught between the prongs of chagrined admiration and stubborn male pride. She *would* bend to him and not solely for his vanity, although he was honest enough to admit that played a part, but because she must for her own safety.

He dropped the hand nestled against her cheek but did not move away. Blood royal when England was the haunt of wild, woad-daubed folk coursed within him. "The mistake is yours, Lady Joanna. I said you will have to *seem* to be. The object here is appearance, not reality."

Her surprise was gratifying, as was the slight flush of embarrassment caressing the skin he had himself so lately touched. And so wished to touch again. Instead, he tucked his hands behind his back and watched her.

"I misunderstood," she murmured. "My apologies."

Instinctive honesty almost prompted him to assure her no apology was needed—or merited. But he had long since learned the greater virtue of discretion.

He nodded once, brusquely. "Very well. In service to this . . . illusion, it would be just as well if you could manage to behave as a proper woman."

"A proper woman who is a mistress?" The notion seemed to confuse her. That damned English morality, he supposed. The ineffable but stubborn sense of what was fair and just, honorable and right that seemed to blossom in the very air of the scepter'd isle, resisting even the stink of corruption wafting from on high.

It was just as well the training of a warrior involved a great deal of patience.

"On Akora," he said, "the term would be concubine, and it is an honorable one. There are women who, for whatever reason, do not marry or if widowed, do not marry again. However, they and their wedded sisters adhere to the same code of conduct, which you will have to learn. As a woman, you are pleasant, submissive, obedient and demure. Your only proper role is to serve the man to whom you belong. You have no other wish and certainly no other concern."

She stared at him for a long moment. The corners of

her mouth twitched. "You can't possibly believe there are women like that."

"You see, this is the problem. You have no idea what women are like."

"I *am* a woman. I grew up surrounded by the women of Hawkforte, I have observed women in society, and I have traveled rather extensively. I can assure you, the creature you have just described does not exist, at least not anywhere I have ever been. If she does exist on Akora, I can only conclude that Akoran women are of an entirely different species from that with which I am familiar."

"I daresay I have far more experience in the world than you do, and the vast majority of women are happiest when they are as I have described."

"Happiest? The only women I have known who could be called happy are those at Hawkforte. They are good, sensible countrywomen. They work beside their husbands in the fields and pastures, even on the fishing boats. Some have businesses brewing, weaving and the like. They would scoff at the very notion of serving a man unless it was a tankard of ale he was wanting and he was paying for it. But they share their lives with their men, they care for them and for the children they nurture. I have seen them in the long twilight of a summer evening or around a winter fire, when day is done and there is rest at last. Men and women together, they seem to shine from within and their laughter is hearty."

Something moved within him, some deep current of yearning. It seemed to rise higher and higher, cresting somewhere in the most secret reaches of his soul, before slowly ebbing away. Even then the echo of it remained like foam left behind on a wave-strewn beach.

Quietly, he said, "Then Hawkforte must be an unusually blessed place. But I do not speak of country folk. We are bound for the royal court. As there are proprieties to be observed in London, so are there in Ilius. Your presence

will cause tongues to wag as it is. If you are less than cir-
cumspect in your behavior, it will be all the worse."

She took a deep breath and closed her eyes for just a
moment. When she opened them again, he saw that she
was resolved. "I will do my best."

He nodded curtly. "Good. I have been lax regarding
your behavior because of your injury and because there
has been no one to observe you save myself. Once we
reach Akora, that will change. To begin with, in my presence you will not speak unless I speak to you directly in
such manner as to require a response." He waited while
she absorbed this, thankfully without comment. "You
will rise when I enter a room." Still nothing although he
thought her eyes were sharpening. "Because of the presumed intimacy of our relationship, it is proper for you
to address me as *kreon* rather than the more formal title
of *archos*."

He braced himself. Her Greek was too damn good
and she was learning Akoran with amazing speed. It was
likely she would—

"*Kreon?*" Joanna repeated. Her brows knit together,
making her look rather like a golden kestrel he had kept
as a boy. "Doesn't that mean . . . master?"

"That is its very ancient meaning. Words evolve over
time, you must know that. Nowadays, it is merely a term
of respect for the man to whom a particular woman belongs." He was speaking more quickly than usual, trying
to allay her anger but not succeeding entirely.

Even so, she kept what he had to regard as an admirable rein on her temper. Her hands were only curled,
not actually clenched. "I would be very interested in
knowing how the word with its original meaning came
to be used in such a way."

"I believe it has to do with the period immediately after the eruption on Akora but that hardly matters now.
After all, it was three thousand years ago."

"You said some people survived. What were they like?"

"Peaceful... they pastured animals and fished. They were artists."

Her gaze drifted around the beautifully decorated walls of the cabin. "Apparently, Akorans are still artists. That surprised me. All I had ever known of Akorans was that they were warriors."

"That is also true."

"But the original inhabitants were not warriors. So it must have been your ancestors, the ones you said came shortly after the eruption, who were warlike. What must that have meant to people already devastated by the destruction of their world to suddenly have bands of warriors arrive among them? They would have stood no chance at all, would they?"

Too damn smart by half.

"They would also not have survived had my ancestors not come when they did. The heat of the blast destroyed almost everything on the island. Not only most of the people but every boat and every stand of forest from which more boats might have been made were gone. The very ground was seared, incapable of growing food for several years. But for my ancestors, those left alive on Akora would have starved to death."

"So your people came as rescuers?" She looked openly skeptical.

"No," he said quietly, "they came as conquerors. It was our way. In time, my people themselves were conquered elsewhere but not on Akora. There we prevailed to the benefit of all."

And with that she would have to be satisfied for he did not intend to say more. Already, he had told her more than any *xenos* should know.

"Do as I have told you," he said, "and we have a chance of success. Do otherwise..." He shrugged, leaving her to imagine for herself what would happen in that case.

His strategy seemed successful for she paled. "If I make a mistake..."

"You will not," he assured her quickly. "I will see to it."

"But to pose as someone I am not ..." Small white teeth worried her lower lip. "Companies of actors come to Hawkforte from time to time. I always marvel at such skill that transforms a plain, ordinary fellow into a victorious king, a chilling murderer or the like."

"No doubt the trappings play a part, the scenery, costumes and the like."

"I suppose ..."

"And then, of course, actors rehearse. They practice what they are to be."

They looked at one another. The freckles across the bridge of her nose were fading, no doubt because of her stay in the cabin. But they were still visible and he supposed they would bloom again once she was back in the sun. Vaguely, he remembered that freckles were not considered fashionable among the *ton*. Neither was plain speaking. It seemed the social proprieties did not come naturally to Lady Joanna Hawkforte.

His gaze dropped to her mouth. Her lips were full, soft and rose-hued. He had a sudden, piercing need to know how they would feel beneath his.

"It would be just as well," he murmured, "if you did not look like a startled doe every time I come near you."

"Don't," she murmured, but stiffly, for the callused palms of his hands, roughened by rein and hilt, were cupping her face. He had no idea whether she was objecting to the characterization of herself or his imminent action, nor did he care. Her hair felt like silk twining around his fingers. The scent of her filled his breath. All the days of her floating through his mind and his dreams. Days of keen awareness, rising desire and the strange, faintly stunned realization that he was not entirely in control of the situation. But he had to be, absolutely and without question. There was far too much at stake—a kingdom, a future, the fates of thousands in whose service he was pledged. Beside all that, his private inclinations counted for nothing.

And yet, he had told her the truth. If they were to succeed, her presence must be both explained and excused. The weakness of a young man who could be pardoned a small lapse since it only concerned a woman and not anything of true importance. A whim, an indulgence, he could be forgiven that by most at least, if not by some.

His dark head bent, his hard mouth brushing hers but lightly, swiftly as a finger might be grazed across a surface suspected of being too hot. Returning, he lingered, savoring her softness, the stiffening of surprise yielding slowly, perhaps grudgingly, but yielding all the same. He moved a hand, clasping the back of her head, holding her still for him, and moved the other very lightly along the slender curve of her arm, scarcely brushing delicate skin, strength and persuasion mingling together.

She moaned softly, her lips parting on the sound. He tasted her, swiftly, then deeply. The sweetness of strawberries still clung to her but he was little aware of it. The taste and scent and touch of Joanna herself eclipsed all else.

Her breasts were full and tantalizing against his chest, the nipples firm through the thin fabric of the tunic, which was all she wore.

All she wore. And the bed scant paces away. It would be so easy . . .

The vessel slipped into a trough between waves, emerged, found another. All unnoticed, the sea had roughened. He caught hold of the table near them, and of her, an arm wrapped around her waist.

Her eyes were very dark and within her he felt a great stillness.

Like the doe?

Or like the hawk when it soars unmoving on currents of heated air. Just before it strikes.

"Play the part," he said.

She nodded. "For my brother's sake."

And he knew just then in the sudden, roiling sweep of the vessel over the sea that she lied.

Or perhaps he merely hoped that she did.

chapter

SIX

✴

$\mathcal{J}$HE SCENT OF LEMONS woke Joanna. She sat up slowly, clinging to the remnants of a dream that faded even as she tried to remember it. Still half asleep, she looked toward the open portholes. The sky was the hazy blue of early morning before the sun burnishes misty night to fair day. The breeze entering the cabin was warmer than it had been the previous morning, which in turn had been warmer than the morning before it. But it was not the heavier, almost torpid touch of the air that had awakened her nor the advent of the day. It was the smell.

She had been taken from dreams by the scent of lemons. Or perhaps they had been the dream. Sitting up farther, she inhaled deeply and had a sudden flashing sensation, more than mere image or memory, of the long lawn at Hawkforte reaching down to the sea with herself seated on the grass enjoying the sweet indulgence of lemonade.

Curiosity drove her from the bed. She slipped a tunic over her head, ran fingers through her tangled hair, and glanced toward the door of the cabin. In the three days since Alex had informed her of the role she would have to play on Akora, he had continued to bring her meals as always. His behavior during their brief encounters had been scrupulously correct. He did not touch her even accidentally. He most certainly did not kiss her again.

More's the pity.

She really did have the most contrary mind. It must have come from having grown up without the strange, hollow strictures society imposed. Here she was on the verge of fulfilling her dream of entering the Fortress Kingdom and all she was able to think about, continually and incessantly, was that kiss. It wasn't as though she had never been kissed before. She had been . . . once. By an overeager stable boy. At least this time she had behaved with rather more sophistication and aplomb, which was to say she had not hauled off and broken Darcourt's nose.

The problem was that she hadn't even thought to do so. Not that plenty of other possibilities hadn't danced through her head. How remarkable that she had reached the exalted age of twenty-four without ever suspecting herself to be in possession of so vivid an imagination.

Perhaps all those years in the company of the women of Hawkforte were responsible. She knew in the same way of knowing what a red sunset meant and when an ewe was ready to lamb that men, their bodies and their hungers could be enticing. But the knowing had not prepared her for the reality, not even the tiny slice of it in one solitary kiss. Of course, Alex himself might have something to do with that. What was it he had said? The women on Akora were kept too well satisfied to stray? She supposed she shouldn't know what that meant but she did, or at least she had a fairly good idea.

My, it certainly had gotten much warmer. Better to think about the lemons.

There was a breakfast tray on the table, proof yet again that she was sleeping shockingly late. Most likely that had something to do with her restless nights. She ignored the food, ignored as well the little shiver that went through her at the thought of Alex being nearby while she slept, and dragged a stool over to one of the portholes. Standing on it, she craned her neck out, turning it this way and that until head, shoulders, and a goodly share of her torso were hanging out over the sun-splattered water.

It was thus that Alex found her when he came down at midday. He sighed deeply enough to tell her he was there. She withdrew with as good grace as she could manage and assumed a look of cheerful innocence.

"Beautiful day, my lord." She hadn't quite gotten round to calling him *kreon* but she was resolved to manage it once they reached Akora. Anything for Royce.

His eyebrows were quite extraordinarily eloquent. She had almost learned to chart his moods, some of them at least, by the rise and fall of those ebony wings.

"Some people might think it overly risky to stick half their bodies out the porthole of a ship moving as fast as this one."

This close to her goal, she was in an extremely good mood, so much so that neither his sardonic drawl or the surge of sensual awareness he provoked troubled her. At least not much. Brightly, she said, "Isn't it a good thing the world is made of different sorts? There's use even for the foolishly cautious, I'm sure."

"But you'd be hard pressed to say what it might be." He set a tray on the table, frowning at the untouched breakfast.

Joanna nodded in thanks but made no attempt to sit. "I smell lemons."

He glanced toward the portholes. "Is that what it smells like to you? Interesting. The lemon groves will be full now, almost ready for picking. But the wild thyme is in flower, so is the oleander. Both add their scents."

Excitement building in her, she stared at him. "Are we so close then?"

"We saw land an hour ago, no more than a slight thickening on the horizon, but the wind is blowing right."

So she had smelled Akora before seeing it, and not the scent she thought of as land, loamy with a hint of rock, redolent of people and animals, which could be disconcerting after a time at sea. This was different, a seductive perfume of scents beckoning her.

Longing filled her, unexpected and startling in that it seemed a misplacement. Hawkforte—its sights, smells, sounds, memories—was home. Not these strange isles born of the fiery earth. And yet the yearning that swept her so suddenly, carried on the scent of lemons, was akin to the yearning for home. As though the isles called to some part of her so long hidden, so unknown that it had almost despaired of ever being heard.

Absurd. She was there to find Royce, nothing more. The yearning she felt was for him. The lemons—and yes, now she could also smell the thyme and was that oleander?—the scent was more complex than she had thought, made of fragrances layered one upon the other. Yet for all that, the perfume of Akora was a pleasant novelty of no consequence. Alex was watching her. She had, again, the sense that he saw beyond her skin.

"When I am away from Akora any length of time," he said, "I smell her in my dreams." It was the most personal comment he had ever volunteered and she was startled by it. So much so that she said the first thing that came into her head.

"Why do men refer to their countries as though they were women?"

He looked surprised that she did not know. "Because we are born of them."

"Then why ships, why are they also called she?"

He smiled a little, cautiously as though unwilling to reveal too much. "Because they bear our dreams?"

She almost asked, "What do you dream?" But she stopped herself. Already, they were too close. Just then she knew in the quicksilver way of memory that it was not the lemons that awakened her. It was Alex, invading her dreams.

Reaching for a chart from the case, he said, "You can see more now."

Questions forgotten, she stared out the porthole. A soft gasp escaped her. Just ahead, still distant but clearly visible, rose a rocky escarpment that seemed to leap directly out of the surrounding sea. For a moment she was reminded of the white cliffs of Dover but these were different, being far more massive and steeper. Nor were they white but some mottling of colors she could not yet make out.

Alex came to stand beside her. She felt the warmth of his bare chest close against her back as though touch could reach against space to taunt.

"It will be several hours yet before we dock," he said quietly.

She nodded but did not look at him. After a few moments, the cabin door closed behind him. She exhaled deeply and found no relief.

Time passed but she had little sense of it. While her body stirred heedlessly, her mind sought distance from the moment, back in that ancient epoch when the island kingdom had been ripped apart.

What had it been like, that terrible night? Had there been any warning, any chance to flee? Alex had said his forebears had arrived in the aftermath. Why had they come to a place of such devastation? What had they found?

The wall of cliff grew nearer until it dominated the western horizon. Massive heights of twisted and distorted rock rose before her. There was not one color but many—purple, brown, red, mauve, cobalt, putty, sea green—blurring together at the edges but still distinct, reminding her of the streaks of separate stone that ran like veins through marble. She had a sudden thought of rock melting in catastrophic heat and felt again the horror that had struck this place. More time passed and still she stood at the porthole. The cliffs appeared unrelenting. Nowhere did she see even a hint of beach where a boat could be pulled in, much less a harbor.

The longer she stared, the more Akora looked to her a fortress designed to keep out all the world. By comparison, the battlements of the strongest castle appeared but a weak gesture of defense. Yet even the mightiest walls contain some chinks. Late in the morning, the cliff face that had seemed a monolith was interrupted by what appeared to be a narrow inlet. So Joanna would have thought it, had not she seen the map. What the Europeans far offshore with their spyglasses had assumed was only a small bay was in fact the twisting, hidden entrance to the drowned center of Akora.

Shortly after midday, they entered it. Scarcely had they done so when she heard a knocking against the hull and pulled herself up yet farther to stare down at the water. At first she could see nothing but after a moment or two, the knocking occurred again. As she watched, a large boulder loomed suddenly just above the surface.

Joanna gasped, fearing a blow that would rip open the hull, but a moment later she stared in amazement as the vessel struck the rock only to send it floating lazily away across the water. Bewildered, she looked more closely and saw that many such boulders drifted throughout the inlet. Floating rocks? Yes, of course, they must be pumice, such as the much smaller chunks she had seen washed up from time to time on the beach below Hawkforte, rock so filled with pockets of air that it weighed almost nothing and did not sink in water. This, too, would be more of the legacy of the vanished volcano.

A short time later, they passed beyond a farther turn in the inlet and came suddenly into a vast open sea. Land curved away from them on either side, vanishing into the distance. Far across the water, miles away, Joanna thought she made out what might be islands but they were still too distant for her to be sure.

The shores of the Inner Sea were vastly different from the cliffs beyond. Fertile fields gleaming green and gold in the sun ran down to the water that was itself a brighter blue than the ocean they had just left. Long, silvered fish darted beside the boat and seabirds flew overhead, their haunting calls drifting on the scented air.

She felt the barque tack eastward and realized they were turning toward the large island where the capital of Ilius lay. Up on a distant hill she caught sight of what might be a farmhouse, looking not unlike those she had seen in Greece, with whitewashed stone walls gleaming beneath a tiled roof. But it was far away and they were passing quickly; she could not be sure it was anything other than a slash of exposed limestone.

Of the gleam of white that appeared shortly close to the shore she had no such doubt. Her breath left her as she found herself staring at a small, perfect temple glistening in the sun. It looked both like and unlike temples she had seen. White columns rose to a peaked roof sheltering a portico that yielded to the dark shadow of a hidden interior. But the walls were not the stark white she had seen amid the ruins of Attic Greece. They were vividly painted on their lower portions with what appeared to be a continuation of the surrounding landscape. Vines twined up the columns, and just beneath the peak of the roof the statue of a woman in a long flowing skirt gazed out over the water.

Excitement gripped Joanna as the reality of where she was sank in. She had truly reached the hidden kingdom, overcoming obstacles generations of would-be explorers, conquerors, traders and adventurers had found too daunting. She was there, in a world where the past that so fascinated her was not lost in the mists of time but remained vividly alive.

Now if only her brother did the same.

Her smile faded, exhilaration vanishing as quickly as it had come. She shut her eyes, breathing a silent prayer for Royce, yet another of a thousand such prayers she had offered up in recent months. When she opened her eyes again, the little temple and its goddess were gone. She turned away from the porthole and busied herself gathering up her few belongings. That swiftly done, she sat down on the bed and schooled herself to wait. Soon enough the effort proved beyond her and she returned to look out again.

She told herself it was merely sensible to learn as much of the terrain as she could. But already she suspected the perfumed air carried on it a potent spell.

Ilius came upon them suddenly. For some time, Joanna thought the habitations glimpsed through the porthole were becoming more frequent but even so she was not prepared when they rounded a curve of land and the city lay before them. Her thirsty gaze tried to drink it in all in an instant and, of course, failed.

This much she saw: There was a deep harbor at waterside from which several dozen stone quays jutted, a third of them occupied by vessels of varying sizes, some almost as large as the *Nestor*, others looking too small to ever venture beyond the Inner Sea. Neat rows of whitewashed buildings rose in tiers one above the other, sharing space with flowering trees and bushes heavy with white, pink and yellow petals. Roads picked a way among them, rising with the broad hill until they passed through high, deep walls on which watchful men paced. Beyond the walls she could make out towers, loftier than any she had ever seen, gleaming white in the sun.

"The topless towers of Ilium," she murmured and grimaced. Who but the bluestocking Alex had called her would think of Christopher Marlowe's immortal line at such a time? Yet it fit somehow.

Had she been asked to describe Troy, it would have

looked like this, powerful and beautiful in the sun. Never mind that people said it was just a story. It had been real to her since childhood and now it seemed before her, but undefeated, the topless towers unburned, no face having come to launch a thousand ships against it.

She sighed and inhaled deeply, drawing the scent of the place into herself. Lemons again, stronger than ever, and with them the thyme and oleander. But also the scents of a harbor that were no stranger to her than the scents of Hawkforte down by the water. The salt sea and the tang of fish, wet hemp braided into rope, stone and pitch, all mingling with the spicy aromas that flowed from the multitude of windows thrown open to the magnificent day.

The tide was incoming and carried them with it. She caught sight of people moving along the piers and the streets beyond. Her curiosity almost unbearable, she watched them, scarcely blinking as the ship moved ever nearer to shore.

They were dark haired for the most part and their skin, when not bronzed by the sun, held the olive tinge she knew well from journeys around the Mediterranean. But here and there she caught sight of some who looked curiously fairer. At such a distance and with the vessel still moving rapidly, she thought it likely she was mistaken. Despite Darcourt's comment on nudity, she saw none. Men and women alike were garbed in simple, sunbleached tunics although the men's tended to be much shorter than their feminine equivalents. The exceptions were the soldiers, of whom there seemed to be a great many. They wore the same pleated kilt that graced Darcourt's form so disconcertingly, and looked to a man supremely fit, but she scarcely noticed them. Some were boarding or disembarking from vessels along the quays, others were strolling apparently at their leisure among the shops and stalls that fronted on the water. In that regard, Ilius reminded her of virtually every port she had ever seen, including London itself. Yet there was no denying that the differences far outweighed any similarities.

Most immediately to her startled eye, she realized that everywhere she looked, whether along the docks themselves or up into the town rising all the way to the palace itself, she saw no glimpse of the poverty so common in London. No children clustered to beg, no women stepped from the shadows in search of custom, no painfully thin dogs slinked about. There were no evil little warrens of stinking lanes with buildings so decrepit that they leaned into each other, blocking out the sun as effectively as they crushed all hope. No heaps of garbage and offal, nothing except the gleam of whitewashed walls and the dizzying scent of nature triumphant.

They were close enough for her to see the pale green foam on the waves licking against the stone blocks of the piers when Darcourt returned. His easy manner of earlier in the day was gone. She felt a pang of loss as she looked into features that were aloof, withdrawn and even stern.

With a flick of his powerful wrist, he shook out the neatly folded bundle he carried, revealing a long, hooded robe of finely woven white wool. "You will wear this when you disembark. There will be a covered litter on the pier. You will be taken to my quarters in the palace. I must meet with the Vanax. It will likely be very late before I return. The servants will make you comfortable."

Joanna absorbed all this in silence. She reminded herself that he was accustomed to giving orders. That she was in his debt. That she cared for nothing beyond finding her brother.

The robe was a single piece without any opening. To don it, she would have to put it on over her head. About to do so, she looked at Darcourt. His expression was unreadable. She had no hope that hers was as contained.

"Will you speak with the Vanax about Royce?"

A flicker of surprise moved behind those crystalline

eyes. "We will speak of what we speak of." He moved toward the door.

He meant to leave, just like that. As though all her fear and dread, all her determination and desperation meant nothing. What of the promise he seemed to have made to her when he said they would find Royce? Was that, too, meaningless?

"Wait! I have to know. What will you do to try to find Royce? What will *we* do?"

He turned, the hard line of his mouth even sterner than it had been. "*We?* You will do what is necessary to avoid the trouble your presence is otherwise certain to cause. That is all you need concern yourself with."

"You cannot possibly expect me to just sit back and do nothing. I have waited far too long and risked too much to be able to bear that."

The moment the words were uttered she knew she had made a mistake. He crossed the room in three quick strides. Before she could draw a breath, his hand closed on her upper arm, not the one that had been injured but the other. The wound was almost healed; he had checked it himself several mornings before when he had come in with breakfast and found her sleeping deeply. Even so, she had almost awakened, murmuring softly in her dreams and turning toward him. He preferred not to dwell on that. Angry or not—and just then not was not an option—he would never touch her in any way that could harm her.

"Have you learned nothing about Akora?" he demanded. "Have you understood nothing?"

"You told me little enough—"

"More than you have any right to—"

He broke off, abruptly aware of the confusion of his thoughts. The barriers were too great; a lifetime of training, of assumptions so deeply ingrained that he didn't question them, about *xenos,* about women, about everything he was supposed to do and be. And yet were those not the same barriers he was committed to lessening, the same assumptions he was determined to challenge?

What could he say to her? That when they left the *Nestor* they would be stepping into a perilous situation made worse by her presence? That already he was distracted by mounting concern over his ability to keep her safe? That since that one kiss they had shared, he had needed every ounce of his formidable self-discipline to keep from touching her again?

They would be sharing a bed. That he did not even consider telling her; she would discover it soon enough. To do otherwise would alert the servants that something was not as it should be. Most, perhaps even all, of the palace staff were loyal. But these were uncertain times and it would take only one traitorous heart to make the situation even more dangerous than it already was.

Left to himself, he would never have agreed to bring her to Akora. But she had forced the issue and ultimately the decision to let her remain on board had been his. He had rejected the alternatives, all for good reason, but in doing so he had made her his responsibility.

He would protect her from the threats that lurked on Akora, from her impulsiveness and even, he thought grimly, from his desires.

But he was damned if he would explain himself to her. As a half-*xenos* child growing up in the royal court, he had learned long ago to keep his thoughts private. There were no exceptions to that, not even among those he loved most. It had never occurred to him that he might one day wish for that to change.

Abruptly, he realized that his hand was still around her arm. He had not intended to touch her, it had just happened. Smothering a groan, he released her and scowled deeply.

"You are not ignorant. I have told you that as a woman you must be—"

The twist of her lips could not be mistaken for a smile. "—pleasant, submissive, obedient, and demure. Believe me, I haven't forgotten."

"You just have no intention of behaving as you should."

She stared at him for a moment. He caught a glimpse of the worry she felt for her brother, the dread moving behind her eyes and had to fight the impulse to draw her to him, this time with no thought but to give comfort. Her shoulders slumped as some of the anger slipped from her. "I have the best of intentions. If they were all that mattered, I wouldn't be concerned."

"But you are." He, too, was finding it hard to hold on to what was surely the proper annoyance of a man faced with a woman whose ideas of propriety were so different from his own. Fascinatingly different, though he was loath to admit that even to himself.

"Having come this far, I don't see how I will manage to sit by while you or someone else tries to find Royce."

Despite himself, he felt a spurt of sympathy for her. Were their positions reversed, he would find such passivity the worst torture. But why was he thinking of that? He was a man, she a woman. Their positions were never going to be reversed. They were etched in tradition, culture and plain common sense.

"What did you think you would be doing?" he asked gently. "Wandering over hill and dale, beating the bushes for him?"

A sudden, wistful smile tugged at the corners of her mouth. It very nearly undid him. "You know," she said, "I can see myself doing just that."

His smile was rueful. "Unfortunately, so can I." The back of his fingers brushed her cheek gently. "Joanna, you must know that cannot be."

Her name seemed as natural on his tongue as if they had been intimate for many years. He had a sudden, startling urge to hear her say his own.

Madness.

Their gazes locked. Mere inches separated them. It would require only the slightest effort for him to lower his head and taste again that warm, tantalizing mouth . . .

Nestor nudged the dock, swayed gently on the swell, and settled into her accustomed berth as though she had never left it. The men on deck cheered as they always did at journey's end. There were answering shouts from the quay where passersby, recognizing the vessel, welcomed their prince back from his foreign adventuring.

Alex had a sudden impulse to order the ship turned around, put back to sea again. That, more than anything else, told him how perilous was the ground that rocked beneath his feet.

Duty and Honor. Mere words to some men. Life to him.

He straightened and let the mask of who and what he was slide back into place. More than ever, it was his shield. "Play the role," he said, and strode from the cabin without looking back.

ℋE WENT DIRECTLY to the palace, not waiting for a horse or escort but climbing the high, cobblestoned road with purposeful speed. At the top stood the proud gate framed by rearing stone lionesses. There were no lionesses on Akora. The statues were another sort of memory, this one of the land from which his ancestors had come. As a child, he had fallen into the habit of passing a quick, fleeting touch over the rear paws of the lioness who stood to the right when entering the citadel and those of her sister when leaving. They were a touchstone of sort, reminding him of what was real, what really mattered. As a boy, he had leaped high to reach even the lowest paws of the lionesses. As a man, he had only to reach up his hand. A fleeting smile touched the mouth that quickly grew stern again.

Beyond the gates lay the courtyard of flat hard-packed soil sprinkled by a recent rain so that no dust rose from it even on what promised to be a warm and sultry day. Fronting upon that vast expanse was the palace, which was vaster yet. He had been in several in Europe but never one that reminded him of the royal house of the Atreides. It was, to begin with, far older, with parts dating back three thousand years.

In unbroken line through all the centuries, the lords of Akora had maintained this, the most outward symbol of their power. Nothing was ever allowed to deteriorate or be forgotten or even be merely discarded. Legions of dedicated priests and priestesses saw to that. Should he choose to do so, he could walk into chambers where his most remote ancestors had stood, looking through windows that had revealed to them a seared and destroyed landscape only just returning to life. He could in his mind's eye see as they had seen and see, too, the fulfillment of their most fiercely held dreams. It took very little effort under such circumstances to envision a future born of the determination to keep Akora as strong and proud as generations of his forebears had found it.

It was a vision, he knew, shared by the man he had come to see. His pace quickening, Alex passed between the high fluted columns painted a vivid red, past the immense double doors of beaten bronze and incised wood thrown open as was the custom and into the first of the many assembly halls that formed this most public part of the palace. Inner columns lavishly decorated with twining vines held up a roof so high it seemed to challenge the sky it was painted to resemble. Against blue dark enough to be almost black, stars shone in the familiar patterns of the constellations as they appeared on the night of the spring equinox when day and night were perfectly balanced and the Great Mother prepared to shower mortals with the bounty of the earth's fertility. Along the walls, frescoes depicted the rites of sacrifice that revealed the sacred behind the seemingly ordinary tasks of tilling and sowing. In the center of the hall, a circular fountain spilled forth from one of the many streams deep underground. Water sparkled in the sunlight pouring through the high windows.

Guards stood at attention as the Prince of Akora passed, but Alex took no notice of them. Nor did he pause to acknowledge the intent glances of the courtiers always drawn near to the source of power. He left whispers in his wake as he continued on through the next assembly room and the next until he came at last to what was, relatively speaking, the smallest and most intimate of them all. Even so, it was large enough to hold the Carlton House crowd and then some. It was also unrelentingly masculine. Here the bull god held sway over all else, his image honored in frescoes and statues alike, his mighty head with horns tipped in gold dominating the wall above the throne that at the moment was empty.

No courtiers had been allowed this far. Only a handful of guards kept vigil on the stone battlements beyond the hall. Alex did not slow but walked past the throne to lightly touch the wall to its left. The door there was so cleverly painted as to seem to merge into the fresco but it was not truly concealed. Everyone knew of the door; only a very few could use it.

Beyond lay the private sanctum of the Vanax and what was arguably the ultimate center of power on Akora.

It was a surprisingly simple chamber free of any hint of excess. The white stucco walls were only modestly decorated with a geometric border near the ceiling. The floor was of plain, uncovered flagstone that held the cool of night far into day. A single large table stood by the window that took up most of one wall. The man who sat behind it looked up as Alex entered. He was about thirty, only a few years older than Alex himself, also ebonymaned and with hard, sculpted features that broke suddenly into a smile signaling both relief and genuine pleasure.

Rising swiftly, the Vanax Atreus, scion of the House of Atreides and chosen ruler of Akora, went to embrace his half brother. The two men were of a height and both equally honed by a life of hardship and training. They pounded each other on the back with enthusiasm that would have broken smaller folk.

"You made good time," Atreus said. "I didn't count on you before next week."

Alex grinned to see his sibling for once free of the worried frown that too often of late had shadowed his countenance. "Matters fell into place more rapidly than I had hoped."

Atreus nodded. Close enough in age to have grown up together, they had shared both the trials and adventures of young manhood but the bond between them went far beyond mere camaraderie. Each had been set apart virtually from birth, Alex because he was half-*xenos,* Atreus because he was fated to rule. Each might have been condemned to the loneliness of isolation had it not been for the other. From their childhood days in the Women's House to the long days and nights of manhood training high in the comfortless hills above Ilius they had woven ties of love and loyalty that would never be broken.

With such fidelity came understanding. Even as he touched hammer to gong to summon a servant, Atreus glanced again at his half brother. "So your mission was successful, good. But then what troubles you?"

Alex sighed. "You're too damn perceptive. It's eerie sometimes."

Atreus laughed, gestured to the pair of high-backed chairs near the window and took one himself. "Nonsense, it's just that I know you too well."

He broke off as a servant entered, bowing respectfully. "Wine," he said, "and something to go with it." Turning back to his brother, he asked, "Is English food still as bad as you've told me?"

"Worse, if possible. We were scarcely out of the Channel before the men were stirring up *marinos*."

Atreus laughed, his dark eyes flashing with amusement. "Still, I've a mind to experience it for myself someday, assuming the circumstances are ever right."

Alex nodded but did not comment directly. The servant returned, setting a blue-glazed ewer of wine and two matching goblets on a small inlaid table along with a tray of bread and cheese. He bowed low and withdrew. Atreus filled the goblets, handing one to Alex, who took a slow, appreciative sip.

"If the French had a gleaning of what our vineyards produce, they might not have sent only the one expeditionary force."

"It's just as well they don't, in that case. We have enough to deal with as it is."

Atreus took a sip of his wine, studied the goblet absently and said, "It's been quiet enough, all things considered, perhaps too quiet."

"The Council—?"

"Continues as before. Of the six, three seem predisposed to support me. The remainder . . ." He shrugged. "It's ironic that the youngest on the Council is also the most resistant to change, but then you remember how Deilos was even when we were boys."

Alex nodded, considering the son of one of Akora's oldest and most noble families with a lineage that could almost, if not quite, match that of the Atreides themselves. The boy who had always seemed most concerned with his dignity had grown into a cold and watchful man whose noble bearing masked what Alex believed was an arrogant, unbending nature. High nosed, the *ton* would have termed him, but he would not have lacked for like-minded souls among them.

"It is even more ironic because Deilos has more reason than most to know the wisdom of your policies. He has been outside Akora."

"His travels do not seem to have endowed him with the wisdom you have found."

Alex smiled wryly, wondering if his brother would think bringing home a *xenos* woman was particularly wise. Unwilling to dwell on that just then, he asked, "What about Troizus?"

Atreus shrugged broad shoulders lightly covered by a summer-weight tunic of unbleached linen. "He is as close-mouthed as ever but grumbles behind his hand. Rumor has it Deilos has suggested a marriage between their houses."

Alex's eyes narrowed slightly as he contemplated what that would mean. "Surely Deilos would consider it lowering to marry into Troizus's clan? We both know he has aspired higher."

"Without success. Kassandra will not consider him, nor am I inclined to try to persuade her."

Both men smiled at the thought of their younger sister who could, when she was so inclined, appear the very epitome of Akoran womanhood yet who had a full measure of the Atreides pride and will, not to mention what had come to her from her English forebears. Like Alex, she was half-*xenos* but the burden of that lay much more lightly upon her, perhaps because as a woman she would never be expected to lead.

"That leaves Mellinos," Alex said. "What are his objections?"

Atreus grimaced. "He claims to stand for Akoran values and traditions, to be determined not to see them undermined by what he refers to as 'feckless' change."

"Change essential to our survival."

"You see that," Atreus replied, "as do I, but there are many more like Mellinos who will fear any alteration in what they have always known. Change threatens their power, their prestige, their very identity. They will do anything to prevent it."

Alex's eyebrows rose. He stared at his brother directly. "Anything? That is very strongly put. Everyone knows that while the Council is expected to express its views freely and frankly in private, once the Vanax has decided, objections are to be put aside. *That* is an Akoran value and tradition."

"Perhaps I will host a dinner party," Atreus said with a smile. "I will invite you and Mellinos both. You can debate each other. I have no doubt as to the winner."

"If you were convinced words would settle this matter, you would be a good deal less concerned than you are right now."

"I thought I was the one who was supposed to be too damn perceptive. Which brings me back to my previous point. What troubles you?"

Alex took another swallow of his wine before setting it aside. Quietly, he said, "Remember the Englishman I mentioned to you, Royce Hawkforte? Last year, he made a bid to be allowed to come here. With conditions unsettled there as well as here, it wasn't an opportune moment for any such effort, as you and I both agreed. Now it seems Hawkforte was not inclined to take no for an answer. He left England nine months ago, told his sister he would be back in three and hasn't been seen since."

"There could be any number of explanations for that. After all, Europe is at war."

"True, but the Foreign Ministry has refused his sister any assistance in determining his whereabouts. If he had been captured or killed on the Continent, it is likely the British would know and have no reason for keeping quiet about it."

"But if he reached Akora, even if he was washed up dead on our shores, I would have known."

"Ordinarily, I would agree but these are far from ordinary times."

Both men sat silent for a few moments before Atreus said, "There are rumors, nothing more substantial than that, to the effect that those opposed to change have established a base from which they can move against me should they feel that is necessary."

Alex stood up abruptly. He walked over to the window and looked out at the curve of the harbor visible from it. The familiar scene should have brought him some measure of peace. Instead, it only heightened the anger stirring within him. Hands clasped behind his back, he said, "That is treason."

Atreus came to stand beside him. "There are some who would say that what I plan for Akora is treason."

Alex shot him a quick, hard look that gentled when he saw the understanding in his brother's eyes. The Vanax had far too keen a mind not to realize the implications of the course he was choosing for himself and his kingdom. It was a course he had determined on with the greatest care and only after much contemplation. Alex knew that because he had played a key role in helping his brother to come to the place where he was now.

"The world is changing as it has never done before," Alex said. "Nothing, not the invasions of the barbarians, the fall of Rome, nothing has equaled the upheaval that is upon us now. This new 'industrialism' that is sweeping out of England will engulf the world. If we try to stand against it, we will be swept away."

Atreus nodded. "You don't have to persuade me of that. The books you've brought as well as the machinery have more than convinced me."

"You see it but why don't others, especially those like Deilos, Troizus and Mellinos? Akora has always survived by remaining strong and that has always required change. We used to fight with bronze swords, now we use steel. Gunpowder was unknown here, now we make our own. Our ships are larger, more agile, and better armed than ever before. This nonsense about Akora always remaining the same has no basis in reality."

Atreus made a gesture of assent and returned to the window. "True enough but you will agree the course we are set on will mean change of a very different sort than what we have known in the past. It won't be merely a matter of strengthening our defenses in order to hold the world at bay. Instead, we will become much more a part of that world."

"In careful, measured steps," Alex reminded him. "And always with due regard for our heritage. After all, the whole point of this is to protect what we hold most dear."

Listening to him, Atreus smiled faintly but his expression was serious when he said, "I could bring you into the Council. It has been numbered at six now for a long time but there is nothing to say it must be only that many. There have been times in our history when the Council has been larger."

"But there has never been a time when a *xenos* has served on it."

Atreus looked at him chidingly. "You are hardly that."

"Half-*xenos* then. When it comes to the Council, many would consider that the same thing."

"Yet it is well known there is no man I trust more than you."

Alex's voice was husky as he said, "I thank you for that. But I still think it best if I remain behind the scenes. There may be advantages to my being able to come and go without accounting for my movements to the Council as I would have to if I joined it."

"You may be right. Do you really believe Royce Hawkforte could be on Akora?"

"His sister believes it. Indeed, she is absolutely convinced he is here."

"You spoke with her in London?"

"No," Alex said slowly. His attention was drawn by the line of guards and servants approaching the palace gate. Among them, bobbing gently, came a covered litter.

"Not in London," he said. Even as he watched, the curtains on one side of the litter parted ever so slightly. Torn between laughter and the sinking thought that Joanna was going to have an even more difficult time playing the proper woman than he had thought, Alex did not notice the Vanax's swift, assessing look.

But there was no mistaking Atreus's cool amusement when he asked, "Just what have you brought back from England this time, my brother?"

chapter

SEVEN

✳

$\mathcal{P}$EERING FROM BETWEEN the curtains enclosing the litter, Joanna struggled to contain her amazement. Seeing Ilius from the sea had not prepared her for the reality of the city itself. Everywhere she looked, vivid colors and designs leaped out to delight the eye. The walls of most buildings were painted in a palette of rich creams, blues, reds and greens. Many were also decorated with exquisite murals. Even as her litter passed along one street, climbing toward the palace, she saw several young men in the process of creating yet another mural on the outside of a nearby house. This one appeared to be of a magnificent garden that blended seamlessly with the real gardens flourishing throughout the city.

Every house and shop sported large urns of flowers by the windows and doors. Flowers even cascaded from the roofs and from baskets hung high on poles. Behind many of the buildings she caught glimpses of small orchards and kitchen gardens. A few dogs had the freedom of the streets and here and there she spied cats napping in the sun or lazily washing themselves. But other animals—mainly goats, chickens and a few pigs—were kept neatly tethered or penned. The streets themselves glistened in the sun, as though they had been scrubbed clean.

Her initial impression of a city far cleaner and more uniformly prosperous than any she had ever seen before was only confirmed as the procession climbed higher and higher above the harbor. Here, closer to the palace, the houses were larger, a few so much so that they might qualify as mansions. But save for their size, they seemed little different in their design or decoration from the abodes of more ordinary citizens. The huge gulf between rich and poor that she was accustomed to seeing in England and elsewhere was absent.

Startling though it was, that discovery was driven from her mind by the sudden appearance, around a bend in the road, of the vast gate leading to the palace. She gaped at the twin lionesses guarding the entrance, each the height of half a dozen men standing foot to shoulder, and barely caught herself before she would have stuck her head out of the litter entirely, the better to see such marvels. With a groan for the restrictions of propriety, she flopped back against the pillows of the litter but could only stay there a few moments. Quickly enough she was back at her perch, gazing through the finger-wide slit in the curtains that was all she felt she could allow herself.

Scarcely had they passed through the gate than Joanna had to remind herself that she was no country naïve. She had traveled widely, even visiting France in her fifteenth year during the too-brief hiatus in the seemingly endless warfare that had gone on since the French Revolution. While so many Englishmen and -women of the aristocracy who would normally have made the Grand Tour languished at home instead, she had seen Greece and even the Levant. The wonders of the world were no mystery to her; she had gazed upon many of them in person. Yet nothing had prepared her for what lay beyond the lion gate.

The entire top of the hill above Ilius appeared to have been sheared off by a giant's hand. Where the peak should have been was an immense courtyard framed on three sides by a palace of such beauty and grace as to steal her breath. Columns painted in the brilliant hues of sunrise rose three stories to a blue-tiled roof that covered what must surely have been several acres. The outer walls were a bright, sun-drenched white save where they were decorated with the geometric patterns she was coming to recognize. Beneath the eaves of the roof, at regular intervals, jutted the carved horns of bulls. A broad staircase led up to the central entrance where double doors, larger than any she had ever before seen, stood open.

But the servants carrying her litter did not go in that direction. Instead, they turned off toward the western wing of the palace. Even at a brisk trot, several minutes passed before they crossed the courtyard and approached another, slightly smaller staircase that gave entry to that side of the building. The litter slanted as the bearers climbed the steps.

Joanna heard the low murmur of voices just before the curtains were parted. Preferring not to be seen reclining on silken pillows, she stepped out quickly. The robe made movement a little difficult but she managed well enough. The moment she did, the bearers took up the litter again and withdrew. She was left standing alone with a slender woman of middle years simply clad in an ankle-length tunic, her dark hair, sprinkled with silver, twined in braids that were wound round her head. The woman clasped both her hands in front of her and bowed very slightly from the shoulders. Straightening, she looked at Joanna with sharp-eyed curiosity that was swiftly concealed.

Speaking slowly as though addressing a backward child, and gesturing to explain her words, she said, "I am Sida, lady, servant in the house of the Prince Alexandros. Please to come with me."

"Thank you, Sida," Joanna said briskly in the same language. "I am Lady Joanna Hawkforte. Akoran is still new to me so, please, feel free to correct any mistakes I make."

She had made none as was evident by the servant's unconcealed surprise. "You speak very well, lady, for a—" The older woman broke off, flushing slightly.

"For a *xenos*?" Joanna asked with a smile. "It is kind of you to say so but I am certain I have a great deal to learn." Without further ado, she tossed back the hood of her robe and stepped into the cool interior of the palace. Light streaming in through the many windows illuminated a chamber that was both elegant and welcoming. Plaster benches fitted along the walls were covered with vividly embroidered pillows of varied shapes and sizes. Low tables held bowls overflowing with fruit or flowers. Near the door, water spilled from the stone head of a dolphin to collect in a shallow basin on the floor before trickling away down a concealed pipe.

Gesturing to the water, Sida said, "It is the custom, lady, to bathe the feet when entering an abode."

In a climate that must be warm almost all the time and inevitably would sometimes be dusty, that seemed an eminently good idea. Moreover, it was in keeping with what she had already noticed about the Akorans' penchant for cleanliness. Her boots having vanished along with the rest of her clothes at the beginning of the voyage, Joanna was barefoot. She stepped into the cool water, holding up the hem of her robe. When she had stepped out again, Sida had a towel ready to dry her feet.

"Thank you," Joanna said but took the towel and performed the service for herself even as she imagined what Mulridge would say if she had allowed someone else to do it for her. At the thought of her stern but kindly friend, a sudden and utterly unexpected wave of homesickness struck her. In the excitement of the journey, she had spared little thought for those left behind save to hope the letter she had written explaining her intentions would provide at least some comfort. That Mulridge, Bolkum and the others would still worry she knew full well but there had been nothing to do about it.

But now that she was actually on Akora, the enormity of what she had done struck hard. She was thousands of miles away from everyone and everything she knew. Although Alex had promised to help find her brother, he had said nothing about what would happen after that. Most particularly, he had offered no assurances that she and Royce would be allowed to leave the Fortress Kingdom. Worse yet, as certain as she was that Royce was out there somewhere, waiting to be found, fear still ate around the edges of her confidence. It was possible he was not, in which case she would have to deal with the anguish of losing the only remaining member of her family alone and among strangers.

Something of her thoughts must have shown on her face, for Sida took the towel from her and said gently, "You have had a long journey, lady. It is well for you to rest and refresh yourself."

Her throat too thick for speech, Joanna nodded and allowed herself to be led away.

The apartment to which she was taken was reached by an interior staircase to the topmost floor. From there, the windows offered magnificent views of the town, harbor, and beyond to the Inland Sea. So clear was the day that Joanna could make out far in the distance the shadowed hump of one of the trio of small islands that bore such dread names.

Sida guided her past several spacious formal rooms to an inner suite that comprised a sleeping chamber, a lavish bath and what was apparently Alex's private study. As the servant left to fetch refreshment, Joanna's natural curiosity revived. She seized upon it as a shield against sorrow and allowed herself to be distracted by her surroundings. Despite the temptation of the many shelves of books and scrolls along the walls, she only stood at the threshold of the study and looked within. To actually enter it without invitation seemed discourteous. The rest of the suite she examined more closely, taking note in particular that there appeared to be only one bedroom.

The sound of Sida returning distracted her. The servant placed a tray on a table near the windows. "Please, lady," she said, gesturing to the chair, "sit. I have brought you *marinos,* very good, and a wine from Prince Alexandros's private stock."

She had also brought small rounds of freshly baked bread, a bowl of cherries, and a large slice of golden cheese. Joanna's stomach rumbled. With a small twinge of conscience, for she thought she really ought to be too concerned about Alex's meeting with the Vanax to even think of eating, she took her seat at the table.

Sida smiled her approval. She poured a straw-colored wine into a goblet before withdrawing. "I will return shortly, lady."

Joanna nodded absently, far too busy savoring the *marinos* to notice much else. Having not eaten all day, she would have done justice to far less sumptuous fare. As it was, the meal set before her seemed fit for a king.

Or a prince. Hearing Sida refer to Darcourt as Prince Alexandros had been a shock. His men had called him *archos,* apparently a military title, and there was still that matter of *kreon* to cope with. But *prince* drove the point home quite effectively. Her daring at importuning him as she had done—following him about London, stowing away on his vessel, insisting that he help find her brother—was coming back to haunt her. Not to mention that kiss—

Oh, no, she wasn't going to think about that. She'd already done so quite enough. Now was the time to be mature and sensible, most particularly if she was to have any hope of convincing him to let her help look for Royce. She was considering how to manage that when a faint movement out of the corner of her eye caught Joanna's attention.

It was only a little flicker of the curtain that concealed a small archway she had not noticed before but it was enough to make her aware suddenly that she was being watched. That singularly unpleasant sensation coupled with the warnings Alex had given her about the need to hold up appearances made the fine hairs on the back of her neck rise.

Instinct told her to launch herself straight across the room, throw back the curtain and haul the miscreant out without delay. But better sense warned that was not how a concubine would behave. Weren't such creatures far too worldly for any such action? A concubine would be used to being looked at. She wouldn't be disconcerted in the least. Indeed, she might simply be amused by it.

Joanna tried a faint laugh but it sounded hollow even to her ears. She settled for a sigh she hoped was appropriately languid. For good measure, she twirled the stem of the goblet between her fingers until it threatened to spin away from her. Setting it down just a little abruptly, she slanted a glance at the curtain. It was parted even farther. She could definitely see an eye.

"You might as well come out," she said. "We both know you're there."

There was a moment's hesitation before a stunning, dark-haired woman stepped into the room. She was an inch or two shorter than Joanna and a handful of years younger. Her hair was midnight black and cascaded in curls down her back. She wore a simple ankle-length tunic of pure white that left her arms bare and emphasized the lush swell of her breasts above a tiny waist. Her eyes were dark-fringed and large, her skin like cream touched with a drop of honey. There was something tantalizingly familiar about her straight nose and full mouth but Joanna was far too preoccupied just then to try to figure out what that might be.

A beautiful woman in Darcourt's quarters. Oh,

heavens, she should have thought of this. That he wasn't married hardly meant he would lack for female companionship. How to explain her presence? And worse yet, how to ignore the sudden, startling flare of jealousy that surged within her?

Joanna cleared her throat and stood up. All too mindful of the shapeless robe she wore, she wished it might at least have pockets to hide the hands that were suddenly clenching and unclenching.

She was about to speak when, to her surprise, the woman blushed—beautifully, of course—and smiled. "I am so sorry. You must think me the rudest person on earth. It was just when I heard the servants chattering about you, I was overcome with curiosity."

English. The stunning Akoran woman spoke fluent English with an accent that would have been perfectly at home in Mayfair.

"I... uh... really there is no need..."

"Oh, but there is!" With a quick, graceful step, the woman came forward. "I have so longed to meet an Englishwoman. If I have managed to offend you in just the first scant moments of our acquaintance, I shall be utterly devastated."

So earnest did she appear that Joanna found herself smiling in turn. "I'm not offended, truly, just surprised. I am Lady Joanna Hawkforte."

"And you are English?"

"Through and through."

"Wonderful! The servants said you were but I could hardly credit it. Oh, my manners! I am Princess Kassandra of the House of Atreides."

"Princess..." Instinctively, Joanna began to curtsey only to be stopped by Kassandra's gentle laugh and her hands on her shoulders.

"Oh, none of that! We don't stand on such formality, especially among women. Men can be stuffier about such things but then you know how *they* are."

It wasn't posed as a question, which was just as well because Joanna might have felt compelled to admit that she had scarcely any idea. At any rate, no reply seemed required as Kassandra continued on happily. "I am Alexandros's sister, in case you were wondering, his younger of course, which he has a rather bad habit of not letting me forget. As though that weren't enough, there is Atreus as well. He's our half brother and really wonderful as is Alexandros truly, but the two of them have a tendency to be rather overprotective, not to mention always believing they know what is best."

"I see—"

"I've been absolutely longing to visit England. Well, really, to visit anywhere but most especially England. Alexandros brings back the most wonderful books and tells me the most delightful stories but, of course, that isn't the same as actually going there myself, is it? I dream of seeing Mayfair, shopping along Bond Street, visiting Ackermann's, buying sweets at Gunter's, and all the rest. I even want to stroll along St. James's though Alexandros says I couldn't because all the gentlemen's clubs are there and it's considered improper for a lady to even ride down the street in a carriage. What nonsense! Or should I say fustian? I do try to keep current with what people are saying but, of course, it's really impossible at such a distance."

She sighed deeply. "It is all so strange and wonderfully exotic, so mysterious. And now, to actually meet someone from there—" She broke off as Joanna laughed. "Oh, you must think me foolish."

"Not at all," Joanna assured her swiftly. "It's just that those are the same words—strange, exotic, mysterious— that I would use to describe Akora. London, on the other hand, seems ordinary."

In deference to Kassandra's enthusiasm, she did not add that London had many flaws. Ilius, by contrast, seemed immensely more beautiful and congenial.

"Ordinary to you no doubt," Kassandra said, "but you are a woman of the world. You actually *live* while I..." She sighed again, then grinned a bit abashedly. "Oh, listen to me, I sound like the greenest girl. Never think for a moment that I am complaining about my circumstances. I know my good fortune. It is just that I envy Alexandros, being able to come and go as he does, while I must remain here."

"Because you are a woman?"

"Yes, because of that." She looked at Joanna cautiously. "How much do you know about Akoran society? I mean about the position of women and . . . well, everything? Did Alexandros explain very much to you?"

The corners of Joanna's mouth lifted. Even on such short acquaintance, she liked Kassandra. There was a naturalness about the young woman Joanna had found missing among the young ladies of the *ton* she had encountered during her brief forays among them. For all her high rank, the Princess seemed completely unaffected.

"He said women were supposed to be obedient and...demure, that was it. Oh, and something else about having no thought except to please the man to whom they belong."

Even as she spoke, Joanna wondered if she was being too flippant. She was, after all, a guest and it did not do to criticize the ways of another. But a quick glance at Kassandra indicated the Princess understood only too well what she was saying.

"Alexandros would say that and no doubt he believes it. Or at least, part of him does. The thing to remember is that here in Akora nothing is ever quite as simple or straightforward as it looks on the surface. We are a very old culture with layer upon layer of history and tradition. But don't be concerned. When you have been here longer, you will understand a good deal more."

"I certainly hope so," Joanna murmured even as she wondered just how long Kassandra imagined she would be staying. The young Princess seemed to take her presence in stride, asking nothing about the reasons for it. But she had made that comment about Joanna being a woman of the world...

Deliberately, she said, "I haven't actually known Prince Alexandros very long."

"Really? Still he brought you back with him, which he's never done before even though no doubt he's had other concubines in England. There will be eyebrows raised, of course, but then there always are, at least in certain quarters. Don't let it trouble you any. Personally, I think it's marvelous that you're here. If you have the patience for it, I have endless questions. Oh, I know! I'll help you get to know Akora and you can teach me about England. Do you think that would be fair?"

"Eminently," Joanna said, hoping Kassandra did not notice how the easy reference to concubine made her blush. The young, unmarried Princess was a good deal more frank that a counterpart of hers in England would have been. Was that merely her nature or were Akoran women in general more accepting of such things? Yet one more mystery about the Fortress Kingdom to puzzle over.

"I would love to talk about England with you," Joanna said, "and to learn about Akora. Where should we start?"

"With clothes."

Both young women turned swiftly to see Sida returning, her arms piled high with glorious lengths of cloth. The servant smiled as she beheld their surprise.

"The Prince Alexandros remains closeted with the Vanax but he sent word that the Lady Joanna requires a wardrobe, her own having been left behind. I have taken the liberty of making a few preliminary selections for your consideration, lady."

Kassandra shot her new friend a startled look. She tried but could not entirely repress a soft laugh. "You came away without clothes? How impulsive of you. Or should I say how impulsive of my brother?"

Perhaps it would be best to cultivate a tan, the better to conceal her blushes. Quite at a loss as to what to say, Joanna focused her attention on the fabrics. They truly were glorious. As Sida spread them out around the room, draping them over chairs, tables and the vast bed, the chamber took on the appearance of Ali Baba's cave. Joanna had difficulty remembering that she had always loathed being fitted for clothes.

"If you would remove your robe, lady?" Sida asked softly.

Joanna did as she was bid only to quickly regret it. One look at her in Alex's tunic had Kassandra grinning broadly. Sida's eyebrows shot up so far they seemed to disappear into her hair but the servant managed to refrain from comment. However, she did turn away hastily and took a moment to compose herself.

"Better and better," Kassandra murmured, but her good humor faded a moment later when the tunic slipped enough to reveal the still ragged slash of the wound on Joanna's arm.

"Heavens!" Kassandra exclaimed. "How ever did that happen?"

"A little accident," Joanna said, quickly tugging up the sleeve. "It's nothing."

Kassandra did not comment further but her brow furrowed. Joanna could almost see the questions revolving behind her eyes. To distract her, she said, "So many beautiful fabrics. I do hope you can advise me as to what would be best."

"Oh, I'd love to. One of the many disadvantages of being a virgin is that I can only wear white, but I dream of the day when that color will be banished from my wardrobe."

"Is that likely to be soon?" Joanna asked, partly from curiosity but mainly to draw attention away from herself. She had the sinking feeling the Princess saw too much.

"Not if I have any say in the matter," Kassandra replied

cheerfully. "Atreus says I am a romantic but I don't care. I want to marry a man who utterly thrills me, not to mention one who is sympathetic and understanding about my dream of experiencing the world beyond Akora."

Sida made a clucking sound of disapproval that prompted a laugh from the Princess. "Oh, I know, my views are horribly shocking. It's just as well I am in no rush to wed for no proper warrior would have me." Her expression grew more serious as she added, "At least not for myself. Not for who I really am."

"Mistress thinks too much about such things," Sida said as she held up a length of fabric and compared it to Joanna's skin and hair. "There was a day when such matters were decided between men. A proper young woman was not informed until all was settled."

"But times are changing, Sida," Kassandra said cheerfully. "And they are going to change a great deal more. Besides, admit it, how many maidens really didn't know who their husbands were to be until they were told formally? For that matter, how many maidens went to their marriage bowers still maidens?"

"I have no idea, Princess," the older woman said stiffly but an instant later, her manner softened. "But I do know you worry needlessly. The right man will come along, just you see."

"It's perfectly fine with me if he doesn't. The Vanax just might be persuaded someday to grant my wish and allow me to travel. But if I marry, a husband will have authority over me. I'll be lucky to see the light of day." She shivered at the thought.

"Is marriage truly so bad on Akora?" Joanna asked.

"Of course not," Sida replied at once, but Kassandra was close on her heels.

"It is fine for some women, perhaps even most. Indeed, it may have to be fine for me someday. After all, I do have certain responsibilities."

"You mean you would make a political marriage?"

"If I had to . . . How I hope it does not come to that! But it is expected I will have children. After all, being half-*xenos* it is especially important that I do so."

That surprised Joanna. She would have thought that the Akoran aversion to *xenos* would have meant the opposite. But before she could question Kassandra about it, Sida whipped a string from her pocket and began taking measurements.

"Just stand up a little straighter, lady. That is good. This will not take but a minute." She murmured numbers to herself, nodding when she was satisfied.

"Akoran styles are generally simple," Kassandra said. "I'm sure we can have a complete wardrobe made up for you in just a few days."

"I really don't want to cause a lot of bother. Anything will be fine."

The two other women sensibly ignored this and began discussing fabrics. For all her lack of personal experience, the Princess had an expert eye. She unerringly picked the materials Joanna most liked and discarded those she thought less appealing. Even so, the pile left to be made into clothing for her was scarcely smaller than the original.

"That is too much," Joanna protested, just a little weakly. She started to blurt out that she didn't expect, or rather hoped not, to be on Akora very long. Catching herself, she said only, "I won't have use for all that."

The Princess was about to answer her when suddenly she went very still. A moment passed before Joanna noticed and then she was startled. Kassandra's entire, ebullient personality appeared to have vanished. In its place was an immense silence that seemed to hold her at its center. Her eyes were focused not on the palace room and its occupants but on some inner landscape unseen by others. Even as Joanna watched, Kassandra's breathing quickened so much as to be visible. As though from a great distance, she said, "You will be here a long time."

Sida stopped in the midst of folding a length of fabric and stared at the Princess. For a moment after she had spoken, Kassandra seemed to stop breathing entirely. Sida went to her and gently touched her arm. "Princess . . ."

Just that, nothing more, but it was sufficient. Kassandra stiffened, then shook herself slightly. She blinked several times before taking a deep breath. With a quick glance at Joanna, she smiled. "What was that you said?"

"What I said—?" What she had said was of no consequence at all. It was what the Princess had said that interested her a good deal more. "Why did you say I would be here a long time?"

Kassandra looked away, uncomfortably, Joanna thought. "Did I? My mind must have wandered. Do forgive me."

She sounded very tired, suddenly, and looked quite pale.

"You should rest, Princess," Sida said. Without waiting for a response, the servant turned to Joanna. "If you will excuse me, lady, I will accompany the Princess back to her quarters. I will return shortly."

Kassandra managed an apologetic smile but all the light seemed to have gone out of her. She offered no objection when Sida took her arm and gently led her back toward the curtained archway.

Alone, Joanna looked at the soft flutter of the curtain as it fell behind them. She waited until their footsteps died away, then went over to the curtain and peered behind it. A corridor led off into the distance, lit by high windows cut into the stone walls. A private means of coming and going, separate from the public spaces of the palace. Such passages existed in many great houses in England. Hawkforte itself boasted several. But unlike such passages as she knew, these were not concealed except only most moderately behind a curtain that would not have deterred anyone determined to discover the private route. Public privacy. It was a new idea for her and startling in what it suggested about the Akorans. That they did not rely on secrecy or other such measures but rather on courtesy, including the good manners that allowed public figures to have some semblance of private life.

An interesting notion but not to compare with the far more startling behavior of the Princess. Kassandra. What parent with any knowledge of Greek lore would name a child for the doomed princess of Troy, condemned to prophesize the future but never to be believed? Unless, of course, the name had other meanings for the Akorans, some of those layers upon layers the Princess had mentioned. Joanna was pondering that when Sida returned.

"Is the Princess all right?" she asked the servant.

"She is resting, lady. If you permit, I have just a few more measurements to take for your clothes."

"Is she subject to sudden spells?"

Searching about for something, Sida shook her head. "The Princess is very healthy, lady." She continued lifting lengths of cloth . . . searching. "Now where did I—"

"What are you looking for?"

"My measuring string. I am certain I left it here somewhere."

The measuring string. Not much different from that which seamstresses at home used. About a yard long, marked with notches . . . pale in color . . . the marks very dark, the better to stand out clearly . . .

"Under that amber silk," Joanna said. "Right over there, on the stool."

Sida spotted it with evident relief. She took the remaining measurements efficiently enough but it was clear to Joanna that her mind was elsewhere. Much as she would have liked to ask Sida more about the strange occurrence with Kassandra, she realized the servant would not be inclined to answer. Rather than put her in the position of refusing, or dissembling, Joanna kept silent.

When Sida left, taking the lengths of cloth with her, Joanna almost called her back to ask if she knew when Alex was likely to return. Better sense stopped her. If she actually were Alex's concubine—a hugely, purely theoretical *if*—and further, *if* they had come away from England with such impetuosity that she had no clothing with her and *if* he had broken with hallowed custom to bring her to Akora—given all those many *ifs*, then surely she would reasonably assume that he would hurry to her side at the earliest possible opportunity and not need to ask at all.

If.

Shrugging the thought aside, Joanna took a deep breath and turned her mind to Royce. Her efforts to find him while still at sea had failed but now that she was on Akora, surely there would be some glimmer, some hint of where he might be found. Willing herself to calm, she reached inward but found only the confusion of her thoughts and worries. That would not do. With an impatient shake, she tried again, still without success. The fear that there might be nothing left to find welled up in her suddenly, making her body go rigid and her breath catch.

Frustration filled her and with it the hard edge of anguish. A measuring string she could find, a newspaper, silly, inconsequential items. But not her brother; for all her love, he remained beyond her reach.

As he might be beyond the reach of anyone.

A vision of him darted like quicksilver through her mind, standing in the library at Hawkforte, the room they both loved best, laughing away her concerns.

"I'll be back by Christmas, sister mine, never fear . . ."

Christmas come and gone, smoke curling from the chimneys, snow on the ground, the sea grey and heavy. They had celebrated the season as usual but there was no heart in it for her, no joy. The winter had been long and seemingly endless. She fell to counting days.

"I must go... there are reasons... things aren't as they should be..."

Spring and the awakening of the earth that had not touched her as it usually did. She had merely gone through the motions, trying to reassure those around her, knowing they, too, worried.

"The government is... unsettled. Prinny can't make up his mind about anything... he wavers this way and that. There are elements... foolish... impulsive... influencing him..."

The news from the Continent was uncertain. Wellington held firm on the Peninsula, it seemed. But Napoleon remained, even more aggressive since the birth of his son and heir earlier in the year, a demigod of war whose appetite for conquest seemed insatiable. Britain, with ambitions of its own, still unreconciled to the loss of its American colonies, turned hungry eyes toward Australia... India... perhaps Akora?

"Have to hope they're more sensible on Akora. But then, they'd have to be, wouldn't they? Having survived so long."

"Be careful, for God's sake. You know the rumors..."

"Know Darcourt's father made it, must have, and there are other rumors, chit, some even you don't know about, believe it or not." That flashing smile that never failed to transform what was otherwise a rather serious, albeit very handsome face. A quick chuck under her chin such as he had done since they were children. A final warm hug and he was gone, swiftly down the stone steps of the entrance to the house that had nurtured them both, onto the fine black gelding he preferred over any coach. He'd turned halfway down the long, chestnut-framed drive and waved to her. She had forced a smile and waved back but already a tiny kernel of dread had begun to form within her.

Royce...

He was so strong, so vital, so central to her life. If he were gone from the world, surely she would know it.

But she did not. To the contrary, when she let herself look inward to the stillness at the core of her being, she could almost...just almost... touch him.

Her fingers were pressed against the window frame. Joanna jumped a little, recalled to the here and now with a jolt. She stared at her arm, stretching out, and her hand, touching stone. Stone that for just an instant had felt damp and cold. But the stone she looked at was dry and still held the warmth of the sun.

The air was soft and fragrant, not chill and clammy. The room was lit by the glory of the setting sun, not dark with only a tiny bar of light. She was clean, dry, rested, not...

Royce.

He lived and she had, somehow, reached out in an instant of time and made contact with him in some way she had never understood yet still accepted. Her brother lived and joy filled her but hard on it came dread. Despite his great strength and will, he was weakening.

Time was running out.

While she sat, cosseted in the quarters of a Prince.

Play the role, Alex had said.

Her hands clenched into fists. She hit them against the stone wall until pain finally pierced terror and released resolve.

EIGHT

$\mathcal{T}$HE PRIESTESSES WHO KEPT VIGIL at the sanctuary of the Moon had burnt their final offerings of the night and sought their rest before Alex left his brother.

He and Atreus had lingered late, talking over the events of recent months and what they might presage for the future. Much was known to Alex from letters carried by trusted couriers that had flowed back and forth during his most recent visit to England, but there was no substitute for discussing matters face-to-face. Their speech was frank and far-ranging. The situation was as Alex had concluded, volatile and approaching what might well be a critical moment.

Atreus, being a sensible man, had retired at last. Alex had found reasons not to do the same. A passing thought of Joanna asleep in his bed was enough to send him down to the beach below the palace. There he walked along the foam-strewn sand, well aware his steps were watched by the ever-attentive sentries in the guard towers but putting them from his mind as he found at least some semblance of solitude.

Too soon, it chafed. Too often, his mind turned back to the silken bed and the woman in it.

Madness.

He had real, serious concerns to occupy him. Now was hardly the time for dalliance, nor was a woman with serious matters of her own the proper object of his designs.

She would not like what he had to tell her. That there was no word of her brother would hurt her deeply. No doubt that was part of why he lingered on the cooling sand long after the moon had set and only the stars remained.

In England, he had known silent nights. Long hours of darkness when it seemed as though nothing in the world stirred save himself. Nights when the chill would finally drive him back inside to stoke the fire and take the heat of a woman.

Nights on Akora were different. Tree frogs hummed just beyond the beach. Fruit bats fluttered, unthreatening to anything save the savory treats they sought. Were he to look, he knew he could find the foxes who hunted at night and the owls who did the same. There was even the occasional splash, a playful porpoise or a ray, possibly even an octopus although they rarely ventured near the surface.

Why was he thinking of such things? He needed to go inside, get some sleep and prepare himself to deal with the challenges facing his kingdom, his people and his family. On the other hand, he could just sit on the beach all night. Chances were he'd doze at some point. His training as a warrior had prepared him to get by on very little rest. He would be fine.

Coward.

The word, come unbidden into his mind, stung. He strode back up the beach, stopped, turned again to look at the water, dark now that the moon slept. Dawn would come soon enough.

She would be asleep.

There was no need to wake her. Indeed, it would be a kindness not to do so. It was a man's duty to treat women kindly but in her case, he also found it a natural inclination. The idea of her being sad or afraid or in want caused something inside him to twist painfully.

And yet, right beside that was the hunger she prompted. The twin drives to possess and protect could cause problems for a man. This was well known and no boy came of age on Akora without being counseled by the older men as to how to deal with such conflict. Discipline was the key. A warrior controlled himself. A warrior exercised restraint. A warrior had enough sense not to stray into the path of temptation.

A warrior also faced up to what had to be faced.

She would be asleep.

He would gain the morning, at least, and then there would be pressing duties to require his attention. He and his men had been too long from the training fields. It would be good to be back there, sweating and straining, honing his skills. Good, also, to remind anyone in need of such reminder that the Prince of Akora, strong right arm of the Vanax, had returned.

It was very quiet in the palace. The servants had long since sought their rest, the courtiers were mercifully absent and the sanctuaries were silent. Even so, he avoided the public rooms and walked swiftly through the private corridor that connected the various family quarters. At either end were the apartments of the royal brothers, in between was Kassandra's.

At the thought of his sister, Alex smiled. He would see her on the morrow, indulge her thousand or so questions, and remain noncommittal on the subject of her longed-for visit to England which, thankfully, was Atreus's decision.

She would hear of Joanna and want to meet her, which, now that he thought of it, would be a good way to keep both women occupied, if somewhat risky. Kassandra had shown, of late, a certain discontent that might be simple boredom or might be something more. She had little interest in her formal duties and none at all in marriage. Alex knew there were times when she rode for hours, often at a gallop, leaving her escort trailing behind her as though she was in flight from an existence she found too constraining. He was sympathetic to that even as he doubted there was any real solution. She was, after all, a woman.

As was Joanna, a woman who was accustomed to managing her family's manor and who did not hesitate to go in search of her missing brother. Fuel for frustration's fire, but not to be helped. Once Kassandra knew an Englishwoman was in residence, there would be no way of keeping them apart short of locking them up, which would make them both very unhappy, therefore was cruel, therefore forbidden.

So much for the "warriors rule" aspect of Akoran society, Alex thought with a grimace. It was a useful enough fiction in the outside world but when it came to day-to-day life...

And night-to-night. He had reached the private entrance of his apartment. Cautiously, he moved the curtain over the archway aside slightly and looked within. He was merely being careful not to wake Joanna, so he told himself. But a glance at the bed quickly had him frowning.

It was empty.

Hell and damnation!

Throwing aside the curtain, he strode into the room. If she had decided to take matters into her own hands, gone off somewhere...

Dread filled him, drowning out even perfectly proper rage. For a torturous moment that seemed to go on and on, he turned this way and that, scanning the room. So anxious was he to find her that he almost missed the slim shape folded into the shadows near the window.

A quick exhalation of breath and he was beside her, looking down at the woman asleep on the bench.

She had a huge bed to stretch out in and she preferred a cramped bench. She had every reason to rest soundly, trusting him to handle the matter of her brother—she did trust him, didn't she?—and she slept frowning as though worry had chased her into dreams. Worse yet, bending closer, he saw the track of tears along cheeks pale in starlight.

The tightness in his chest was startling. He scooped her up, cradling her in his arms, and carried her over to the bed. She stirred slightly but did not wake. Laying her down, he eased the silken covers back until he could slip her under them. She looked very small but he did not make the mistake of thinking her weak. She had the spirit of a lioness, one of those who guarded the city gates and padded through the legends of his people. But even lionesses had bad moments.

Slowly, he sank down onto the bed beside her and took a slim hand in his. Turning it over, he stared at the long, slender fingers, the deceptively fragile bones. His thumb rubbed over her palm. The skin there held a slight roughness, from reins perhaps? Although it might have been from wielding a shovel or hoe. He suspected she would be a fierce gardener.

The English ladies he had known were forever slathering themselves with creams, avoiding the sun, and doing everything possible to keep their skin soft and unblemished. Any hint of manual labor was considered déclassé in the extreme. He had never managed to get used to that.

With a deep sigh, he slipped her hand under the covers. But when he tried to let go of it, her fingers closed around his. She murmured something. He couldn't be sure but it had sounded suspiciously like his name.

For the first time since setting foot again in the home of his heart, the balm of peace stole over him. It was deceptive, of course. Nothing had changed. The moment was perilous, the crisis loomed. But for just a little space of time, he could set that aside. The bed beckoned. He ignored it and the fire in his blood as well. For this

woman, he would sit through the remaining hours of the
night, heedless of his own needs, and simply hold her
hand. Rather to his surprise, that was enough.

For now.

JOANNA WOKE SUDDENLY toward dawn. No gentle waking this but rather the shock of her mind certain that
something was very wrong.

She had slept. It was morning, if just barely.

Hours had come and gone, and she had failed to
speak with Alex, to tell him what she knew, to insist—no,
that would not work, to persuade him—to act *now,* without further delay.

Shamed by her weakness, she left the bed quickly
and was standing halfway across the room trying to decide what to do when she realized she had no memory of
getting into the bed in the first place. But she did remember . . . something . . . strong arms, gentle reassurance . . .
closeness that soothed and comforted her.

Alex had been there. He had come in the night and
placed her in the bed. Had stayed with her? It was
damnable that she could not remember, even worse that
she had been so weak as to sleep in the first place.

Frustration warred with confusion. Why did she not
wake when he came and went, first bringing her breakfast on the ship, now making sure she slept comfortably?
How could she sleep through that? Why did he make her
feel so utterly safe? And so deeply unsettled?

It didn't matter. Sternly, she reminded herself that
nothing did except Royce. He was alive. She had felt his
presence. Given enough effort, she could find him. But
not sitting in a palace, sleeping in a silken bed.

"Alexandros is out on the training field," Kassandra
said as she came through the archway. She looked well
rested and relaxed. All sign of the strange episode the
previous day seemed to have vanished. "He's liable to be

there all day. I was wondering if perhaps you would like to go riding? You ride, of course? I understand all English ladies do but sidesaddle, is that right? How very strange that must be. I can't imagine sitting that way on a horse without falling off. Perhaps you could show me except we don't have any of that sort of saddle. Can you ride without it? Not without any saddle, I mean, just without that kind?"

"Yes...I can...I do, at least around Hawkforte. Side-saddle is awkward but—"

"Oh, good! I'll show you all my favorite places, at least those not too far from the palace. Alexandros would be displeased if we ventured really far. We can take lunch with us. A picnic, it's called?"

Feeling just a little dazed, Joanna said, "A picnic, yes, but I really need to speak with Alex...with Prince Alexandros. It's urgent actually."

Sida made a small sound suspiciously like a snicker but one quick, hard glance from Joanna left the woman looking abashed.

"I must speak with Prince Alexandros," Joanna said again, this time very firmly. She raised her head as she spoke and looked straight at Kassandra.

"I see," the Princess murmured. A moment passed, no more, before she gestured toward the archway. Instantly, the two young servants hurried through it. Sida was close behind them for all that she moved with dignity befitting her position.

Left alone, Kassandra said, "Will you tell me what is wrong? I may be able to help."

The temptation was great but still Joanna was uncertain. She liked the young Princess and was inclined to trust her. But Alex had said just enough about the situation on Akora to make her realize it was precarious. She had no real idea of how much she should reveal...or how little.

Kassandra saw her quandary. She glanced at the bed

where only one side was turned down. Quietly, she said, "I have misjudged the situation, have I not? But then perhaps that is understandable. Alexandros is a very clever man. He knew we would all leap to the obvious conclusion, so he simply let us."

As Joanna watched, the Princess walked over to the window and stared out. With her back still turned, she said, "He told Atreus the truth, I suppose."

"I don't know. I was asleep when he finally returned last night. I tried so hard to stay awake but—"

Abruptly, Kassandra turned to face her. Gone was the lighthearted, exuberant Princess. In her place was a woman of seriousness and courage.

"There is something I think I must explain to you. When I was born, my parents called me Adara. It means beautiful. I suppose it is the sort of name doting parents give to a child."

Joanna shook her head slowly. "Why are you called Kassandra now?"

"Because when I was still very young, it became obvious that I had a... gift, I suppose you could call it, although there are times when it seems anything but that."

"Kassandra...?" Princess of doomed Troy. A tragic figure lost in the mists of blood-drenched time. "You can... see the future?" It seemed incredible, the far side of unbelievable, yet Joanna knew too well that the world held far more than most people ever glimpsed. She had grown up with the truth of that, woven as it was into the very air of Hawkforte.

Kassandra nodded. "The name I was given then is a reminder of what happens when people refuse to recognize such gifts and do not heed the wisdom they bring."

"Because no one would believe the original Kassandra when she said Troy would fall?"

"That's right."

Silence drew out there in the silken bedroom of a Prince filled with the bright glow of a cloudless morning.

Into that hushed brilliance, Kassandra said, "I have seen the fall of Akora."

"*No.*"

Quickly, Kassandra went to Joanna and took her hand. She led her over to the bench beneath the window. "Listen to me," the Princess said urgently. "Nothing is written. Nothing! Except that the Creator of us all loves us. My brothers know it is within our power to change the future. With every breath they take, they work to prevent what I have seen."

Joanna's voice shook. She felt swept by a great coldness. "Are you certain they can succeed?"

"I am certain that with the warning we have, we can step away from what would otherwise be and create something far better."

"I pray you are right." Joanna's voice was hushed, strained with the shock of what she had just learned. For all that she had been in Akora only a short time, already she appreciated its unique beauty and serenity. In a world riven by violence and turmoil, such a place had to be protected at all costs.

"How have you seen its end?" she asked quietly.

"Weakened from within, falling prey to conquerors from without. It is an old story and holds a certain irony for Akora was conquered once before in just that way."

"The volcano."

"Alexandros told you of that? Yes, that is what I meant. But that time nature was responsible. This time it will be man." She was silent a moment before she said, "I regret to say this but what I saw involves soldiers in red coats marching beneath a flag of red, white and blue on which three crosses are layered one over the other."

"The Union Jack," Joanna murmured, "with the crosses of St. George, St. Andrew and St. Patrick." Horror filled her. "You have seen the British invading Akora?"

"So it seems," Kassandra said gently. "Do you have any idea why they would do such a thing?"

"I don't . . . at least not exactly, but I know this is a time of turmoil in Britain. The king is insane, his son is regent and frankly that one's character leaves much to be desired. We have been at war with France almost twenty years. Napoleon has everyone terrified though they are loath to admit it. It stands to reason that there could be elements in the government, or perhaps seeking to become the government, who would look to foreign adventure to restore pride and buttress security. That may be why Royce came here—"

"Who is Royce?"

Abruptly, Joanna realized she had revealed more than she had intended but she could not regret that. What the Princess had told her was so alarming that ordinary caution no longer applied.

"Royce is my brother. He left England for Akora nine months ago. Royce served with the Foreign Office, but I don't believe his mission had official sanction. That is not surprising given how uncertain everything is now. It may be that he was attempting to work quietly, behind the scenes as it were. At any rate, he has not returned and I am deeply worried about him."

"That is why you came here?"

Joanna nodded. "I have heard the stories about Akora, I know how *xenos* are treated. But the very fact that your and Alex's father was not killed gave me some hope."

Kassandra let out her breath slowly. She seemed deep in thought, as though wrestling with a difficult choice. Finally, she looked at Joanna. "I think we should ride later. This morning, I would like to show you Ilius."

The Princess's sudden switch from a matter of such seriousness to one of such seeming frivolity startled Joanna. "I hardly think—"

Before she could continue, Kassandra stood up and looked at her very firmly. "Why don't you put on one of the gowns Sida brought and we can go."

It was not a request. The daughter of the royal house

had decided this was a good moment to tour Ilius. Joanna fought for patience. The young woman seemed to have sense and intelligence. She could be an important ally. Nothing would be served by antagonizing her.

Even so, it was only with the greatest difficulty that Joanna acquiesced. She chose the garment that happened to be on top of the pile Sida had left without even glancing at it. In the bathroom, she washed hastily, dropped the gown over her head, tried to make some order of her hair, gave up and went back to join Kassandra. The Princess was shifting through the clothes to find a pair of sandals.

"Oh, you look marvelous," the Princess exclaimed.

Joanna glanced down at the gown of sea green silk that left her arms bare and swirled lightly about her ankles. "It's very comfortable," she said, tugging on the sandals. "Shall we go?" The sooner they went, the sooner they would be done and she could set about finding Alex. In the meantime, she could decide what to say to him.

They used the private corridor to reach a small door that opened a short walk from the lion gate. The vast courtyard in front of the palace was much busier than it had been when Joanna saw it the previous day. People were arriving, some singly, others in small groups. They were heading purposefully toward the large staircase that led to the main entrance.

"Who are they all?" Joanna asked.

"Some are nobles, come to see and be seen, exchange the latest news, promote their pet causes and keep an eye on everything the Vanax does. Others are merchants who are here basically for the same reasons. Some will be coming to attend Council meetings, which by law must be open to the public. Then there are those who are going to the law courts in that wing over there. The mint is there as well for anyone with precious metals to refine. So, too, will those who are looking for capital go there. Many business arrangements are made in side rooms off the mint."

With a laugh, Kassandra concluded, "It is said that there are no strangers on Akora for sooner or later, everyone meets at the palace."

Thinking of how Prinny would object to one of his residences being used by ordinary folk for their own purposes, Joanna asked, "The Vanax does not mind?"

"Atreus? Of course not. According to our traditions, the palace belongs to the people, not the sovereign, so the people feel perfectly free to use it as their central meeting place. The privacy of our quarters is respected but anyone has the right to go anywhere else."

The other side of that seemed to be that the Princess could leave the palace without fuss or formality. No one approached them although quite a few people nodded pleasantly as they walked down the long road leading into the town. Once again, Joanna was struck by how clean everything was, how orderly yet also how beautiful. Everywhere she looked she saw healthy, well-fed people who wore an air of contentment as readily as a smile. Yet the scene was far from peaceful for in her mind's eye she saw the terrible future Kassandra had glimpsed and felt the sharp stab of anguish deep within.

"This is the clothing district," Kassandra said as they entered a street that seemed filled to bursting with stalls displaying fabrics in every hue of the rainbow. "Many very talented tailors and seamstresses live here. Our clothing tends to be simpler than your European garments but we take great pride in the cut, the way the cloth flows and how it is stitched."

"Fascinating," Joanna murmured, wondering how much longer she could bear to indulge the Princess's whim. She truly did not want to be rude but neither did she see how she could pretend an interest in Ilius, lovely though it was, when far more pressing matters filled her mind. She had to find Alex, tell him of Royce and—

"Jean-Paul, Marie, ici s'il vous plaît. Vite, vite!"

Joanna jerked her head sharply in the direction of

the voice. It was a woman who spoke, one dressed much as herself in a deceptively simple but quite lovely tunic. The woman was several inches shorter than Joanna and plumper. She had thick, curling chestnut hair tied back by a ribbon, sparkling eyes and pretty, sun-warmed features. At the moment, she looked somewhat harassed.

The objects of her attention were two small children, a boy and a girl, playing nearby. They looked up in response to her summons and came to her quickly as she had asked. She smiled and ruffled their hair before noticing that she had an audience.

A little abashed, she spoke in Akoran but with an accent. "Your pardon, Princess, but zees children, I tell them to stay inside just for a leettle while so they not get so dirty before they go to school but what do they do—?" Her shrug and her accent both were purely French.

Joanna gave Kassandra no chance to respond. Instead, she addressed the woman. *"Vous êtes française, madame? Une française ici sur Akora?"*

The woman looked surprised but answered readily enough. *"J'étais française mais maintenant je suis Akoraine."*

"What does she say?" Kassandra asked. She spoke mildly with no apparent surprise.

"She says she was French but now she is Akoran."

Whirling around, Joanna faced the Princess. "I have heard of the French expeditionary force that vanished in Akoran waters several years ago. Do not tell me they included women and children among their crew. Besides, they are all presumed dead because of Akora's well-known policy of slaying any foreigner hapless enough to land upon these shores. How then is this woman here?"

Very gently, Kassandra said, "Look around, Joanna. Really look. See not just what you expect but what is."

Bewildered, Joanna nonetheless glanced in both directions up and down the street. At first, she saw nothing to explain the Princess's strange instruction. But then her eye fell on a man hurrying out of a small lane. His skin gleamed with an ebony sheen. He was talking cheerfully with a young man who might have been his son, so closely did they resemble each other.

That was puzzling enough but there, at the other end of the street, she caught a glimpse of a woman with reddish hair. And above, hanging out of a window to call to a friend, was a man who was unmistakably blond.

They were only a relative few among the dark-haired Akorans but they were definitely there.

"You ride," Kassandra said. "Do you also breed horses?"

"Yes," Joanna replied dazedly, "we breed horses at Hawkforte."

"You are careful not to inbreed, are you not? After all, inbreeding weakens the line. It leads to disease, still-births, all manner of problems."

"Among horses," Joanna said slowly, ". . . and among people."

Kassandra smiled. "How then do you imagine we have stayed strong and healthy for thousands of years if we were truly sealed away from the world?"

"You don't kill *xenos*."

The Princess nodded. "It is our great secret. Truly, we do not want the world coming here for we cherish what we have and wish to protect it. But no *xenos* is harmed on Akora. On the contrary, we go to the greatest lengths to assure they will be happy to stay, settle down, and have children. We even," she added with a smile for the French woman, "go quietly to fetch their families so that they may be reunited and all live together here. Marguerite can tell you about that."

Delighted at the opportunity to describe what was surely the most dramatic event of her life, the French woman nodded. "Men come into our village three years ago, take *mon mari*, my 'usband, Felix, and other men away, they say for ze 'onor of serving the Emperor. *Phht* for such 'onor! 'ow I weep when 'e go, fearing I never see 'im again. Day and night I work on our little farm and try to look after *mes enfants,* my children alone. Then I am told Felix, 'e iz lost. Oh, *mon Dieu!* Such sorrow I 'ave never known. When the strangers come a fortnight later, at first I do not believe them. Felix is alive, they say. They 'ave a letter from 'im. In it, 'e says things only I will know so I believe the men, they are telling the truth. 'e says 'e is in a much better place, peaceful and 'appy. I should go with the men. I am still very afraid *mais dans le désespoir . . .* 'ow do you say? But in despair? We are so poor, we 'ave nothing and my children, they 'ave no future. I pray to the Virgin to protect us and we go."

"They brought you here," Joanna said softly.

Marguerite nodded. Very seriously, she said, "At first, I think perhaps we 'ave died. Felix, 'e tells me 'e thought the same. But we 'ave not. Instead, now we can begin to truly live." With a bright smile, she gestured around at her neat little house and the stall before it. "Always it was my dream to make beautiful clothes but I 'ad no chance. Now, not only do I make them, I can wear them *aussi.*"

Joanna's eyes stung. She told herself it was from the brightness of the sun, not the sudden, stunning vision she had of men, women and children lifted out of lives of poverty and despair, transported into a world of peace and beauty.

But hard on the thought came the realization that Alex had known all this and had not told her. He had let her go on believing the lie about Akora.

"Where," she asked between gritted teeth, "are the training fields?"

"About half a mile in that direction," Kassandra said and, being at heart a prudent woman, quickly stepped out of the way.

chapter

NINE

✴

ALEX SAW HER COMING across the wide field beyond the barracks. She was on foot, the glorious mane of her hair flowing behind her. Sida must have done her work, for Joanna was wearing some frothy green thing that suited her very well. Watching her would have been a pleasure if not for two unfortunate factors: she was coming to him in a place reserved for men and she was in obviously high dudgeon.

Akora's Prince waved off the man he had been about to fight and resheathed his sword. Bare-chested, sweat-streaked, he took a moment to savor the loose-limbed ease that was the gift of strenuous physical effort. A morning of slashing and stabbing had worked out many of the kinks left by his months in England. He felt a new man, well able to deal with one Lady Joanna Hawkforte.

Until, that was, he saw that behind the anger in her hazel eyes she looked bruised.

"You knew," she said while she was yet some distance from him. She spoke clearly and loudly enough for the men standing nearby to hear, and she spoke in English. She did not wait for him to speak first; she did not address him as *kreon*; indeed, she observed none of the requirements of propriety. Her appearance aside, there would be no question that this was the *xenos* concubine the Prince was said to have brought back with him. An oddly ill-behaved woman, appealing to be sure, but not at all properly schooled. Which would make men wonder why he had bothered with her when there were lovely women aplenty on Akora. Spirit was all well and good in a woman but a certain decorum was expected, too.

Without a word, he closed the distance between them, took her arm, and began leading her in the direction of his tent set up near the edge of the field. She tried to jerk away but he merely tightened his grip, not enough to be hurtful but firmly all the same.

"If you want a scene here," he said quietly, "you can have it. But it will serve no good purpose and only complicate matters yet further."

She glared at him but pressed her lips tightly together and went.

It was cooler in the tent, the high sun filtered through deep blue linen that rippled in the breeze from the Inner Sea. Joanna ignored the low couch Alex gestured to and remained standing.

Never taking her eyes from him, she said, "You don't kill *xenos*."

He poured a goblet of chilled water from a mist-covered ewer, offered it to her, shrugged when she refused. The muscles of his throat worked as he drank. When he was done, he set the goblet back down in a gesture that was very measured, very controlled. As was his voice. "I gather you have met Kassandra."

Joanna jerked her head in assent. Confronted by the sheer physical beauty and overwhelming masculinity of the Prince of Akora, she was finding it shamefully difficult to concentrate. Angry at herself, at him, at the whole damnable situation, she wrenched her attention back where it belonged. "She took me on a little tour of Ilius. The French dressmaker was a particularly interesting discovery."

Alex's smile was rueful. "How like Kassandra. She wouldn't tell what every Akoran knows is to be kept secret but she would point you in the right direction so that you could discover the truth for yourself."

"Secret be hanged, why didn't you tell me?" She took a deep breath, fought to steady herself and failed. "You let me believe Royce could have arrived here and been killed. You did that knowing it wasn't so!"

Her sense of betrayal stabbed at him, all the more so for his conscience knew it to be deserved, at least partly. Fury swirled in his gaze—at her, at himself, at the whole bloody circumstance—and something else, something very hot and primal too long denied. Almost snarling, he said, "Do you think you are the only one with duties and obligations? I am not one of your fat, pampered British princes! I *serve* Akora. It is my sworn duty and my privilege to protect her—to the death, if need be." Fighting for control, he picked up the goblet again. As she watched, unwillingly fascinated, his hand closed on the beaten metal, slowly and inexorably crushing it.

"Your brother is British. Do you have any idea what that means to me?"

She did, just then, in sudden, shocking clarity. "Kassandra believes the British will invade Akora." Her stomach clenched. For a horrible moment, she thought she would be ill.

He tossed the ruined goblet aside without notice. "My sister told you that as well? She must have really taken to you. No matter. Yes, she has seen not just the invasion but the British conquest of Akora. Knowing that, do you seriously expect I would have encouraged your brother to come, much less that the Vanax would have permitted it?"

"But Royce would never be a party to harming Akora! He has been fascinated by this place since he was a child."

"And men seek to possess what fascinates us. We are driven to it. It is our nature."

His nature. Beneath the training and discipline, the formidable self-control, the dedication to duty, he was only and utterly a man. A truth he had denied too long.

Ten days at sea... discovering the woman shorn of social restrictions and stiff propriety... the gamine creature who sat cross-legged reading Homer and dangled out portholes to catch a glimpse of a forbidden world... who laughed and challenged and somehow slipped past his defenses without him even realizing...

Ten damned, endless days.

And nights.

He had tried. By all the gods, he truly had. But his hands were on her shoulders and he was drawing her to him even as the responsible, disciplined part of his nature looked on in blank amazement.

Her mouth was soft, sweet, lush. The taste and scent of her filled him. He couldn't get enough of whatever it was about her that so fascinated him—courage, beauty, intelligence, a certain prickly defiance that melted so appealingly into pure passion.

For an instant, she stiffened as though to push him away. His breath caught on the horns of conscience but in the next heartbeat, she made a low, utterly female sound and relaxed into him. He groaned with relief and deepened the kiss. That first time on board ship her response had been innocently tentative. Not so now. She met him hotly with hunger that fed his own.

Her breasts were full and soft against his chest. He slipped his hands around, cupping her, rubbing his thumbs over her distended nipples through the delicate fabric of the gown. She shivered and clutched at his broad shoulders, her hands sliding down to find and learn the powerful muscles of his back. Her head fell back as his mouth claimed the base of her throat, raking her with his teeth even as he wrapped a steely arm around her hips and drew her even more tautly against him.

She smelled of honey and eucalyptus, sea air and

pure woman. Her hair was silk tumbling over his hands. Her slim arms tightened around him and he felt her strength. No languorous concubine this, no woman of tutored skill and artful responses. There was honesty at her core. He drew back slightly, saw the need that turned her eyes smoky, and crushed her mouth with his.

The world tilted. She clung to him as shock coursed through her and passion drove away the last feeble stirrings of reason. She did not care that they were sheltered by no more than a tent, in broad daylight and surrounded by his men. Nor that fate seemed poised to decree them enemies. Their lives were their own and destiny whatever they made of it.

Life was too precarious. It could vanish into a calm sea struck by a sudden storm or down a drive with a wave and a smile. The past was memory, the future hope, and nothing was truly real except the moment.

She wanted this man in her arms, in her body and in her heart. Wanted the white-hot need that sprang between them with a desperation that stunned her. She was trembling, on the brink of a leap into the unknown when memory stabbed sharp and relentless.

Stone, that for just an instant had felt damp and cold.

How could she? How could she, even for a moment forget the peril her brother faced and dally—that was what she was doing—dally with a man who might well consider himself her brother's and her own enemy. What low and craven wretch had she become to be a slave to passion's perfidy?

"I cannot—" The words were torn from her even as she struggled to tear herself from the embrace of the man who still, despite all, so tantalized her.

"We cannot—" He said in almost the same moment and abruptly let her go, standing a little apart and staring at her in disbelief he quickly tried to mask.

Alex took a deep breath, stunningly aware that he had scarcely managed to stop and was within a heartbeat of reaching for her again. What insanity was this? Never, not even as an untried boy, had he felt so susceptible to a woman. Under the very best of circumstances, he would not amuse himself on the training field, for pity's sake, where duty demanded strict diligence. Much less would he do so in such a perilous time when so much hung in the balance and even the most loyal men might be tempted to doubt a self-indulgent leader.

Yet he had come astoundingly close. With a muttered curse, he turned away, went to the tent flap and yanked it open. A single command sent several of his men scrambling.

Moments later, he stepped into the chariot brought for him, took the reins of the pair of greys who drew it, and gestured to Joanna.

"Come."

Painfully aware of the guarded but curious glances directed her way, praying her cheeks were not as fiery as they felt, she stepped from the relative shelter of the tent and quickly took her place in the chariot. Doing so, she avoided touching the hand he extended to her and instead took a firm grip on the railing. That was just as well for in the next instant, the horses surged and she gasped as the light, highly maneuverable vehicle designed for the pounding rush of battle seemed almost to leave the ground, so powerfully did it leap forward.

She clung, scarcely breathing, scrambling to deal with the extraordinary reality in which she found herself. She was in a chariot—a chariot!—racing from the training fields of the Akoran army to the royal palace. She, Joanna Hawkforte, who had lived what was to her a life of remarkable ordinariness. Her days had followed a simple but satisfying order, overseeing the activities and accounts of Hawkforte, following the flow of the seasons, deeply rooted in the same routine followed by the legions of women who were her ancestors.

Until now.

She touched a finger to her lips tentatively, felt the tingling lingering there, and tightened her grip on the railing. She stood behind Alex. Alexandros. Mayhap it would be wiser for her to think of him that way. Alexandros, Prince of Akora. Bare-chested, the powerful muscles of his arms and back flexing as he controlled the horses, his skin gleaming in the sun as he took them speeding over the land.

Warm skin, hot even, the feel of it still on her hands. The taste of him still on her mouth. The need . . .

Please God, she was not going to think about that.

They thundered into the courtyard in front of the palace, dust spraying in all directions. A young boy ran forward to take the reins Alex tossed to him and led the chariot away. She felt, for she dared not look, the gaze of the people coming and going. Quickly, before he could touch her again, she went up the stairs leading to the family wing. He was close behind her.

At the top of the stairs, she turned, delving for courage. He looked so . . . formidable. Yes, that was it. He was inches taller than she was and in superb condition. But there was more, his nature, the custom of command and the responsibility that went with it. His eyes were narrowed, watching her.

"We have to talk," she said, and heard her voice as though from a great distance.

He nodded once, curtly. In silence, they climbed the steps to his private apartment. It was cooler there, freshened by a steady breeze that came through the broad windows cut into the thick stone walls. No one was about. In the silence, she could hear the faint drip of a water clock.

Time fleeting.

"Royce is alive."

Alex turned, looked at her. A lock of ebony hair fell over his forehead. Without warning, his eyes softened. "I know you want him to be."

"No. Listen." She pressed her lips tightly together, searching for the words that would convince him. "Kassandra has a gift . . . or a curse. Have there been other women in your family with unusual abilities?"

He was frowning, perplexed. "A few—"

"In my family as well. But more than a few and going back centuries to the very beginning of our history. We are accustomed to it." She laughed very faintly. "As much as one can ever be."

Another breath, confidence growing. She could do this. She had to do it.

"I would wager that if you searched your family history, you would find that no one in your line showed such abilities until about seven hundred years ago."

He was very quiet for a moment, a stillness deep within him. "Why then?"

He had not corrected her. She was right, as she had known she would be. Relief surged in her. "Because that was when members of my family came here. At least some of them stayed. Having met Kassandra, I have to wonder now what exactly they brought with them."

"These gifts—"

"Not in every generation but often enough and always among women, not men. They seem somehow to come when there is need although no one pretends to understand that. At any rate, I am one of these women, in my own way, much smaller and simpler than Kassandra's."

She drew herself upright, took a breath, let it go on a silent prayer. Please let him believe her. Let him understand. Let him act.

"I can find things. It began when I was a small child. A lost toy, a puppy asleep in a cupboard, a misplaced bonnet. It was all very simple at first. Then when I was six, the miller's son went missing. Everyone was frantic. The search went on for two days and nights. I knew him, we played together. I wanted so desperately for him to be found. Something in me... reached out. I don't know how else to put it. I felt him. He was cold and so afraid, trapped in the earth but I knew where. *I knew*. He was in a sinkhole that had opened up about a mile beyond Hawkforte where he had wandered. Thank God no one thought me odd. Hawkforte's people knew of such things, even welcomed it in me. And my parents..." She broke off, the pain of loss still too acute even after all these years. "My parents were wonderful. My father remembered the tales he had heard about my great-grandmother. He helped me to understand, to cope."

She spread her hands, her eyes on his. "Believe me, please. Royce is alive but he is imprisoned and he is... weakening. He must be found soon."

Alex was silent for a long moment. He was torn, still struggling to control his hunger for her and struggling as well to accept what she was telling him. Clearly, she truly believed what she was saying. But could he? Could Royce Hawkforte possibly still be alive?

"Joanna... there has been no word of him. You know now our policy toward *xenos*. If Royce had reached here, he would have been reported to the appropriate authorities at once. Moreover, an English lord would have been brought to the attention of the palace. We have been on the lookout for him ever since he told me of his wish to visit Akora, but there has been no word of his coming."

He spoke gently, truly dreading the thought of hurting her. Yet it seemed inevitable. Even if she was gifted as she said, and he was prepared to believe that, the odds of her being right were infinitesimal.

"He is here," she said unflinchingly. "I am absolutely certain of it."

"We would know—"

"You should know. That is not the same." She frowned. "Why do you not know?"

He stiffened, watching her with unwilling fascination. She was intelligent. He was only beginning to understand how deeply that shaped her being.

"Royce is here," she said slowly, stating what was for her a given, "and the Vanax of Akora does not know it. Someone is concealing that knowledge from him, probably the same person who is keeping Royce a prisoner. Why? To what purpose?" Her gaze narrowed, focused on him unerringly. "Who would dare?"

"What makes you think—?"

She made a quick, dismissive gesture with her hand. "Don't. There is no time for this. Please, just be honest with me."

It was the "please" that did it. That and the look of yearning in her eyes. Yearning for her brother, for truth, and dare he hope, just perhaps for him as well. So she had felt in his arms. So she lingered in his memory.

Slowly, he said, "These are difficult times for Akora."

"Because you believe Britain will invade?"

"Partly..."

He needed a shower and a change of clothes. More to the point, he needed time to gather his thoughts and decide exactly how he was to deal with this woman who was so much more than he had expected.

"Stay here," he ordered. "Do not go anywhere, do not do anything. Understood?"

She nodded once, grudgingly he thought, but it would have to be enough. Seizing clothes from a chest, he disappeared into the bathing room.

When the door had closed behind him, Joanna let out her breath and sat down quickly on the edge of the bed. Better that than fall down. Her legs had the consistency of the beef jelly Mulridge used to insist she eat if she was feeling poorly. Her head felt stuffed as though with the cottony milkweed seeds that would drift like clouds on hot, sultry summer air across the fields of Hawkforte. There was a distant buzzing in her ears like the drone of busy bees.

All that and her breasts felt unaccountably heavy, the nipples acutely sensitive, while between her legs she was undeniably damp.

Breathe ... in ... out ...

She could hear water flowing in the room beyond, cascading down over rippling muscles, over the perfect contours of his extraordinary body, over every inch of that taut, bronzed skin.

Breathe ... in ... out ...

He had listened to her; she should be glad of that. He had not, as she had feared he might, dismiss her claim to being able to find that which was lost. Indeed, he seemed to have taken it in stride. But when she had realized that something was not as it should be ... then he had suddenly decided on a shower.

Droplets of water sliding slowly down ...

Oh, for heaven's sake! She was not some addled girl to moon over an entirely natural reaction to an incredibly handsome man. If only she could think of it that way. Entirely natural, nothing extraordinary, no reason to feel as though the world itself had rocked beneath her feet.

She paced back and forth across the cool flagstone floor, the green silk fluttering around her legs. Beyond the broad windows was a scene of seemingly perfect peace and prosperity. Ships rode at anchor in the harbor or cut purposefully across the smooth blue water of the Inland Sea. Wagons and carts trundled up and down the roads. Beyond the city, ripening fields gleamed golden in the sun.

It looked like paradise. Wherein was the serpent?

The water stopped. She turned, glanced at the door, and quickly looked away. Minutes passed.

She closed her eyes, summoning strength, and saw suddenly a snake, small and green, curling its way past the garden wall beside the old keep at Hawkforte, searching for birds' eggs, no doubt, or other delicacies. Twisting, twining, its lithe body never stayed still, its tongue flicked constantly in search of direction. How many times had she lain on the wall in the warmth of the summer sun, drowsily watching such small moments of high drama and incipient tragedy?

"Joanna . . . ?"

Alex was looking at her with concern. She took a quick, hard breath against the tightness of her chest and tried to smile. "I was just thinking."

His hair was damp, curling in ringlets around his head to emphasize the chiseled beauty of his features. He wore a simple tunic of unbleached linen belted at his waist and ending midway down his thighs. In his right hand was his sword, sheathed in beaten bronze. He laid the weapon on top of a chest and looked at her.

"There's a part of me that wishes you wouldn't do that."

"Do what?"

His smile was rueful. "Think." Quickly, before the lightning that flashed in her eyes could reach her lips, he added, "Note I said a part of me, not all, and I have the sense to know it for a fool's wish."

"You are not a fool." She spoke a little huskily, stumbling as she was over outrage, chagrin, abashed pleasure and the still-stirring hungers of her body.

He ran a hand through his hair, thoroughly distracting her. "I have felt one of late, but never mind. So, are you hungry?"

The mere thought of food made her stomach clench. "Only for information. You were going to tell me why these are difficult times for Akora."

His glance was quick and penetrating, leaving her shuddering within as though she had been touched. "Was I?"

"Or perhaps you weren't, but if you do not, I shall be left to my own conclusions."

He was silent, daring her, she thought. Very well, if he wished to drop the gauntlet, she would not hesitate to pick it up. Kassandra had not been willing to tell her how *xenos* were received on Akora but had shown her. Perhaps Alex felt a similar reticence.

"When Kassandra told me about her vision, she said she saw Akora weakened from within but this time by man rather than by nature."

She looked at him expectantly but his features were unreadable. Still, not for an instant did he take his gaze from her.

Gesturing toward the window, Joanna said, "Everything here looks so peaceful. Meanwhile, the world outside Akora is in turmoil, has been for centuries really, but now there is something more . . ." She stared out at Ilius and the countryside beyond, seeing what was there but seeing also what was not.

"In England, factories seem to be springing up everywhere. Every day brings some new innovation. Nothing seems able to contain the change sweeping over us."

"Nothing will contain it," Alex said quietly. "Do the names Samuel Slater or William Cockerill mean anything to you?"

Joanna thought for a moment. "Cockerill does. He caused a bit of scandal a few years ago when news leaked that he had gone to France, taking with him plans for machines that had been England's alone. I remember Royce talking about it."

"Slater did the same thing but his destination was America. Such men leave no doubt that it is impossible to build boundaries around knowledge. That is a lesson Akora needs to absorb, and quickly. In the past, it has been sufficient for us to keep our defenses strong, to acquire the latest in weaponry and be well prepared to use it, but soon that will not be enough. Power will come as surely from a steam engine as from a gun. If we allow ourselves to remain as we are now, it will be only a matter of time before the tide of change sweeps us away."

"I have seen this new industrialism in parts of England. Mines scar the countryside, factories brutalize the workers. It is a fate I would not wish for anyone."

"Nor do I. We must find a way to make use of this new kind of power in our own way and for our own benefit. My brother believes that can be done, as do I, but"— he hesitated for a moment—"but there are others on Akora who oppose any change. They see any threat to the status quo as a threat to their position, and they are determined to stamp it out."

"Despite the wishes of the Vanax?"

Alex nodded. He had come to a decision while wishing the heat of passion could be washed away as easily as the sweat of training. Joanna Hawkforte was unlike any woman he had ever known. It would be folly not to recognize that . . . and use it. Even so, it was only with difficulty that he said, "Once the Vanax decides, all opposition should cease. But there appear to be members of the Council whose lust for power outstrips their sense of honor."

He was telling her things no other *xenos* had heard, Joanna thought. She spared a moment to savor that before turning her mind to the seriousness of the situation. "How many members? Enough to truly make a difference?"

"Three possibly out of six. They are named Deilos, Troizus and Mellinos. Apart from the royal House of Atreides itself, they represent the wealthiest and most powerful families on Akora."

"Still, they are only three men. Can they really pose a danger to Akora itself?"

"Ordinarily, they probably could not," Alex acknowledged. "But there is another factor. In the last year or so, a group has arisen that is demanding greater change even than what the Vanax contemplates. Its leader has gone so far as to say they want to bring revolution to

Akora, such as has occurred in America and France. As yet, we have no way of knowing how much influence this group has among the people but their numbers seem to be growing."

"Then your brother is caught in the middle, on the one side reactionaries who want no change and on the other rebels who want sweeping change?" No wonder Kassandra envisioned Akora weakened from within. The situation was such as no country would wish to face.

"Regrettably that is true but Atreus is a brave man and a wise leader. I have no doubt he can see Akora through this difficult period safely. I intend to do everything in my power to help him."

"Even as I intend to do everything in my power to find Royce."

They stood in the silence that descended, looking at one another. Alex saw a woman of courage and honor who stirred his blood even as she won his admiration. Were he to have no concern beyond his own wishes, he would not hesitate to claim the right to both possess and protect her. For her part, Joanna saw a man who seemed to have stepped directly from a legend into her dreams. Were the world a different place, it would have been so easy to forget all else and yield to the soul-deep hunger he ignited within her.

But the world was the world and duty a harsh taskmaster.

"I suggest," Alex said quietly, "that we cooperate." Despite the yearnings of his heart, he would put both Joanna's rare gift and her desperate desire to find her brother in service to Akora. What price he would have to pay for doing that would be only for him to know.

"An excellent idea," Joanna replied, and determinedly ignored the protest of her heart. Sympathetic though she was to Alex's desire to protect Akora, Royce had to come first. She would do anything—and deal with anyone—in order to find her brother.

He smiled and reached out a hand, gently stroking the curve of her cheek. She fought to conceal the tremor that raced through her. A shadow of regret moved behind his eyes but Joanna did not see it. She had looked away an instant before, lest he see the yearning she could not conceal but knew she must deny.

chapter

TEN

✳

$\mathcal{H}$IS DECISION MADE, his resolve should have been firm. That it was not told Alex all too clearly how in danger he still was of succumbing to temptation's lure. He took a step back, focusing on the wall over her shoulder. Anything to blank out his vivid, wrenching awareness of her. "Can you get a stronger sense of where Royce might be?"

"I can try." Joanna still felt the brush of his fingers over skin that seemed hypersensitive. Pleasure skimmed through her—light, tantalizing, filled with yearning. "I need to concentrate in a quiet place, undisturbed." She hoped he would take the hint and leave her so that she might have some time to gather herself back together.

But he did not leave. Instead, he said, "There is a chamber here in the palace. Kassandra uses it sometimes when she is seeking visions. She finds it helpful. Perhaps you would, too."

Curiosity got the better of Joanna, that and the need for something, anything to help her focus as she had never done before. The miller's son had come to her so simply when she was a child and since then there had been nothing of such dire consequence. Nothing until now to help her prepare for what would surely be the effort of her lifetime.

She could find newspapers and measuring strings with confidence but when it came to finding her brother, uncertainty threatened to overwhelm her. "I would like to see the chamber."

Alex glanced around, spied the dark blue cloak Sida had brought in along with another pile of clothes, and laid the garment gently over Joanna's shoulders. He felt her stiffen beneath his hands and removed them quickly. "This way." Drawing aside the curtain over the archway, he waited for her to precede him.

She went swiftly, holding the cloak closed at her throat to give herself the illusion of concealment. A foolish notion since in truth she felt more exposed than ever before in her life.

Windows high in the stone walls of the private corridor admitted sufficient light to see clearly. The passage appeared to run the length of one wing of the palace. At the very far end, almost beyond the limit of Joanna's sight, she thought she could make out what might be the entrance to another apartment. Of the archway midway down the corridor there was no doubt. Between it and Alex's own quarters was a recess a little more than the height and width of a man. It gave way to a small, curving staircase. They followed the steps down to a narrow landing where Alex paused for a moment. He gestured to a wooden door.

"We are on ground level here. Beyond there is a small path that leads into the city."

He took a lantern from the hook near the door, lit it, and continued on down the steps. Joanna followed gingerly. The bright airiness of the apartment seemed more appealing by the moment.

"Where are we?" she asked after a few moments. Her voice echoed hollowly.

"Near the caves under the palace."

She stared at his broad back and tried not to shiver. There were caves near Hawkforte. She and Royce had been forbidden to go near them, which, of course, assured that they would. But they had been sensible about it, never venturing in very far before being overcome by the satisfying delight of terror so beloved of children.

This was different. With each of Alex's long strides they were descending farther and farther into the earth. Already, the palace seemed all too distant. There was no sound save for their footsteps on the stone floor. When those suddenly died away, Joanna's throat tightened. The smooth flagstones laid down who knew how many ages past had ended. Cool, damp earth lay beneath their feet. She could feel it through the thin leather of her sandals. Feel also the tightness of her breath as only a thin circle of light held stygian darkness at bay.

"I really don't think—"

"In here." Alex bent his tall frame as he stepped through a narrow opening in the cave wall.

Joanna followed but only because to do otherwise was to be left in the smothering dark.

Beyond was a chamber, its dimensions lost in shadows. The air smelled not salty like the sea, but familiar all the same, reminiscent of the mineral springs in Bath that she had visited four years before. Alex went round to lamps set in wrought iron brackets along the walls and lit them one by one. As the chamber filled with light, Joanna gasped. She was standing in a space the size of a cathedral with a soaring ceiling carved not by man but by the hand of nature. Far above her, slender cones of sparkling white, pink and green crystals hung down like fantastical chandeliers. Similar cones grew from the floor itself, seeming to form aisles that led to a deep rock ledge at the far end of the chamber.

Slowly, well aware that her legs were shaking, Joanna moved closer to the ledge. A crystal so large she could not have wrapped her hands around it rose up out of the rock. In the light of the lamps, it glowed with a deep, pulsating red as though the heart of the earth itself were caught inside.

"What is that?" she asked. Instinctively, she kept her voice low. In such a place, it seemed sacrilegious to speak loudly.

Alex set the lamp he carried on the ledge. He, too, spoke quietly. "It's a ruby."

Joanna stared at him in amazement. "A ruby? But it can't be. It's too large by far. If it were a ruby, it would be—"

"The largest in the world? Yes, quite probably. Others, smaller to be sure, have been found in this cave and nearby. Mostly, we find diamonds." He glanced at her and almost laughed. "Shocked? How did you imagine we pay for our ventures into the larger world and what we acquire there?"

"I didn't . . . that is, I suppose I should have realized . . ." Chagrined she had not considered so obvious a matter, Joanna was struck suddenly by the implications of what she had just learned. Akora was not merely strategically placed to control access to the Mediterranean, it was also a land of riches such as men would go to extreme lengths to possess. And it was threatened by conflict from within. Were such information to reach the proper ears in England, it might well prompt the very invasion Alex was determined to prevent.

Why had he told her? Did he truly trust her so much? Much as she wished to believe that, a far less appealing alternative taunted her. Perhaps he had no intention of letting her leave Akora.

"You will be here a very long time."

She would not think of that, could not. Whatever Kassandra had seen, her visions were only one version of a possible future. Nothing was written.

Except that she had to find Royce.

"Kassandra focuses on the ruby," Alex said. Her face, framed by the hood of the blue cloak, was pale and serious. A few stray wisps of honeyed hair drifted over her skin. Her mouth looked very soft. He remembered how she tasted and reached deep for control.

Why had he told her of the diamonds? From what he had seen with Kassandra, the ruby truly might help. Telling her of that was justified but the diamonds . . . that was the bragging of a boy.

Her voice sounded hollow in the vast chamber. "What is this place?"

"It was used as a temple long ago. Most of the people who survived the volcano did so because they reached here."

"Is it still used for worship?"

"Not ordinarily but when a new Vanax is chosen, he is consecrated here."

A dozen questions perched on her tongue but she asked none, afraid he would answer and she would wonder again why. Better to think only of the moment and the need.

She looked at the ruby doubtfully, unsure of what to do or how to begin. It was so large, so beautiful, born as it was of earth and fire. How right that it was still here, in the place of its creation. He said it helped Kassandra but how? Her gift seemed so much vaster, terrifying really, whereas Joanna's own felt so small in comparison. Still, she had found the miller's son, snatching him from death.

Never mind the other time when she had reached out through the fury of a storm, desperately seeking the parents who were gone.

Never mind.

And yet, if she was honest, she would admit even then she had felt the brush of . . . something. So gentle, tender, filled with regret yet somehow joyous. The rare times she let herself think of it, it comforted.

But please God, let her not find anything like that as she went in search of Royce.

The ruby would be cold. If she touched it, she would not feel the fire. Yet it was there all the same, she was certain of it. Leaning just a little closer, she stared into the heart of the gem.

A short distance away, Alex watched her. He was glad she had not asked to be left alone for he would not have considered it. But neither would he crowd her. If nothing else, he needed a little space between them to shore up what passed for his increasingly laughable self-control.

Just then, the look that flitted across her face almost made him groan. He wanted nothing more than to snatch her into his arms, to keep at bay anything that might sadden or frighten her.

Oh, yes, that was all he wanted. The sudden, fierce memory of her pliant against him, her mouth soft and welcoming, that meant nothing. Nor did the temptation to lay her down on the gentle earth and take what he so desperately hungered for.

His fists clenched against the instinct to reach for her, Alex turned away. His gaze wandered sightlessly over the cavern. His mother had brought him here first when he was still so young a child that he could just barely remember. She had held his hand and spoken gently as she always did, telling him about the people—her people— who had found the cave. Her stories made the images come alive even now, men and women gathered to celebrate the blessings of Mother Earth, huddled to escape her wrath, clinging to life as their world was torn apart. He saw it through her eyes, felt it, and glimpsed in that moment what the coming of the warrior had truly meant to Akora.

Meant especially to her priestesses, shattered by what seemed the failure of their faith, suddenly shorn of power, subjugated by the conqueror. Then had the law been decreed: Warriors rule, women serve. But centuries and the quiet strength of the women themselves had wrought a transformation. More change was coming—not enough for some, too much for others—but change nonetheless. Its success would depend on the trust between men and women, their mutual respect and their willingness to work together for the land they both loved.

As he and Joanna might work together. Scarcely thought, the notion was rejected. She was *xenos*. He could gird himself to make use of her ability because he knew he had to but there could never be anything more.

She looked so slim, almost fragile standing there gazing into the ruby. Surprised to find he had come full circle and was staring at her again, he tried to look away and gave up the effort rather than admit that he simply could not. The hood had slipped from her head, revealing the glory of her hair. She seemed resolute, free and utterly female. Had the priestesses of old been like that? Were they still when they gathered for the women's rites?

Kassandra would know; he could ask her. Just as he could have asked her to accompany Joanna to the cavern rather than go himself. He had not because Joanna was his ... that was, she was his responsibility. He had brought her to Akora. He would see to her himself.

And wonder in the meantime what she saw.

JOANNA CLOSED HER EYES, seeking calm, finding only dread. There was nothing save the ruby itself, the ledge it rose from, the wall behind the ledge, and her own hands clenched in frustration. She shut out the sight, forcing herself to breathe deeply and rhythmically. Somewhere was the peace she sought, and desperately needed, but it remained beyond her reach. The harder she strove to find it, the more elusive it became.

She looked again at the ruby, staring at it so intently that it seemed to burn into her mind. When she closed her eyes again, she saw behind them the same shape glowing in brilliant green. Opposites, no more reconcilable than were her own desire and duty. Tears stung her eyes. She swiped them away impatiently and redoubled her efforts.

Time slowed until she lost all sense of its passage. There was only the desperate striving of her own will amid the dizzying whirl of opposing forces seemingly set on thwarting it. A dull throb began in the back of her head, radiating upward to pound within her skull. The muscles of her neck and shoulders clenched. Inch by inch, the column of her spine began to throb. Pain filled her and still she could not let go. Royce was out there somewhere, that she knew. The ruby might be the best, if not the only, hope she had of finding him. She could not give up.

Despite the coolness of the cavern, her skin felt clammy. Nausea swept through her. She clutched at the ledge, trying to steady herself, and felt the hot burn of tears down her cheeks.

"I can't . . ."

She was caught hard against steel, held with careful strength. He cursed softly, under his breath, yet she heard him.

He had waited so long, stopping himself a dozen times as he saw the struggle playing out within her. He had to use her, absolutely had to. She was the best tool he had to discover the whereabouts of those traitorous to the Atreides and to Akora. But in the end he could not stand what he saw. Call it weakness, call it cowardice, at that moment he had no care save for her. She was so pale, trembling even, when impulse overwhelmed all else.

"It's all right," he said, willing the words to be reality. "You have done all you can."

"No! I have not. Let me go! I must—"

"Must what?" He turned her in his arms, staring down

at her, sweeping over the fierce glitter of her eyes, the stiff stature of her body. Even now, she would not yield. "Exhaust yourself? Make yourself ill? You are very close to both. What good will that do Royce?" He took a breath, willing calm, finding it as elusive as control. "It was a mistake to bring you here."

"Kassandra uses the ruby."

"You are not her, your gift is not hers. Mayhap for you there is another way."

She stared up at him. "I am not less than her." Behind the words were others, both fear and plea: *do not disbelieve me.*

He shook his head, trying to clear it, finding he could not. There was a strange confusion, clouding all else. Sweet heaven, how he desired her! "What does that mean? Less than her? You are not her, she is not you. We will find another way."

"There is no time." Her voice broke, her strength with it. She bent into his chest and sobbed, great convulsive shudders he feared would tear her apart. He held her desperately through the storm, crooning nothings, stroking her hair, straining for some means to reach her.

At length, it passed.

She raised her head, sniffed hard. Her eyes were red and swollen, her body limp. Her voice sounded husky and raw. Embarrassment kept her from meeting his gaze. "Royce is my only family. That's odd really. There have always been numerous Hawkfortes but of late we seem to have shrunk." She smiled, or tried to, but the effort wobbled and she gave it up. "There are cousins, distant ones, in America. They went there decades ago."

He stroked her hair, cupping the back of her head, blindly grateful that she was just a little calmer. "In time to be rebels?"

"Oh, yes, they were that. Still are, I suppose. They suspect the worst of Britain, believe we are plotting to take them back. But it doesn't matter. We are still family, however distant."

"Miles count for little." He hesitated, aware of the hurdle that still must be jumped each time he told something of himself. "My parents are also in America."

The gambit worked; she was distracted. "In America? Why?"

"For the same reason I go to Britain."

She did look at him then and he felt a spurt of relief such as he could scarcely credit, for behind the wan despair in her eyes he saw the woman of strength he knew her to be, still there, still strong, only needing a little comfort. Whether she would take it remained to be seen.

"To gather information?" she asked.

"And acquire whatever seems of interest. My mother loves it. Like Kassandra, she always yearned to travel."

"What of your father? Wouldn't he rather go to England?"

"And appear where he is assumed long dead? Hardly." Still talking, and with his arm firmly around her, Alex moved toward the entrance to the cavern. "Besides, he enjoys America. He's said the only place he would have liked to be washed up other than Akora is Boston."

Joanna laughed weakly, surprising herself. How remarkable that anything could be amusing under the present circumstances. She knew what Alex was doing but could muster no more than muted resentment. She had failed and a dark wave of despair hovered only waiting to engulf her.

"You will rest," he said and she saw they had left the cavern, were at the foot of the steps leading up to his apartment. Just then it seemed a mile away and straight up. With a sigh, she put her foot on the first stone tread only to gasp softly when the world swung away from her.

"Put me down." What was meant as a demand

emerged as little more than a squeak. Grimly, she pressed her lips together and determined not to make another sound until she could do so without humiliating herself further.

He climbed, easily, lithely, no hint of exertion hastening his breath. She was not a will-o'-the-wisp woman. Though slender, she regarded herself as sturdy. He should not have been able to carry her so effortlessly. That he could and did sent a small shiver through her she did not want to acknowledge.

"Cold?" Alex asked.

She shook her head and began counting the steps. There were fifty-four of them not including the ones she had missed at the beginning. She concentrated on that information as though it had some actual significance.

They had reached the apartment. Through the wide windows she could see the sun almost crowning the peaks of the mountains on the distant island, tranforming hazy green and blue to pure gold. Another day almost gone, another night almost come.

"I must try again."

His arms tightened around her. "You will, but not just now. Now you will rest and eat."

He set her down on the bed and stepped back quickly to her relief, or so she told herself. With long strides, Alex crossed the room, picked up the hammer that hung from the side of a gong of beaten bronze, and struck it lightly. "Sida will see that you have whatever you need."

He could not look at her just then, not at the proud but weary set of her shoulders, the paleness of her face, the spill of gold over her shoulders. She was close, he had only to cross the room again, ease her gently back onto the bed. She was lost, he could see that, and afraid. With just a little persuading, she would come to him.

Self-loathing washed cold over hot desire. Without another word, he turned and strode from the room.

✳

Sɪᴅᴀ sᴘᴏᴋᴇ ᴛᴡɪᴄᴇ before Joanna heard her. The servant stood, hands folded in front of her, face wreathed in concern.

"Lady?"

Slowly, Joanna reached through the fog of confusion and dread to focus on the older woman. She had no memory of Sida entering the room, only of Alex leaving. "What is it?"

The servant's frown deepened. "Are you all right, lady?"

Was she? No, she didn't think so, but admitting that would only make it worse. "I'm fine, just a little tired."

Mulridge would have turned her mouth down at the corners and produced a glinty-eyed stare at so transparent a deception. Sida merely clucked. "A warm bath, perhaps?" Without waiting for Joanna's agreement, Sida helped her up and directed her firmly toward the bath. "I will send for food. You have had a long journey. It is good that you rest."

"That seems to be all I do," Joanna muttered, but she went. Her head still pounded and every muscle in her body ached. The hot water helped but she emerged from the bath still dogged by an anxious weariness from which there was no respite.

A thin white tunic dropped over her head, she sat as Sida directed. The food was delectable as always: a shrimp bisque lightly touched by sweet pepper, freshly baked bread, and a salad of seaweed threads Joanna was curious enough to try. It proved surprisingly good but she set it aside unfinished as she did the rest of the meal. By the time she got up from the table, the mountains westward across the Inland Sea looked bathed in fire. It would be dark soon. Already she could see a few stars high above. The sounds of the palace were muted. Far off in the distance, she heard the sweet song of pipes soaring into the gathering night.

Longing filled her, harsh and bittersweet. She blinked away tears, furious at herself for being so weak. To sit and do nothing in all the days since she had left England. To fail the one time she did try. And now...to what? Slip into the big, welcoming bed as her body ached to do? Seek the escape of sleep? Her spirit rebelled at so craven a retreat. Before she could think twice, she seized the blue cloak, swirled it around her shoulders and left the room.

There was still enough light to find her way down the stairs that led off the private corridor, at least so far as the landing and the door Alex had pointed out earlier. She opened it cautiously, feeling the rush of warm night air, and stepped outside.

The moon had risen. By its light, she could make out the path that led down toward the city. Rather than follow it, she turned toward the courtyard in front of the palace. At this hour, it was almost empty, the crowds having gone home. Several young boys were raking away the traces of a busy day, their slim bodies casting long shadows in the moonlight. They paused as she passed but said nothing.

She walked with no clear notion of where she was going, only that she had to be doing something. Since her arrival, she had seen little of the palace beyond the private quarters. As there seemed to be no prohibition against her wandering about, she climbed the main staircase. At its top were high fluted columns painted red and framing immense double doors, easily twenty feet in height and almost as wide. They were open, revealing a vast chamber beyond. She stepped in cautiously, uncertain of what she would find or the appropriateness of her being there. But as still no one appeared to dissuade her, she yielded to her intense curiosity and took a long look around.

The ruins she had seen in Greece, magnificent though they were, had not prepared her for the living reality of Akora. Clearly, this was an audience chamber, one that could hold thousands. It was impressive by virtue of its size alone but there were none of the accoutrements of power she would have expected, the lavish displays of wealth and military might intended to awe and subdue. Instead the assembly hall seemed designed to welcome and even relax.

The moon, rising farther, illuminated the fountain where water burbled gently beneath the painted sky, but it was the figures on the walls that compelled Joanna's attention. She walked slowly, staring at the murals. They appeared to depict rites taking place in fields, some with a view of Ilius itself in the background. While she could not completely understand them, they reminded her a little of the old country customs preserved in places like Hawkforte. The first seeds of the year were still sown with murmured prayers and the last cornstalks were made into dolls hung high in trees. She saw no harm to such things and indeed, would have missed them.

But here she saw far more, men who appeared to be priests leading the people in prayer and, most remarkably, women performing the same tasks. At these last she stared long and hard. She had never seen a woman lead a religious service. How very strange that she should find that depicted here, in the land where "warriors rule, women serve."

Still puzzling over that, she stepped behind one of the many vine-entwined columns that held up the ceiling of the vast hall to get a better look at a section of the mural. She was still studying it when the voices broke her concentration.

Two men were speaking, one seeming to override the other with strident insistence.

"I tell you, we cannot wait much longer. The Atreides

grow stronger by the day. Soon they will crush any who
dare to oppose them."

The other man spoke too low for Joanna to be sure
what he said but it sounded like a demurral promptly rejected by the first.

"You can't be that blind! You know what the exalted
Alexandros carried in his hold this trip. Do you imagine
those cannons truly are only to protect us from *xenos*?
You believe that of a man who is half-*xenos* himself?"

At the mention of Alex's name, Joanna pressed
against the column, the better to conceal herself, and
dared a quick peek around the curve of stone. In the
shadows between silver streams of moonlight, she saw
the two men. The taller of the two also appeared to be
older. His hair was tinged with grey, his face sagging toward jowls and his brow creased into what appeared to
be a permanent frown.

"I don't...that is, it is impossible to say but—"

The younger, smaller man shook his head emphatically. Large, flitting eyes rested above the blade of a nose.
He had a whippet body, lean and tense, that even as he
stood seemed poised to erupt into motion. "There is no
but. We stand at the crossroads. If we fail to act now, we
will lose all we hold most dear."

"I share your concern, Deilos," the older man said
rather wearily. "But precipitous action will avail us nothing. I counsel caution and—"

"Caution." The younger man's contempt rang clear.
So clear, indeed, that he must have heard it. With a
visible effort to control himself, he said, "Forgive me,
Troizus. I feel so intensely about this matter that it is dif-
ficult for me to understand the hesitations of others.
However, of course, I respect your views."

No, Joanna suspected, he did not. Plain, sensible
country wisdom told her he threw out the assurance as a
gesture lacking even the pretense of sincerity. Arrogance
ruled him and, right beside it, fierce impatience.

They spoke a short time longer but too softly for her to hear. She watched until both men left the assembly hall, parting near the red columns to go their separate ways. Only then did she let herself consider what she had just witnessed: Troizus and Deilos, two of the counselors Alex had said were opposed to the Vanax's plans to bring change to Akora, the one cautious but the other pushing for some sort of immediate action. Were she to lay odds as to who would prevail, they would favor the younger for he seemed by far to possess the stronger will. Moreover, she suspected that in his arrogance and impatience, he might not be deterred by the older man's reluctance but could act instead on his own.

Swiftly, with no attention now for the glories of the palace, Joanna returned to Alex's apartment. She went from room to room looking for him only to give up in defeat. Frustration gripped her. She strode to the windows in the bedroom, looking out at the city etched in moonlight. Where could he be? The previous night, he had returned so late she had not even awakened. As determined as she was to avoid that happening again, she could not bear to wait long hours to tell him what she had learned. Deilos was planning something, she was certain of that, and she doubted very much if Troizus's disapproval would deter him. Time might be of the essence.

Glancing toward the curtained archway, she considered going in search of Kassandra. There was a chance the Princess might know Alex's whereabouts but there was also a good possibility that Kassandra did not know about Deilos and the other Council members. Joanna did not want the responsibility of telling her, not if there was any other option.

Was there? She had tried desperately to find Royce and failed. Why then would she believe herself capable of finding Alex?

True, even as he drifted through her mind she recalled

the warmth of his smile, the deep caress of his voice, the very touch and taste of him. That didn't mean she would be any more successful. He was closer, very close, somewhere in...near the palace but her need to find him did not compare with the life-and-death urgency she felt to locate Royce. Yet but for that one tenuous glimpse, her brother remained beyond her reach whereas Alex...

In some distant region of her mind, scarcely knowable, something flashed like quicksilver, here, gone, returning again. Gleaming against darkness, bright, flowing...wet...

Water but of a kind unlike any she had ever seen, alive with light not laid upon it but buried deep within as within the currents of her mind.

How could her imagination conjure such a sight? Surely, she had never encountered anything of the sort yet now she could almost feel it.

No, not almost. She did feel the cool, flowing shiver of the glowing water as it spilled over her hand, transforming her skin so that it, too, radiated light.

Her skin? Or Alex's? Skin to skin, unsure where one ended and the other began, yearning to be even closer to him...

Even as he turned and looked over his shoulder as though puzzled, seeking in the darkness for something he thought he had heard or felt, yet was not there.

Joanna gasped, fighting for breath. She was on her knees, clinging to the silken covers of the bed while waves of shock tumbled through her. Against all her expectations, she had found Alex. Only her own ignorance about Ilius had kept her from knowing exactly where he was. How could that be? How could she possibly reach out and find a man who little more than a fortnight ago had been a stranger to her, when she could not find her own brother?

The question haunted her even as she fought to ignore it. She had neither time nor energy to puzzle over such things. Quickly, she pulled herself upright and stumbled over to the gong. The hammer reverberated softly as it struck the beaten metal.

ELEVEN

SIDA APPEARED MOMENTS LATER. One look at Joanna and the servant hurried to her. "Lady, what is wrong? You look ill."

Joanna held up her hands both to ward Sida off and reassure her at the same time. "I'm fine, truly. Only tell me, is there someplace near here where the water glows as though there is light caught inside it?"

The older woman stared at her in bewilderment. "Lady—?"

"I know it sounds very strange but can you think of anywhere like that? Water that looks almost like liquid silver"—the image was vivid in her mind even as she puzzled over it—"but thinner than silver would be and with a touch of green almost as though there were something alive within it?"

"Do you mean the Pool of Sighs? If you wish to see it, perhaps Prince Alexandros will—"

"The Pool of Sighs?" What she had seen existed, it was real. Excitement filled her. "Where is it? How do I get there?"

"It is difficult, lady, especially at night. There is a path from this wing of the palace—"

"The path that goes to the city?"

"Yes, but you must veer off to the left before you reach the city and go down toward the shore. It is rocky there and can be dangerous in the dark. Please to wait for Prince Alexandros to take you."

"He's there now," Joanna said boldly. "I must join him."

The servant looked startled. "But he left no such instructions."

"Not for you perhaps, nonetheless I must go. The moon is very bright. I'll find the way."

Before Sida could try again to discourage her, Joanna hurried from the room. She sped down the narrow stone staircase to the landing and went out the door. This time, she followed the path toward the city. The moon rode high, graced by slender streams of cloud drifting across it. So brightly did it shine that she could have opened a book and read by the illumination. Or plowed a field as had been done times uncounted at Hawkforte when the planting and harvest moons bestowed their gifts.

Before the path turned downward to the city she saw where it forked off to the left. Carefully, she followed what was little more than flattened grass. Sida had told her true; the way was difficult. Several times she paused to listen to the sea washing the white strand below the palace hilltop. Pebbles rolling beneath her feet slowed her yet further. To the west, the Inland Sea looked vast but tranquil. Moonlight carved a watery road leading to some unfathomable destination.

The air smelled of jasmine and wild grasses. Whenever she paused, Joanna thought she could still hear the distant song of the pipes. The direction was elusive, for the sound seemed to come from everywhere and nowhere.

She went on, almost falling once so that her heart thudded violently but finally finding her way gingerly down the path to the shore. There she paused, listening to the gentle lap of the waves and the occasional splash of something out in the water. A little distance down the beach, the sea cut inward. She followed its path a short way until, coming over the crest of a gentle rise, she saw what could only be the Pool of Sighs. It was exactly as she had seen, water gleaming with inner light. *As though the moon had drowned,* she thought and tried to ignore the shiver such thought evoked.

Beside the pool, staring into it, she saw Alex. He stood in shadows but there was no mistaking him. Startled, she realized she already knew the tilt of his head, the shape of his broad shoulders brushed by thick ebony hair, the way he planted his feet firmly apart when he was thinking. Knew, too, that he was aware of her.

"Joanna?" He sounded hesitant, not quite willing to believe the evidence of his own eyes. A short time before, he had thought her near. Now she truly was, as though conjured by the desire he strove so desperately to contain, desire that had driven him from her side when his every instinct was to stay to comfort and protect her. Desire that had brought him to this place of seemingly unearthly beauty where he sought but failed to find some measure of peace.

He should have been surprised yet was not. Gathering within him over hours and days, really from that first moment when he found her on board *Nestor,* was a sense of inevitability he could no longer deny.

She stepped closer, the dark blue cloak swirling around her. Moonlight bathed her features. To Alex, she looked cast in silvered light.

"Sida told me of this place."

"How did you know I was here?"

"I saw you." Quickly, she added, "I know, it sounds unbelievable and indeed, I feel it to be so. I seek Royce and find you. What sense does that make? No matter, Sida said this place is called the Pool of Sighs. Does that mean people sigh over its beauty?"

She had found him? He felt a fierce pleasure at this

evidence of the connection between them even as he admitted inwardly that her power was disconcerting. Still and all, any man of sense knew the power within women. Hers just showed more obviously.

"Not precisely. There is a legend, of course, as there seems to be for everything on Akora." He spoke very softly as though not to alarm her even as he stepped closer.

She looked around at the pool, the dark rocks enclosing it, at him. Her gaze lingered, as though touching. "A legend?"

He took a breath, felt his own power running in his blood. Softly, across the small distance still between them, he said, "Eons ago, Lady Moon had a lover."

"*Lady* Moon?" She tested the sound of it on her tongue. "Not the Man in the Moon? How very odd."

He came closer still, almost, not quite, touching her. "No, it is not. You know that." When still she looked at him, he shrugged. "You bleed with the moon."

Warmth swept her cheeks. Her eyes dropped, rose again, and met his in challenge. "That is not spoken of."

"It is here on Akora. We are far more sensible about such things. Lady Moon shapes the tides, including those that flow within women. Eons ago she had a lover. He became curious about the Earth and one night, he leaned too far down from his heavenly perch. He fell into this pond and drowned. When the moon is high and the wind is right, you can still hear Lady Moon sigh over her lost love."

"How romantic."

The tartness of her response made him chuckle. Lady Joanna Hawkforte thought little of romance, it seemed. No misty-eyed naïf this but a woman of hardheaded practicality. Or so she liked to fashion herself, she who had thrown aside all care and caution to journey to a hidden kingdom on a desperate quest. Who stood before him now, wreathed in moonlight, beguiling.

"You prefer reality to romance. So do I, I confess, but only because I think ultimately it is far more exciting." He dipped a hand into the pool, raised it draped in radiance. "There are tiny creatures in this water who absorb the light of the sun during the day and radiate it back at night. I have seen them under a microscope. You can do the same, if you like. Think of it, a universe of creatures so small we would be completely unaware of them if not for the trick of nature that makes them beautiful to us."

He took Joanna's hand, drawing her down beside him, and slowly trickled the glowing water into her palm. She gasped, startled by the sensation of holding cool light. Several drops began to slip between her fingers. She caught them in her other hand and bent to replace all the living water in the pool.

"They can't survive outside of there, can they?" she asked.

"I suppose not." Her care for even the smallest life touched him. They knelt in silence for a few minutes, looking down into the pool.

Staring into the silver depths, Joanna concentrated on breathing slowly and steadily. Her awareness of Alex was so acute as to be almost painful. Her lips, her hands, her arms, truly all of her felt his touch as though memory shimmered on the edge of tantalizing reality. Moment by moment, heartbeat by heartbeat, she had to fight the urge to turn to him, this man who lived for duty but bent the rules of his culture and upbringing to help her, who awakened her to needs she had never before acknowledged, who treated her with unfailing gentleness and patience when he so easily might have done otherwise. He had even, lest she forget, gone so far as to offer her a look through a microscope, apparently assuming she had both the intelligence and curiosity to appreciate it. What English gentleman would think to do the same?

A small laugh escaped her. She met Alex's questioning glance and sobered. Reluctantly, she said, "I heard Deilos and Troizus talking. They are two of the counselors you told me about, aren't they? The ones who oppose change?"

Beside her, Alex stiffened. He had assumed her safe in his apartments, not wandering about in the night encountering men who might well be enemies. His mistake was not one he would make again; assumptions regarding Joanna Hawkforte were foolishness itself. With calm he was far from feeling, he asked, "They are, but how did you happen to cross paths with them?"

She shrugged as though with no regard for how close she had come to danger. "I was restless and decided to explore the palace. I was looking at the murals in the hall beyond the red pillars when they came by."

"They saw you?" He waited for her answer, girding himself for the possibility that he would have to move against Deilos at once before he could pose a threat to Joanna.

"Oh, no, I'm sure they didn't or they would never have spoken as they did. I was behind a column. They seem to be in disagreement. Deilos believes they must act immediately while Troizus is more cautious."

Alex relaxed very slightly. The situation was not as bad as he had thought. Bad enough, to be sure, but not as bad as it could have been. "I have known Deilos since we were both boys. He was never content to wait for anything."

"Then he has not changed." She brushed aside the hair falling across her cheek and turned to meet Alex's steady gaze. Tremors of awareness whispered through her as she realized how very close they were. She found herself staring at the hard curve of his mouth and looked away hastily. "He told Troizus he respected his views but he clearly does not. Perhaps I am wrong but he seemed a man brimming over with the need to act . . . and soon."

"Did he say anything else?"

"He knows about the cannons you brought back."

"That was inevitable and, being so, Atreus informed the Council earlier today. Deilos knows perfectly well they are to defend Akora from outside invasion."

From British invasion, Joanna thought, and shuddered with revulsion at the thought. "He sounded as though they were a personal threat to him." She paused, waiting for him to confirm or perhaps try to deny what she already had concluded for herself and what had sent her in search of him. Deilos's urgency, his demand for action now, could only be explained if he had reason to fear the Atreides strengthening their defenses.

Alex brushed the last of the water from his hands back into the pool and rose. With deliberate casualness, he said, "Don't let Deilos concern you. He will be dealt with when the time comes."

Joanna also stood but cautiously, too aware that she was not entirely in control of herself. Too aware of everything really, the breath of warm night air on her skin, the pressure of fabric against her nipples that were unaccountably sensitive, the lingering scent of jasmine, above all, the memory of what it had felt like to reach out, seeking Alex . . . and find him.

"Deilos does concern me," she said. "I know perfectly well that he represents danger heaped on danger. You don't have to treat me as though I were a child to be protected from that truth."

"Believe me," he murmured, "I am all too well aware that you are not a child." He turned to go.

What it had felt like . . .

She reached out not with her mind this time but with her hand, brushing down his forearm to catch her fingers twining round his. "Wait."

He stopped, breathing deeply, fighting himself. Slowly, he raised their entwined hands and looked at them, slender against strong, pale against dark, each the complement of the other as though deliberately matched. Desire became a roar within him but it was honor that spoke. "There are limits, Joanna."

She let the warning go like the water running between her fingers, with due notice but no regrets. "Life is very precarious, isn't it?"

"I told you, there's no need to fear Deilos."

"Not him, all of it. I lost my parents, I may have lost my brother." Her voice caught. "I come here to a place filled with peace and beauty only to find it, too, is threatened. It seems we truly have nothing but the moment."

His eyes were gentle, filled with comprehension, yet still he said, "What we do in all the moments shapes the future."

"Ah, yes, choices and their consequences." She stepped closer, still holding his hand, lifting his arm weighted with muscle around her waist so that she stood within the curve of it. Too vividly, she remembered how very hard it had been to move away from him in the tent scant hours before. Ever since then, she seemed to have been moving toward him. "Too often, I have done nothing."

His eyebrows rose though whether from her words or her actions she could not say.

"You? I would say the contrary, you do not hesitate to act."

"You'd be surprised." She paused, still unsure how much of herself to reveal, to give. "I've stayed with the safe and familiar all my life, rarely venturing a toe out into the world and then quickly deciding it wasn't for me. I've scarcely ever taken a risk or dared anything until just recently."

"That doesn't sound like you."

"I think it wasn't. I think this is me." Quickly, before she could reconsider, she raised herself on tiptoe and touched her mouth to his. His lips were firm, slightly parted, warm and oh, so, tantalizing. And surprised, very surprised. He stiffened and began to pull back but she tightened her hold on his hand and pressed closer, melding her body to his. "I found you."

Against her lips, reluctantly, he smiled. "That you did."

"So easily...so amazing..." She let go of his hand, half afraid he would use it to push her away, and twined her arms around his neck. "I can't settle for safe anymore."

"Joanna..." He took hold of her waist, truly meaning to put her from him, but somehow the intention was lost in the thrumming heat of his blood as he responded helplessly to her touch. Helplessly. He, a man of experience and discipline. The very notion seemed startlingly odd yet there was a poignant pleasure in the sense that events were moving beyond his control.

He cleared his throat, tried again. Gods, she felt so good, so right! He had to fight that somehow, had to overcome the passion that flowed like a deep, remorseless wave within him. "Joanna, desperation drives you. I understand that. You fear for your brother and long to find him. Life seems very bleak right now. But later, you would regret this—"

He broke off. The greatest will in the world could not have compelled him to continue when she was raining light, quick kisses over his jaw, along the corded column of his throat, lingering over the pulse she found pounding there. Her unbound breasts pressed against his chest, full, tantalizing. Somehow his hands had slipped to the curve of her hips. Through the thin fabric, he could feel the exquisite softness of her skin and the heat of her, reaching out to him.

"I will regret nothing, Alex. Nothing so long as I do not deny this." Her arms closed around him fiercely. "I *found* you...and, I think, myself."

Duty, that cold bedfellow, made a final, feeble try but he was scarcely aware of it. Another, equal imperative had taken over, driving out all else.

He bent his head, his mouth brushing over hers again and again, the kiss deepening even as she gave a husky little moan and wrapped her arms around him. Lost in the taste of her, he lowered them both to the welcoming ground. The bed of moss was cool and lightly scented with the essence of the earth. She gazed up at him and for a fleeting moment, all the brightness of the moon was reflected in her eyes. Stray wisps of cloud moved across the sky, wrapping them in gentle concealment. She smiled and he felt a surge of joy that sent him spiraling back in time as though he were once again a feckless boy and this his own first time to discover the power of a woman.

"We," he said as he held his weight above her, "are going to go very slowly." He touched his mouth to her throat and felt her blood leap in answer, raised his head again and saw that her smile had deepened.

"Are we?" Her hands slipped down his back, lingering over the hard bone and powerful muscle. She felt transformed even before the deed was done and exalted in a way reason could not explain. But then reason had no role to play there in the veiled moonlight beside the living pool. "I already feel as though I have been waiting all my life for you."

He breathed in sharply, exhaled slowly, and looked at her so fiercely that her own breath caught. "It is not wise to say such things under these circumstances."

"Oh, forgive me. I bow to your superior wisdom." Laughter rose in her, little bubbles of happiness bursting on the surface of the miracle that was happening. He wore a tunic that ended at mid-thigh. With very little effort she could tug it up. Boldness shimmered through her. She was leaping high, exhilarated to discover that she could fly. His skin was very hot and when she touched him, he shuddered.

"Gods, woman, you will not undo me!"

She clasped his face between her hands and arched so

that her nipples brushed the hard wall of his chest. "I am already undone. It is only fair you join me."

"Already?" His smile matched her own. "I perceive you are an innocent after all."

Genuinely surprised, she paused in her delighted discovery of so much of his body as she could reach. "You doubted it?"

"I thought it would be useful if you were not since you were to pretend to be my mistress."

Her smile returned. "I have yet to call you *kreon*."

"Somehow it does not matter any longer." He heard himself speak as though from a distance. Her skin was exquisitely soft, her touch enticing. His blood roared. He grasped handfuls of her gown and freed her long, slender legs. Instinctively, she parted them, making a place for him.

"I need to see you," he groaned. ". . . Touch you."

"So do I . . ." She sat up, her hands on his, urging him. Together, they drew her gown over her head. The riot of her hair spilled like pale gold over skin opalescent as the moon. His hand trembled as he reached out, gently brushing the silken curls away, staring at what was revealed to him.

"You are exquisite," he said thickly. He had known feminine beauty in many forms but never had loveliness moved him as it did now. His desire for her was acutely physical and vastly more. He wanted her here and now beneath the moon on the bed of moss and a thousand years hence.

She sat up on her knees, facing him with pride and just the smallest shadow of embarrassment he found endearing as she triumphed over it. "I think you should know," she murmured, "I am not a particularly patient woman." And with that her slim but surprisingly strong hands drew his tunic from him. For just a moment, the garment dangled from the tips of her fingers before dropping, quite forgotten.

"Oh, my . . ." Her gaze drifted over him in a way a dead man would have found encouraging. "You are . . . superb."

Grateful for the shadow that concealed just how superb she made him feel, he said quietly, "You have nothing to fear from me, Joanna, truly."

Her hand reached out and brushed the hard line of his jaw in a caress of such piercing tenderness as to touch the very core of him. "I would not be here if I thought otherwise, Alex."

Relief flowed through him and with it sheer delight at her beauty, her boldness and above all, her honesty. "That is just as well," he said with a grin, "for you have a very long way to go before we can truly say you are undone."

She looked at him in surprise that gave way swiftly to a soft gasp of shock as he gathered her to him. Gently but implacably he lowered her back onto the ground. "Being undone," he murmured as his mouth grazed her throat and trailed lower, "may involve more than you suspect."

"More . . . really? *Alex* . . ." She arched against the hard wall of his body as he cupped her breasts, his tongue grazing over her distended nipples before suckling first one, then the other.

"Much, much more," he said and proceeded to show her exactly what he meant. With no more than the brush of fingertips and of breath, a flick of his tongue and the constant, tantalizing heat of his body all along her own, he brought her swiftly to a peak of expectancy that banished reason. A lifetime of caution and care unraveled with stunning speed. Every inch of her skin felt acutely sensitized. He blew very lightly on her nipples and she moaned helplessly, her fingers digging into his massive shoulders.

"No more."

He raised his head, dark eyes dancing, and smiled. "No more? We've scarcely begun." At her look of mingled astonishment and alarm, he laughed and soothed her with a kiss that made her forget all concern and yield herself eagerly to the delights he offered so passionately.

Sweet heaven, she was so responsive! Watching her discover what she was capable of experiencing enthralled him. So fascinating was she that he could almost ignore the molten thrumming of his own need. Almost. Moment to moment, heartbeat to heartbeat, he felt his control shredding like so much chaff driven onto the wind.

He wanted desperately to wait, to draw out her pleasure to the utmost and give her everything he possibly could, but the molten passion of her own response proved more than he could endure. He could feel her teetering just on the brink, her whole body arching beneath his, pulled taut with need even as his own overcame him at last. Groaning deeply, he drew back just enough to enter her. She was blazing hot, wet and tight, but the moment she felt him, her sleek inner muscles flexed in welcome. He gasped as she took him, her hips rising, unflinching as he drove past the barrier of her innocence.

Joanna's eyes opened very wide, staring up at the moon. Heat thrust deep within her, stretching and filling her more than she would ever have believed possible. There was no pain, only a piercing sense of rightness that stunned her. And with it a mounting delirium that drove out all thought, reason, memory, even her own sense of herself as separate and apart. There were only the two of them moving as one, bathed in silver radiance that finally, gloriously exploded deep in the very core of her being. Dimly, she was aware of Alex surging within her, of his own husky groans mingling with her soft cries. She clung to him as the waves of release swept over them both.

THE MOON HAD MOVED HIGHER in the sky when Joanna next took note of it. She returned to herself as though she had ventured a great distance away into some unknown realm where dream masqueraded as memory.

Or did it?

Had she really come down to the beach, found Alex and, despite his obvious scruples... *seduced* him? Had she truly thrown all caution and propriety to the wind, cast away a lifetime of good sense, and embraced the most shocking conduct right along with the man himself? Had she, in short, behaved in a manner even the most charitable soul could consider nothing less than *scandalous*?

Dazed, she marveled at the realization that seemed to grow within her with each breath. Yes, she had, and truth be told she felt quite wonderful about it.

Still scarcely awake, she smiled. Alex lay close beside her, the lingering heat of his skin a contrast to the gathering coolness of the night. She turned slightly, looking at him, and felt a deep upswelling of affection that in its own way rivaled the so-recent tumult of lustful discovery. Affection and respect, incandescent passion and delight, all that and perhaps more she had yet to discover...

...Her mother, standing in the great hall at Hawkforte, a soft gown of white muslin billowing about her in the breeze from the open doors. Beyond a day of bursting summer, no hint of warning shadow.

Her father, tall, so handsome, an arm around his beloved wife, the two swaying together in the motes of dust dancing in the sunlight.

> *Come live with me and be my love,*
> *And we will all the pleasures prove*
> *That valleys, groves, hills, fields,*
> *Woods, or steepy mountain yields.*

Marlowe again. Her father had loved the doomed playwright, dead in a tavern brawl long before his time.

Death so often came early, sneaking up out of sun-filled days, lurking around unnoticed corners.

"Don't go," Joanna begged, child and woman, locked in dream and memory, and reached out a frantic hand, finding warm, solid flesh.

"Of course I will not go," Alex said, voice thick with the remnant of sleep. He caught her fingers, touching them to his lips even as he gathered her to him. He had awakened suddenly for no apparent reason but just in time to hear her plea and feel the distress within her. Distress he moved instantly to soothe. "Hush, everything is all right. What troubles you?"

Not what had passed between them, he hoped. He truly did not think he could bear that.

"I must have . . . dreamt and thought myself awake."

Dreamt of loss, again and of death, if he was any judge of the demons haunting her. Suddenly heedless of his strength, he crushed her close, holding her along every inch of skin as though he could absorb her torments and destroy them. She was on her back, gazing up at him and he above, unknowing of how fierce he looked just then. How enthralling.

"I am alive, Joanna, and I am not going to die. Be assured of that. Before long, we will laugh over vanquished fears."

Despite herself, the corners of her mouth twitched. "Have you Kassandra's gift then?"

"No gifts at all, not like that at any rate, and praise God for it. But I've a strong arm and a keen will. A multitude of possible futures lie before us. When fortune favors, we pluck the one that suits us best."

She believed him, God help her, or perhaps it was merely that her yearning was so strong as to seem transformed into reality. No matter. Her hands clutched at his shoulders, so broad, so strong, blotting out the dark. Instinctively, her hips rose.

He groaned deep in his throat. She watched the pulse

leap there, fascinated. Felt, too, the leap between her thighs and herself, in response, sliding so easily into the sweet, hot enthrallment of desire.

"It is too soon," he said.

She grinned, country girl that she was, and moved again, savoring him. "I think not."

Alex arched his brows. "Shameless, utterly shameless."

"Oh, heavens, I hope so."

His laughter exploded. He hugged her close, delighted and relieved all at once. What a woman! Beautiful, intelligent, provocative, daring... He would have to remember how he appreciated her daring next time she did something foolhardy. For the moment, it was enough to see her smile.

Well, no, not really enough. Not even remotely.

And not, as it turned out, too soon after all.

chapter

TWELVE

T HERE WAS PALE LIGHT and a smell she knew, cold and
dank, hard. Stone.

There was pain and a weariness so great it almost
stopped her breath.

There was a window, small, blocked by iron bars
through which it was just possible to catch a glimpse of
what lay beyond. A ditch and a stone wall, then a field
dropping away to water gleaming in the growing light.
Across the water, more land and a tower, tall and slender,
revealed white in the new day.

One more endless, hopeless day.

Rage... bitterness... despair... But withal, life.

"Royce."

The cry was wrenched from Joanna. She sat up, heart
slamming against her ribs, breath gasping. Tears were hot
on her cheeks. She rubbed them away fiercely even as she
struggled to understand where she was... and where she
had been.

She heard the sounds of the palace, servants moving
about, petitioners and visitors already arriving, and farther off the noises of the city. She smelled the sea, the
pots of flowering thyme beyond the windows, the
nearby lemon arbors. She was draped in silk. Dimly she

recalled Alex pulling the sheet over them both when at last they tumbled into sated sleep.

She might as well have been in paradise but she tasted, ashen on her tongue, the brutal knowledge of captivity.

Water splashed in the bathing room.

Long limbs flashing, she leaped from the bed, crossed the chamber in quick strides and thrust open the door.

Alex stood before the basin, looking into the silvered mirror on the wall. Except for the narrow towel knotted around his waist, he was naked. Droplets of water clung to the broad expanse of his chest, glistening on bronzed skin, trailing slowly down chiseled muscles. His ebony hair curled damply at the nape of his neck. Soap softened half the hard line of his jaw. The other half was bare and smooth, freshly shaven. She had a sudden, piercing memory of the roughness of his skin against her breasts in the soft hours of the night. Lingering astonishment at herself, at him, at them together threatened to overwhelm her before it flattened before the onslaught of urgency.

"I've seen where Royce is."

He went very still, staring at her an instant in the mirror before nodding abruptly. She was pale, her honeyed hair tumbling in disarray around her shoulders and the sheet she clutched in front of her concealing very little. Inevitably, his body stirred. With quick swipes of the razor, he finished shaving, then plucked a hand towel from a nearby shelf as all the while, his mind turned over and over. Since waking, he had thought of little save what to say to her, what to do. Never before had he needed to concern himself with such matters but then he had never known such a woman as Lady Joanna Hawkforte. Women were for pleasure, nothing more. He had always understood that, always been in complete control. No longer. The reality of what had happened between them left him stunned . . . and wary. He was careful to mask his thoughts before turning to her.

Drying his face, he said, "Come and sit down. Tell me what you saw."

So distracted was she that she failed to notice she had not wrapped the sheet around herself. He was treated to a tantalizing view of her long, tapered back and luscious bottom as he followed her into the bedchamber. He took a deep breath and gestured to a chair beside the table.

Her hands twisted in the folds of the sheet. "Royce is in a cell with bars across the windows. Beyond there is a ditch and a stone wall. Farther off, I saw what seems to be a green field that runs down to water. On the other side is a slender tower of white stone."

"On the other side of the field?"

"No, across the water. I could just make out the tower." Unaware of the desperate plea brimming in her eyes, she gazed up at him. "Royce is sick and in pain. He is close to despair but he *is* alive. Today, at least, right now. Who knows for how much longer?" Her voice broke. She turned away in a futile effort to hide her anguish.

Alex's hands clenched into fists, the only way he could stop them from reaching out to her. Much as he longed to believe he was still in sufficient possession of himself to hold her and offer only comfort, he knew better. Besides, there was no time. Quickly, he moved to the chest and withdrew a tunic. As he dressed, he said, "I don't want you to be alone. I will send Kassandra to you."

Her head jerked around. "Why? Where are you going?"

"To speak with Atreus."

He dropped the towel, slipped the tunic over his head. Her mouth was very dry. God help her, she had to concentrate.

"Do you recognize the place I described?"

"I . . . may." Again, a fragment of hesitation. He reached for his sword belt. Buckling it on, he said, "This is progress, Joanna, truly. Take hope from it."

Hope. Faint, weak, and no substitute for action. "I want to go with you." She was on her feet, kicking aside the sheet that threatened to trip her, her eyes never leaving him. "I can help. The closer I can get to Royce, the better able I will be to find him."

Alex took his sword from its accustomed place on the top of a chest near the bed. From long training, he automatically drew the blade from its scabbard, confirming that it came smoothly to his hand. Steel gleamed in the morning light. He replaced it and slid sword and scabbard together into the leather sheath attached to his belt. All this was the action of mere moments but in them, Joanna's attention was distracted. She stared at the weapon, trying to remember when she had seen Alex actually wear a sword. A dagger, yes, as a customary part of his garb, but not a sword except on the training field.

"You are going to fight."

He stopped and looked at her, his expression carefully blank. "I am going to see Atreus, as I said."

"Wearing a sword?"

"Surely it has not escaped your notice that we are warriors here?" What might have been sarcasm was softened by a smile. But then that was the Akoran way, wasn't it? A warrior would not do harm to a woman, not even with words.

Again, she said, "I want to go with you."

"Joanna..." He spoke very gently, his voice a caress. As implacable as all his caresses. "You know that cannot be."

"I know no such thing. I have gotten this far. Why can't I come with you?"

He sighed, a supremely male sound, and looked heavenward for an instant, as though the answer might appear somewhere in the region of the ceiling. When it did not, he looked at her again. "Because it is too dangerous. You know that, I know that, let us not pretend there is any confusion about it."

"You do understand how infuriating I find this? To

sit by and do nothing while you take all the risk is intolerable to me."

"Because you are a woman of honor and strength, yet you forget I have been trained for this. As some men are farmers and some tenders of flocks, some scribes and some smiths, this is my occupation."

"You are a warrior." Her throat was thick. He spoke so simply as though it was the most natural thing in the world that he had been trained to kill and to lead other men into battle. So natural that he would perform this duty no matter what the cost, even if it meant his death.

"Kassandra's name was changed when her nature became evident," she said. "I marvel that yours was not as well."

Cautiously, as though he already knew he would regret the answer, he asked, "What do you mean?"

"Why, they should call you Hector, of course. I should have realized it sooner. He was like you, unswerving in his devotion to duty and honor. He lived by the warrior's code and he died by it because other, lesser men were not so noble."

She had thought to anger him and damn the cost but his response surprised her. The corners of his beautiful, sculpted mouth twitched and his gaze was suddenly filled with tender amusement. "I am no doomed prince of Troy to die at the hands of an Achilles. Hector's hallowed name is wreathed in the gildings of legend. Somewhere under all that there may have been a real man but I doubt he would recognize himself."

"You would die for duty, do not deny it." Even as she could not deny the sickening horror the thought of his death provoked in her. This man she had neither right nor reason to think of as other than an enticing memory to warm her in the years to come.

"Of course I would but believe me, I have a vast preference for helping the other fellow die for *his* duty." Succumbing to temptation that had been building by the moment, he brushed the back of his hand along the silken curve of her cheek. "Why, Joanna, I believe you are concerned for me."

"Do not make light of this!"

"Perish the thought." His voice was a rough caress. He bent his head, his mouth brushing hers, returning, claiming. The fire, so recently tamped, exploded in an instant, taking them both by surprise. In a heartbeat, she was caught against the hard wall of his chest, her arms twined fiercely around his neck, lips clinging, bodies straining. The sheet, forgotten, fluttered between them in the breeze from the high wide windows.

"My God," Alex muttered as his callused palms slid down the silken smoothness of her back to cup her buttocks. "You make me forget everything."

"It isn't me," she countered. "It's you...can't think . . ." He felt like warm steel in her arms. She had to remember that and remember, too, how he had looked on the training field, a man of lethal skills honed to perfection. And behind all that, a mind keen and sharp as any blade.

Not Hector, please God.

The sword at his belt jabbed between them even as duty did the same. He stepped back quickly. She watched reason's return deep within his vivid eyes and knew the moment when he regained control of himself.

"Stay here in the palace or close by," he said, his voice almost normal. "When I can, I will send word." He kissed her once more, hard, and was gone.

Joanna watched the curtain over the arch until it stopped fluttering behind him. Slowly, consciously, she forced herself to breathe. Her mouth felt acutely sensitive and her knees were unaccountably weak. Or perhaps not so unaccountably. The past twenty-four hours had been...eventful. Grimacing at the understatement, she made her way to the bathing chamber. After a longing glance at the tub, she chose the shower instead. The

spray helped to revive her. By the time she turned off the
water and toweled herself dry, she no longer felt quite so
caught in a dizzying maelstrom of emotions that threatened to career out of all control at any moment. Even
so, she jumped slightly when she returned to the bedchamber to find Kassandra waiting for her.

The Princess looked concerned but determined to
conceal it. "Alexandros said you were awake. He suggested you might enjoy exploring more of the city."

"Was that before or after he asked you to play
minder?"

"Pardon?"

With a sigh, Joanna relented. She was not naturally
sharp tongued and even if she were, she certainly would
not take out her feelings on Kassandra. "I'm sorry. It's
just that I despise having to depend on someone else to
do what I would much rather be doing myself."

Kassandra's smile was immediate and understanding.
"I feel the same way but sometimes it is unavoidable.
Now, tell me, what has Alexandros gone off to do?"

"Figure out where Royce is, I hope."

"You have seen him?"

Joanna nodded, her expression somber. "Finally and
not very helpfully, I'm afraid. But then what did I expect? That there would be a signpost to announce where
he is?" Her voice broke. She looked away quickly.

Kassandra's touch was gentle on her arm. "What did
you see?"

Briefly, Joanna told her. "Does it mean anything to
you at all? The green field and water, the white tower?"

"I'm afraid not. But you must have faith. Alexandros
knows these islands far better than I do and he will do
everything possible to find your brother."

"I'm sure he will." Yet it was so very hard to wait, so
dreadful to feel helpless.

"Come," Kassandra said briskly, "let us pick out

something for you to wear. There is so much yet you have not seen."

Joanna agreed but she could muster no enthusiasm. It was Kassandra who plucked the tawny silk tunic from the pile in the chest, dropped it over Joanna's head, and wove matching ribbons through her hair that did little to tame the wild mass but were lovely all the same. Looking in the mirror, Joanna had difficulty recognizing herself. The woman who stared back at her seemed worlds away from the sensible creature who plodded through muddy fields, helped birth colts, shared cider with farm wives, and would have been content to live out her days within the fair fields and proud walls of Hawkforte.

Or would she?

As a child, she had dreamt of traveling to distant realms, most especially fabled Akora. It was only after her parents' sudden deaths that she had retreated into the safety of the dear and familiar. Hawkforte had been her sanctuary, but had it also been her prison?

Kassandra was looking at her curiously. With an effort, Joanna repressed the shock of a hitherto unsuspected revelation and gestured toward the door. "Shall we?"

"Where are we going?" she asked when they had left the palace. After passing through the lion gate, they turned toward the city but shortly left the road leading to it and instead followed a wide path leading up the slopes of another hill almost as tall as that upon which the palace itself stood.

"There," Kassandra said, and pointed ahead to a graceful colonnade gleaming white in the sun. "The actors in the royal troupe are rehearsing this morning. I thought you might enjoy watching them."

As a distraction went, Joanna thought it better than most. She had always been fascinated by the players who came through Hawkforte and thought that if London had one redeeming grace, it was the plenitude of its theaters. But to actually see a play performed on Akora...even under the present circumstances that was exciting. The theater resembled those she had seen in Greece, a horseshoe-shaped auditorium consisting of stone benches set in tiers beneath the open sky and facing a platform separated from the audience by a large arch through which the play was viewed. Several actors were just taking their places on the stage. Kassandra and Joanna found seats near the scattering of people gathered to watch.

"The play is *The Trojan Women* by Euripides," Kassandra whispered. "Are you familiar with it?"

"I saw it in Athens a few years ago. I was struck by how modern it seems, especially how vividly it depicts the atrocities of war."

The Princess nodded. "I think the Vanax had a particular reason for choosing it to be performed now."

Watching as the tale unfolded of lost Troy, of slain warriors and enslaved women, Joanna could not help but be caught up in the timeless anguish of the wives and mothers mourning those they had loved even as they looked forward to a future that promised only more suffering. For ten long years, so legend told, they had patiently endured a war not of their making, loyally accepting without question the decisions of their men, keeping to their hearths as was proper. For their reward, all they had held dear was gone. Homes, husbands, children, everything was lost.

As Andromache, Princess of Troy and wife of the slain hero Hector, suffered her child to be torn from her arms and hurtled to his death beneath the battlements of the once proud city, Joanna felt the hot trail of tears on her cheeks. Beside her Kassandra bit back a sob. Around them, the small audience gathered for the rehearsal sat utterly still and rapt, the women obviously moved and the men grim-faced, intent on every word.

When at last the Trojan Queen, Hecuba, was led

away into captivity, no one moved for long moments. There on the green slope above beautiful Ilius lingered the memory of a tragedy so profound that it could still sink talons into the soul.

"Did the Vanax choose this work for the reason I think he did?" Joanna asked as they stood and began making their way out.

Kassandra looked back at the now empty stage where the shadows of the actors still seemed to move. "As a warning to our people? A reminder that the peace and security we have here are not inevitable? Atreus does very little by chance, so I suspect you are right."

"He truly believes Akora may be invaded?" The very thought, especially coming on the heels of the play they had just watched, was repellent.

"There is that but remember, all those who fought at Troy regardless of which side they were on were our ancestors. They spoke the same language, worshipped the same gods, shared the same roots. At its heart, Troy is really about what happens when a people turn against themselves and betray what has made them great."

Some little distance from the theater, when they were alone, Kassandra added, "Atreus is in a difficult position. If he accuses Deilos and the others of plotting rebellion, they will simply deny it and accuse him, in turn, of defaming them unjustly. The first, most important requirement of the Vanax is that he give justice to all, so that would be very serious. But by ordering the performance of this play, Atreus sends a message few will miss. Deilos certainly will not."

"Is it wise to warn him that the Vanax knows what he is plotting?"

"I have to believe so," Kassandra replied. "There may be a chance that Deilos will reconsider but I doubt it. Given his impulsive nature, it is more likely he will be provoked to act."

"Before he is truly ready?"

"Exactly. Atreus pushes him to move precipitously and thereby make himself more vulnerable."

Despite the warmth of the morning, Joanna shivered. "It seems a risky gamble."

"Anything we do at this point, even if we do nothing, brings risk. I am sure Atreus and Alexandros together thought long and hard before choosing this course of action."

"I have to confess, I feel guilty about bringing yet another problem here. Royce is my brother and very dear to me. It is only natural that his well-being be my prime concern. But I realize it is a distraction to Alex at a time when he certainly doesn't need that."

Kassandra stopped and looked at her in surprise. "I do not understand. You and Alexandros have become lovers, have you not?"

Joanna's cheeks flamed, prompting the Princess to sigh. "Oh, dear, I have put my foot in it, haven't I? Alexandros tells me the English expect young unmarried girls to be astoundingly ignorant. I do apologize if I have upset you, but for heaven's sake, never suggest to Alexandros that he should not be helping you in this matter. He would be terribly offended."

"But it is not his responsibility."

"Of course it is. Alexandros understands that full well." Kassandra looked at her, puzzled. "Are Englishmen truly so different? They can share the bed of a woman and have no care for anything that troubles her?" She frowned at so distasteful a possibility.

"I don't know," Joanna admitted. "But I suspect some are like that. Others, men of character, would be different."

Kassandra nodded emphatically. "A man who takes pleasure with a woman and does not see to her needs, in bed *and* out, is no true man. Indeed, he is at the same level as a goat."

Joanna coughed to conceal her surprise. Virgin that she was, Kassandra seemed to have very clear-cut ideas about the relationship between men and women.

"Are all young ladies on Akora so . . . well informed?" she asked tentatively.

Kassandra's dark eyes flashed with amusement. "Let us just say that on Akora ignorance is never considered a virtue."

"I am very grateful to Alex for his help," Joanna said quietly. "If you wouldn't mind, I'd like to return to the palace. He may have learned something about Royce's whereabouts."

"Of course, whatever you like."

But when they reached the palace, and Kassandra sent Sida to see if there was news, the servant returned with word that the royal brothers remained behind closed doors.

"We could go riding," Kassandra suggested as she sat on the edge of the bed, watching Joanna pace back and forth.

"You don't have to keep me amused, truly, although I do appreciate your company." Indeed, left to herself, Joanna feared she would not be able to contain the dread threatening to smother her. Too vividly, she recalled again and again the sensation when she at last found Royce . . . the pain and despair, the feeling of life ebbing away.

"I can't simply do nothing," Joanna burst out. "If our positions were reversed, Royce would be moving heaven and earth. Yet here I am, useless."

"Hardly useless. Without your gift, no one would have any idea where your brother is or even that he remains alive."

"But what I saw is no real help. A white tower. How many of those are there on Akora? Dozens? Hundreds?"

"I don't know," Kassandra admitted. "Quite a few, no

doubt. But you saw more than just a tower." Jumping up suddenly, she rang the gong for Sida. "I have an idea. You can draw, can't you? I understand all proper young Englishwomen learn to draw."

"Some with more success than others," Joanna muttered, but she didn't reject the idea. Perhaps she could draw some semblance of what she had seen. Anything would be better than simply waiting.

Sida arrived quickly, went away again, and returned with a sheaf of paper and a box of charcoals. Kassandra placed both on the table and gestured to Joanna. "Just take your time and put in as many details as you can manage."

Awkwardly, Joanna tried to do so. Her first efforts were clumsy but little by little, the image she had seen began to appear on the paper. When she was satisfied at last that she done the best she could, she held out the drawing to Kassandra. "Does it mean anything at all to you?"

The Princess frowned. She studied the picture with obvious attention but just as obviously, it meant nothing to her. "I'm sorry—" She broke off and laid a finger on the narrow expanse of water Joanna had drawn between the sloping field and the distant white tower. "Is this supposed to be a river?"

It was Joanna's turn to frown. "I'm not sure . . . I don't think so. Unless you have a river on Akora that is very wide."

"Not so wide as you show here. It could be . . ."

"What?"

"I don't want to mislead you—"

"Never mind about that! For pity's sake, if you have any idea at all of where this could be, tell me!"

"Joanna, I could be wrong. It's just that . . ." Kassandra stared at the picture again. "Our three small islands—Phobos, Deimatos and Tarbos—are close together. I'm not sure but—"

"We need a map."

"Yes," Kassandra agreed. "Come." She hurried into the chamber Alex used as his office and quickly found the same map he had shown to Joanna on board *Nestor*. "Look here," Kassandra said as she spread it out on the table. "From the eastern shore of Deimatos it is possible to look across to the western shore of Tarbos. I have sailed through the strait between them. It is wide as you have shown but not so wide that a tower on the other side would not be visible."

"Do you remember such a tower?"

Kassandra shook her head. "It was several years ago. I was a child and I might not have noticed anyway. As you said, there are many towers on Akora. But no other place I can think of where it is possible to look across a broad expanse of water and see an opposite shore."

"Then Royce is on Deimatos, somewhere on its eastern shore!"

"Yes, possibly, but I don't understand—"

"Understand what?"

"You told Alexandros what you have told me?"

"Yes, of course, but I hadn't made any drawing."

"That shouldn't matter. Alexandros knows every inch of Akora's coastlines."

"You think he recognized what I described," Joanna said, astounded.

"No, at least perhaps not. I don't really know."

"But you suspect. You think he figured it out for himself. But he would have told me. He wouldn't have left me believing he had no idea of where Royce is."

The two women stared at one another. Gently, Kassandra took Joanna's hand. "My dear friend, for I consider you that and hope you feel the same way about me, if Alexandros had told you where Royce might be, what would you have done?"

"Gone there, of course."

"Despite all danger, just as you came to Akora?"

"Royce is my *brother*!"

"As Alexandros is mine. He would want you to be safe. Indeed, he would insist on it."

"He can insist all he likes. He has no right—"

"Does he not? Did you lie with him of your free will?"

"That has nothing to do with—"

"It has everything to do with it! I know Alexandros. He would never—*never*—have lain with you if he hadn't been absolutely certain it was what you wanted." Kassandra took a step back, stared at Joanna, and said, "You chose him. You decided he was the man you wanted and you took him. Did you think to do that and then go on as though nothing had happened?"

"If you must know, I didn't think at all. In fact, I am not absolutely certain I remember how to think. I seem to have left that faculty behind in England along with all my good sense, assuming I ever possessed any."

To her horror, her eyes filled. She turned and hurried from the office. In the bedchamber, she stopped and gazed out the broad windows at the city below. It all looked so beautiful and so normal yet to her the bright day seemed brittle, as though it might shatter at any moment.

Kassandra laid a hand on her arm. "It is almost time for the women's prayers. Would you like to come with me?"

A few scant weeks before, offered an opportunity to observe a religious ceremony on Akora, or for that matter to observe anything at all in the fabled kingdom, Joanna would have leaped at the chance. It was a measure of how desperately worried she was that she could only smile faintly and shake her head.

"Not this time, thank you."

Kassandra nodded. Quietly, she said, "There are so many paths in life, so many times when we must choose among opposing futures. At each fork in the road, it is so difficult to know which way to go. In the end, I think the best any of us can do is follow our heart."

Joanna's eyes met hers. "Alex wants me to leave this to him, doesn't he?"

Kassandra shrugged. "He is a man. Is it really necessary to say anything more?"

"I suppose not." The Princess was turning to go when Joanna asked, "Was it only for diversion's sake that we saw the play?"

For just a moment, Kassandra's eyes looked huge and fathomless, as though they were windows into eternity. Then she blinked and there was only gentle understanding. "Do you remember that I said nothing is written in stone? We cannot change the future but we can choose which future will be ours."

Long after the Princess had gone, Joanna remained at the window. Her gaze followed the winding road leading up to the theater where the past still lived and down to the city in its glorious present. Once each had been an unexplored possibility waiting to be discovered.

What awaited her here where the road divided?

Go? Stay?

Please Alex? Anger him?

Be what he wanted?

Be herself?

He was not Hector but he expected her to be Andromache, tamed to her hearth.

The wind shifted, blowing from the sea, and she was reminded suddenly of how it did just the same at Hawkforte, rippling over the shale beach below the old stone walls. Odd how little she had thought of home since leaving there, but perhaps in some sense she hadn't left at all. Hawkforte would ever be in her heart.

The strength of generations stirred within her. She went from the silken chamber and did not look back.

chapter

THIRTEEN

✴

"MAKE HASTE," Alex said. He stood on the stone quay, monitoring his men's preparations to sail even as he tried not to keep glancing up the road to the palace. He had been very clear with Joanna, despite her ability to so cloud his mind that he could barely put two coherent thoughts together. There was no reason to believe she would disobey him.

No reason at all except Joanna herself.

He raised a hand, signaling to the man closest to him. "Search the ship, bow to stern. Make sure no one . . . extra is on board."

The man was a disciplined warrior; his mouth barely twitched. "As you say, *archos*."

She couldn't possibly try to stow away again. All the same, it did no harm to be sure. When the man returned a short time later with assurances that no one was on board *Nestor* who should not be there, Alex did not relax his vigilance. He continued to keep a close eye on the palace road until all was ready. Even then he was the last to leap from pier to deck as *Nestor* raised anchor. Taking his place at the oars, he did not completely put aside his concern until the stone quays of Ilius faded from sight.

Out on the Inland Sea, a freshening breeze filled the

sails. With the men staying at the oars, they made excellent time. The sun was slipping beneath the western hills, bathing the water in fiery gold, when they dropped anchor in the small, secluded harbor on the southern shore of the island of Tarbos.

In almost complete silence, the men of *Nestor* unloaded the equipment they would need, distributed it among themselves, and moved out rapidly into the pine forest that fringed the island. Alex took the lead. Although they had no concern about detection at this point, they spoke little. No words were needed, for each man knew exactly what had to be done.

An hour after leaving the harbor, they emerged onto the edge of a sandy beach that ran along the western end of the island. Alex gestured silently. As one, his men dropped down, concealed beneath the fringe of low bushes and the rise of the small dunes. He joined them, taking a spyglass from the pack he carried. By the light of the moon, he carefully studied the opposite shore.

Despite its name that evoked memories of fear and terror, Deimatos was a pretty island. It boasted pleasant beaches, several small harbors, deep forests and a warren of caves that, according to legend, still contained religious shrines that had survived the volcanic explosion that created the island and its two companions. A traitor could hide an army in those caves. Best not to dwell on that now. Best simply to get the job done.

He put the spyglass away, raised his hand and gestured forward. As one, his men moved onto the beach and into the water. Moments later, they were swimming swiftly and steadily toward Deimatos.

They came ashore under cover of darkness, hugging the shadows cast by the moon. Quickly, they moved off the beach and regrouped in a copse of trees. Alex spoke quietly. The men divided into two groups. One headed up the beach while the other remained on the shore with Alex.

*

HER FATHER HAD CLAIMED she was born knowing how to sail. Joanna thought of that as she made a minute adjustment to the rudder of the boat she had appropriated—stolen was such a harsh word—and looked out over the silver path of the moon. Perhaps he was right, for she could not remember a time when she had not felt as one with wind and water. Even after her parents' deaths, when her pure pleasure in the sea was gone, she had still felt its call deep within her.

Which was just as well since sailing in unknown waters at night could be tricky. She did not know the currents or what rocky shoals might lie in wait for unwary sailors. That being the case, she turned north out of the harbor and continued in that direction a goodly distance before tacking west on a course that would, if she had read the map right, round the northern coast of Tarbos well offshore. *Nestor* was still in dock when she departed. She was counting on Alex taking a more direct approach that would keep her well out of his sight.

Counting, too, on the time at sea to help her settle in her mind what she should do. She was not so naïve as to believe that she could free Royce by herself. She would have to meet up with Alex, a prospect that was nothing less than daunting. At least she had a fair idea of where he was going, somewhere opposite the white tower on the west coast of Tarbos. Find the tower, locate the spot on Deimatos across the reach from it and she would have her objective.

But that proved more easily said than done. Despite the moonlight, deep shadows obscured much of the shore of Tarbos. Once she reached Deimatos, the shadows would be her friends but in the meantime, they were a source of growing concern. What if she couldn't locate the white tower?

Dread was growing in her when a flash of white off

the port side caught her straining eyes. At first, she thought it might be only one more of the limestone outcroppings that littered all the islands. Scarcely breathing, she tacked in closer to shore than prudence dictated until her heart suddenly gave a joyful leap. There it was, just as she had seen! A slender white tower rising up directly opposite Deimatos. Suppressing a shout of relief, she tacked round toward the island she was certain was Royce's prison.

Fortune favored her. She was able to run the small skiff almost all the way up onto the beach. Leaping out, she grabbed the line and straining with all her might, hauled the boat the rest of the way above the tide line. She had no idea how long she would be or if the boat would be needed again but she was taking no chances. Quickly, she found fronds fallen from the palm trees that edged the beach and did all she could to conceal the boat. It would not escape close scrutiny, but she had to hope a casual glance from someone on board another vessel passing by would arouse no suspicion.

The sheer enormity of what she had done sank in suddenly. She ran for the shelter of the trees and slumped against a sturdy trunk until her heart stopped thundering. By the brightness of the moon, she could make out the field ahead of her and some little distance from the shore, a long stone wall. Quickly, she stepped out into the silver glow, stood for a moment, then moved on.

$\mathcal{I}$DIOT. IMBECILE. Dimwit and dullard. Alex considered that truly, when it came to Joanna Hawkforte, his brains or what remained of them had descended to his nether parts where they failed to function very well at all.

Of course she hadn't stowed away again. How much more creative and daring to *sail alone across unknown waters in the dead of night into God only knew what danger.*

And the worst part, absolutely the worst, was that he should have known. All the warning signs were there—the proud will, the intelligence, the courage. The utterly infuriating disregard for anything resembling proper womanly deference to the authority of the male.

Really, when all was said and done, he had only himself to blame. Which was just as well since law, custom and his own inclination forbade his retaliating with anything other than, at most, a stern talking-to. As though that would do an iota of good.

However, there was no prohibition against him taking prompt action in the interest of her safety. A vengeful smile lit his eyes. Between one breath and the next, he darted out of the concealment of the trees, sprinted easily, leaped and brought her down with what would have been a jarring blow had he not rolled at the last moment and taken most of the force of it onto himself.

Even so, she let out a small shriek that he felt perfectly justified silencing by the simple expediency of putting his hand over her mouth at the same time he twisted, angling her under him. She lay on the ground, her eyes very wide as she stared up at him. He lifted his hips slightly, determined to conceal that he was rapidly becoming aroused, a reality he was loath to admit even to himself. For just a moment—a bare, scant moment as he duly noted—she looked startled. Then he saw the light of relief replace surprise.

It was good that she had no fear of him. He just had to keep reminding himself of that. "I'll take my hand away," he said, his voice very tight with the effort to remain calm as befitted a man, never mind however bewildered and bedazzled he might be. "If you promise to keep quiet."

She nodded once, curtly. It would have to do.

Slowly, he removed his hand but continued to glare down at her. Very low, so that neither enemies nor his men could hear him, he said, "I could tell you how incredibly foolish you have been but I don't imagine there is any point to that. You truly are a law unto yourself, aren't you, Lady Joanna?"

He stood up, pulling her with him, and moved immediately back into the protection of the trees. His men, ever loyal, averted their gazes.

"I'm sorry," Joanna said when she was finally able to respond. She could feel the waves of anger moving off him and was deeply shaken. Still, she was not about to lie. "I had to come. You must realize that you stand a far better chance of finding Royce with me along."

Alex spoke through clenched teeth. "I realize a great deal, none of it appropriate for discussion now."

"*Archos*—"

He turned, seeing one of the men he had sent ahead to reconnoiter.

"We have found the cell as you described, *archos,* but it is empty."

"Empty?" Joanna exclaimed. She stiffened beneath Alex's hand. "But it cannot be. Royce is there. I know it!"

"He may have been there," Alex said, still gripping her arm. "But he is no longer." He pulled her closer, ignoring the temptation of her nearness as best he could. Still, it made him speak more harshly than he might have. "Your presence endangers this mission. At least have the sense to keep silent and do as you are told."

He saw the fire in her eyes, braced himself for her response, but saw, too, how she fought for control and won. Under other circumstances, he would allow himself to take pride in her strength. Just then all he could think of was getting her off Deimatos unharmed.

He gave an order. His men formed up, effectively surrounding and engulfing Joanna. She shot him a look of pure chagrin but stayed silent. They moved out along the track of the stone wall, heading inland. They had traveled at a swift pace for about a half hour before Joanna could no longer contain herself. She caught up with Alex who was in the lead. "Where are we going?"

He did not so much glance at her but continued staring straight ahead. However, he did unbend just enough to impart a small fragment of information. "There are caves."

She puzzled over that for a moment. "You think Royce has been moved into them?"

"If I wanted to hide someone, that's where I'd do it."

He said nothing more nor did he give her any encouragement to do so. All the same, she could not resist just one more question. "Do you think someone knew we were coming?"

His only reply was a shrug. He might have been out for a Sunday stroll in Hyde Park, so little concerned did he appear. That they could be walking straight into a trap with Royce as the bait did not seem to perturb him in the least. She had to run a little to keep up with him, which put her a little out of breath. Only that, not deep concern growing in her by the moment.

When she opened her mouth to speak again, he said, "If they do not know, your chattering will give them ample warning."

That silenced her. She did not say another word for the better part of an hour. They were heading inland, away from the broad field she had seen running down to the beach and deep within the pine forest. Deep, too, within the night muted in black and grey, its palette that of sound and smell rather than sight. The perfume of pine needles crushed beneath their feet mingled with the scent of fecund earth and farther off the salt tang of the sea. Muted rustlings in the bushes heralded their passing but did not interrupt the cacophonous chorus of tree frogs that set the very air to vibrating.

Joanna concentrated on keeping up. Alex set a swift pace over ground that was often rough. Several times, she caught him glancing at her. Her response was always a confident smile. Sunday stroll, indeed. She could play that game as well as he did. Indeed, pride demanded that she do so. Yet pride threatened to be in short supply when they paused at last on the slope of a hill and she saw before her a clump of bushes partly concealing the entrance to a cave.

A very dark cave. This time there would be no bright torch to light the way, only a single, small oil lamp lit by tinder and flint Alex drew from the snug canvas package that had kept it dry. Holding the lamp, he drew her directly behind him. "Stay close. At the first sign of trouble, drop down and keep out of the way. Understand?"

She nodded, not trusting herself to speak. Silently, she followed the faint glow of the lamp into the earth. At first, the blackness was so complete that she felt it swallowing her and had to fight down a surge of panic. Her fear eased just a little when she realized that she could see the dim flame of the lamp a few feet ahead. Behind her, she could hear the muted footfalls of Alex's men following them. Throat tight, she forced herself to move forward.

They had gone only a short way from the cave opening when Joanna realized the temperature was dropping. A chill ran down her back that had only partly to do with fear. For a brief time, she distracted herself with thoughts of the soft, warm cloak she should have brought along. While yet she imagined it around herself, Alex stopped without warning. She walked straight into his broad back, only just managing to contain an exclamation of surprise.

His arm was suddenly around her waist, an iron band that brooked no resistance. He handed the lamp to one of his men and spoke very low, his breath close against her ear. "Stay here, do not move."

"My brother—"

"Will not be well served by you getting in our way."

He was gone then, between one heartbeat and another,

his men following in tight order. Behind, he left the lamp, all that stood between Joanna and the darkness that threatened to engulf her. For long moments, she was aware of nothing save her own rapid, gasping breath. Dizziness hovered on the edges of her mind before pride and will came to her rescue. Only when she was breathing more normally did she realize that she could hear nothing from deeper in the cave, no sounds of fighting, no voices, nothing. She truly was alone.

But she had the lamp and, feeling its weight, she reassured herself that it was still almost full of oil. The tiny light would burn for some time yet. What would happen after that, she would not think.

Better instead to think of Royce. He was somewhere nearby, he had to be. She believed that but did not know it in the way she had known he was in the cell. Desperately, she closed her eyes and sought her brother as she had so many times before. But the sense that had been so strong scant hours before was now entirely absent. She was trying too hard. Whenever she truly tried to use her gift, it eluded her but when she simply relaxed, it seemed to happen of its own accord.

Relax. In a cold, dark cave with only a tiny flickering light for company and not knowing what might be happening to her brother or to Alex and his men.

Sooner sprout wings and fly.

Still, she tried. Staring into the pale flame, she made a valiant effort to empty her mind of all concern and dread. The harder she tried, the less success she had. Her breath was painfully fast again and she was trembling from the combined effects of fear and cold when a sudden sound riveted her attention.

Voices. In the utter stillness of the cave, they sounded like thunder but in fact they were very faint and still some distance off. Hope flared within her. Perhaps Alex and his men had overcome Royce's captors and were returning with him. She was holding the lamp out at arm's length, the better to see whoever might be coming, when an alternative possibility occurred to her. Perhaps more than one group of men was moving through the caves. Perhaps Alex was nowhere nearby and she was about to be discovered.

Quickly, she jerked her arm back and pressed herself against the wall. The voices grew closer. Torchlight flared. She blinked against the sudden brightness and peered out at the approaching shadows. For so they appeared, long, thin shadows cast by the torches several of the men carried, resolving quickly into the shapes of the men themselves. There were half a dozen in all if she didn't count the figure slumped between two of them.

The lamp in her hand shook violently. Suddenly terrified that the wavering flame would draw attention, she hesitated only an instant before snuffing it out between her fingers. Never mind the blackness that closed around her. There, in the glow of the torches, was Royce.

But oh, dear God, not the Royce she remembered. Even from a distance and in darkness, she could see that he was pitifully thin. He hung between the men holding him, barely able to put one foot in front of the other as he was dragged along. Long, unkempt hair partially obscured his features but she knew him beyond doubt. Her brother, her friend, all the family she had left. But for the fierce brake of her will, she would have hurled herself at his tormentors heedless of any danger. The pain of seeing him so abused was almost more than she could bear. So great was it as to banish all thought of her fears. Without hesitation, she followed the wavering light of the torches deep into the cave.

They emerged into a chamber almost as large as the one beneath the palace. Joanna hung well back, pressed against the wall along a ledge that led downward into the chamber. There other torches burned and more men were gathered. In the shadows, she seemed to see several other passages leading off in different directions. Truly, Deimatos possessed a labyrinth of caves. It would be so very easy to become lost in them.

She would not think of that, absolutely not. She would think only of Royce, who was still being held between two of the men although he appeared to be barely conscious. How could he be otherwise after months of captivity during which he had suffered obviously terrible deprivation and now to be dragged belowground into temperatures that were chilling, at the very least? He could not possibly survive imprisonment under such conditions. The thought roared through her. It was so very obvious. He was half dead, much as her heart rebelled at the thought. Why then would his captors have brought him here?

Here to the cavern in the earth where torches flickered around a thick, broad slab of stone set in the very center looking almost like an . . . altar. Why would they—?

A strangled scream rose in her throat. Her brother's captors were not as men should be. Rather they were horned beings with the faces of . . . bulls.

Masked. They had to be masked. There was a rational explanation for virtually everything in this world, even if it was sometimes startling, and this was no exception. They were not half man, half bull like the legendary beast who dwelt beneath the palace of Minos, King of Crete. They were simply men wearing masks. Men dragging her brother toward the stone altar. Men with knives, one shining suddenly as it was lifted high in the light of the torches.

"No!"

She did not think nor did she hesitate for there was no time. Safety forgotten, she leaped from the shelter of the stone wall and screamed again, *"No!"*

She was halfway to Royce, close enough to see the dawning of recognition in his poor, thin face when the bull-men seized her.

*

THE TOP OF HIS HEAD was coming off. Distantly, he remembered that he had been told of just such a phenomenon. The older men who trained the novice warriors had spoken of it. Given sufficient provocation, a warrior could transform into a being of savage battle lust with no thought, no urge, no purpose except to kill. Berserkers, the Vikings of lore called such men, and it was as good a name as any. Never had Alex imagined he could experience such madness yet it came upon him the instant he saw Joanna captured.

Kill. Kill over and over. Kill without mercy. Kill until the earth ran red with blood.

Kill until she was safe.

Nothing else mattered. Nothing else was. Except some tiny remnant of sanity that still lingered deep within the mind of the Prince of Akora.

He breathed, deeply, again and again, sucking in air as though reason traveled on it. He had to—had to—regain control of himself. In his present condition, he would accomplish nothing except get Joanna, Royce and possibly his men killed.

Breathe—

They were dragging her off, four of them, four dead men walking though they did not know it. That left a dozen or so guarding Royce.

"Take them," he said to his men, no further instruction being needed. Hard on the order he went, deep into the caves, into darkness, following where they took her.

IT WAS GETTING WARMER. What an odd thought under the circumstances, but her mind seemed intent on it. Perhaps it kept her from being more terrified than she already was.

Did Royce still live? She had no idea and indeed, no reason to hope except that he was still there in her sense of him, not like the distant whisper of their dead parents she still felt from time to time. She had, at the least, forestalled his death and that meant there might still be a chance for Alex to rescue him. As for herself...

She bit back a cry of pain. Dragged over rough ground, falling several times to her knees, she was quickly bruised and bleeding. The men did not slow but continued until the passage opened up suddenly into another chamber. It was much smaller than the first and far less dark. She could hear water running somewhere nearby. It sounded fast and deep. An underground river? That would make sense if this was, as it appeared to be, a military post hidden deep within the caves. Torches affixed to iron brackets glowed darkly against the shields secured to the walls. Nearby were racks of swords and other weapons. Sleeping pallets were laid out around the sides of the chamber. A large wooden table framed by benches dominated the center. Dishes were scattered across it. They struck the floor with a clatter, swept aside by one of the bull-men. Having cleared the table, he pushed Joanna on to it.

Bewilderment filled her. She knew yet did not know, did not want to. She had heard of such things, of course. Even growing up motherless, women spoke among themselves. But there were no men capable of such a thing at Hawkforte. Had there ever been, there were husbands, brothers and sons aplenty to deal with them. Yet she knew.

Terror roared down her spine. She clawed out, desperate, driving on instinct for her assailant's eyes. There was no shirking, no delicacy. She meant to blind him if she could, even better kill him if only she had a weapon of any sort. And then... what?

There were four of them. She had no chance, not really, but she couldn't think of that. She would fight to the last gasp of breath, the last beat of her heart, the last, piercing thought of Alex.

Oh, God, Alex. How could something so incandescently wonderful be turned into such horror and debasement? Time only for that single question shouted in her soul before her gown was pulled up, her wrists manacled by hard fingers. Still she fought, lashing out with her legs until her ankles, too, were seized, pulled apart. She heard grunting, smelled the odor of exhaled wine, blackness whirled deep in her mind.

And flew apart to the sound of steel and screams.

She was released so suddenly that she slipped from the table. Landing on the hard-packed dirt floor of the cave, she scrambled to her knees and stared, bile rising in her throat, at the scene before her.

One of the bull-men was dead or the next thing to it. He lay unmoving, a bloody heap on the ground. She studied him for a moment, untouched by pity. He had gotten what he deserved. Of far more matter were the other three.

They and the one who fought them. Her throat closed before she could cry out his name, and just as well for she was Hawkforte enough to understand that in combat, the smallest loss of concentration could mean disaster.

As a child, she had delighted in watching Royce and his fencing master as they practiced outside in the bailey yard or on dank days in the great hall. Alone, her brother had yielded finally to her stubborn pleas and taught her something of swordplay. She had even become passably good at it.

Good enough to recognize that now she watched deadly genius. Alex was big, hard muscled, supremely fit. All this she knew and more. Knew the sound and scent of him in the dark, knew the flavor of his skin and the husky way he moaned when the heat was upon them both. This was just one more discovery, that was all.

There was no need for the coldness that seeped through her, as though inch by inch she was turning to frozen stone, unable to move or even so much as glance away.

In the flickering shadows of the torches, he looked like a god of war, merciless, implacable and yet for all that so strangely beautiful. The other men fought; he danced. Or so it looked, a terrible dance of death played out to a primal rhythm she could not hear but felt rippling under her skin, as though the very air hummed with energy that entered her with every breath.

The masked men were hardened warriors amply trained. That was no surprise on Akora where it seemed almost every man was trained for war, but they knew how to fight together.

Alex knew how to fight alone. He, too, had trained but differently, not only with the body but with the mind as well, and that, in the end, could be the stronger weapon.

And yet there were three . . . no, two of them.

Two. Just that suddenly and seemingly simply. His blade moving so swiftly in the dance, striking without warning, going deep. Fire fell on ruddied steel.

Just two. But all the more savage with their number halved. They roared in rage, surging forward, driving Alex farther back into the cave.

Joanna stumbled to her feet. She was dizzy, aching, and tripping over the damn gown but she did not hesitate. Desperately, she looked round, saw the racks of weapons, and seized a short sword. It dragged her arm down, making her realize how weak terror had left her. That simply would not do. Spine straight, she followed the grunts of the men and the clash of blades until they were all but drowned out by the roar of rushing water.

A river, as she had thought, and on its bank a battle. Here, too, torches flared illuminating a scene that might have been snatched from the bowels of hell. In smokey light, over the thunder of water, the warriors fought. The pair still left were fueled by rage and desperation. They knew now that their opponent was more than them and if they had souls at all, they would be afraid. But there were still two and they would take courage from that. Be emboldened by it. Be driven to attack faster and harder than ever before, edging Alex back ever closer to the river's edge.

Sweet heaven, why was she just standing there? She had a weapon and God knew, she had the will. Grasping the sword hilt in both hands, she raised it high and rushed at the men.

Alex faltered the barest instant before redoubling his attack. God's blood, she truly would drive him mad. Or to drink. Or both. He had the fools just where he wanted them, desperate yet still overconfident and here she came—

What was that she was yelling? Some sort of battle cry. It sounded . . . old and rather impressive actually. Her color was up, he could see that even in the torchlight and she had a grip on that sword that suggested she knew how to use it. Well, why not? She was Lady Joanna Hawkforte, not some simpering drawing-room ninny. A woman to set a fire in a man's heart and fill him with pride so great it hurt.

She looked damn angry and . . . good. Not cowed because the bastard who was already dead had tried to rape her while the others waited their turn. Don't think about that, not now. Just let it move through him, stoking the rage that flowed down his sword arm straight into the blade.

The red mist was gone. He felt cooler, in control, just where he needed to be. Or at least he did until one of the pair turned, saw her, and slashed his weapon in her direction.

He got himself a slicing cut down his sword arm for that bit of effrontery. The lady had no sense at all but plenty of bite.

"Joanna, get back."

Miracle of miracles, she obeyed. He almost regretted not being able to pause long enough to savor the moment. Perhaps later. Just now he had other business.

He glimpsed her face, resolute, waiting. No trembling, no revulsion. Relief joined everything else and drove him on.

One left. One tougher, more skilled or perhaps merely luckier than the others. Definitely cannier for he turned just then, chest heaving, eyes glittering behind the bull mask, and made a grab for Joanna.

If he got her, if he used her as a shield . . . Alex's heart almost stopped, only to start up suddenly a moment later when he realized she had been prepared for exactly that move, had anticipated it as a warrior would and had moved out of reach in ample time.

"You should be able to take a woman," she said, almost pleasantly. "Unless you think I'm faster than you, more skilled, better."

It was a good ploy, Alex acknowledged, even as his gut clenched. A truly disciplined warrior would ignore the scorn of a woman and focus on the real threat, another warrior. But this piece of scum was likely to do just the opposite. Clearly he was tempted but some instinct for self-preservation stopped him. To attack Joanna he would have to turn his back on Alex and that, even scum knew, was a very bad idea.

"I wonder," she said, "back there in the cave, would you have taken your turn or would you have been unable?"

A roar of mindless rage broke from the bull-man. He lunged at Joanna even as Alex cursed viciously and went for him. She eluded the attacker just as easily the second time as she had the first and in the process, gave Alex a ready opening to finish him off. This he did with savage speed, then turned on her.

"You idiot! You maddening, insane, infuriating

woman! What the hell do you think you were doing? Could I not manage them? Was I not already? You had to put yourself in danger, *taunt* that scum, *encourage him* to come at you?"

His sword was back in its scabbard somehow. He was walking toward her somehow even though echoing terror had him in so firm a grip he marveled that he could move. His hands were on her shoulders and he was dragging her to him before he could even begin to think.

She was in his arms, real and solid, delicate and strong all at the same time. Her fingers tangled in his hair, drawing him down. Her mouth took his, hot and demanding. Against his lips, she murmured, "What would you have had me do?" The kiss deepened, heated; they broke apart both gasping. Her eyes glittered. "Cower under that damn table and let you fight four men all by yourself?" She nipped his lower lip, soothed the tiny hurt with the stroke of her tongue, drove him onward to sweet madness. "You saved me. I'll never forget how you looked, terrifying and wonderful." Her hands slid down the iron muscles of his back, cupping his buttocks, squeezing hard. "You're magnificent, incredible, but don't you dare blame me for helping. If something had happened to you, if you had—"

She was trembling, this woman who desired him so boldly and yielded so generously. She was shaking in his arms at the thought that something might have happened to him. Odd how his heart seemed to be expanding in his chest. In another moment, he would forget all else and draw her down onto the ground.

The damp ground still drinking the blood of enemies.

That he could forget that even for scant moments astounded him. He shook his head to clear it even as her gaze cleared. Hoarsely, she said, "Oh, God, Royce! I cried out because those men were about to kill him. I didn't know what to do except try to distract them but—"

"Hush." He soothed her gently, pressing her head

against his broad chest and stroking her hair. "I left my men to deal with them. Have no fear, Royce will be safe by now."

"Thank heaven! But I have to see him, after so long, I can't wait—"

"I know, it's all right. Come, we will leave this place, but you stay very close to me and if anyone else comes along, do not think for even a moment to put yourself in the way of harm because if you do—"

He broke off, frowning. Beneath his feet, very faintly, the ground vibrated. Earthquake? He had heard of such things but they did not occur on Akora. Even as the question formed in his mind, instinct took over. He pulled Joanna down at the same time he dropped, pushing her under him so that his body completely covered and sheltered hers.

"What—?"

The cave heaved with the force of the explosion that ripped through it.

chapter

FOURTEEN

✴

WALLS AND CEILING ALIKE shook violently as the air roared. Rocks, some the size of carts, crashed down. Blinded by clouds of dirt, Alex held fast to Joanna. Mere seconds passed before the ground steadied but they felt like eternity. In the aftermath, silence, made all the starker for what had preceded it, descended unbroken save for the still random falling of a rock here and there and a sound it took Joanna a moment to place. Waves. She heard the slosh of small waves across the cave floor. The river was washing up over its banks.

Cautiously, Alex got to his feet and held out a hand to her, drawing her up beside him. Almost all the torches had fallen and gone out. Only one remained, still in its iron bracket but lying on the ground. Alex grabbed it before it, too, could be extinguished and held it high. Through the still-swirling clouds of dirt, they surveyed their surroundings. Where there had been an opening to the chamber beyond there was now only a solid wall of fallen boulders.

"What do you think happened?" Joanna asked. Her voice rang strangely in her ears yet it sounded calm enough, for which she was profoundly grateful. She was not going to think of the weight of the earth pressing down above them or of the impenetrable darkness lurking just beyond the pale circle of flame.

"Gunpowder, several barrels' worth probably, either accidentally or more likely, deliberately."

She turned and looked at him in the flickering torchlight. His face was streaked with dirt as hers must be as well. There was a bruise on his forehead, reminder of how very close he had come to much more serious injury or worse while protecting her. She swallowed against the tightness in her throat and reminded herself that she was of Hawkforte. "Whoever was holding Royce blew this place up?"

He nodded, relieved that she was taking their situation well. But then he had counted on her doing so. They were both going to need their minds clear if they were to have any chance of escape. "To conceal their activities, most likely. Trapping us was probably only a side benefit."

"I'd have to say they got lucky." For surely they were well and truly trapped. Yet Alex seemed remarkably unconcerned. Warrior training, no doubt. Acknowledging fear is the first step toward surrendering to it.

Still holding her hand firmly in his, he moved closer to the river that was returning to its natural course. "Atreus and I explored these caves when we were boys."

"Were they in use then?"

"No, this is all very recent and unauthorized. At any rate, I think I remember this river."

"Think?"

He shrugged. "Underground rivers aren't all that rare but this one looks familiar."

"If you're right, do you know where it goes?"

"It surfaces not far from where we entered the caves." His hand tightened on hers. "Can you swim?"

The question was reasonable but it startled her all the same. So basic a part of her and yet he did not know it. She answered simply. "Yes."

"I mean really swim. The current is fast and there are

stretches, some long, where we won't be able to surface for air."

And it would be dark. Very, very dark.

Don't think of that. Think only of Alex, of being with him again in the sunlight.

"I can swim very well."

He looked at her a long moment, seeing the hollowness of her eyes. Seeing also the proud courage in the tilt of her head and the set of her shoulders. "All right." He propped the torch against a nearby boulder and took hold of the hem of her gown. Before her startled gaze, he tore a long strip from all around the bottom, then pulled the fabric hard between his hands, testing it.

"This is good silk, strong. It will do."

"For what?"

"The greatest danger is that we become separated."

In the dark. "I'd rather we didn't."

"Very wise. I'm going to tie one end of this around your waist and the other around mine. We'll go into the water together. You should be able to feel when I surface and do the same."

"You said there are stretches when we can't?"

He nodded. "Two long ones. I'll tell you when we're about to enter those."

"You remember them so clearly? How often did you and Atreus swim this river?"

"Until we decided neither of us would ever be able to best the other. It took quite a while."

"Should I comment on the utter insanity of what the two of you did or would it be better for me to just let that go?"

"Under the circumstances, you should probably just let it go. But be comforted, we were well and thoroughly punished when our father found out."

"Really? What did he do?"

"Set us to muck out the stalls by ourselves for a solid month."

She who had mucked out her fair share of stalls at Hawkforte could not help but be amused. Until he added, "The palace stables house upwards of three hundred horses."

"Good lord, you must have done nothing but muck."

"Eighteen hours a day. Our father said if such labor was good enough for Hercules, it should be good enough for us."

"It's a wonder he didn't make you perform all twelve of Hercules's labors."

"I wouldn't have minded capturing the girdle of the Amazon queen," Alex said, and bending, brushed a lingering kiss over her mouth. "Ready?"

Silence seemed the better virtue just then. She nodded, took a deep breath and followed him into the river.

The water was cool but not unpleasantly so. She had swum in far colder water without ill effect. But not in the dark. Not underground.

Don't think, just swim. The current was strong. They were carried swiftly from the ruined chamber. Joanna cast a glance over her shoulder in time to see the last flicker of torchlight vanish.

Darkness more complete than any she had ever known enveloped her. Her heart beat frantically and her breathing quickly became ragged. That would not do. Too soon, life itself would depend on the steadiness of her breath. She let the current take her and swam just with her legs and with one arm, enough to keep her head above water. With her other hand, she held fast to the bond of silk connecting her to Alex. He was in front and slightly to the right of her. Only the knowledge of that, the sense of connection to him, allowed her to push back the glittering edge of panic threatening to overtake her.

So dark. She could shut her eyes and see more light, tiny patches of red behind her lids. Open, her eyes saw nothing, no hint of shadow or shape, no movement, absolutely nothing.

The river curved unexpectedly. Taken by surprise, Joanna grazed rocks below the waterline along the bank. Wincing, she forced herself to let go of the cord and swim hard toward the center of the river. Or what she hoped was the center.

"Are you all right?"

Alex's voice came as a burst of bright light into the darkness. He sounded strong, certain and blessedly near.

"I'm fine," she called quickly. "How much farther?"

"A way. We'll stop in a moment."

Around another curve and she blinked, thinking her eyes were playing tricks. Suddenly, the darkness was... greenish?

Alex drew them both toward a small ledge that came down to meet the water. It and the surrounding walls were covered with fan-shaped lichen that glowed softly in the gloom.

"Incredible," Joanna murmured. She rested her forearms on the ledge and tread water as she looked around. Slender silver rivulets flowed down the walls and into the river. The rhythmic plink of drops and the murmur of the river itself were the only sounds. Her voice, even her breath seemed an intrusion.

"Life always seems to find a way," Alex said quietly. "I suppose these are related somehow to what lives in the Pool of Sighs." For a moment, he looked entirely engrossed as though nothing occupied his mind save the mystery of the tiny, glowing life.

"Did you ever think to be a scholar instead of a warrior?" Joanna asked.

He looked at her in surprise. "What made you wonder that?"

"Your interest in things and your"—her smile was just a little chagrined—"your patience." She might have said his gentleness for it astounded her that despite his great strength and the years of training for violence, never did he make her feel other than safe and protected.

Such was the complexity of the man that even now, in such perilous circumstances, she felt oddly detached from danger.

"I did think of it," he admitted, "but it was never a real possibility and besides, I was also drawn to the life for which I was intended."

"Perhaps someday you can combine both."

"Perhaps, if Akora is secure enough."

They were silent for a moment before Alex said gently, "We must go on. The next stretch is difficult. The ceiling of the cave descends to the level of the water. There is nowhere to rise for air."

Joanna's stomach tightened. The dark was bad enough but to be without air... "For how far?"

"Far enough to think you may not make it, but you will." He drew her closer, held her fiercely for a moment before letting her go. "Fill your lungs deeply, let go... again..." Three times, he directed her to inhale. Each time she managed to do so just a little bit more. On the third try, he was satisfied. With a quick smile, he plunged back into the water. Joanna followed.

Darkness again, as thick as before but this time burdened by the knowledge that she was well and truly trapped. She could not even rise into the air. Her lungs felt like stone, so heavy they would surely draw her down. Rather than think of that, she concentrated on swimming fast enough to keep up with Alex. He set a swift, steady pace, not so fast as he undoubtedly could have sprinted but more sustainable over distance. That, more than anything else, told her that they truly did have far to go.

The desperate need to breathe grew more urgent with every passing moment. She hung on, trusting this would end, trusting in Alex to bring them through safely, trusting they would both stand in the light again, even as her lungs scorched and she feared each time she lifted her arms and brought them through another stroke that it would be the last.

Finally, just when she knew she could go no farther, she felt herself drawn upward. Blessed, merciful air filled her lungs. Gasping, clinging to Alex, she breathed again and again until at last the horrible sense that she was about to drown eased. Only then did she realize that Alex was holding her up, treading water for them both even as he regained his own breath.

"I'm fine," she said, coughing only a little. "Let me go, I can manage."

She could not see him but she felt his hesitation. "Are you sure?"

"Yes, absolutely. It was ... challenging, but I'm fine."

His low chuckle sent a quiver of pure pleasure down her spine almost as though he had touched her. "A woman of courage," he said, "and thank the gods for it. From here, we go on through another cave where there is some light from the same kind of source as before. After that, we will have to make another passage without air but it is shorter."

She nodded, already dreading what would have to be yet encouraged by the thought that the worst was behind them. That hope proved well founded as they negotiated the second airless passage without difficulty. Indeed, when Alex surfaced, drawing her with him, Joanna was surprised for this time she was girded for far worse. Greatly relieved, she smiled broadly, ignoring that her teeth chattered. "We're almost out, aren't we?"

"We are. It is night, of course, but I believe the moon is still up. You will know when we approach the opening in the cave because there will be a hint of light. Given how long we have been in the dark, it will probably look much brighter than it really is."

She nodded, eager for them to continue but still Alex hesitated. "When you see that, you must prepare."

"Prepare? For what?"

"As I told you, the river surfaces not far from where we entered the caves. It just happens to do so as a waterfall."

He was joking, he absolutely had to be. After surviving an explosion and a swim through underground caverns including the long stretches without air, he could not possibly mean they were going to hurl out into empty space.

"You've done some diving, haven't you?"

"A little at Hawkforte. A very little."

"The river empties into a deep pool with a sandy bottom. You'll be fine."

Oh, certainly. In fact, she was better able than ever to appreciate why he and his brother had done this sort of thing for *fun*.

"I hope you won't mind my saying so," she said very low, "but I think your father fell several labors short."

"Our mother felt the same way. Ready?"

No, but that hardly mattered. She puffed out a breath, sucked it back in and followed him.

Scant moments later she heard the deep-throated murmur of water and almost immediately thereafter realized the impenetrable veil of darkness was thinning. She could make out faint contours of the rocky walls around them and even catch, just up ahead, a hint of sparkle on the water.

Moonlight. They were almost out. Any minute now and—

"Headfirst," Alex shouted over the gathering roar of the falls. "Push off the bottom as soon as you hit it."

Hit. Bad choice of word. It would have been better if he'd said touch or brush or encounter or—

She was outside suddenly, engulfed in the silver brightness of night painful to her eyes, and she was falling, fast and furious, her stomach seemingly plummeting several yards ahead of her. She glimpsed the blur that must be Alex, saw him go into the pool and had time only to draw a partial breath before she struck the water herself. The shock stunned her into furious action. If she touched bottom, she never felt it, only fought with all her strength to regain the surface. An instant later, she broke free and was engulfed in Alex's arms. Swiftly, he swam with her to the edge of the pond, levered himself out and lifted her free.

"We did it," he said as he carried her, gathered high against his chest. "By God, we actually did it!"

Joanna spit out a great spurt of water and stared at him. "Don't sound so surprised. You've done this how many dozens of times?"

He laughed with inexpressible relief. "When I was young and foolish. Never did I imagine doing it again, much less with a woman I should not have allowed into such danger."

"Allowed?" Her voice was very soft, almost caressing. Under other circumstances, Alex might have been lulled. If he had been unconscious, for example. As it was, he stopped in mid-step, looked down at her, and said soothingly, "Joanna, we can argue the point up one side of that particular mountain and down the other, or we can find ourselves a nice soft patch of moss, collapse onto it, and figure out what to do next. As a trained warrior, and speaking strictly from a strategic perspective, I recommend the latter."

She sighed, coughed up a little more water, and said, "Truth is, I don't think I have a good argument in me right now."

He gave her a little squeeze. "Truly, the gods are merciful."

A few moments later, Joanna realized Alex was still carrying her. "Why don't we stop?"

"We will, just a little farther."

He paused finally deep within the wood that bordered the river. The canopy of trees was so thick that scarcely any moonlight penetrated. They were wrapped once again in obscurity.

Alex laid her down gently but did not rest himself. Instead, he drew his sword from the scabbard still at his side, gathered up handfuls of moss, and began to dry the blade with meticulous care.

After observing him for several minutes, Joanna said, "You think some of the men who took Royce may still be at large."

He glanced up, nodded once, and resumed his task. "I think my men killed those who had your brother but someone remained to set off that explosion. It is simply good sense to be cautious."

"We must find Royce." She struggled to sit up, realizing only then the extent of her exhaustion.

Alex placed a hand on her shoulder, urging her back. "The moon is about to set. We will not go stumbling around this island in the dark, not knowing what enemies may lie in wait."

Loath though she was to admit it, Joanna knew he was right. Even so, she resisted giving in. The one glimpse of Royce in the cave haunted her. She had a desperate, driving need to know that her brother was safe. Until then, true rest was impossible.

Alex set his sword on the ground beside them and lay down next to her. He gathered her into his arms and held her firmly until finally, grudgingly, she began to relax against him.

"In warrior training," he said, "we are taught that it is wisdom to know when to expend strength and when to conserve it."

Joanna roused from creeping drowsiness to ask, "How old were you when you began training?"

"I was six."

"So young? What must your mother have thought?"

"I don't know," Alex admitted. "But that is the normal age for a boy to leave the women's quarters and live among men."

"Didn't you miss your mother?"

"No, I can't say that I did. But then, I still saw her most every day for morning and evening meal, and before bed."

She raised herself up slightly, looking at him. "I thought you said you left the women's quarters."

"I did, but it's really just a symbolic departure. Not all that much actually changes." When she continued to look at him, puzzled, he said, "You've been on Akora long enough to know that we preserve our past best by compromising with it."

"Yes, I suppose I do know that. We try to do something of the same in England but not so successfully."

England. A subject for another time, not now, but all too soon. "You should try to sleep," Alex said quietly.

She nodded against his chest, soothed by his voice, which seemed to float away little by little, carrying her with it. She drifted, not truly asleep but not fully awake either. Her mind played and replayed the scenes of the past few hours—Royce, the bull-men, Alex's combat with them, the explosion, the river, and finally their desperate rebirth back into the world. How very close they had come to dying there in the dark.

She murmured something Alex could not make out. Drifting himself, he responded instinctively, soothing her. She quieted and relaxed more fully against him. So astounding a woman, so brave, so determined. So English.

So loyal to her brother.

He turned onto his side, looking at her in the starlight. Her hair had dried. It fanned out around her head like rippling silk. On impulse, he plucked a strand, twining it around one finger, capturing it.

Her lips were slightly parted. His gaze slid over them to watch the deep rise and fall of her breath. Her gown, too, had dried but the tawny silk did little to conceal the beauty of her form. The fragrance of her, all woman, all Joanna, filled him.

All too soon.

She had passed through a terrible ordeal and was exhausted. Conscience demanded that he let her rest.

But conscience just then had competition from another source.

He had fought for her. It was a primitive thought unworthy of a man of wisdom and control, but damn it, that was how he felt. The memory of the red mist that had engulfed him lingered, fueling the desire that was never far beneath the surface when he was near her. Or away from her. Or anywhere in between.

All too soon.

His mouth brushed the sweet curve of her cheek. He wasn't quite sure how that happened but it did. She murmured softly and drew closer.

Conflicting loyalties threatened to draw them apart, hers to her brother, his to Akora. Was it truly dishonorable to seek to bind her to him by any means possible?

Her throat was slender and warm. He could feel her life's blood pumping beneath the velvet smoothness of her skin. Desire thrummed within him. His hand cupped her breast, feeling the nipple harden. He glanced up quickly. Her eyes remained firmly closed. She appeared deeply asleep yet the corners of her luscious mouth curved upward.

There really was only so much a man could take.

The gown slipped so easily from her shoulders. Her skin glowed pale as alabaster, not cool like stone but warm, so warm beneath his lips. Just another moment or two and he would draw back . . .

Her legs shone smooth and sleek. He stared at them and at his hands, seeing the tawny silk gown bunched in his fists. He had drawn it up all unknowingly, baring her to his eyes and his touch.

He was achingly hard, consumed by the need for her but more than that, overwhelmed by the desire to assure the connection formed between them beside the Pool of Sighs could not be broken.

Lady Moon had a lover but he fell from a high place and drowned, leaving her to sigh over him ever more.

He was not Hector, much less some fragment of legend. He was himself, plain and simply, Prince and warrior but above all a man. A man who ultimately could not resist the dream of beauty and strength, courage and gentleness before him.

He watched her face as he settled between her thighs.

SHE DRIFTED as though free of the weight of her body, carried on the wind. Drifted through memory and dream, through darkness into light. Hot, shimmering light that drove away all fear, all thought, leaving only stark sensation.

She gasped and reached, finding broad shoulders, hot skin, and the sound of her name, husky, deep, shivering through her.

"Joanna, so beautiful . . ."

Her eyes opened, reflecting his. *Alex*. Companion in danger and adventure, friend. Lover. She arched long and luxuriously. "So good, come into me . . ."

He moved, slowly, deeply. She stared up into his taut features, saw the control, the discipline, saw both shatter. And smiled.

"*Joanna* . . ."

Rising, so fast, so suddenly, no lingering ascent this but a relentless driving to a peak that rolled on and on and on. She knew she cried out, knew he swallowed the sound, knew her body clenched furiously, claiming him in fierce exaltation.

And then knew nothing more.

chapter

FIFTEEN

✳

"CHIRRUPPP . . . CHIRRUPPP . . ."
 Joanna stared into blackness. Sleek, glossy black . . . feathers. And quizzical black eyes above a yellow beak pecking at the ground just beside her.

"Chirruppp . . . chirrupp . . ."

Morning. Blue sky, white clouds, sunshine on nearby water. She was lying on the ground. Something heavy held her down. Very hard and heavy, warm and oh, so familiar.

"Alex."

At the sound of her voice, the bird moved off, not far but just enough to make the point. She watched him go in the moments before she became fully awake.

Turning onto her back, she stared at the dark head nestled against her shoulder. Her lover's lean cheeks were roughened by a night's growth of beard. The morning breeze lightly ruffled his ebony hair. He looked very . . . dear. Yes, that was the word and the cause, no doubt, of the tightness she felt in her chest.

And of the wish, so small and selfish, to hold the world at bay, to forget for just a little time the relentless claims of duty.

It was an unworthy thought for them both, and yet

there on the golden sand in the break of day, it glittered with enticement.

She slipped from beneath his arm and sat up, getting slowly to her feet. Her intent was to put some distance between them but she did not get far before the silken cord held her fast. She stared at it in bewilderment, realizing all in a breath that she had forgotten about the cord, the desperate swim through the river, the terrifying darkness. Forgotten it all in the incandescent fire of what followed.

A shiver moved through her, belying the warmth of morning.

Desperate suddenly, she knelt down and reached for the sword at Alex's side. She would slip it out just the smallest way and use the sharp blade to cut the cord. But before she could do more than touch a finger to the scabbard, a hard, sinewed hand clamped down over hers. She winced with pain that was gone so swiftly it might have been imagined.

"Joanna..."

"I was just going to cut this," she said, gesturing to the cord.

He followed her gaze, nodded and sat up with the same swift readiness that had brought him from dreams so suddenly. Dreams of her that lingered, echoing in his body and his mind. For just an instant, he was tempted to refuse, to keep her tied close to him. An unworthy thought. An impossible wish.

The deed done, he rose. "The pool is over there."

She nodded and glanced away rather than risk continuing to look at him. They walked back toward the pond in silence, without touching.

Joanna heard the rush of the waterfall before she saw it. For an instant, she relived the plunge out of the cave as though it were happening again. Hard on it, she took a breath and plunged again.

"I must see Royce."

He was silent for a moment that seemed to stretch on

forever. She gathered herself and looked at him. He was just beyond her arm's reach yet seemed farther, as though somehow distance already grew between them.

"Yes," Alex said, "of course."

"You understand . . ." She spoke impulsively, with no real notion of what she intended to say, but it didn't matter. Before Alex could respond, another voice rang out.

"*Archos!*" They both turned to see one of Alex's men hurrying toward them.

"The Englishman from the cave," Alex called, "is he all right?"

"Yes, *archos,* and on his way to Ilius." The man ran up, his eyes warm with relief. He did not look at Joanna. "We brought our own boat over this morning but also found a skiff on the beach. Several of our men took it back with the *xenos.*"

"Good. What of the bull-men, any sign of them?"

"None, *archos.* Our efforts to enter the caves after we heard the explosion were fruitless. Praise the gods that you are well."

"Tell the men to prepare to sail at once."

The man inclined his head and was gone, running swiftly back through the trees.

Alex turned to Joanna. "We must go."

She nodded, not trusting herself to speak. They walked down to the beach together. On the narrow path, their bodies brushed twice. Each time, she struggled against the temptation to reach out to him, to feel the warmth of his hand holding hers, to lean on his strength and be comforted by it.

Long before she took her place on the deck and watched the sails fill, the brilliant day was darkened by the shadows within her heart.

AND YET, joy came as it will, crowding out all concern if only temporarily. On a brisk wind, with the men pulling hard at the oars, they reached Ilius swiftly. Joanna was on the quay before the anchor touched sandy bottom. Propriety be damned, she gathered up what was left of her skirt and ran. The courtyard of the palace was crowded as usual. Heedless of the startled looks, she elbowed her way through the milling mob and dashed up the stairs to the family quarters. There she paused, realizing suddenly that she had no idea where to go.

Where was Royce? He would have been brought to the palace certainly but then what? She was looking around anxiously when the touch of a hand at her elbow almost made her leap out of her skin.

"This way," Alex said. He had come up behind her so swiftly and silently that she had no awareness of his presence. Belatedly, she thought how her departure from the quay must have looked to him and his men. She truly did not want to embarrass him but neither could she bear to wait to see Royce a moment longer than necessary.

"He is in the guest quarters," Alex told her with calm she had to think admirable. Still holding her arm, he guided her down the corridor. The doors to an apartment she had not seen before were open. Servants were coming and going. A white-haired woman stood beside the large bed. Beyond, wide windows stood unshuttered to admit light and air.

Her throat clenched, Joanna entered the room. She could scarcely breathe and was shaking so hard she feared she would fall. Only Alex's hand kept her upright. Slowly, she approached the bed.

The man lying on it did not stir. He was covered by a sheet that could not conceal the extreme thinness of his form. Hair that might have been gold was a tangled mat of indeterminable color. His features were concealed by a heavy growth of unruly beard. But for all that, she knew him just as she had in the cave. She did not need to see the long thin scar, souvenir of a misplaced fishing hook in a boyhood accident, on the hand visible above the sheet to tell her this was indeed her brother.

"Royce." She fell to her knees beside the bed. All the pain and anguish of the past months welled up in her. Tears slipped, first slowly, then in a rush. She wept with anguish at his state and relief at his survival. Wept and wept until her cheeks burned with the salt of her tears. Through the storm, she was aware of Alex's hand resting gently on her shoulder, of his quiet voice murmuring comfort to her, anchoring her to the world of reason and ultimately drawing her back into it.

As she rose and wiped her eyes, he nodded to the white-haired woman who said gently, "I am Elena, lady, senior among the palace healers. Your brother has suffered but he is a young man and strong of nature. He will recover."

"He is so thin—"

"From starvation, not illness. Good food will restore him."

Hands balled into fists, she turned to Alex. "Why would they have starved him? Wasn't it bad enough that they kept him captive? What kind of monsters would do this?"

"I don't know," he admitted quietly. "But we will find out and they will pay."

"You don't know? But—" She stopped abruptly, aware they were not alone.

Alex drew her aside into a corner of the room as Elena and her assistants discreetly busied themselves.

"I understand what you are thinking," he said, "that Deilos and perhaps the other reactionaries on the Council are responsible for this. But you must realize, with the caves sealed and the bodies of the bull-men unrecoverable, we have no actual evidence of anyone's involvement."

"Who else could it be?"

"The rebels, possibly. You can be certain that is what

Deilos will claim. Perhaps your brother, when he awakens, can tell us more but in the meantime, we must go very carefully. The Vanax must be seen to administer justice to all. If Atreus makes accusations that cannot be substantiated, or even allows them to be made, he will only add to the challenges against him."

When she would have protested further, Alex said, "We must wait and hope that Royce can provide the evidence we need."

Her quick mind leaped ahead, seeing the danger from those who might wish to assure her brother never spoke at all. "He must be guarded."

"Yes, he must and so must you. You were also there. Whoever is responsible cannot know what you saw or heard."

"Nothing of any use," she said bitterly.

"Nor did I. Whoever they are, they are very careful."

He was thinking about that, and of what it might mean, a few minutes later when, having left Joanna, he sought his brother in the Vanax's private chamber. There they spoke long and urgently as the day waned and night settled over Akora.

JOANNA REMAINED at her brother's side. She resisted Elena's urgings that she get some rest although she did take a few minutes to bathe and change her clothes. Seated beside Royce, she held his hand and spoke to him softly, talking of their childhood together, of how much he meant to her, of how concerned she had become about him, but above all, reassuring him that all would be well now. He was safe and free. She spoke until her throat ached and finally, in the deep of night, exhaustion overcame her. She slumped into sleep beside him and never knew when Elena gently draped a blanket over her.

She was dreaming of the black bird when the scream awoke her.

Royce sat bolt upright in the bed, his eyes wide open, an anguished shout coming from his throat.

"Joanna!"

Torn from slumber, she reacted with pure instinct, embracing him fiercely even as she tried to calm him. "Royce, I'm here! It's all right. You're free, it's over!"

For a moment, he seemed not to hear her but quickly enough the dazed incomprehension of his gaze turned to startled recognition. Hard upon that came despair. "Joanna, no! Tell me I dream, you are not here."

His strength gone but still deeply agitated, Royce fell back against the pillows, gazing at her as though he hoped she would vanish before his eyes.

Bewildered, she seized his hand and said urgently, "I am here, you do not dream, but why that should be of concern to you, I do not understand. You are in the palace, Royce, the palace of Akora! And you are being well cared for." She gestured to Elena who had risen from her chair near the bed. "I am promised you will recover. Surely, this is cause for joy."

He motioned her closer. So faintly she could barely hear, he said, "We must speak alone."

Softly, Joanna said, "I don't think anyone else here understands English."

"Can't be sure . . . Can't trust them. Speak alone . . ."

Joanna looked to the healer. "Elena, would you mind? My brother and I have been apart for so long, we would like some time for just the two of us."

If the older woman thought anything amiss in such a request, she did not show it. Instead, she nodded at once and left, closing the doors behind her. Joanna caught only a glimpse of the guards who had already taken up their post in the corridor beyond.

"We are alone. Now brother, please, tell me what concerns you."

"That you are here. It is bad enough that I am but

that you . . ." He broke off, struggling against the weakness that threatened to overcome him. "My God, Joanna, the only comfort I have had all these months is the thought that you, at least, were safe."

"As I am now and so are you. Royce, if you are thinking of the old stories about the fate of *xenos* here on Akora, they are not true. The Vanax will do us no harm. His own brother, Prince Alexandros, led the mission to rescue you."

Royce's mouth twisted in a sneer. "The exalted Marquess of Boswick. Don't make the mistake of trusting him. He is no friend of ours."

"But he is! He risked his life to free you."

"From the captivity ordered by his brother? What sense does that make?"

Joanna shook her head, thinking she must surely not have heard him properly. He could not possibly have meant—"Ordered by *whom*? Whom do you think responsible for what happened to you?"

"The Vanax . . . Atreus, Darcourt's brother and the sovereign he serves so well."

Shock burned through her. "No, Royce, you are mistaken! Neither Alex nor his brother had anything to do with imprisoning you. They knew nothing of your whereabouts."

"Then how was I found?"

"I found you. You know I have that gift. I was certain that if I could be close enough to where you were, I would be able to find you, and I did. As soon as I described your location to Alex, he set off with his men to free you."

"He told you that?"

"No . . . I went along. I wasn't supposed to but I did. I saw everything that happened. There were men wearing bull masks. They had taken you from the cell where you had been kept into caves deep underground. I think they meant to kill you . . ."

She broke off, overwhelmed by the memory of how close they had all come to death.

Royce grasped her hand with a hint of his old strength. "I don't know what Darcourt told you or why, but I do know who was responsible for my being in that damn cell and it was the Vanax, no one else."

"How can you know that?"

"Because the guards boasted of it. They bragged that they were doing the bidding of the Vanax himself."

"Are you sure you understood them?"

Royce nodded. His voice was weakening but his eyes still burned with certainty. "I heard you speak to the healer. You must have realized what I did, that Akoran shares roots with the ancient Greek we learned as children. With effort, I could understand what was being said."

"Even so..."

"For pity's sake, Joanna, I know what I heard."

"But he could not have...I am certain of it. Alex would know if his half brother was involved and he would—" Would what? Tell her? But his loyalty was to Akora, not to her. She would be the world's worst fool to forget that.

"Alex? You are so familiar with Darcourt?"

Oh, God, let him not think that, not now. "No... somewhat...it does not matter. Royce, you are exhausted. You must sleep."

She feared her brother meant to resist but the little strength that had returned to him was gone. Although he fought it, sleep proved irresistible. She said a silent prayer of thanks and stood up, walking over to the windows. Moonlight shone brightly over the sleeping city but she scarcely noticed.

She had not thought beyond the moment of finding Royce. He had come to Akora for a purpose that, once freed, he might wish to pursue. She naturally would remain at his side. There would be no need to part from Alex . . . at least not yet, not with so much still left unsaid, undecided . . . unknown.

Alex had said she had nothing to fear from him. Had he lied? Or spoken only in the heat of passion? She simply did not know, nor could she, for she did not know the man, not really. Nor well enough. Indeed, she scarcely knew herself when she was with him.

She was alone now, save for her sleeping brother, and she remembered very well who she was: Lady Joanna Hawkforte, a countrywoman of no pretensions, impatient with the vanities of the *ton*, content with the well-ordered rhythm of her days. A woman who had embarked on an extraordinary adventure for the highest purpose and who would see it fulfilled no matter what the cost.

She stayed, watching Royce sleep, but did not close her eyes again. If her brother was right, if the Vanax really was responsible for his captivity, Royce remained in terrible danger and would so long as he was on Akora. Beside that, nothing else could matter.

With the first grey light of morning, she rose and went in search of Alex.

He was not in his quarters nor was there any sign that he had been. The bed was untouched, the covers still pulled smooth. She took a breath and turned her mind to finding him.

In daylight, the Pool of Sighs looked ordinary. It gave no hint of its secrets, Alex thought. He stood, staring into the water, but turned when he heard the light footsteps coming down the path. Hands clasped behind his back lest he yield to the temptation to touch her, he asked, "How is Royce?"

"Still asleep but better, I think. He woke in the night."

"And was distressed. Elena told me."

As she had told him that the lady and her brother wished to speak alone. Elena knew no English but she understood well enough when there were secrets to be imparted. What had Lord Royce Hawkforte said to his sister? What had required such privacy?

"He is very glad to be alive, of course," Joanna said.

Her gaze slid past him and in that moment, he knew that she lied. Oh, not that Royce regretted living but that he had not said as much. They had talked of other things.

Britain's plans to invade Akora, perhaps?

"Did he say why he came here?"

"No, he didn't." Truth? Or not? He could not tell.

"Or anything about who held him captive?"

She hesitated and he had the fleeting impression that she wanted to unburden herself, to confide in him in some way but instead she shook her head. "Nothing of use. He is very weak. Obviously, there is no possibility in his present condition of his being able to fulfill whatever purpose brought him here. Therefore—" She took a breath. "I think it best that we return to England."

The words fell between them, cold and hard. Did he fancy that she flinched? He knew he did but hoped she did not see.

"We have excellent healers. Elena and—"

"Yes, I know, but England is home and that is where I believe Royce should recuperate. It was terribly ill-advised of him to come here, we both realize that and he surely does, too."

"I see . . . ," he said as he grappled with the urge to re-fuse. She had given herself to him, therefore she was his, therefore she could not possibly be the one to walk away.

Except that she was. Out of loyalty to her brother? Out of a desire to prevent discovery of why Royce had come to Akora? Or simply because what had passed between them was, for her, an interlude without lasting meaning?

He could not believe how much that last possibility

hurt. To distract himself as much as for any other reason, he said, "I have spoken with Atreus."

"The Vanax..." Did he imagine she gave the title a particular twist? "And what does he say?"

"He is very glad Royce is alive, of course." Deliberately, he parodied her words, then waited to see if they would have any effect.

Her eyes flashed. He saw it, there in the early morning light. Joanna Hawkforte was angry but he did not know why.

"Is he? How good of him. And he has no objection to Royce leaving...?"

There was the crux of the matter. Atreus could forbid it easily enough. He had the power and they had discussed it in the long hours of darkness over several pitchers of wine. His brother was very understanding.

"None, of course. He wouldn't dream of it."

"And you...?" she asked.

"Your loyalty is to your brother." Not a question, though it easily could have been; only then it might have sounded far too much like a plea. "As is mine to Atreus." For good measure, he added, "We have always known that."

"Please...," she said, her voice falling to a whisper and her hand...Oh, yes, he was not mistaken about that. Her hand reaching out.

He would remember that, reflect on it. But just then he took a step back. His pride needed that small victory.

"We each have our duty, do we not?" he asked.

"Oh, yes, ever that." She looked very pale, her back straight, her eyes... he could not read them.

"I will arrange a ship," he said quickly, before he could say something altogether different.

"Thank you," she said, very properly.

Damn her.

"Joanna—"

She sniffed and the sound alarmed him. She wasn't

about to cry, was she? Not his indomitable woman of Hawkforte?

"I am getting a cold," she declared. "Probably from being in the river."

He pretended to believe her. It was easier that way for both of them.

SIXTEEN

✴

T HE HOUSE SMELLED of lemon oil. Not of lemons as Akora had but of the essence of polished furniture, attentive servants, order and sensible domestic custom.

Home. Joanna tried the word in her mind as she stood in the entry hall. Unsurprisingly, the notion did not fit, for Hawkforte was home, not the house in London to which she and Royce had come directly after docking in Southwark.

Still, it would have to do. Her brother was insistent. He had to meet with various people; he did not specify whom. He would not withdraw to Hawkforte to engage in any sort of "convalescence," he had said with an expressive curling of the lip. He was not some "damn invalid" but was well on the mend and would be perfectly fine. There was no reason to fuss.

Had she not loved him so dearly, she might have been tempted to pummel him. During the voyage to England, Royce had regained some of the weight so cruelly taken from him but he had also pushed himself very hard, insisting on being out of bed and on deck at all hours. No doubt the sun and fresh air did him good but Joanna suspected it was the confinement within the four walls of his cabin that he could not bear.

She turned to see her brother entering the house aided by Bolkum Harris. Or more correctly, that stalwart fellow was trying to aid him. Royce waved off the offer of a shoulder to lean on and made his way unassisted. He stood for a moment in the hall, taking a long look around as though to recollect and savor every detail. With a faint smile, he said, "Nothing has changed."

"And why would it?" Mulridge inquired. She came down the stairs in a swirl of black bombazine and high dudgeon. "A fine uproar you've caused."

Royce looked startled for a moment, then threw back his golden head and laughed. It was the first time he had done so since his rescue and the sound thrilled Joanna. She was smiling as her brother swept Mulridge into a hearty hug.

Mulridge, too, grinned with delight and relief that belied her words. "Put me down, you big oaf. What do you think, going off as you did and this one"—she turned her stern gaze on Joanna—"traipsing after you with all the sense of a day-old hatchling?"

Royce did as he was bid while regarding his sister, who did her best not to squirm under the combined force of such scrutiny. "On that we can certainly agree. I have yet to hear the full details of what transpired but," he warned, "I will."

Joanna ignored the sudden flutter of concern deep within her. "This *day-old hatchling* succeeded in doing what she set out to do," she said. "Royce is home, safe and sound, and that's all that matters. Now, if you will excuse me, I need a bath." In fact, she did not, having made ample use of the shower in her stateroom on the vessel that had brought them to England. However, it seemed an opportune means of escape.

"I should think so," Mulridge said, looking slant-wise down her long nose, "not to mention some proper clothes. What is that you're wearing?"

"A gown in the Akoran style. It is quite comfortable, far more so than English garments." Halfway up the stairs to her chambers, Joanna turned and looked at her brother. Pointedly, she said, "I hope you won't overdo just yet, Royce. You are far from fully recovered."

Satisfied that she had succeeded in pinning attention where it belonged, she continued on her way. Below in the hall, Mulridge pounced. "Look at you, gaunt as a hawk that can't hunt. Bolkum, hurry below and tell Cook we need a meal, all of his lordship's favorite dishes. Go on now, there's no time to waste."

Smiling at Royce's feeble efforts to deflect the care even he knew he could not possibly avoid, Joanna hurried to her rooms. After more than a week of keeping up a brave face for her brother, as well as deftly sidestepping his more probing questions, she desperately needed some time to herself. Still, that was not to be, at least not yet. Hard on her heels came several maids dispatched by Mulridge. They brought hot water for her bath, warm towels and curious looks. This last they tried their best to mask but Joanna could hear them whispering among themselves the moment they finished their tasks and the door closed behind them.

She could hardly blame them for their curiosity. When last they had seen her, she had been sensible Lady Joanna, as like as they to plunge her hands into the good brown earth of Hawkforte and coax life from it, to share a jug of cider on a hot summer day, and dance around the bonfire on All Hallows' Eve. As familiar as the proverbial old shoe, she would have harbored no surprises for them or, she had thought, for herself.

How very wrong they all had been. The woman who looked back at her from the mirror above the dressing table might have stepped from legend. Honeyed hair curled by the humidity of days at sea flowed untamed halfway down her back. Hazel eyes appeared immense against skin touched by gold. Whereas fashionable garments attempted to recreate the flowing lines of classical garb, hers bore the stamp of authenticity. She was covered decently enough by the standards of the day, but even her relatively untutored eye could perceive the sensuality and awareness in her gaze, her bearing, even the simplest gesture of her hand tried before the mirror. A souvenir, she thought, of Akora, and blinked when her vision blurred.

Ridiculous. She would not cry again, absolutely not. Enough tears had been shed on the voyage home. Home. There it was again. Her heart longed for the balm of Hawkforte. She could lose herself there in the ripening fields, the rhythms of the season, the smiles of old friends.

Lose herself so lately found.

She, who bore the gift of finding but who had come so surprisingly to the discovery of her own self.

Twin to Hawkforte itself was the duty it embodied. The woman in the mirror would understand that. Women like that had carried in their marrow the knowledge that duty mattered over self. Long after life ended and the body moldered, the legacy of duty properly fulfilled would remain. It was a kind of immortality.

Had Helen thought of that? She who had launched a thousand ships and burned the topless towers of Ilium? Had she wondered if she would be remembered?

A headache hinted behind her eyes. She looked away from the mirror but carried the image of the woman within it, within herself.

After her bath, dressing in English garb felt awkward. She had trouble with the buttons of the simple tunic-style gown she plucked from the wardrobe. Her fingers felt clumsy, the gown itself seemed too heavy hanging from her shoulders, the little sleeves ending at an elbow cuff constricted too tightly and the skirt caught around her legs when she moved. Worse yet, the color was a muddy green like summer algae on a dwindling pond. What had she been thinking when she had it made?

No answer being forthcoming, she hurried from the room. Too long away from Royce and she worried about him, a tendency she supposed she was going to have to get over. He was recovering and he would resume his normal life. So, in some fashion, must she although she shied from thinking how that was to be contrived.

Her brother awaited her in the smaller of the two dining rooms customarily used when the family dined *intime*. He had also bathed and changed. The frock coat she remembered as fitting him impeccably hung on his thinner frame as did the waistcoat beneath it. But she could not deny that he was much improved from the skeletal figure she had wept over. He was freshly shaven as he had been since leaving Akora, his features as sunkissed as her own. His hair, which she had trimmed for him on the ship, was brushed back from his brow like a golden mane. Of even greater importance was the light of determination and strength in eyes that matched hers in hue. He was the brother she remembered . . . almost.

Royce studied her as she studied him. He frowned. Ten days of seeing her in the Akoran garb that suited her so startlingly well made the deficiencies of her English garments all too evident. "I don't recall that dress."

She took the seat held out for her by the footman and busied herself with her napkin. "Is there any particular reason why you should?"

"I suppose not. I never paid any attention to such things." He sounded surprised by the lapse, he who had otherwise been so caring a brother.

"Neither did I," Joanna said cheerfully. "All I cared about at Hawkforte were clothes that were comfortable and didn't look dreadful if they got a grass stain or a splatter of mud on them."

"You feel differently now?"

She settled the napkin again, felt the constriction in

her chest of clothes, place, lies. No, not lies, merely omissions. They had always been close, brother and sister. She wished they could be again.

"People change, do they not?"

"I wondered about that. If you would change, I mean. Not that I wanted you to be one more ninny-hammer but I thought you might be happier if you broadened your perspective somewhat."

"If I was not so much at Hawkforte?"

"That occurred to me. I deeply regretted not being in London during the one Season you consented to. If you had enjoyed it more, perhaps you would have returned."

"I doubt it since I find the *ton* exceedingly tiresome. Besides, there were matters on the Continent requiring your attention."

"I never explained to you what they were."

"Good heavens, you did not need to. Napoleon was trying to blockade Britain. The very notion that a vessel, having visited a British port, could be seized the next time it dropped anchor anywhere Boney controlled was absurd. Nevertheless, it stirred up a good deal of trouble for him before fading away." She looked at her brother astutely. "Trouble that perhaps did not stir entirely on its own?"

Royce grinned, looking suddenly very much like his old self. "There was never any getting around you, which I hope you realize is the prime reason I haven't told you much about my wanderings in recent years."

"Nor of your work for the Foreign Ministry."

"Joanna . . ." He looked hesitant, even abashed. Slowly, he said, "I haven't been working for the Foreign Ministry precisely."

She was surprised and not. Often she had wondered how he managed to serve an institution so defined of late by rivalry and mediocrity. With all the changes of government seen in recent years, was any ministry ably run? Yet the kingdom stumbled on.

"There is a group," Royce said slowly, "of men dedicated to the well-being not of any party but of the nation as a whole. I am proud to number myself among them."

"A group? Whig or Tory?"

"Both and neither, transcending party and even personal interest. You will admit these have been turbulent times?"

"Extremely so. Do you really mean some men have managed to put aside their personal ambitions to serve the greater good?"

"I think it is the genius of our nation that such is so. At any rate, there are those of us looking beyond the presently unsettled circumstance to a time when a government of true ability will hold sway."

"And in these present circumstances, you form... what? A shadow government?"

"Let us just say we find a way to influence events."

"Does Prinny know?"

"He... suspects. That is enough."

"You took an even greater risk than I realized by going to Akora."

"Because I didn't have the support of the Foreign Ministry? They would have done nothing in any case. But let us speak of risks and Akora . . ."

Joanna grimaced, seeing too late that she had trapped herself. "I would rather not."

"You stowed away."

"They were not selling tickets."

"Somehow you convinced Darcourt to let you complete the voyage."

"He is a gentleman."

"A paragon, apparently. At any rate, you got yourself there. I salute you, not only for rescuing me, for which I am profoundly grateful, but for managing the journey itself. I must say, the experience seems to have suited you."

She glanced up at the footman, signaling him with

her eyes to begin the service. "Aside from the pure joy of finding you alive, to see Akora was the fulfillment of a life's dream. It stands to reason it would suit."

The first course was trout, presented in a wrapping of golden pastry. She took a forkful of the succulent fish, remembered the complex flavors of *marinos,* and reached for her wine.

"You learned more of Akora," he said, "than I did or so it seems."

"Alex was very . . . generous."

Royce put down his fork. He, too, drank. But only for a moment. The eyes, turned on her, were full of a lifetime's love but that did not conceal the essential strength of the man. He, too, was Hawkforte.

"You really believe in him, don't you?"

Her throat was tight. She swallowed with some difficulty. "Let us just say that I want to."

"But you understand why I cannot? Prince Alexandros is either in league with his brother or a fool. Either way does not reflect well on him."

Gently, because she so loved Royce, Joanna said, "There is another possibility."

"That I could be wrong? Actually, I would like to believe that but I know what I heard."

"In a language you were still learning and under circumstances so harsh as to easily breed confusion."

Royce was silent for several moments during which she was glad to see that he ate a good portion of the trout. For herself, she had no appetite. The dishes were removed and the second course brought, a fricando of beef sautéed with mushrooms and tomatoes in the Italian style that was a favorite of her brother's. He smiled when he saw it and took a bite with relish.

"I think I had dreams about this," Royce said when he had swallowed. He took another bite before returning to the matter at hand. "If I had overheard the guards only once or even twice, I would agree that I could be mistaken. But I heard them speak of doing the Vanax's will many times."

Joanna had no immediate answer for that. She moved the food around on her plate and tried to imagine what it must have been like for her brother, there in that cell day after day, listening to the conversation of men who were well-fed and could walk in the sun.

"I don't quite understand . . ." she said slowly. "They stood outside your cell on repeated occasions and talked among themselves of how they were doing the will of the Vanax?"

"They boasted of it."

"To each other? Why would they boast of it among themselves?"

"I suppose they were anticipating the rewards they would receive."

"For serving the Vanax? That is the part I cannot grasp." She hesitated, all too aware of how much she had not told her brother, torn between the desire to be honest with him and dread of what that could mean. "Royce, there are rules on Akora, fundamental rules that are the legacy of the Akorans' experience over thousands of years. Chief among them is that women are never to be harmed. They are revered as the givers of life."

"I thought women were expected to be submissive to men."

"Well, yes, there is that although it's all rather more complicated. I think it has to do with the people who were on Akora first, those who came afterward and how they all blended together but that is for another time. At any rate, for an Akoran man to harm a woman is an act of intolerable shame. I find it difficult to believe that men capable of behaving in such a way would be chosen by the Vanax to serve him directly. If nothing else, the potential for public scandal would be too great."

Royce did not mince words. He waved away the footman who was about to refill his wineglass and demanded, "Are you saying you were harmed by them?"

"No, but they did try. I have been reluctant to mention this because I did not wish to upset you, but Alex is more deserving of your trust and gratitude than you know. Not only did he save you, he also saved me."

A pulse beat in her brother's jaw. "From what?"

"Four of the men who were guarding you caught me in the caves where you were taken. They were about to ... violate me when Alex arrived." As Royce's face darkened, she hurried on. "He fought all four of them, at tremendous risk to himself, and I was unharmed. We got away but the cave was sealed off by an explosion. Their bodies could not be recovered so it is not possible to know for certain who they were but I cannot believe they would be trusted to serve the Vanax."

"Darcourt killed them?"

"Yes, he did."

She watched the struggle within him and saw the moment fairness won. "Good," Royce said, albeit grudgingly. "However, that doesn't really change anything. The Vanax doesn't take his half-*xenos* brother into his confidence. There's nothing surprising about that."

"Alex and his brother are very close, and Alex himself is far too intelligent to be any man's dupe. There has to be another explanation."

Royce picked up his crystal goblet, turning the stem as he regarded the ruby wine. "What do you imagine it might be?"

She sipped her own wine before answering. "I am in something of a quandary. Going to Akora as I did, being there, I learned more about the Fortress Kingdom than is known beyond its shores. Because you were a captive, even you who were there far longer would have had no opportunity to learn as I did."

"Why does this cause you difficulty?"

"Because I don't feel able to reveal all that was told to me. The Akorans and particularly the royal family of the Atreides have good reason for keeping their secrets. I can only say that it is believable to me that there could be men on Akora operating against the will and interests of the Vanax. On the chance that you might escape, or perhaps even that you might be allowed to do so, it is possible you were deliberately given false information."

She had half expected her brother to immediately reject such a thought. It seemed too serpentine, a twisting conspiracy beyond the straightforward grasp of good Englishmen. But Royce surprised her. Instead of dismissing such a possibility, he listened thoughtfully. And promptly unscrambled what she had been trying so hard not to say.

"There are factions on Akora working against the Atreides."

"Is that a question?"

"No. It's the only explanation that fits what you are—and are not—telling me. We've always thought of Akora as a fortress completely unified against the outside world. The Akorans themselves have gone to great lengths to encourage this view. I began to have doubts about it when I found myself in the Inland Sea right before I was captured. The discovery that Akora isn't even intact geographically, that it is instead a group of islands, made me consider all aspects of it differently."

"You realize even that knowledge, in the possession of a *xenos*, can be a threat to Akora?"

"Do they feel threatened?" he asked.

"Given what is happening in the world beyond them, how could they not?"

"Then why were we allowed to leave?"

"I don't know," Joanna admitted. "But being half-British and knowing much of Britain, Alex would understand the implications of keeping us against our will."

"You think he encouraged his brother to let us go?"

"I think it possible."

Royce looked at her closely. "He is a man for duty then, above any personal consideration?"

The wine was cool on her parched throat. She let it linger, delaying her answer. "I have no notion what you mean."

He did not respond but merely smiled slightly. The smile faded when she said, "Royce, I hesitate to speak of this but given what you have told me...perhaps it is as well you and your colleagues know what governs all the Akorans do these days."

"And that would be?"

She took a breath, prayed what she was about to do was right, and leaped. "They believe they may be the target of an invasion from Great Britain."

She waited then for him to exclaim over such absurdity. Britain was engulfed in war on the Continent, fighting Napoleon took all their resources, they were in a struggle for their very survival. Why would they look elsewhere for yet more conflict?

Moments passed and no such reassurance came. Instead, Royce looked at her with a penetrating directness that sent an odd chill through her. She knew in an instant why he had gone from home and family, into the midst of deadly conflict.

Without expression, he said, "They know of that?"

From cold to hot, she felt herself suddenly fevered as though in a dream turned nightmarish. "You mean it is true?"

The Lord of Hawkforte set his glass down, leaned back in his chair, and asked, "Why else would I have gone to Akora?"

chapter

SEVENTEEN

✴

𝒥OANNA SLEPT BADLY that night. Even with the windows opened wide, her bedroom was hot and stuffy. The bed itself felt lumpy, the sheets scratched, and a mouse nibbling in the wall behind her head nearly drove her to distraction. At length she gave up, donned a thin wrapper, and went downstairs. On the way, she peeked in Royce's room. It was empty, as she had expected.

The hall that cut through the center of the house from front to back led to a small garden secluded behind high walls. There roses shared space with kitchen herbs near the spreading branches of an old apple tree. Royce sat beneath the tree, his back against the gnarled trunk.

"Can't sleep?" he asked when she approached.

Joanna shook her head and sat down beside him. The grass felt cool and damp but even outside the air remained very still. "You?"

"Off and on. It's getting better." In the moonlight, she saw him smile. "Who knows, by winter I may be sleeping inside again."

"I certainly hope so." His effort to dismiss what she knew to be an embarrassment touched her. "It was to be expected, you know, after all you endured. Considering what might have been, this is not so very much, is it?"

"The fact that I break out in a sweat if I am within four walls for very long? No, all things considered, I suppose not. It could have been far worse. Would have been if you had not come."

"If Alex and I had not come," she corrected gently.

He inclined his head in acknowledgment but said, "I leave for Brighton in the morning."

"The Prince Regent is there?"

"So Bolkum tells me and he seems as well informed as always. Apparently, Prinny has found being Regent harder than he expected. His hand is sore from signing so many documents, his head throbs and he seeks the curative powers of salt water. Much of society follows."

"Brighton is not so very far from Hawkforte. Why not stop there a few days?"

"Unfortunately time is fleeting. But I am sure you are anxious to be home."

"I thought to remain with you."

"Joanna . . ." He spoke gently, robbing the words of any sting. "I do not need a nursemaid."

"That is fortunate as I have no intention of being one. However, it did rather seem to me that you might need a friend. We were ever such, were we not?"

Her brother looked away for a moment. When he faced her again, his voice was a little rough. "We were and always will be that. Still, I am mindful of the risks you took for me. I would not place you in danger again."

"In Brighton? Good lord, Royce, what do you expect might happen? That I could be struck down by a runaway sedan chair along the promenade?"

"Joanna, these are turbulent times."

"Well I know it. For all that I have been a countrywoman, I am no one's fool. If someone truly is plotting an invasion of Akora in the midst of all we already face, then there is madness afoot and that is always dangerous."

"Yet you are bound and determined to go, are you not?"

"Royce, I went to *Akora*. Surely you understand Brighton holds no terrors for me."

He laughed and tried no further to dissuade her. Indeed, she had the impression he was relieved to have the matter settled. In the quiet of the garden, where the nighttime sounds of the city seemed faint and distant, she said, "I have been thinking."

"Heaven help us."

A playful swat had him in retreat. He settled back to listen.

"I am, as I said, a countrywoman at heart. Sophisticated folk might look down their noses at that but it has advantages. In a place such as Hawkforte, people get to know each other very well. There is little room for pretense or subterfuge."

"And so . . ."

"I have never met Spencer Perceval."

"The Prime Minister. No, I suppose you haven't."

"But I have read much about him. He hates Catholics."

"That he does and makes no secret of it."

"When was the last time we had a Prime Minister who hated Catholics or any particular group, for that matter?"

"I don't know," Royce admitted. "Some of them may have but—"

"They kept it to themselves, sensibly enough. It has become the English way. We have discovered that when people are allowed to follow their own consciences, they generally do a good job of it. Now along comes Perceval."

"Bubbling over with hate."

"And with intolerance in general. I hear he has a cold, ungenial nature."

"That has been my experience with him."

"Yet he clings to power, for how much longer, do you suppose?"

"Until the Prince Regent feels secure in his own authority."

"Next year, when the restrictions on the Regency expire, what do you suppose the Prince will do?"

"Craft a government of his own liking, is the general assumption."

"Led by Perceval?"

"It is widely assumed that Prinny prefers his friends among the Whigs to Perceval and the Tories."

"But if Perceval could deliver a magnificent coup, say British control of Akora, his hold on power would be strengthened greatly."

Royce was silent for a moment. Slowly, he said, "Yes, gods, Joanna, you should be sitting in the Lords, not me. All this you put together in the rustic bliss of Hawkforte?"

"We get *The Times,* you know."

"Oh, *The Times,* I should have realized. Seriously, you have a gift for intrigue. It is a marvel you did not take London by storm."

"In my muddy green? Besides, I have a tendency to speak my mind."

"You could be married by now, well settled with a man you care for, children even."

Her breath caught, not at the image he conjured but at the sudden, unbidden yearning for all she had left behind in the Fortress Kingdom. Quietly, she said, "I do not think I was meant for that."

"Nonsense, you would be a wonderful wife and mother."

"Thank you but had I been so congenially settled, how would I have gone in search of you?"

And found not only him, but her own self.

"Even so—"

"No, even not. Morning comes soon. Let us seek what rest we can. It is cooler here in the garden."

"Mulridge will be appalled. Bad enough I sleep here."

"Mulridge will understand. She always does."

"Go to sleep then, sister mine. Tomorrow, into the lion's den."

"Today," Joanna murmured as she curled on the soft ground. Just then, curiously, on the edge of dreams she caught the scent of lemons.

BRIGHTON LAY in brilliant sunlight beside sparkling water. It was a pretty town, Joanna thought, though no match for Hawkforte. Once an old fishing village of black flint cottages and dozing dogs, it bore the mark of having grown too rapidly for its own good. The streets running down to the Strand were crammed with houses available for rental, clubs, theaters, and inns including the famous duo, the Castle and the Old Ship where the most popular assembly rooms were to be found. In winter, so she heard, it was a sleepy place but now with summer having come and brought the Prince Regent with it, Brighton burst at its seams.

It also got above itself, quite literally, thanks to the remarkable dome, an immense structure said to stand fully sixty-five feet in height at its center, that floated over the town. Beneath it were the royal stables, housing horses who surely lived in more exalted circumstances than those to be found anywhere else on earth. After a while, people probably got used to the dome but Joanna couldn't imagine how. Each time she glanced out a window or ventured outdoors, it startled her anew.

Royce had borrowed a house from a friend. It was set a little apart from the bustle, behind stone walls and with its own garden but with a good view of the town.

She was grateful for that, even as she struggled to cope with the challenge her loving brother had thrown at her.

"Do not tell me," he had said in the carriage coming down from London, "that you are afraid?"

"Only of boredom. Do you have any idea of the sheer tedium behind even the simplest gown?"

"No worse than that required for a frock coat. Besides, your muddy green hurts your eyes now that they have been opened. I can tell."

"All right, I admit it, but not Mme. Duprès. Please God, not her."

"She is the milliner of the moment."

"She is a tyrant by all reports. Besides, she must be far too busy."

"I sent a note."

From the Earl of Hawkforte informing the fashionable dressmaker that her services were required for the outfitting of his sister. Damn the man.

"I told her cost was no consideration."

"She will bankrupt you. Some parvenu manufacturer will end up owning Hawkforte."

He had laughed, appalling creature that he was, and offered her no relief. Mme. Duprès was there, salivating behind her smile, when they pulled up before the house they were to occupy. She had not left in the three days since.

"A triumph," the plump milliner chortled. She got off her knees, wincing, and surveyed Joanna who stood stoic-still, determined to give the tyrant no satisfaction.

"My brother is mad, you know," Joanna said. "Any moment now, I expect him to be declared such."

Three days had accustomed the madam to such announcements. She merely chuckled. "His lordship is a generous man. Would there were more like him."

"There are," Joanna asserted. With a sweeping gesture of her arm that almost knocked over the harried apprentice loaded down with fabrics each more glorious than the last, she indicated the high windows and the world beyond. "Out there is a veritable townful of Incomparables beseeching your services. How can you deny them?"

"My assistants are seeing to them," Mme. Duprès said with simple practicality. "You are my special project."

"God help me."

"I think He already has." She studied the young woman, and the aura of feminine knowledge and confidence she radiated. Munching on a cucumber sandwich offered by an awed tweenie, Madame remarked, "I perceive this will be a very interesting summer."

"The Chinese have a curse: 'May you live in interesting times.'"

Madame absorbed that unfazed. "*Chinoiserie* is all the rage. Wait until you see the Prince's Marine Pavilion, mam'selle. It will astound you."

Not after Carlton House, Joanna thought, but as it turned out she was wrong.

"It was," Royce explained as he stepped down from the carriage and turned to offer his sister a hand, "a rather pretty little farmhouse when the Prince Regent first espied it almost twenty years ago. He is said to have liked the view."

Joanna stared dumbstruck at what lay before her. The dome should have prepared her yet it had not. Before her was a vast mansion in the neoclassical style set a scant hundred yards or so from the water's edge. Around it, spreading over many acres, were outbuildings of every conceivable purpose or none at all. The sun was setting, illuminating the scene with a ruddy glow added to by the burning flambeaux positioned along the gravel driveway where guests were arriving.

"Is it like this every night?" Joanna asked.

"Sometimes more. This looks to be a crowd of fairly modest proportions." In dry understatement, Royce added, "Prinny does not like to be alone."

There was no risk of that on this night. Entering the
Pavilion on Royce's arm, Joanna did her very best not to
gape. Mme. Duprès had warned her, after all. Still, she
was hard set to resist the thought that she had somehow
stepped across continents. Everywhere she looked, everything her eye touched, was Chinese. Here was a world
of pagodas and dragons set among lacquered cabinets,
bamboo furnishings, paper lanterns, porcelain and palm
trees. No surface was left untouched. Walls, ceilings, and
everything in between glowed in an explosion of dazzling crimson and scarlet, teal and emerald, sapphire and
gold. It might have been exotically beautiful but there
was simply too much, too many rooms stuffed too full as
though the Prince Regent had constructed Ali Baba's cave
rather than a palace.

"Amazing," Joanna murmured. Even as she spoke,
she became aware that they were the object of a great
many eyes. Men and women alike broke off their conversations in mid sentence and stared. Not at her, although
a few got around to that, but at Royce. Indeed, they
gazed at him as though at an apparition.

"It seems," Royce said quietly, "Mme. Duprès kept
her word."

"And her silence, but then you paid her well enough
for it." For the three days during which Joanna had been
pinched, poked and pinned, Royce had kept to the back
garden of the Brighton house, reading dispatches sent by
friends he did not name, and breaking off only to eat and
sleep. Though still somewhat thin, he looked vastly more
like his old self.

Certainly no one had difficulty recognizing him.
After the initial shock of his presence, a throng of people
quickly surrounded them with exclamations of surprise
and delight.

Royce bore the happy tumult good-naturedly, accepting the welcome even as he deflected questions as to
where he had been. This continued until the crowd

parted abruptly, clearing the way for their royal host. Joanna observed the Prince Regent with interest. At Carlton House, she had caught only a glimpse of him. Now she saw before her a man who would celebrate his forty-eighth birthday in a matter of days, his age belied by round, almost cherubic features that were virtually unlined and the fine brown hair of a child, all startlingly at odds with the corpulence of his body. He looked like an angel run to fat, stuffed on too many sweet buns, syllabubs and sauces. He wore a long-tailed coat of dark blue superfine with a high turnover collar framing his face to the lobes of his ears, a waistcoat of contrasting crimson and buff trousers mercifully more loosely cut than had been the style a few years before. His cravat was tied exquisitely, his cuffs shot and the whole a picture of style that veered just short of dandyish.

He also looked displeased, at least in the grey eyes, which were small in the largeness of his face but the bow-shaped mouth smiled charmingly. "Hawkforte, the devil! Where have you been keeping?"

Before Royce could reply, the Prince Regent rushed on. "Damn good to see you. D'you know how long it's been since I had a jaw about the old Greeks? These numbskulls"—he gestured to the assembled listeners—"don't know Homer from Herodotus."

"It's good to know you keep up your reading, Your Majesty," Royce said smoothly. His hand tightened at Joanna's elbow. "May I present my sister, sire, Lady Joanna Hawkforte?"

She made her curtsey, rising to find the Prince Regent looking at her assessingly. "Very nice use of that nainsook. Mme. Duprès's work?"

Joanna nodded. "Madame was most helpful."

"She's another who seems to have gone missing, least these last few days. More than a few ladies in a tizzy over that, let me tell you. Really, Royce, you might have sent word you were in Brighton."

So that was the source of the Prince's annoyance. The man who read Homer in the original Greek and could converse on all aspects of literature with rare erudition was sensitive to a fault, at least when it came to his prerogatives.

"Had I followed my inclination, Majesty," Royce said, "I would have come at once to pay my respects. But"—he leaned forward a little, as though imparting a confidence—"I was a tad indisposed and thought it best not to intrude upon you until my health was properly restored."

The Prince Regent shuddered slightly. "Hate illness, hate anything to do with it. Good of you to think of that. Come along then, there's much to show you. Made a few changes about the place since you were last here and I've got more planned, much more. Have to give you a look at what's in store. Not so much on the inside, rather like what I've got here, but a whole redo of the exterior in the Mughal style. You familiar with that, India and the like? Quite extraordinary, really."

They moved on but did not get far before a slim, pale man stepped in front of them. Austerely dressed, almost entirely bald save for a powdered fringe around his ears, he pressed together lips so remarkably thin and colorless as to appear missing altogether.

"Perceval," the Prince Regent said without enthusiasm. "Look here, Hawkforte is back."

The Prime Minister bowed. "Your Majesty, milord . . . Lady—?"

She was introduced and promptly ignored. Perceval gave his attention to Royce. "You've been the source of much speculation, Hawkforte. Rumor had you dead."

"Rumor is an untrustworthy fellow, Prime Minister."

Perceval flushed, which made him look only a little less like a cadaver. "Even so, we must talk. I'm sure you've had fascinating adventures."

"Rather dull actually. Didn't get about much."

Joanna choked, which earned her a startled look

from the Prince Regent. Nonetheless, he extracted them adroitly, thereby winning her instant gratitude.

"Have to go into all that later, Spencer. Promised Hawkforte—and Lady Joanna, too, of course—to show them the plans."

The Prime Minister seemed well acquainted with the nature of "the plans." He rolled his eyes and muttered something about the expense but the words faded as Prinny pressed on, drawing them in his royal wake.

They saw the plans, laid out on a table in the Prince's private sitting room which looked better suited to shelter a Khan, and exclaimed over them. Fairly enough, Joanna thought, for the elaborate drawings of the new exterior were remarkable. That the Prince Regent had exquisite taste could not be denied. It was, however, unsuited to the English countryside as though his was a soul set down in the wrong time and place.

In between comments about the plans, Royce and the Prince exchanged a few quiet words. Across the wide table, Joanna did not catch all of them but it sounded as though her brother was reassuring his sovereign.

They returned to the ballroom as musicians of the Tenth Light Dragoons struck up a lively tune. The band was one of the Prince's favorites and most kindly said to be notable for their sheer volume. Prinny went to join them at once, beating time enthusiastically against his plump thigh. Royce and Joanna could not have followed had they been so inclined for they were surrounded instantly by dozens of guests eager for conversation with them.

Recalling how she had been ignored so studiously at the Carlton House fête, Joanna could not but marvel at her sudden popularity, which she attributed entirely to her connection to Royce. Yet when the press of the crowd separated them, she continued to find herself surrounded by a good many young gentlemen who inexplicably seemed intent on making themselves pleasant.

She was rather enjoying being in the center of a cluster of young bucks, some of whom were undeniably witty and charming, when a ripple went through the room, interrupting conversations and redirecting gazes, including her own.

Caught in laughter, she stared at the man who stood alone at the entrance to the ballroom. He was dressed in black save for the flashes of white at throat and wrist where she had felt his lifeblood pulse. The garments, though superbly tailored, were incidental; power was his natural garb and he wore it devastatingly well. His hair, like thick silk beneath her fingers, as she recalled, was drawn back, emphasizing the purely masculine beauty of the features she had studied as he slept. He stood head and shoulders above almost every man there except her own brother, his height affording him a clear view of the room. Detachment gleaming in the eyes where she had found her own reflection, he surveyed the crowd, his gaze coming finally and irrevocably to rest on Joanna herself.

The jolt of that instant connection robbed her of breath even as excitement she could not deny surged through her. The Chinese ballroom in its dizzying excess, the cacophony of music and voices, the heat and smells of the summer night all vanished in an instant. Only one reality remained: Lord Alex Haverston Darcourt, Marquess of Boswick, Earl of Letham, Baron Dedham had returned to England.

chapter

EIGHTEEN

✦

$\mathcal{T}$HE CROWD PARTED not from any instinct of courtesy, Alex was sure, but from the simple urge for a better view. No one would want to miss this, including the simpering fops who had been gathered about her far too closely and attentively. The *ton* remembered, he was certain, the set-down the Marquess of Boswick had delivered to Lady Joanna Hawkforte at Carlton House. They would be eager to see how this new and enticing incarnation of the lady dealt with him, and he with her.

Truth be told, he was rather eager to see that himself.

He crossed the room with steady, swift strides and stopped directly in front of her. From the corner of his eye, he saw Royce take a step forward as though to intercept him. Her brother stopped when Joanna lifted her chin and smiled.

"Alex," she said with simple directness. "It is good to see you."

Only her eyes said how very good it truly was. Even so there was a quick, collective intake of breath as those standing nearest absorbed this shocking bit of familiarity and awaited his response.

Alex smiled, inclined his head in a bow, and took her hands in his. "Joanna, beautiful as always."

Meaningful looks flew along with whispered asides to the unlucky ones caught beyond eavesdropping distance. They *knew* each other, very well apparently, how well being a matter for delicious speculation. Just where had Lady Joanna been these past several weeks during which Darcourt had also been absent from London? Could they possibly have been... *together*?

Darcourt and the Lady Joanna. Darcourt the elusive, bane of ambitious mothers and their chicks, scion of an ancient and powerful name, and of the even older mystery that was Akora. And the Lady Joanna of Hawkforte. Hawkforte of renown, also ancient, also illustrious, wreathed in history and legend of its own.

He knew the *ton,* had studied it at length, for collectively the men and women who comprised it wielded great power in England. He knew how shallow and crude they could be, how cruel and empty. And how prone to infatuation. How quickly they could seize upon a moment, an event, a vicarious tidbit of excitement and make it their own.

He raised her hands, holding her eyes, and brushed a lingering kiss over her fingers curling around his own. He might have stood in Whitehall and shouted his intentions for the world to hear, so clearly did he make them known.

To all but Joanna and just possibly Royce who was looking murder at him. It was a delicate moment calling for subtlety but receiving instead the Prince Regent, barreling toward them with sheer delight.

"Darcourt! Marvelous, absolutely marvelous! What an evening for reunions! Know Lady Joanna, do you, and her brother? Royce—" He beckoned, smiling like the puppeteer he was said to fancy himself sometimes, drawing them all together. "Splendid." Turning, the Prince Regent broadened his smile to include the man hovering nearby, frowning so heavily Joanna had the fanciful thought that his face would sink right through the floor.

'It is splendid, isn't it, Perceval? Two old families, two
old friends, of mine at least, and a lovely new one—" He
inclined his head most graciously to Joanna, bestowing
upon her the mantle of royal approval. That did not escape the dour Prime Minister but his attention was focused much more on Alex and Royce who, whatever
their personal disagreements, stood side by side regarding him with identical expressions of sardonic challenge.

As like as two peas, Joanna thought even as she
sought to contain the tumult of emotions, the delight,
longing, joy and apprehension that had erupted in her
the moment Alex appeared. Alex! Here, in England, and
intent on... what? Had he come solely out of service to
Akora or dare she hope his feelings for her played some
role?

She would have liked an opportunity to try to find
out but the Prince Regent had other plans. They and the
rest of the assembled guests were ushered into a vast
chamber in which all illumination had been extinguished but for that provided by a few candelabras held
high by liveried servants. Heavy curtains were drawn
over the windows to exclude any stray light from the
torches outside or even the moon. When all the guests
had entered, the last faint flames were snuffed out, leaving them in utter darkness. Bewildered, Joanna found no
enlightenment in the anticipatory ooohs and aaahs of
those assembled, most of whom seemed to know what
was about to transpire. Moreover, she was struck by concern for Royce. How well could he manage in a room
that must seem as dark and confining as the cell in
which he had dwelt for so long? Instinctively, she took
his hand.

"Don't stay," she whispered. "Whatever this is about,
no one will notice if you slip out."

Behind her, she was aware of Alex, comfortingly
close, and knew he could hear but there was no helping
that.

Royce's hand tightened on hers. "Don't be silly," he responded *sotto voce*. "There is no reason for me t leave."

She knew that was not true but lacked any means c persuading him. She could only wait with the severa hundred other assembled guests for whatever it was th Prince intended to unfold.

It came suddenly with a crash of sound that mad her gasp, followed swiftly by strange, multicolored light illuminating the end of the room nearest to where the stood. Indeed, they were close enough for her to perceiv that a screen of sorts, perhaps of gauze, had been ex tended from floor to ceiling and wall to wall. As the mu sic continued in such a manner as to make the spin tingle and raise the hairs on the back of the neck, th whirling lights began to resolve themselves into fantast cal shapes. She gasped again as what appeared to be headless horseman appeared out of nowhere and seeme to ride down upon them. As the figure grew grotesquel large, Joanna instinctively tried to back away only t come right up against Alex's broad chest.

"Easy," he murmured. "It's nothing more than ligh magnified by glass behind the screen, a magic lanter show."

Relief filled her and with it just a little embarrassmen She had heard of such things, who had not? They were a the rage of late. But never had she experienced one or full apprehended what it could be like.

"The Prince is tremendously fond of these spectacles, Royce said quietly. "His always have a special flavor."

A moment later, Joanna saw what her brother mean The horseman vanished, replaced by writhing spectres c the dead, skeletons and all other manner of terrifying fig ures that rose, grew huge, advanced, retreated, seemed t dissolve into one another and finally vanished into th floor as the music surged and the audience applaude wildly.

Joanna scarcely heard the applause. She could think only of Royce. Throughout the display, his grasp of her hand had tightened until now her fingers were caught in a painful vise. She knew he was entirely unknowing of what he did and took that as an indication of his own extreme discomfort.

"We must leave," she said and turned to Alex, seeking, in the light of the few candles that had been relit, to communicate her concern to him. He saw her concern immediately and glanced at Royce who stood unmoving, sweat gleaming on his strained features. Without hesitation, Alex opened a path for them to the nearest door. His size and strength, as well as the habit of command, made him do so as naturally as he did all else. Within moments, they were out of the room and walking swiftly toward a brace of French doors that led to the garden beyond.

Once outside, Royce recovered quickly. A few deep breaths, a hard shake of his head and he seemed his old self.

"Quite a performance," he said dryly. "Prinny has outdone himself."

"He seems to have a certain preoccupation with the dead," Alex remarked. The two men resumed their study of one another as combatants will in the moments before mayhem ensues.

"I suspect most royals are uneasy these days," Joanna said hastily. "And have been ever since revolution unleashed the guillotine. They fear the same could come here."

"Tends to create a certain anxiousness," Royce agreed without taking his gaze from Alex. "But perhaps you on Akora feel immune from any such worry."

Oh, dear, Joanna thought, *already.* She had to admire her brother. Only moments after suffering what clearly had been a very uncomfortable episode he had rebounded sufficiently to be on the attack.

"Are you asking if we fear revolution on Akora?" Alex asked with deceptive mildness.

"If, as I have been told," Royce replied with a glance in Joanna's direction, "your brother could not have been responsible for my captivity, then someone on Akora is trying to stir up trouble for you and your family."

"My brother responsible . . . ?"

Hawkforte had done it deliberately, Alex realized. The canny bastard had dropped his sledgehammer of an accusation without warning specifically so that he could assess his reaction to it. As tactics went it was brilliant, if damned uncomfortable.

"That is absurd," Alex said when he was certain he had a sufficient grip on himself. His gaze shifted to Joanna. "You knew of this?" Her only answer was a nod but it was enough. "That is why you were in such haste to leave Akora?"

"Please," she said, "try to understand. I had to assure my brother's safety."

"Still, you could have told me . . ."

It hurt that she had not but there was relief as well. As absurd as the accusation was, at least it made her behavior understandable.

"You would have denied it," she replied. "Besides, we both know you have had your own doubts."

"What doubts?" Royce asked. He had remained silent through the exchange, watching them both, but now he clearly was driven to speak.

"About you," Alex said bluntly, "and why you went to Akora. When we spoke last year, I made clear any such attempt would be unwelcome."

"You did," Royce acknowledged. "What you left unclear were your reasons for saying so."

"They should have been evident. Akora does not welcome *xenos*." At Royce's chiding look, Alex corrected himself, "Officially, but those *xenos* who do come remain

Such was not your purpose. You intended to return to England."

"Of course I did after, I hoped, meeting with the Vanax. I wanted him to understand that there are those in England who wish only peaceful, friendly relations with Akora. I hoped to open a channel for further discussion."

"Why didn't you tell me this directly?" Alex demanded.

"Because you were immediately against my going and I wondered why. Were you truly working on Akora's behalf or your own?"

Joanna breathed in sharply. Instinctively, she moved between her brother and the man she knew he had just insulted profoundly. It was an understandable gesture on her part but unwise just the same. Each man glared at her and moved to lift her out of the way.

"Oh, for heaven's sake," she said when both had hold of her. "I am not a wishbone. Put me down."

They obeyed, looking at each other warily as though startled to have reacted in so identical a fashion.

"Perhaps," Alex said tightly, "you would like to explain why you think me capable of betraying Akora?"

"I didn't think that...entirely," Royce replied. "It simply occurred to me that you might consider being a Prince of Akora, subject to the rule of your brother, less appealing than being governor in your own right of a British-controlled Akora."

For once, Alex looked utterly taken aback. Into the silence that followed Royce's admission, Joanna said quietly, "Sadly, there are men who would choose such a course. Alex is not one of them."

"You are half English," Royce said. "If Perceval were to succeed in his plans to take over Akora, you would be the logical choice for royal governor."

"Hardly that, as I would be dead. Never would I live to see Akora conquered."

Royce looked at him for a long moment. What he saw
must have convinced him. Quietly, he said, "Perhaps my
sister has not misplaced her trust." It was a huge admission
for him. A little of the tension that had gripped Joanna
from the moment she realized her brother and Alex were
to come face to face eased but she remained cautious.

"This is hardly the best place to talk," she said. With
the magic lantern show concluded, more guests were fil
tering out into the gardens for a breath of fresh air before
returning to the gaming tables and whatever other en
joyments the Prince had planned. The festivities were
likely to go on to the wee hours of the morning.

"Prinny will be offended if we leave too early," Royce
said. He handed Alex a card. "This is our direction here
in Brighton. I suggest we meet when we are less likely
to be observed. The constable of the watch makes his
rounds at three o'clock and again at four."

"I will come in between."

He turned to leave but before he could do so, Royce
said, "I have not thanked you for rescuing me and for
protecting Joanna."

Slowly, Alex took the hand that was offered. The two
men stood for a moment regarding one another before
going their separate ways.

Joanna remained with her brother. She was still con
cerned about his well-being and he seemed disinclined
for them to part even temporarily. Several times she
caught him casting censorious looks at the young bucks
clustered around her and could not help but laugh at
the sheer absurdity of it all. She who so scorned society
looked set to become its darling. Heaven help her.

Before the novelty of the experience grew too tire
some, she turned her attentions to being pleasant to the
Prince.

That proved a surprisingly easy task. For all the sto
ries she had heard about his dissipations, on this night

the Prince Regent seemed intent on exerting his charm.
The discovery that she, like Royce, was fluent in ancient
Greek transported him. Ignoring most of those gathered
about him, he plunged into a remarkably erudite discussion of the Greeks that so fascinated Joanna she lost track
of passing time. Alex joined in and though he spoke not
at all of Akora, his knowledge of matters Greek delighted
the Prince, as did his friendliness. It was after midnight
by the chiming of the clocks before she noticed people
were beginning to flag. Wigs askew, makeup smudged,
they soldiered on with bleary-eyed stares. Of the Prime
Minister there was no sign; Joanna heard in passing that
he had gone home, claiming indisposition.

Two A.M. had come and gone before she and Royce
departed. The night was clear and pleasantly warm, the
air freshened by the breeze from the sea. The sway of the
carriage proved all too relaxing. Joanna woke with a start
as Bolkum drew the horses to a halt in front of the house.

"You aren't accustomed to such late hours," Royce
observed.

Alighting from the carriage, Joanna said, "A bit of tea
will revive us both."

"You have no doubt Darcourt will be here?"

The question surprised her. "Of course not, do you?"

"Some," Royce admitted, "although he is not what I
expected."

"A Prince prepared to betray his country?"

"You yourself said there are men who would not hesitate to do so."

Joanna had not chance to reply before the front door
opened to reveal Mulridge looking at them sternly.

"Fine time to be getting home," the black-garbed
woman said.

"It is a fine time, Mulridge," Royce said. "The stars
are shining, the night is balmy and the company"—he
dropped a light kiss on her cheek—"is delightful."

Mulridge did try but she was no proof against such gallantry. "Oh, well, then off to bed with you—"

"Actually, we await a visitor," Joanna said. "But that needn't concern you. I'll make the tea."

"A visitor? At this ungodly hour? And who might that be, I wonder?"

"A Prince," Royce replied with a perfectly straight face. "It's all the rage you know. Royalty loves to go calling in the wee hours."

"A Prince," Mulridge repeated chidingly. "Am I supposed to believe that—" She broke off, looking from one grinning face to the other. Grimly, she said, "And I'll just bet I know which one it is, too."

Before either could reply, she ruffled her long black dress, cast them both a stern look and headed off toward the kitchens. Over her shoulder, she said, "*I* will make the tea."

While Joanna went upstairs to restore herself, and cast a longing look at the bed, Mulridge did as promised. Joanna returned to discover not merely tea but a tray of sandwiches and cakes that she was far too nervous to touch. In the plentiful distractions of the Prince's pavilion, she had managed not to dwell on the thought that Alex was coming *here*, to the house, and that he and Royce would be talking. About affairs of state, of course. She had no reason to believe anything else would be discussed, most especially since she intended to be right there to make sure it was not. This was not the time for matters of a personal nature so liable to misinterpretation.

Smoothing her hair for perhaps the twentieth time, she glanced at the clock on the marble mantel of the family parlor, situated toward the back of the house for greater privacy. Bolkum had laid a small fire more for cheer than the heat that was not needed. Gas lamps added their own glow. It was half past three. She had heard the constable of the watch pass thirty minutes before and knew he would return in a like amount of time. Royce was in the garden. She waited a while longer, then went out to join him.

"Alex should be here at any time."

He nodded. "Bolkum is in the front hall. He will admit him."

"Do you really think all this care is needed?"

"I think we stand on the edge of a precipice. If Perceval should succeed at his scheming . . ." He shook his head at the thought where such madness would lead.

"It isn't enough to be fighting Napoleon? The Prime Minister wants to take on a war with Akora, too?"

"He may flatter himself it would be an easy conquest."

"Then he knows nothing of Akora."

"That's the problem," Royce said. "Hardly anyone does. In their ignorance, men like Perceval can imagine anything they like."

She thought of the cannons in *Nestor*'s hold and shivered. Whatever internal disputes might threaten, Akora was still superbly prepared to defend itself against invaders.

Through the open windows of the back parlor, she heard the clock chime again. Beyond on the street, the constable called his greeting.

"Four o'clock and all's well."

Perhaps for him but not for Joanna. Alex was late. "He is coming," she said. "I know it."

Kindly, because he loved her, Royce replied, "He may have been delayed."

They waited until half past four. When still there was no sign of Alex, Joanna went into the front hall. She thought Bolkum might have fallen asleep and not heard the knock but the faithful fellow was sitting crouched on a chair, as bright-eyed and alert as though it were high noon.

"Be light soon," he said.

She stood, staring out through the etched glass panes on either side of the door. "Something has happened."

Blessedly, he did not doubt her but stood matter-of-factly. "Want me to have a look?"

Did she want Bolkum to try to find Alex? Better that she try herself and so she did, quietly, with confidence she had not possessed before. Deeply, she reached within herself for the strange, sometimes elusive power she knew dwelt there. She thought of Alex, letting memories of him seep through her, the sight and sound, the touch and taste, the essence of Alex.

Where was he?

Her fingertips twitched. She could almost feel the smooth heat of his skin, the way his chest rumbled when he laughed while she lay with her head against him, listening to the steady beat of his heart. They had lain like that beside the Pool of Sighs and again on Deimatos after the escape from the caves. The air had smelled of damp sand and grass crushed beneath their bodies, of night-blooming jasmine and the ever-present perfume of lemons, of—

Blood.

She could smell the iron tang of blood. Taste it in her throat. Feel it on her own skin.

"*Alex!*"

Royce came running from the garden. Bolkum was holding her gently by the shoulders as Mulridge flitted nearby, watchful and alarmed. "I knew this would happen," the older woman declared. "It was always in her but never so strong before. Needed bringing out, it did."

"What's wrong?" Royce asked gently as he took her from Bolkum, staring into her eyes, steadying her with his gaze.

Still choking on terrible knowledge, she said, "It's Alex. He's hurt, that's why he isn't here. But he is somewhere nearby, I'm sure of it."

All her life, from earliest memory, she had counted on Royce. After their parents' death, that had only been more so. Now he did not let her down. The remnants of his suffering seemed to vanish before her eyes. He was the Lord of Hawkforte, heir to generations of men and women who had risked much, dared greatly, and triumphed magnificently.

"We will find him," Royce said, and gestured to Bolkum who followed him into the dying night.

Mulridge went into the kitchen. Instinctively, Joanna trailed after her. She had some time, she had no idea how much, but Royce would succeed, of that she had no doubt.

"Hot water," Mulridge said, "that's always useful." She hung a large pot on the hearth. To Joanna, she directed, "Go get the chest."

She did, finding it where they had left it when they arrived, in a spare room of the Brighton house. It was a very old chest, no one really knew how old, made of oak and bound in iron. The wood was deeply pitted and darkened by uncounted age. The iron fittings were loose but still served to hold the wood together. There was a tradition that the chest had been a gift to a Hawkforte bride from a woman who was a great healer. Joanna's mother had kept medicines and bandages in it. Her father's mother had done the same and hers before her in an unbroken line that vanished into mist.

The very weight of it in her arms was a comfort. She brought it to the kitchen where steam rose from the boiling water. Mulridge had laid out towels on the wide worktable. "Soon," she said, and began tearing lengths of linen.

Before the pile was very large, the back door to the garden opened. Royce stood there with Bolkum. Between them, they held the slumped form of Alex.

Joanna did not scream. She was rather proud of that even as she rushed to them. "He'll be all right," Royce said quickly as he and Bolkum maneuvered Alex into a chair. He was conscious and aware enough to look at Joanna and grimace. There was blood on his mouth and on his brow above one eye which was swollen shut. But all that was as nothing to the blossom of crimson on his shirt just below and to the left of his heart.

"They missed," he said, and turned the grimace to a grin.

"Damn you," Joanna said even as she reached for his shirt and without ado, ripped it apart. "Damn, damn, damn you. You walked, didn't you? Without a carriage or driver, without anyone. What were you thinking?"

"That I was in civilized England?"

"Fool, damn, damn fool."

He had been stabbed, the blade entering between two ribs. Another few inches and it would have pierced his heart. Oh, yes, they had missed, but scarcely.

Time stopped. There was nothing but the urgent need to care for him. She did not think, hesitate, or ponder. She merely acted as she had learned from tenderest childhood, at her mother's side, not even realizing what she absorbed.

"Your grandmother taught me," her mother had said on some soft spring day too long ago. "As she was taught."

She was not alone. There in the kitchen of the Brighton house, she might have been at Hawkforte. Other women were with her, sisters of her soul clustering near. They lent their strength with ancient wisdom.

"You're very good at this," Alex said. A lesser man would have been stunned by the attack. He was merely surprised.

"How many were there?" Royce inquired.

"Six, I think. Three got away." He sounded disgusted.

"The constable will find the others."

"I suppose." It was no matter. Three dead bodies unexplained would cause talk of the hysterical variety. But the message would be well understood by those to whom it had been sent.

"Joanna is right, you should be more careful."

"I will be . . . now." He looked to Royce. "This is more serious even than I thought."

"I can say the same. A direct attack on you indicates a
ertain level of desperation."

"Or determination. We were seen talking together, af-
r all."

"Wait," Joanna interjected. "Are you both saying you
think the attack on Alex has something to do with
kora? But there is no evidence of that. It could have
een ordinary cutpurses."

"Unfortunately not," Alex said. "I recognized them."

Both Hawkfortes looked at him in surprise. "You
id?" Royce asked.

Alex nodded. "They were dressed as Englishmen but
key fought as Akorans." He gestured to the wound on
is chest. "This was done by an Akoran blade."

"But who—?" Joanna murmured.

"Likely the same people who imprisoned me," Royce
aid. He looked at Alex. "You trust your brother?"

"With my life."

"Then it is someone else."

Joanna gave a small sigh of relief that her brother had
ealized his captors had not worked for the Vanax but had
ought to slander him. That, at least, was progress.

"They are resourceful," Alex said. "Enough to come
ere, which also means they are determined to carry out
heir mission."

"Then they will show themselves again," Royce said.

Alex's face hardened. "And when they do . . ." The
vo men exchanged a silent look of understanding.

"Enough," Joanna intervened. "You need to lie
own," she told Alex firmly. Neither his natural male ar-
ogance nor her brother's sense of propriety would dis-
uade her. Alex was not going anywhere except to bed.

"I'm fine," he began, but to her surprise, Royce sup-
orted her.

"She's right. We're all weary and you are also injured.
is daylight now . . ." A glance out the kitchen windows
onfirmed this. "If you are seen in such a condition, it

will only fuel speculation and perhaps connect you
those three dead bodies the constable will find, if
hasn't already. That would be an unneeded distraction

Reluctantly, Alex assented to the wisdom of this.
allowed Royce and Bolkum to help him up the stairs a
into a spare bedroom. Mulridge bustled after them, tu
ing down the covers, fluffing the pillows and genera
assuring their guest would be as comfortable as possib

Joanna remained without. She had strained I
brother's tolerance to the limit, she thought. Ensconc
her lover in the house was one thing, hovering over
bed could be considered quite another. The smile :
bestowed on Royce when he emerged was filled w
gratitude.

He saw it and opened his arms. She went into th
and was comforted. The smell of blood was gone,
placed by the freshness of a new day.

chapter

NINETEEN

✴

THAT DAY SHE SLEPT THROUGH in large part. Waking in the soft light of afternoon, Joanna sat up abruptly. Her one thought was of Alex and how he fared. She darted from the bed, seized the wrapper at the foot of it and while pulling it on, hurried from the room.

A tentative knock at Alex's door bringing no response, she peered within. The curtains were drawn, plunging the room into deep shadows. She could just make out the vague shape of the man asleep in the bed.

Barefoot, she approached. When her eyes had adjusted sufficiently, she saw that he was lying on his side facing her. The sheet, his sole cover on so balmy a day, was pushed down to his waist. The bandage around his chest shone starkly. She bent closer, confirming for herself that the linen wrapping was unstained. The bleeding had not resumed. Carefully, lest she disturb him, she reached out a hand and lightly touched his brow. No fever.

Relief filled her. Hardly aware that she did so, she sank down on the bed beside him and touched her lips to his. "Alex...thank God." He stirred, turning over onto his back. His mouth softened, drew hers in even as his arms enclosed her. The kiss was more sweet than

sensual, a gentle affirmation of life and love. When
ended, she was nestled beside him, her head on l
shoulder.

"A good way to wake," Alex said with a smile. I
glanced toward the curtained windows. "What tir
is it?"

"I'm not sure ... not quite time for tea but close t
perhaps."

"Amazing, I can't remember ever sleeping so late
He began to sit up but was stopped by the gentle pressu
of her hand on his chest.

"When was the last time you slept long enough?"

"A while ago," he admitted.

"It's just as well we all rested." She touched his fa
lightly. The bruising around his eye had gone down co
siderably. He looked very much his old self. Lying the
on the bed was dangerous but she could not bring hers
to move. Not quite yet.

"Alex ... why did you let us leave Akora?"

His expression remained carefully impassive. "Wh
makes you think it was my decision?"

"Because in this matter more even than any oth
your brother would be guided by you."

He stroked a stray wisp of hair away from her chee
letting his hand linger. "It would be very easy for me
say that you were allowed to go because I care deep
about your feelings and did not wish to cause you pa
by forcing you to do anything you did not wish to d
most particularly stay with me. All that happens to
true but it is not the entire truth."

Even as she absorbed the very pleasant declaratie
that he cared for her, something that in all honesty s
had long since realized, Joanna asked, "There is more?"

"Although I could not be certain of your brothe
reasons for coming to Akora, I was certain of yours
knew you to be a person of courage, honor and trustwe

hiness. I had to hope you were right about Royce, as it now seems you were. The two of you couldn't do anything to help Akora if you were forced to remain there but back here in England you could be invaluable allies."

She raised herself up and looked at him. "In short, ou thought to make use of us?"

"Joanna . . ."

The deep note of concern in his voice wrung a smile rom her. "Be easy, my lord. I am myself no stranger to uty's dilemma."

His arms tightened around her. "I know that now. Royce truly believed Atreus was responsible for his aptivity?"

She nodded. "Guards stood outside his cell and boasted of the rewards they would receive from the Vanax for the service they were doing him."

"That makes no sense. The men of Atreus's personal guard would never behave in such a way."

"That is what I thought." As Alex had been willing to accept her assurances that Royce meant no harm to Akora, even to the extent of risking his own life to rescue him, she would accept his judgment of Atreus. "I also thought that men of such loathsome character would never be in service to the Vanax to begin with. But Royce heard what he heard. In his weakened state, he believed it."

"Understandably enough . . ." Alex thought for a moment, then said, "Whoever held him must have wanted him to believe that Atreus was responsible."

"But why? Was it a plot to embarrass the Vanax, to make it look as though he had violated Akoran custom by his treatment of a *xenos*?"

"I fail to see what that would accomplish. Even if people believed it, which most would not, it wouldn't really change anything. Atreus's power would be undiminished unless—"

He broke off, looking at Joanna. "Unless it was n⟨
Akorans who were supposed to believe Atreus was r⟨
sponsible for Royce's captivity. Unless it was—"

"The British! The ones considering an invasion ⟨
Akora."

"Exactly. A British nobleman, an aristocrat of hig⟨
rank and repute, held captive on Akora, subject to brut⟨
mistreatment at the orders of Akora's leader himsel⟨
Invasions have been launched on less pretext than that.

Even as he spoke, Alex tossed back the covers an⟨
stood, heedless of his nudity. "Royce must be informe⟨
of this, and speaking of him"—he smiled ruefully—"⟨
doubt he would appreciate my abusing his hospitality i⟨
this fashion."

She looked at him with unabashed pleasure. "H⟨
sleeps in the garden. He can't bear to be inside for lon⟨
periods of time."

"I wondered last night at the magic lantern show⟨
Alex caught her hand, his fingers curling around hers. H⟨
squeezed them gently. "Joanna, you know that almo⟨
any other man would have been crushed by what yo⟨
brother endured."

Vastly relieved that he did not pity Royce, a sent⟨
ment her brother would despise, she smiled. With⟨
shake of her hair made wild by sleep, she rose but ke⟨
hold of Alex's hand. Standing beside the bed, she pulle⟨
away slowly.

"I must dress," she said. "You must do the same."

"To face the world."

"This little piece of it at least. You know it is impo⟨
tant you be seen."

"It is important that Hawkforte and Akora be seen t⟨
gether. The *ton* will be titillated to be sure but our enemie⟨
will be alarmed. Frightened men do foolish things."

His nearness was dizzying. Quite literally so an⟨
even now, after all she had found with him, that sti⟨

astounded her. Whatever had happened to her plain and simple self? She stared at his mouth, remembering how it felt on hers.

"The bodies will have been found by now," he said. "Whoever was behind the attack on me is likely to panic." He raised a hand, burnished by the sun, honed by steel, and buried it in the silken mass of her hair. "Go back to Hawkforte."

She started. "What?"

"Go back to Hawkforte," he repeated. "You will be safe there. I will come when this is done."

"You want my help. You need it."

He did not deny that but said, "I want you safe more."

"I thought Akora came first."

"So did I." His mouth took hers, hard and urgent, hot and demanding. She met him with equal hunger. They clung together, all else forgotten, through the space of precious moments.

Until the sound of a footfall on the other side of the door pierced passion's cloud and set them reluctantly apart.

It was a servant, Joanna saw with relief when she peered cautiously into the hall before returning to her own room. One of the maids about her chores, not Mulridge thank heaven, who would have fussed, or worse yet, Royce. She knew her brother bided his time, waiting for the present crisis to pass, but when it did—

She pushed the thought aside and dressed hurriedly. Royce was in the family parlor, chatting with Alex who had beat her down.

"The suspected leader of the reactionaries is named Deilos," Alex was saying as she entered. "Of the other faction, the rebels, we know virtually nothing."

"A difficult situation—" Royce began. He broke off when he noticed Joanna.

Both men rose and bid her good morning. Before she could encourage them to continue with their conversation, Royce gestured to a pile of correspondence on the side table.

"Invitations," he said. His tone was shaded with amused impatience. "Vast quantities of invitations. It seems as though everyone in Brighton has decided suddenly to give a party."

Joanna took the chair Alex drew out for her, sat and helped herself to tea, reconciled for the moment to their damnable protectiveness. At least they were talking with each other openly and honestly. That was a step in the right direction.

"Well, why not?" she asked. "There are no fewer than two princes in town, our own and Akora's. Not to mention the elusive Earl of Hawkforte, back, as the Prime Minister put it so charmingly, from the dead. What hostess could resist that combination?"

"You omit mention of yourself," Royce pointed out. "Yet I have it on good account that there is talk of little else in Brighton today than the lovely Lady Joanna Hawkforte." His gaze flicked to Alex, no doubt as he considered the precise content of that gossip. "Oh, yes, and of those three bodies found near the Steine."

"The Steine?" Joanna asked, preferring to concentrate on that rather than dead bodies.

"The fashionable promenade near the Pavilion. The good folk of Brighton used to dry their fishing nets there. Now it's where society shows itself."

"This afternoon in particular, I would imagine," Alex said. He turned to Royce and said very properly, "My lord, I find myself in the mood for a stroll. May your sister have leave to accompany me?"

Joanna looked to her brother who set down his teacup and looked directly back. Slowly, he said, "I am not inclined to object."

She breathed again, discreetly in the hope neither man would notice her relief, and said softly, "That is very good of you, Royce."

"Why don't you come along?" Alex suggested.

"I think I will." He stood, eyeing them both. "We can present ourselves *en famille,* as it were."

With that pointed reference to his expectations for their future, Royce went out into the entry hall, leaving them to follow.

The day was glorious, bright, buffed and just balmy enough to encourage a leisurely pace even down by the water where heavy sea fogs were known to descend, leaving determined strollers so encrusted with salt they could be compared to Dutch herrings. But not on this afternoon, reveling in its last burst of golden radiance before fading into soft evening. The promenade was thick with gentry and those anxious to be mistaken for it.

With Alex on one side and Royce on the other, Joanna tried very hard not to gape but was hard pressed to manage it. There in the space of a few dozen yards were ladies and gentlemen of the *ton* in all their glory, wealthy *cits* down from London and dressed at least as superbly as their titled "betters," Cyprians in their gauzy garb plying their trade, jockeys still in gaudy silks fresh from the racecourse above on the chalky downs, sharp-eyed "gentlemen" looking for a game of chance, strutting members of the Guard at camp just outside Brighton, resplendent in their scarlet uniforms, and all manner of individuals from the very young to the very old who might or might not be engaged in the time-honored activity of picking pockets. It was, she knew in an instant, Brighton at its very best, bold, bawdy and unabashed.

"Stay close," Royce murmured.

She needed no encouragement to do so. They were approaching a spot along the Steine where the crowd thickened. With a swift glance at Alex, her suspicion was confirmed.

"I wonder why they bother," he said. "There's nothing left to see."

Nothing except his own impassivity. The attack on him and the action he himself had been forced to take in dispatching three men from this world appeared to have made no impression on him whatsoever. Joanna was not fooled. She saw the shadows in his eyes and squeezed his hand gently.

So occupied was the crowd staring at nothing that the trio managed to remain unnoticed. They were continuing on their way when a passing gentleman paused to greet them.

Charles, Second Earl of Grey, was much as Joanna remembered from the glimpse she had caught of him at the Carlton House ball. A slender, well-set man with dark hair and a receding hairline, he had somber features alternately rumored to be the result of his political disappointments or lingering grief over the death of his mistress, Georgiana, Duchess of Devonshire, with whom he had created both a great scandal and an illegitimate daughter. As the Duchess had passed on fully five years before while the political disappointments were of an immediate nature, Joanna was inclined to believe the latter weighed him down more. Still, she admired his commitment to parliamentary reform and was pleased to be introduced to him.

"Lady Joanna," he said, "delighted. I can hold my head up now that I have met the woman all Brighton extols."

Despite herself, she blushed. This business of being a social success was still so new that she found it quite unsettling. All the same, she was not about to succumb to it. "The pleasure is mine, Lord Grey. May I say I have followed your efforts with interest?"

"Have you indeed, madam? Are you of a political turn of mind?"

"More a practical one. It seems foolish to expect people to give all their energy and loyalty to a nation in which they have virtually no say."

Her candor delighted Grey who threw off his solemn mien to bestow a startled smile. "Have the venerable old towers of Hawkforte nurtured a radical?"

"It wouldn't be the first time," Royce interjected. "It's good to see you, my lord." Indicating Alex, he asked, "You are acquainted with Lord Boswick, I presume?"

"Certainly. How are you, my lord? And you, too, Royce? There's been a great deal of concern about you, you know."

"So I've heard. Remarkable how rumors fly about. But tell me, what brings you to Brighton? I thought you avoided this place like the plague."

Grey did not deny that but merely shrugged. "A man cannot always choose his circumstance. You are back in England rather quickly after leaving, Lord Boswick. I thought you preferred to spend the summer months on Akora."

"As you say, my lord," Alex replied, "a man cannot always choose where he is to be."

Grey looked at him steadily for a moment. "Poor Brighton, it seems none of us is terribly fond of it. Except you, perhaps, Lady Joanna? How do you find our Prince's seaside Xanadu?"

"Beyond anything I might have expected, my lord. It seems a fantasy come to life."

"The Prince appears to prefer fantasy to reality," Grey said. "Ah, well, do not let me detain you. If you are at the Pavilion this evening, perhaps our paths will cross again."

"Will we be at the Pavilion this evening?" Joanna asked when Grey had gone off. His bluntness in speaking of the Prince Regent surprised her, as did the sense of disapproval he made no effort to conceal.

"I don't see how we can avoid it," Alex said. "Prinny will expect us."

"Not for another magic lantern show, I hope. One of those was quite enough."

Royce looked out to sea where the sun was going down in glory. "The Prince isn't inclined to repeat himself. He'll have something else in store."

On that rather ominous note, they parted, Alex to his Brighton residence, Royce and Joanna to theirs. But before leaving them, Alex took her hands, raised them to his lips, and bestowed a gentle kiss.

"Until later," he said.

Her heart was still beating much too rapidly when he vanished into the crowd.

"A FINE MAN," Mulridge declared. "I thought as much."

"You thought he was a villain," Joanna corrected. "When he wouldn't help me, you said you weren't surprised."

"That was then. He was very brave about being stabbed."

"He is a warrior, trained to fight and win."

Mulridge fluffed out a towel warmed by the fire and handed it past the modesty screen to Joanna. "Not a bad quality in a man."

Emerging wrapped in the towel and patting herself dry, Joanna glanced at the gown Mulridge had laid out for her. It was a lovely thing, a shade of soft green that highlighted her eyes. Under other circumstances, she would have been delighted to wear it. But on this night, an imp of mischief sat on her shoulder. She wanted something...different.

"The white muslin, I think," she said and wondered what to do with her hair.

Thirty minutes later, when she descended the stairs to find Royce waiting for her, she was satisfied her efforts had been worthwhile. Her brother simply stared. They were in the carriage, on the way to the Pavilion, before he said, "Poor Darcourt."

"What?"

"Darcourt, never stood a chance, flushed like a fox from cover."

"Alex *flushed*?"

"He'd know what I mean."

"Well, I most certainly do not. Alex is as far from a flushed fox as it is possible for a man to be."

"No doubt he thought he was. Knows differently now."

Royce was grinning, looking rather pleased with himself, when his loving sister said, "You know, brother, a wise man might pause to think about the implications of what you're suggesting. If an Alex Darcourt can be brought to ground, surely no man may consider himself safe."

She was rewarded with a look of surprise shading into wariness just as the carriage rolled to a stop before the Pavilion. They joined the assembled guests streaming inside.

Standing at the entrance, her hand on her brother's arm, Joanna had just the smallest qualm about her choice of garb. She was vividly aware of the eyes turned upon her but sought only one particular pair. Sought and found before another heartbeat passed.

"Fully half the population in some areas is applying for relief," the Prince Regent was saying. "It's really quite extraordinary. Wherever do they expect the funds to be found?"

Resisting the temptation to point out that the Prince's own excesses—they were standing in one of the foremost of them—might be tempered in service to his struggling people, Alex glanced toward the entrance.

"We are fighting a war, after all," the Prince continued. "I think it only proper to expect people to keep that in mind and . . ."

He went on but Alex did not hear him. All his attention was riveted on the woman who had just entered the room. Joanna. The woman he knew more intimately than he had ever known any other because she touched some vital part of his soul. Moment to moment, he could recall the sight, scent and touch of her, the breathless way she gasped in the throes of love, the deep richness of her laugh. All so piercingly familiar and yet... not Joanna. A vision out of dreams.

He thought for an instant that the gown she wore was Akoran but quickly saw his mistake. It was in the Akoran style, all right, but cleverly blended with the English. She must have guided Mme. Duprès in its creation, this woman who had paid no mind to fashion. What an artful declaration of her affection for Akora and, he rather suspected, for him. Embroidered all over with white glass beads that reflected the light, the deceptively simple tunic shimmered lustrously as she moved. Her hair was swept up in a cascade of curls that tumbled behind her bare shoulders, held in place by white ribbons of silk embroidered with the same beads. She looked like a princess. His princess. His and his alone.

It was a matter of pride that he retained sufficient control to bow to the Prince Regent. Vaguely, he saw that worthy was startled but, following Alex's own gaze, comprehending. Prinny even went so far as to smile and nod his assent. Not that it mattered. No force on earth could possibly have stopped Alex.

He strode across the room. Joanna saw him coming and stepped a little apart from Royce who of the three was the only one not looking dazed. He grinned at Alex and murmured something that sounded oddly like, "Tally ho." It couldn't have been, of course, that wouldn't have made any sense. Not that it mattered. Nothing did except the overwhelming sense of rightness that flowed through him as he took Joanna's hand and raised it to his lips.

That evening, Lady Joanna Hawkforte was escorted into supper by the Marquess of Boswick, who not incidentally, as the assembled guests were eager to remind each other, was also His Highness, the Prince of Akora. It was all well and good, not to mention entirely proper, that his British titles took precedence but it did no harm to remember that he was *royalty*.

Conversation at the Prince's table was both jolly and erudite. Joanna lost all sense of time and was startled when she realized the servants were clearing the last dishes from the table. Having slept so late, she felt far from tired and was delighted, if just a bit wary, when the Prince leaped up, eagerly beckoning them into another of the seemingly endless series of large, lavish rooms that made up the Pavilion.

"Wait until you see," he said with a grin. "Something really special, great fun."

At least it wasn't dark. Royce was standing off to one side, looking well fed and amused. Alex was at her side. The Prince drew them and a privileged dozen or so others toward the far end of the room. Many more guests followed, crowding in as best they could.

After the bizarre spectacle of the previous night, Joanna was only mildly surprised to see that targets had been set up at the opposite end. Was there to be an archery match? She had to hope only those who were more or less sober, the Prince decidedly not among them, would participate.

Her hopes were dashed a moment later when he seized from an impassive footman an object that sent an immediate murmur of shocked surprise through the crowd.

"That's not . . . ," Joanna murmured.

"An air gun," Alex said. He took her arm and moved her behind him. "My guess is it's his latest toy. Unfortunately, it's also potentially lethal."

Joanna had never seen such a thing before but she

had heard of it. A chamber held compressed air which, when released, shot forth pellets or even an entire ball of lead.

"Alex," she whispered urgently, "he's drunk."

"So is almost everyone here, sweetheart. Time for us to go, I think."

Even as he spoke, Royce joined them. Noting that Joanna was behind Alex, he nodded approvingly. "Time to go."

Joanna stifled a groan. It was uncanny how alike they thought.

"Definitely," Alex said. He and Royce began moving toward the door, drawing her along with them. But before they got very far, the Prince suddenly called out, "Darcourt...I hear you're a crack shot. Have a go at this."

Alex murmured an expletive under his breath that further enhanced Joanna's Akoran vocabulary.

"Here, Your Majesty?" he inquired. "How tragic it would be to damage such exquisite surroundings."

"Oh, but you won't," the Prince insisted. "I have absolute confidence in that." Again, he held out the weapon.

"He's arranged this," Royce murmured. "Drunk he may be, but he means to make a point."

Immediately, Joanna grasped what her brother meant. "Who shoots? The Marquess of Boswick, a peer of Great Britain, loyal subject of the King and Prince Regent, or the Prince of Akora, fierce defender of his homeland?"

Alex hesitated. "Is that what this is about?"

"I suspect so. Look, Perceval is right over there."

So he was. The Prime Minister looked especially dour. His eyes darted from the Prince to Alex and back again.

"In that case, Your Majesty," Alex said. He placed Joanna's hand in her brother's, sent Royce a very private male look that was returned in full, and ignored the rather loud sigh she gave. "I would be delighted."

The crowd rippled with excitement. Immediately, wagers were cast. The odds flew fast and furious, clearly favoring Alex but allowing for everything from the lighting to the distance from the target.

Alex stepped up to the line drawn with chalk on the parquet floor. The target was about two hundred feet away, down the length of the lovely room. He shrugged off his finely tailored coat and handed it to a footman. Joanna shot a sharp look at several ladies who had the effrontery to sigh while staring at him. They looked like ravenous bitches. As in dogs, of course, never would she even think the impolite meaning of that term. Perhaps there was something to Royce's fox hunting allusion after all.

"Pulls just a shade to the left," the Prince advised.

Alex nodded, sighted down the barrel of the weapon and fired. At the far end of the room, one of the targets fell over. A footman hurried to right it.

"A direct hit," the Prince declared when the target was brought to him. "Look at that, dead center."

Even as he spoke, Alex accepted another of the weapons from a footman, raised it to his shoulder, and without pause, fired again. A second target fell, pierced through the center.

In rapid succession, all the targets were dispatched. Again and again, he fired, seemingly without even drawing breath in between. Again and again, he struck directly center.

The crowd was beyond itself. Men and women alike cheered wildly. Joanna looked around at the flushed faces and wondered if they understood what they saw. An Akoran prince fired at a British target. An Akoran prince proved his aim was true. Yet they applauded him.

No, not quite all of them. Off to the side, Perceval

remained stone-faced and glum. Nearby, Grey appeared the same, but then he almost always did.

"Magnificent!" the Prince exclaimed. And then, perhaps because he was drunk, he raised his voice and there in the opulent Chinese room on the edge of the sea, inquired, "Know much about cannons, Darcourt? Fascinating things, I hear."

"Cannons," Alex repeated. Joanna thought he did very well concealing his surprise at the extent of the Prince Regent's knowledge. He lowered the last of the air guns and cast a glance around at the assembled crowd. Quietly but clearly, he said, "Unlike this charming toy, cannons are never a game. They have one purpose and one purpose only, to smash the enemy to pieces, to utterly destroy him, to drive him into the ground and under it."

The gentlemen looked somber as the ladies shivered with delicious excitement.

"How terrible," Alex went on, "to have to turn such weapons against those who should be friends and brothers."

"Absolutely," the Prince exclaimed. He nodded so vigorously his head looked in danger of bobbing off. "Damn well put. Enough enemies in this world. Need to know who our friends are." With a quick, rather clumsy gesture, he embraced Alex. "Old Boswick knew what he was doing, making you his heir." The Prince took a step back and beckoned to Joanna, drawing her to them. "Fine old house, Boswick. Goes all the way back to the Conqueror. Of course, there's older still in this land. Did you know," he asked Alex, "the first Lord of Hawkforte fought beside Alfred the Great? Now that's *old*."

"Fought *and* won," Royce said quietly.

The Prince nodded again. He was red and rumpled, drunk as the proverbial lord but still in command of himself. "The Crown has always been able to count on Hawkforte. Never let us down. Not once."

"There was that time with Richard III," Royce said, smiling.

"No need to dwell on that, my boy," the Prince declared. "No need at all. Well, now this is fine, very fine indeed. Two old houses, three good friends. Damn good evening."

And so it was, Joanna thought, not in the least because they escaped before the other guests took their turns with the air guns.

chapter

TWENTY

✳

$\mathcal{A}$ND SO A WEEK PASSED in Xanadu. That was how
Joanna thought of it. She dwelt in the bright, brilliant light of enchantment shadowed by swirling undercurrents of apprehension. Rising shockingly late every
day, she took long, languorous baths scented with oils,
dressed in gowns of astounding beauty and ventured
out in the company of the two most fascinating men
in England, one of whom was recovering from a stab
wound delivered by assailants still unknown, guided by a
hand perhaps still poised to strike.

She also wrote letters to Kassandra. They were not
sent and she had no idea if they ever would be but they
began when one night, having returned to her room as
usual in the wee hours, she found herself sitting pen
in hand at the desk beside the window overlooking the
garden.

"Royce is asleep," she wrote. *"Alex has left. The night
air smells of the sea. I miss the scent of lemons. We never
had a chance to say goodbye and I think that for the best as
I hope we will see each other again soon. I think of you
more and more.*

"What do you see? How much? You said nothing is written but that the Creator loves us all. It is within our power to change the future. How desperately I want to believe you are correct."

And on another night:

"I had the queerest sense this evening, dancing at the Pavilion. I saw us all as though from a great distance, like a traveler from another era, and imagined what people will say of us. Indeed, imagined they are already saying it as though all time exists in a single, sacred moment. Is this what you feel?"

And on yet another:

"Lately, I have begun to think of you and Royce. Did you see his fate? Or should I say possible fate? What do you see for yourself? Does the God who loves us allow you to see even the paths you yourself may walk?

"Come to England. I know you want to and you would be delighted here."

Over a game of euchre one evening, she said to Alex and Royce, "Kassandra should come to England."

"Kassandra?" Royce asked as he dealt the cards.

"Alex's sister, the Princess of Akora."

"I didn't know there was one."

"Oh, yes, most definitely."

"Odd name. I mean really, Kassandra?"

"It suits her," Alex said, and gave his attention to his hand.

The following morning, they rose early to take the waters. "Vile stuff," Joanna exclaimed, observing what flowed from the brass taps in the drinking room off the baths where apparently sincere men and women were downing pints of the liquid. She was a lady, she absolutely would not spit. But how anyone could stomach such stuff, much less think it healthful, was utterly beyond her.

"Try it mixed with milk," Royce advised cheerfully, as he might since he had no inclination to try so much as a mouthful.

"Die first," Joanna murmured and turned away discreetly, grateful for a nearby bucket.

They went to the theater; amusing, Joanna thought, but no match for Akora's. And to the races, which were rather more exciting. They watched the Prince Regent receive the salute of his own regiment, the Tenth Hussars, processing in all their splendor on the parade ground just outside of town. They were invited everywhere and to everything but stole a few private evenings just for themselves. On these occasions, Royce and Alex talked long into the night while seated in the garden, their voices a quiet accompaniment to Joanna's dreaming, curled up in the spacious swing beside the flower beds.

The August evenings lengthened. There was no sign of Alex's attackers though, Joanna knew, he and her brother were constantly on guard. They contrived between them that she never went out without one, the other, or both.

"To the best of my recollection," she said one evening on the way back from the Pavilion, "it was Alex who was attacked, not me, yet he comes and goes as he pleases while I am beginning to remind myself of one of those women one hears of in Araby kept behind, what is it called, *purdah*?"

"Purdah," Royce reflected, "a curtain or wall behind which the women of the household are shielded from the gaze of men."

"All in all," Alex murmured, "not such a bad system."

He laughed at the glare she shot him but grew more

serious a moment later. "Royce and I have men all through Brighton and the surrounding area looking for anyone who might be from Akora. So far there has been no sign."

"Perhaps they gave up," Joanna suggested.

The two men exchanged a look.

"Perhaps," Alex agreed without conviction.

Several more days passed. Parties began earlier and ran later. People failed for the most part to pace themselves, so inevitably Brighton took on the aspect of an overly tired child on a hot day, sticky and prone to irritability. But toward the middle of the month, the town brightened in a sudden burst of energy as it prepared for the great event of the Season, the Prince Regent's birthday.

"Can't think why they make such a fuss," the Prince said, his eyes alight with anticipation. "Still, awfully nice of them."

No one was so *de trop* as to point out that it was hardly as though there was a choice. Besides, Joanna thought that would be churlish. The good folk of Brighton seemed genuinely fond of their Prince. There were times when Joanna was, too, but not as she dragged herself from bed shortly after dawn on the great day.

"About time you were up at a decent hour," Mulridge muttered as she yanked open the louvered shutters designed to admit the sea breeze.

Raising her hands to block the sunlight stabbing her eyes, Joanna groaned. "I should have just stayed up as Royce suggested. Why did the sea battle have to be scheduled so early?"

The older woman shook her head. "To leave time for all the rest of the falderal? Never heard of such nonsense. A grown man carrying on in such a way."

Alex and Royce were in the parlor, fortifying themselves with tea. Joanna knew they had sat up late again the previous night talking but neither looked any the worse for wear save for the concern that lingered in their eyes. Yet for all that, she drank in the sight of them. Alex was . . . magnificent; she refused to shy away from the word. She could not be in his presence, or for that matter even think of him, without feeling the deep chord of need within her. The few stolen kisses they had shared in recent days only heightened her longing for him.

Royce looked his old self, which was itself cause for elation. Though he still slept in the garden, he had shucked off the outward signs of his imprisonment and appeared supremely fit. At the balls and other events they attended, she saw how the ladies flocked to him. One day he would marry, if only for the sake of an heir, although she hoped profoundly that deeper feeling would guide him. He deserved so much more.

That thought surfaced again in her mind an hour or so later as they joined the Prince Regent on the quay across from the Pavilion to watch the naval spectacular. A bevy of lovely ladies was in attendance, not one among them failing to make herself pleasant to Royce. He bore it all with good humor and occasional flashes of real interest in, Joanna noted, the bolder among them. A few drifted in Alex's direction but his obvious attentiveness to her seemed to discourage them. As it had damn well better.

To be fair, some of the ladies also made overtures to Joanna. She understood that their friendship was within her reach but hesitated to attempt it. She had so little experience with ladies of society, and all of that bad, that she really wasn't certain how to acquit herself. Alex seemed to sense that for he said very softly, so that only she could hear, "Some of them remind me of Kassandra. Good-hearted and with considerable wit."

"It's just that I've never known how to manage among them," Joanna admitted. "All my experience is with countrywomen and they are a different sort."

"Are they really or do they just seem so? These women face the same problems: how to get on in life, how to fulfill the expectations of others while finding some measure of happiness for themselves, how to deal with husbands, children, parents, siblings, all the rest. Is that really so different?"

"Good lord," she replied, turning her head to look at him. "You understand us far too well."

His smile never failed to stir her heart. "I have had the advantage of a loving mother and sister. Perhaps they revealed secrets they should not have."

"No," Joanna said, her eyes lingering on him, "I would say they did very well by you."

To her utter delight, he blushed. She laughed, which drew a chiding look from him. He slipped an arm around her waist and squeezed just the smallest bit, enough to remind her of his strength and will. She responded by settling back against his chest with greatest comfort. He laughed in turn and put his other arm around her. They stood in that position of candid intimacy as meaningful nods flew all about.

"Oh, look," the Prince called out, "here they come."

And so they did, a dozen proud frigates deployed to Brighton especially for the event. Half flew the Regent's colors of blue and buff, the others evinced what to the casual eye might appear to be the French tricolor but was in fact a reversed image of it. Joanna's first reaction upon seeing them was astonishment that so many ships of the line could be put to such frivolous use while Britain remained in a state of war against Napoleon. She said as much to Alex.

"Look around," he said, bending close to her ear. "Care to guess how many French agents are here right now? They will report back that the Prince Regent is loved, that the military rejoices in his name, and that a dozen ships of the line could be spared for this frivolity. Of course, their masters may choose to temper such information before it reaches Bonaparte, who will find it tough as old leather to chew."

"So it's all for the sake of appearance?"

"And the Prince's vanity, which is quite real, some-times annoying and occasionally useful."

She was silent for a moment, doing her own chew-ing. "You know, I really appreciate your willingness to explain things to me. There are men—foolish men—who assume women's minds are not equipped to handle such matters."

"Perish the wretches."

She laughed, then jumped suddenly as the cannon on several of the ships fired at once. The mock sea battle was underway, proceeding to its foregone conclusion of British victory. As the tricolored vessels slunk away in ig-nominy, and the crowd along the piers cheered lustily, the Prince waved them all back toward the Pavilion where luncheon was laid out. Scarcely was it finished than they went by carriage to Race Hill, above the town, where they observed a military review. Joanna coughed on the dust raised by hundreds of horses and men, thrilled to the martial music, and generally enjoyed her-self. But she was grateful for the brief respite offered in late afternoon when she returned to the house.

"Falderal," Mulridge declared again, ignoring Bolkum who had been at the free ale offered at the Castle Inn and was in high good humor. She fluffed her skirt, waving Joanna upstairs. "A nice cool bath is waiting for you."

"Thank heaven," Joanna murmured, grinning at Bolkum who winked in reply.

"Roast ox at the Castle tonight," he said. "You and that lad of yours ought to come by."

"Alex? That lad?"

"That's the one. Fine fellow. Reminds me of some one...Oh, well, long ago."

"We're supping with the Prince but I'll keep it in mind."

"Good," he said and added, "And good to see you getting out and about more."

She paused on the stairs. "Was I such a stay-at-home?"

Bolkum shrugged. "Who could blame you? Hawkforte's a rare place."

"I miss it," Joanna said, and realized just then that she had already parted from it in some essential way. The knowledge left her feeling just a little bruised yet at the same time quite thrilled.

Royce returned to escort her to the Pavilion. Alex was already there when they arrived. He greeted them near the porte cochere. Taking Joanna's hand, he said, "Fair warning, I hear the chef has run amok."

She groaned, thinking back to the Carlton House fête and the absurd amounts of food presented there. "I pray the Prince does not intend to keep us at table until dawn."

"He rose too early for that. Come, he has invited a few friends to exclaim over his gifts before we go in to supper."

The Prince was a child and this was Christmas morning, or so it seemed to Joanna when she stepped into the private withdrawing room set aside to display the gifts of those deemed nearest and dearest to His Royal Highness. Royce had chosen well, she saw, for the copy he had arranged of a rare manuscript in Hawkforte's library delighted the Prince. He exclaimed over the exquisite artwork, admired the calligraphy and had a keen eye for the lavishly embossed leather case studded with jewels.

"Magnificent, absolutely magnificent. The original dates from—?"

"The reign of Alfred the Great, Your Highness," Royce replied. "We believe it to be the work of one of the monks trained in the royal scriptorium at Winchester. The book was commissioned by the first Lord of Hawkforte for his wife who had a great love of nature. As you know, sire, Alfred was as devoted to language and literature as you are yourself."

That nice bit of flattery was received with a genuine smile of appreciation. The Prince, for all his failings, truly did possess a good mind. So good, indeed, that he could not help but be aware that his subjects generally held it in little regard.

A short time later, the turn came to open Alex's gift. It was brought forth by a footman who struggled a little under the weight of the long, rectangular package wrapped in a length of amber silk. The Prince's eyes widened as he beheld it.

"Now what could this possibly be?" he mused.

Slowly, as though he deliberately drew out the suspense, the Prince unwound the wrappings to reveal a magnificent box of rare mahogany carved with patterns Joanna recognized as being typical of Akoran art.

With a quick glance at Alex, the Prince carefully opened the box to reveal inside . . .

"Oh, my! This isn't—? Could it be—?"

His hands shaking slightly, he drew out a sword sheathed in beaten gold that gleamed in the glow of the gaslight. The crowd exhaled sharply as even the most plodding among them recognized what they beheld.

It was a sword out of legend that was old when England was young. A sword that might have been drawn before the walls of Troy, ruddied in the blood of ancient warriors whose names resounded down the ages, noble Hector and lofty Achilles, cuckolded Menelaus and feckless Paris, all of them living forever in song and story.

"It could be Greek," the Prince said as he turned the sword in his hands, examining it. "Yet it isn't, is it?" He looked again at Alex, waiting for confirmation of what he dearly hoped.

"It is Akoran," Alex said quietly, and in those words hung a world of meaning, for every man and woman in the room knew that nothing came from Akora, not the meanest plate or jug, not a solitary coin, nothing but rumor, whisper, and legend. Aside from the centuries-old objects believed to be Akoran that were sequestered at Hawkforte, no one had ever possessed the smallest part of the Fortress Kingdom. Until now.

"Our gift to you, Your Highness," Alex said, and inclined his head, one Prince to another. "We are confident that we place it in good hands."

"I do declare," the Prince said when he had gathered himself sufficiently, "this is the best birthday I have ever had."

For a moment, Joanna assumed he was merely being polite. But then she thought of the barren family life of the Prince, the coldness of his relationship with his father who even while sane had never shown him the slightest affection, his utter estrangement from the despised wife he had been forced to wed for dynastic reasons, and his own spiraling into dissolution that had sundered him from Maria Fitzherbert, the one woman he was believed to have truly loved and even illegally married. This birthday, within months of attaining true power when the restrictions on the Regency finally expired, might genuinely be the best he had ever known if only because it presented him at last with a chance to truly do something of significance—guide his nation through tumultuous times. Just then, she had the sudden conviction that the "Prinny" of whom so little was expected might well surprise them all.

But for the moment he was still their extravagant, pleasure-seeking Prince and supper did not fail to meet his exacting expectations. The banquet hall was hung in scarlet silk complementing the rich tones of the Aubusson carpets. Gold-filigreed chandeliers illuminated the richly carved ceiling and the vast table beneath it covered in the finest white damask, set with silver emblazoned with the royal crest and the Prince's favorite Sèvres porcelain.

Barely were they seated than a veritable army of harried waiters appeared bringing course after course. These they placed down the center of the table to be served à la française, the guests passing the dishes among themselves while the waiters darted about with yet more.

Her eyes rapidly glazing, Joanna watched the cavalcade of trout, turbot, lobster, eel, ham, goose, chicken, veal, salmon, pheasant, rabbit, partridge, lark, beef, quail, lamb, pigeon, and on and on and on, each entrée seemingly prepared more elaborately than the last, everything sauced and garnished, minced and molded, accompanied by endless side dishes and followed by a parade of sweets that convinced her if she could not leave the table soon, she was likely to disgrace herself.

At last, it was over. She had eaten only a very small amount of only a few of the dishes but even so felt inclined to waddle. To add to her discomfort, the room was very hot. In moments, her stomach progressed from vague unease to genuine discomfort.

"If you will excuse me," she murmured to Alex, "I believe I will refresh myself just a bit."

The ladies' retiring room was toward the back of the Pavilion, through a series of rooms so crammed with *chinoiserie* as to make her feel some small degree of Royce's disinclination for enclosed spaces. All the same, the relative freshness of the air away from the crowds and the simple act of moving rendered her more at ease. She was glad, nonetheless, to find the room empty except for a drowsing maid who sat, her head slumped on her chest, lost in dreams. That suited Joanna perfectly.

She slipped past the maid quietly, tended to her needs, then took a seat on a brocade chaise longue set before gilded mirrors. On a table in front of her were arrayed all manner of perfumes in bottles of cut glass as well as silver combs and brushes, gold pins, enameled cases of cosmetics and everything else a lady might equire to repair her *toilette*. She knew she could not arry long. Other guests would be affording themselves he same opportunity. But for the moment, it was bliss o be alone.

Her scalp tingled, reminding her of how long her hair had been held upright in the simple coif she had ashioned for herself, secured at the crown of her head with a ribbon and allowed to fall in curls below her houlders. With an impatient tug, she undid the ribbon, dropping it into her lap. Shaking her hair out, she sighed with relief and reached for one of the combs on the table, only to stop at a sudden sound. The creak of a floorboard, the rustle of a skirt . . .

"My lady—"

She turned, surprised, but it was only another maid, a young girl looking weary from the long day and what was likely to be a long night of cleaning up. She bobbed her head shyly. "Are you Lady Joanna Hawkforte?"

"Yes . . ."

"Beg pardon for troubling you, my lady, but there is a gentleman"—her voice dropped a notch—"in the garden. He sent me to ask if you would join him."

Joanna restrained a smile. How like Alex to grow impatient as she dawdled in the retiring room. "The garden, you say?"

"Yes, my lady, there is a door to it just down the corridor."

Standing quickly, Joanna nodded her thanks. Her discomfort was gone and she was eager to see Alex. But then, when was she not? When this was all over, they would have to sort out matters between them. She shied away from thinking too much about that, yet her mind kept returning to it as she hurried down the hallway and through the door to the garden beyond.

The fresh air felt like a balm after the stuffiness of the pavilion. Scents of the sea mingled with those of night-

blooming jasmine and sweet grasses. She looked around
seeing no one, and made her way deeper into the shad
ows cast by the high hedges and the Graeco-Roman stat
ues on their tall pedestals.

"Alex . . ."

A man cleared his throat. She turned toward th
sound only to find herself facing not whom she had ex
pected, but a stranger.

No, not quite a stranger. There was something abou
him. She could not place it but he looked familiar.

"Sir," she began, meaning to ask if it was he who ha
sent the maid for her but before she could do so, h
stepped more fully into the moonlight. Joanna stared a
the young man. He was about her own age and ju
slightly taller. His eyes were large and moved fitfully. H
had a long, thin nose and a whippet-lean body elegantl
clad in breeches and a frock coat. It was the clothing tha
confused her but only briefly. When last she had see
him, he had been dressed very differently.

"Deilos!"

His smile was chilling. "The familiarity of you En
glishwomen is really quite astounding. I would instruc
you in the proper manner of address but the effort woul
be pointless."

His arrogance made no impact on her. She was fa
too occupied with the shock of his presence. "What ar
you doing here?"

"Did you imagine our fine Prince was the only one t
venture out from Akora? I, too, was trained for such mis
sions. I am no stranger to England although I have bee
forbidden to move in such exalted circles as Alexandro
Still, there is something to be said for keeping to th
shadows."

A cold finger of fear lanced down her spine. "It wa
you," Joanna said. "You were behind the attack on Alex

"Our Prince makes a habit of survival. Quite annoyin

really, but not even his damnable luck can last much longer."

"You are insane to think you can behave in such a manner here. When the Prince Regent finds out—"

"That fat fool? He only knows what is put under his nose. He will be led to do exactly as we wish. But enough—"

He moved to grasp her but Joanna evaded him. She had no doubt that he had lured her into the garden for his own purposes, doubtlessly unpleasant. The longer she could keep him talking, the more chance someone would come along who would hear her call for help.

Her resistance appeared to surprise him. "Don't be foolish. I have men nearby. You cannot possibly evade me. Now come along."

"Like a sheep to the slaughter? I think not." She pretended to stumble and bent down, grasping a fistful of the gravel that lined the garden paths. As a weapon, it was poor indeed but at the moment she had no hope of better.

"What happened to the Akoran prohibition against harming women?" she asked mockingly.

His frown deepened. "A *xenos* should know nothing of our customs. Yet another failing of the illustrious Alexandros."

"Who is a hundred times the man you are—no, a thousand. Is that why you wish to harm him? Because you cannot bear to live with the knowledge that it is he and his brother who will shape Akora's future, not you?"

His features distorted with such rage that for a moment, she regretted going so far. But resolve hardened as he came toward her swiftly and more importantly, without caution.

"You will die as will Alexandros," he snarled, "but not quite yet. Not until you are no longer of use."

The threat to Alex made her stomach clench but she

ignored it and faced Deilos bravely. "As you thought to use my brother to provoke a British invasion of Akora."

He stopped in mid-step and stared at her. "You cannot know that."

"Why not? Did you imagine your motives would be so far beyond understanding? You want to use the British to destroy the Atreides but in the process you will destroy Akora."

His mouth twisted. "Only a *xenos* would believe that." Through with talking, he seized hold of her but just as he did, she hurled the handful of gravel at his eyes. The surprise was enough to make Deilos jerk back even as his bellow of outrage alerted his men. Joanna did not linger but picked up her skirts and ran.

Her objective was the Pavilion and the safety of the crowd, not really a great distance but just then seemingly as far away as the moon. She ran not from ordinary ruffians but from superbly trained warriors, including Deilos himself who recovered quickly and led the pursuit. Even so, she was strong and agile thanks to her healthful life at Hawkforte, and the lights of the assembly rooms were so very close. She might have made it were it not for the twisted and gnarled root of an old tree emerging just far enough above the ground to trip her.

She fell hard, the breath knocked from her, but scrambled quickly to her feet. The Pavilion was so close that she could see people through the ballroom windows that stood open to the warm night air. She would only have to yell—

A rough hand slammed down over her mouth. She struggled fiercely but was no match for the strength and agility of the man holding her. It was not Deilos, she saw, for he stood a little aside, already moving back in the shadows. She was dragged along after him.

"If she attempts to escape," Deilos said clearly in Akoran, "kill her."

With that, he disappeared into the darkness, followed swiftly by his men and their still-struggling prisoner.

*

Alex HAD MISSED HER almost the moment she left. Before Joanna could be more than halfway to the retiring room, her absence chafed at him. At night, returning alone to his Brighton residence as propriety and Royce required, he had to resist the urge to turn back and tarry like a hapless swain beneath her window. Waking each morning, his first thought was of seeing her again. Even as he marveled that he could feel such simple, boyish anticipation, he also enjoyed it thoroughly. Despite the pressures of his mission and the still-lingering mystery of the attack on him, the past fortnight had been an interlude of happiness in a life far more characterized by duty.

But not now. Now her absence troubled him. He was all too conscious of each passing moment and of his own tendency to glance repeatedly in the direction she had gone. An unproductive habit as there was no sign of her.

He looked at one of the clocks on a nearby mantelpiece. She had been absent almost half an hour. That was rather long. Perhaps she was ill. The thought provided the excuse he needed to disengage himself from the Prince Regent and stride purposefully back through the rooms of the Pavilion until he neared the ladies' retiring room. He could not, of course, enter it. Nor did he particularly wish to loiter outside. Just as he was debating what to do, a familiar face appeared.

"Why Alex," Lady Lampert said cheerfully, "how nice to see you. How have you been keeping?"

"Tolerably well," he replied, and bowed over her hand. Her ready gaze and unfeigned good humor reminded him that she was a lady of considerable sense. Not for a moment had she taken their affair as anything more than what it was, a pleasant diversion for them both. Now she greeted him, quite correctly, as an old friend.

"Eleanor," he said, "I wonder if I might ask a favor?"

She heard him out with wry amusement. "I must say,

Alex, it's rather nice to see you so attached. Lust is all very well but if I may be frank, love is better."

"Love, Eleanor? You?"

"Oh, I know, I swore it would never happen. But Cupid has a rare sense of humor. I marry at Christmas. He's poor as a church mouse, plain as a post and utterly brilliant. I adore him. Now, as to that young lady of yours, of course I shall see if she requires assistance. Just wait here a moment."

True to her word, Eleanor returned a short while later. "I'm sorry, Alex, there's no sign of her. Perhaps she has already gone back and you simply missed each other in the crush."

He agreed that was likely but when another half hour had passed and he had yet to find Joanna, his opinion changed. Then he returned to the ladies' retiring room with the Prince's majordomo in tow. That worthy called instructions for the ladies to kindly exit that the room might be inspected. They did so, gathering in an avid cluster to watch as speculation flew about.

Alex entered the gilded chamber feeling just a bit foolish. It was still likely there was a simple explanation for Joanna's absence. She might have gone out to sit in the gardens and he simply did not see her when he looked. Or she might be elsewhere in the vast Pavilion.

But wherever she was, her hair ribbon was not. He bent slowly, plucking up the length of ivory silk where it had fallen on the carpet. Unseen, it had been trampled by several feet, leaving it smudged but still completely recognizable.

Where, he wondered even as he wound the silk tightly around his fingers, would Joanna have gone without her hair ribbon?

And how quickly could he find her?

chapter

TWENTY-ONE

✴

HE WOULD TEAR BRIGHTON APART with his bare hands. Before he was done, the damned town, the Pavilion and all the rest of it would be so much scattered dust.

Or at least that was what Alexandros, Prince of Akora, most sincerely wished to do. The Marquess of Boswick, on the other hand, was managing to maintain at least the façade of calm.

"We will find her," the Prince Regent declared. Despite having been considerably in his cups when Joanna's absence was discovered, and having been up all night since, the Prince looked remarkably cool and collected. He who had always longed for command seemed in his element. Startling though that was, it did give Alex some fragment of hope.

"Fully two thousand men from the regiments are searching for her," the Prince continued. "We have the entire area for twenty miles in all directions marked off in a grid and they are going through it systematically. I am receiving reports every thirty minutes. The fog is a problem but it thins inland and the men are dealing with it quite well. If there is any sign of her, if anyone has seen her or indeed anything of the slightest suspicious nature, we will know of it."

"I appreciate Your Highness's efforts—"

"No thanks are necessary. Even were it not for my esteem for you, Lady Joanna and Lord Royce, I would never tolerate the effrontery of someone absconding with a guest from beneath my own roof. I assure you, this offense will be punished most sternly."

"I look forward to that," Alex murmured, but first and foremost, he looked forward to getting Joanna back where she belonged, which was to say in his arms. Meanwhile, the waiting was intolerable. He had gone out with the men initially but returned in the hope of news. With none forthcoming, he hesitated. Royce was with the regiments. Alex knew he could trust him to do everything possible there. But what if she was not within the area they were searching? What if she already had been removed farther from Brighton?

How? The roads to and from Brighton were good enough as such things went but travel along them remained slow. Checkpoints had been put in place within a very short time of Joanna's disappearance. It would have been extremely difficult for anyone to move her out of the area. Which meant whoever was responsible might be holed up in one of the many farmhouses and cottages that dotted the surrounding countryside. With every building down to the last shed and sheep pen being searched, it was only a matter of time before she was found.

Unless... whoever had her had taken another way out of Brighton.

Brighton on the sea.

Also within minutes of the alarm being given, guards had been sent to the quays. No boats were reported missing and it was inconceivable that any would try to sail, not with one of Brighton's infamous fogs descending like a salt-laden cloud over the harbor. Because of that fog, it had seemed sensible to concentrate the search on land. But now with their efforts fruitless so far, Alex was forced to reconsider. The fog had lingered into morning. A ship a short distance offshore could remain concealed, unseen by the most vigilant eye, waiting to raise anchor and slip away as soon as it became safe to do so.

He had been attacked by Akorans, of whom no trace had been found. Perhaps because they remained at sea, not on an Akoran vessel, which would have drawn far too much attention, but on one of the numerous ships of every description that plied the waters around Brighton. It was a wild card, at best, but he could think of nothing else to do and he had to do *something*.

Slowed by the fog, which seemed to creep and twist around every corner, he made his way down to the Steine where he found the fishing boats in dock, among them a sleek little skiff whose owner was standing nearby, eyeing the shrouded sea morosely.

"Not going out today?" Alex inquired though the answer was obvious.

The young man looked at him, took in the elegant evening garb, and spit in the direction of the sea, the gesture making it clear what he thought of the idiocies of the gentry. "Guess not."

During his speedy walk, Alex had considered and rejected every other possibility, including ships of the royal fleet itself that were still at anchor in Brighton harbor. He had no doubt anything he requested would be made available to him, no matter how ill-advised the request might seem, but it was one of the swift, agile fishing boats that he wanted. The smaller of them were built for the capricious winds and currents of the Channel but they were modeled on larger boats that plied the North Sea and the vast cod fisheries off Newfoundland. Even to an Akoran eye, they were masterpieces of engineering and design.

"Keeping her in dock doesn't put coin in your pocket."

"Aye, an' takin' 'er out in a blind fog won't do me any good neither."

"What if you could have it both ways? Make enough money to replace the boat if you had to and still have a hefty profit?"

The man laughed. "An' wha' if the fish jus' jumped onto the deck, wouldn't that be grand?"

"I want to rent her," Alex said. He named a sum that had the fisherman looking at him openmouthed.

"Say again, guv?"

Alex did. After that, everything happened very quickly.

$\mathcal{D}$AMN, DAMN, DAMN!"

Joanna leaned her head back against the wall of the bunk and squeezed her eyes shut against the tears that threatened to fall. She had struggled through the long hours of night to loosen the rope around her wrists but had succeeded only in badly abrading her skin. Even so, she scarcely noticed. No degree of discomfort mattered when compared to the urgency of escape.

The fog was godsent. She had noticed it just beginning as she was brought to the boat by dinghy shortly after being captured, but had scarcely dared to hope it would delay Deilos's plans. Through the seemingly endless night, the one small bright spot had been imagining his mounting frustration as he remained trapped only a short distance outside Brighton's harbor, near enough to be visible as soon as the fog lifted.

Which it was likely to do as the morning aged. She looked around the cabin she had tried, unsuccessfully, to explore in darkness. Besides the bunk where she lay and the single table and chair bolted to the deck, there was nothing to indicate she was on other than an English vessel, one most recently used for fishing if the smell burrowed deep within the planking was any indication. That did not surprise her. Deilos might be many things, chief among them a traitor, but he was no fool. Once free of the fog, he could mingle with all the other fishing vessels plying the waters near Brighton and likely elude detection.

So never mind the pain in her wrists or her weariness or anything else. She had to get free and quickly.

Determined, she angled herself off the bunk and hobbled, as best she could, over to the desk. She had little hope of finding anything useful but opened the three small drawers all the same, twisting her bound hands to do so. Two were empty of all but a scattering of dust but the third held toward the back a . . . rock. A small, purple-veined rock of the sort that would fit easily in a hand or pocket, picked up on a whim from some distant beach and used, perhaps, to hold down papers on this same desk when they were riffled by sea breeze from the nearby porthole. A rock of such unremarkableness as to be forgotten when the previous occupant of the cabin departed.

Or so she imagined all in an instant as she struggled with her disappointment. Of what possible use was a rock against rope? She needed metal, preferably very sharp metal, to cut through her bonds. The only metal in the cabin was the rim and latch of the porthole and the bolts holding down the desk and chair. The latter were of sturdy steel with smoothly rounded edges. Even if she were to be able to loosen them, they would be of no help to her. But the porthole latch . . . that was a different matter. The latch was dull, probably brass without the care of polish, and looked corroded by the salt air.

She hopped over to the porthole, raised her hands far enough to clasp the latch, and tried pulling it loose. Perhaps if she had not been bound, she would have managed it but as it was, she could not get sufficient leverage to snap the metal free. That left the rock. Resolved, she tried hitting it against the latch but that proved difficult because of the awkwardness of her grasp. Despite striking her own fingers numerous times, she persevered and was finally rewarded when one corner of the latch broke off. Quickly, she grasped the whole and tried again to free it. When that failed, she returned to using the rock until her arms ached, her fingers bled, and she feared any moment her efforts would be heard on deck.

Finally, just when she thought she could not possibly continue, the precious strip of metal broke off and fell to the floor. Quickly, she scrambled to recover it, scarcely breathing until she rubbed a fingertip along the broken metal, confirming its sharpness. Elation at her success drove out all thought of discomfort. Still seated on the floor, she began at once to work the broken metal against the rope holding her hands.

The rope was thick, the cutting edge small. The cabin brightened as she worked. Several times, she glanced up to see that the fog was thinning. Soon, perhaps too soon, Deilos would be able to lift anchor and then . . . Rather than think what that would mean, she returned to her struggle. Several minutes later, a single frayed strand of hemp offered hope to which she clung even as her hands weakened and began to shake. Several times, she dropped the metal and had to begin again. While yet the rope held her bound, her tortured fingers became so numb she feared she would not be able to continue. In sheer frustration, she tried to tear the ropes apart but quickly realized she was wasting what little strength she had left. Desperate, her eyes stinging with sweat and tears, she struggled on until at last, even as mid-morning sunshine flooded the cabin, the rope gave way.

"Finally!" She tore the rope from around her ankles and stood, only to almost sink back onto the floor as her legs threatened not to hold her. Oh, no, that would not lo. Any moment, she would hear the creak of the anchor chain...

As she did just then. Despair blackened the edges of her mind. Surely, she could not come so far only to be defeated? With the vessel quickening to life, she hurled herself against the cabin door, praying against all odds that it would open.

ALEX RESTED THE OARS of the skiff. He had shucked his evening jacket and stock while still on the quay and rolled up the sleeves of his shirt. The heavy, wet fog pasted the linen to his chest. Forced to go very slowly to avoid collision, he had steered around the craft at anchor near the piers until finally he reached open water. Now he paused, bobbing on the outgoing tide and listening intently. So completely was sound muffled that he could hear only the slap of wavelets against the sides of the skiff and his own breathing. All the same, he continued, scarcely moving, straining for any murmur or clank, any angle or creak that might signal the presence of another vessel.

Slowly, he became aware of a rising breeze, blowing from the west and at the same time realized the fog was thinning. With the oars secured in their locks, he took up the spyglass he had sent for immediately before departing and began scanning in all directions. Through the swiftly widening rents in the fog, he caught glimpses of the harbor and shore, of boats lying near the quays, and even of a gull perched on a tiny islet that vanished back into the mists as though into a dream. Off in the distance, he thought he saw one of the ships-of-the-line used in the previous day's celebrations, probably standing guard near the harbor while the Prince Regent was in residence.

Except for the reminder of danger cast by the presence

of a warship, the scene looked idyllic. Certainly, there was
no hint that a woman might be in deadly danger. Indeed,
there was nothing to suggest that Joanna was anywhere
nearby.

Perhaps he had made a mistake. Perhaps she had
been taken somewhere inland and his efforts should
have been directed there. Perhaps she had already been
found and he did not know.

Even as the doubts—and wishful hopes—rose within
him, Alex pushed them aside. The discipline of battle, so
long instilled within him, demanded that he focus his attention on the situation at hand. The time for second
guessing, if it came at all, would be later.

Within the harbor, fishing boats were making ready
to put to sea as were several merchant ships. Before they
did, he returned to scanning the vessels still anchored
outside the port. Those waiting to enter would remain at
station until the tide turned. Those intending to move
on now that the fog had lifted would be preparing to
do so.

One was already getting underway, her captain and
crew speedier than the others or perhaps simply more
skilled at judging the moment when it would be safe to
go. A fishing boat, by the look of it, but with no sign of
nets on the deck he quickly surveyed through the glass.
Several men were visible but they had their backs to him
as they raised the sails. There was another, standing half
in the shadow of an open door leading below. He appeared to be giving orders.

"Turn, damn it," Alex muttered, waiting...waiting...

The man turned.

It was the discipline of a warrior that enabled Alex to
set the spyglass down without breaking it. He flung the
oars into the water and pulled back on them hard, the
powerful muscles of his chest and arms straining with
the fury of one thought only: to reach Deilos before he
could harm Joanna.

*

THE DOOR WAS BARRED from the outside. That was the
only explanation Joanna could conceive for why it
would not open. A cabin door would be designed to be
locked from the inside. This one must have been adapted
to assure that anyone in the cabin would not be able to
get out. Deilos had come prepared.

Giving up on the door, she eyed the porthole. The
fishing boat had not been built with such amenities as
light and air in mind. Slender as she was, she had scant
hope of fitting through the narrow opening. That left the
walls, the floor and the ceiling. A wave of exhaustion
washed over her, fruit of the sleepless night and her frantic exertions. Shaking it off as best she could, she ripped
the thin mattress off the bunk, seized one of the wooden
planks beneath it, and stared at the walls.

They were made of planed wooden boards, fitted
snugly together but without any sort of mortar or plaster
to fill the inevitable gaps between them. On journeys
north to the fishing banks off Iceland and Newfoundland,
the chill wind must penetrate cruelly. She took a deep
breath, grasped the plank from the bunk, and rammed
one end of it between two of the boards. It struck with a
satisfying thud but except for knocking a few flecks of
wood loose, had no effect.

What she would give for an axe, a hammer, anything
with which she could smash her way out of her prison and
do it quickly enough to avoid detection. Pounding away
with the plank was not only likely to be futile, it would
also bring attention from her captors she did not want.

Or did she?

Deilos intended to use her as bait to lure Alex to his
death. Of that, Joanna had no doubt. Beside that, no risk
was too great.

Resolved, she took up the plank again but this time
began pounding on the door itself. Pounding and

pounding, blow after blow, the sound ringing in her ear
until at last, blessedly, she heard the thud of feet, angry
and purposeful, coming swiftly down the galleyway.

As swiftly, she jumped back from the door, grasping the plank tightly, all her being gathered for the one
chance she would have . . . the one moment when . . .

A man flung open the door and stepped into the
cabin. Not Deilos, slightly shorter, stocky, cursing in
Akoran . . .

She raised both arms, inhaled deeply, and swung the
wooden plank directly into the back of his head.

THEY WOULD SEE him soon. Preoccupied as they were
with raising the sails, someone on board the fishing vessel
would notice before too long that a skiff was bearing
down on them.

Without breaking the rhythm of the oars, Alex calcu-
lated the swiftly shrinking distance and compared it to
the accuracy of the weapons they were likely to have.
When he entered what he realized was a lethal zone, he
crouched down a little but made no other concession to
the closeness of death.

The sails on the fishing boat were almost fully raised.
In another moment, they would catch the wind. Once
that happened, he could row as frantically as he liked. It
would not matter, he would never catch them.

He had to stop them now.

A shout rang out from the deck. He looked up to see
men pointing toward him, ducked his head just as one
shouldered a gun.

At least they didn't have a cannon.

That grim thought diverted him just long enough to
notice that there was someone else on deck. A slender
figure, crowned in a tumble of honeyed hair, garbed in
silk, incongruous among the Akoran warriors who, seeing her, were momentarily distracted from their target.

Joanna. Her name was a prayer unuttered for he needed all his breath to continue rowing, faster and faster, closing more quickly than the watchers on deck could have believed possible. Violating every dictum of seamanship instilled in him from tenderest boyhood, ignoring even the most basic instinct of self-preservation, he rammed the skiff straight into the bow of the fishing boat.

The clash of the hulls smashing into each other all but drowned out the shocked shouts of the men on deck. Instantly, the skiff began to take on water. For a sickening moment, Alex thought his effort might have been in vain. But then, through the clearing dust and spray, he saw the shattered planks of the fishing boat's hull. It, too, was admitting the sea, albeit more slowly.

The deck of the skiff was level with the sea when Alex leaped. He grasped the anchor hanging off the side of the larger boat, using it to haul himself up. Even as the guards rushed at him, he drew the sword he had tucked into his belt and attacked. He went for the men with guns first, cutting them down before they could fire. The slashing savagery of his assault carried him steadily across the deck, mowing down any and all foolish enough to challenge him. He saw Joanna, knew she had seen him, and was almost close enough to reach out a hand to her when Deilos suddenly appeared behind her.

Seizing Joanna, Deilos coiled an arm around her neck. "Drop the sword!" He squeezed her throat hard, cutting off her air. "Do it or she dies!"

Alex did not hesitate. Even as Joanna's eyes pleaded with him not to obey, he dropped his weapon and stood, arms at his sides, without even the protection of a shield. Deilos smiled cruelly.

"Take him!" he shouted to his men. As they moved to do so, he slowly but steadily tightened his strangling hold on Joanna. "The *xenos* whore is of no further use. I offer her death to the ancient gods of our fathers, to the

all-mighty bull who will soon trample all *xenos* polluters
of Akora into our sacred soil!"

Joanna heard his words as though from a great
distance. The rush of blood in her ears grew steadily, like
a vast wave threatening to sweep her away. Her lungs
burned and the pain in her throat would have wrung a
scream from her had she been able to make any sound at
all. Blackness seeped from the edges of her vision as col-
ored lights danced and whirled before her. She struggled
against the loss of consciousness even as she used the last
of her strength to try to break Deilos's hold, but both efforts were futile.

The deck pitched suddenly. Deilos lost his balance
and with it, his grip on her. She was hurtled backward,
her starved lungs gasping for air in the instant before she
hit the water and sank.

Down and down and down...Beyond light, beyond
hope...She was going to die. Oh, please, oh, no, not
now. Sorry, so sorry, Alex...

ALEX THREW OFF the men who reached him first, seized
Deilos, and fell with him across the sloping deck of the
boat. Brutally, pitilessly, he pounded Deilos's head into
the wooden plankings, unsatisfied even when the traitor's blood flowed over his hands. Only when more of
Deilos's men reached them did he stop. Standing, he
lifted Deilos's bleeding, gasping form and hurtled him
straight at his oncoming men. Only then did he realize
that Joanna was gone. He paused only long enough to
draw breath before leaping into the water, a single cry
breaking from him.

"*Joanna!*"

"*Joanna...*"

Soft the voice, so soft. So familiar, out of dreams.

"*Joanna...*"

A different voice, deeper, strong, so loving.

"Daughter..."

Above her, the voices were above her. She had to reach them. When she did, she would be safe, loved, protected...

She struck out, straining with strength that was not entirely her own, swimming desperately toward the voices, out of darkness, into light.

HE WOULD FIND HER or he would die. Life narrowed down to those two very simple choices. He would dive until his lungs burst if he had to, but he would never leave her alone in a watery grave. Behind and above him, he heard shouts and turned to see the fishing boat listing hard to port as water rushed into her. She was sinking fast. Deilos's men wasted no time abandoning their leader as they sought to save themselves.

He was inhaling deeply, preparing to dive, when a sudden ripple in the waves ahead stopped him. He stared, scarcely daring to hope...to believe...

"Joanna!"

She heard him but lacked the strength even to lift her head. The wind was rising, the waves mounting swiftly in height. As though from a great distance, she realized that a storm was coming, a summer gale surging up the channel swiftly and fiercely, just like the one that had taken her parents fifteen years before.

And roared through her nightmares ever since.

No nightmare this but stark reality, life to be wrested and won or lost forever. Resistance rose in her, fitfully at first but growing swiftly. With it came resolve. At the very least, she would not go easily.

"Alex!"

He came to her over the swell of a wave, swimming readily. His arm around her was blessedly strong, his chest the comfort against which she laid her head.

"Hang on, Joanna," he said fiercely. "Hang on!"

She did so even as the waves mounted and the wi[nd] became a roar. The determination so valiantly nurtur[ed] within her began to ebb. Though her heart cried o[ut] against it, she knew they could not survive this. No o[ne] could. They would, at least, die together.

Or perhaps not. Over Alex's shoulder, as he held h[er] Joanna saw something dark and smooth bobbing again[st] the greyness of the waves. Wood planking flung loo[se] from the sinking ship. She cried out, pointing, a[nd] sobbed with relief when the capricious sea tossed the[m] toward it.

They clung to the wood and to each other as the f[ull] fury of the storm struck. The wind shrieked and t[he] waves surged, but the little scrap of hope bobbed stead[ily] along. Exhausted, Joanna drifted in and out of co[n]sciousness, but Alex remained alert, his great streng[th] preserving them both. He knew they were moving ea[st]ward and caught glimpses of the coast from time to ti[me] when they crested the waves. But he saw no sign of an[y]one else caught in the heart of the storm. Deilos's m[en] had vanished along with their master, swallowed up [by] nature's fury. Time passed but he had no idea how muc[h.] He alternated between simply trying to stay alive and a[g]onizing over how Joanna could manage to do the sam[e.]

Later—an hour, perhaps several hours—he realiz[ed] suddenly that the wind was weakening. The waves, wh[ile] still huge, were smaller than they had been. The planki[ng] took them more readily, and then almost easily.

Slowly, the sea calmed. Gusts of wind still blew b[ut] no longer steadily and with ever-diminishing forc[e.] The great thunderheads had swept on, farther down t[he] Channel, perhaps to blow themselves out finally alo[ng] the eastern tip of France and the Lowlands.

He looked up and saw through the wisps of traili[ng] clouds the brilliance of blue sky.

As swiftly as it had come, the gale was gone.

"Joanna . . ."

She raised her head slowly and gazed into his eyes.

Live. They were alive.

Dazed, bruised, lost in the sea, but alive.

She laughed, the sound filling her, laughed to the sky and beyond, laughed with sheer joy and triumph. Laughed because it was the best way she could think of to say *thank you*.

Finally, she said, "We're alive."

Alex cleared his throat. "Damn if we aren't."

A little while later, safe in Alex's arms, she looked toward the shore and saw what seemed a vision out of dreams.

Rising above the rich green fields and rocky coast, the proud towers of Hawkforte caught the radiant sun and flung it heavenward.

DROWNED RATS," Mulridge said. "That's what you both look like."

Standing in the cobblestone courtyard, just within the ancient walls covered now in a riot of roses, Joanna stared at her old friend. "You were in Brighton."

Mulridge shrugged. "Time to be back here. Come on then but mind how you go or we'll be mopping up after you for days."

They were cosseted with hot baths, warmed towels and dry clothes, with tea and scones eaten before the fire in the library, with hours of sleep from which they woke to a supper of ruby wine, tenderloins of beef and sweet spears of asparagus from the kitchen garden, fare simpler than the Prince's table but delectable especially when fed to each other on fingertips. But first, before any of that, a messenger on horseback raced down the shore road westward to Brighton.

The last vestiges of twilight were fading from the sky

when the messenger returned. Royce rejoiced tha
they were safe. Loving brother, understanding friend, h
would come to Hawkforte ... *in the morning.*

Night wrapped around the proud towers. Joann
took a taper and held it to the fire, set it to a candlewick
Standing, candle in one hand, she held out the other t
Alex. He took it and went with her wordlessly.

They climbed a coiling staircase so old the stone
sloped gently in the centers where generations of fee
had walked up and down them, and came at last to
room that took up the entire uppermost floor of th
tower.

"This," Joanna said quietly as she opened the iron
bound door and stepped beyond, "is the oldest part c
Hawkforte. Legend has it the first Lord of Hawkforte an
his lady shared this chamber. Ever since, it has been oc
cupied only by the present lord after he marries."

"Are there spirits who would mind us being here?
he asked with a smile.

"They would welcome us," she said, and wen
around the room, lighting the candles set in wall sconce
until the room was bathed in their gentle glow.

An immense bed stood at its center, hung with richl
embroidered curtains and covered with furs. Joann
walked toward it, turned, and faced Alex.

"I love you," she said. "I just thought I ought to sa
that and I wanted it to be here, in this place."

"I love you, too," he replied matter-of-factly becaus
it was that way to him now, a simple fact of his life
Having spoken, he walked toward her, only to b
stopped by a very female smile.

"Wait," she said.

He did though he was not quite certain how long h
could manage it. Her smile deepened as she slowly undi
the tie that held together the neckline of the simple gow
she wore. Without taking her gaze from him, she with
drew first one slender arm, then the other. For a momen

she held the gown upright before letting it fall, baring her
breasts, slipping past her slender waist, slowing on the
curve of her hip before tumbling in a pool of silk at her
feet.

She stepped out gracefully and walked to him. He
swallowed with some difficulty, noting that his mouth
had gone very dry. His hands clenched at his sides, he
fought the urge to touch her. One stroke of a single finger down her satiny skin and he would be lost.

"Your turn," she said and began to ease his borrowed
shirt up out of his trousers. It was only gentlemanly to
help her, which meant he had the shirt shucked off in
seconds, tossed who-knew-where. Her hands caught his
as they moved to his trousers. "Let me," she said with
more of that winsome smile.

By candlelight, they explored the enchanted land
that was each other. Enchanted but just a little battered.
Alex frowned over the bruises on the sleek curve of her
thigh and on her throat, she shook her head over the evidence of his own struggles against Deilos and the sea.
Carefully, he lifted her above him, settled her upon him.
She smiled, a little startled at the sensation, but quickly
decided she liked it. Tossing her hair over her shoulders,
she moved, slowly at first, almost languorously, but that
quickly became impossible to sustain. Swiftly, her heart
raced and her blood heated. She moved more swiftly
then, needing him desperately, watching as he watched
her, battling to wait until she reached...

"Alex."

Fiercely, he turned her, drove deep and true, and moments later shuddered as dazzling bliss seized them both.

They slept, exhausted by the day, and woke in the
depths of night to rain pelting down. Alex got out of bed
and pulled the shutters closed, returning to find Joanna
snuggling under the furs. He joined her, drawing her into
the circle of his arms.

They lay like that some little time, without words,

content simply to be together. Until contentment turned
to sweet, hot need and he laid her beneath him, loving her
with hands and mouth, slowly, so slowly, wanting her to
know with every touch how precious she was to him.

"I love you," she said again as he rose above her, her
hands stroking his powerful shoulders and chest, reveling in the strength of him, the power and the gentleness,
the sense that with this man, no storm could ever truly
touch her. "Oh, heavens, how I love you!"

She drew him to her, gasping as he entered her, for
the sheer beauty of their joining struck her to the core.
She had prayed that day for life and she did so again, this
time for new life, that it might be created in this place
that was so dear to her.

They moved as one to a rhythm ancient as time yet
of their own making. And in the moment when he cried
out her name, she felt her prayer was answered.

It was dawn when they woke again. The rain was
over but the air, whispering through the shutters,
smelled of fertile earth and fragrant grass. The familiar
weight of Alex's arm lying over her brought Joanna smiling from sleep. She turned beside him, loving the
rougher texture of his skin against her own, loving him.
How glorious to wake in such a way.

To wake to . . . morning.

Morning. Royce.

Joanna leaped from the bed, dragging the covers with
her, and wrapped in a sheet, sprinted for the door.

Her hand was on the knob when Alex sat up, instinctively reaching for the sword that for once, was not at his
side. "What's wrong?"

"Nothing, nothing at all, only my brother said he
would be here *in the morning*, which it is, if only barely. If
I know him and I do, we can expect him momentarily."

Even Alex blanched just slightly. He rose as quickly
as she had herself, pulled on his trousers and joined her
at the door.

"This is hypocrisy, of course," he said. "Royce knows our feelings for each other."

She nodded, not denying it yet undeterred. Royce was the best of brothers but there were limits to his tolerance even so. "Later," she murmured, kissed him lightly and fled down the tower stairs.

Bathed, dressed and just a little out of breath, Joanna arrived in the great hall just as Royce rode into the courtyard. Alex was already outside to greet him. The two men clasped hands and spoke briefly before entering together.

"Sister," Royce said with fierce gladness and gathered her to him. They clung together for several moments before he stepped back and regarded her closely. "You are unhurt?"

"A few bruises only. Is there any word—"

"Several bodies believed to be Akoran washed in on the morning tide not far from here," Royce said quietly. "There is no sign of Deilos but that is hardly surprising. The currents..."

Joanna nodded. She knew all too well that some of those lost in the swift Channel storms were never recovered.

"Someday," Royce said, "I hope I will have an opportunity to apologize to the Vanax for believing that he was responsible for my captivity."

"I am confident my brother would tell you no apology is necessary," Alex assured him. "But I believe I owe you an apology for being remiss." His gaze was frankly warm as he looked at Joanna. "There is a matter Royce and I need to discuss."

Royce nodded, looking serious yet pleased, as though it were all quite clear to him. It was not to Joanna.

"And what would that be?" she asked.

The two men exchanged a glance. "The marriage settlement," Royce reminded her gently.

"Oh ... oh!" How suddenly her cheeks could heat and

how surprising, all things considered. "Well, as to that, hate to quibble, but I haven't actually received a proposal.

It was very bad of her, as she knew, but still enjoy able. Instantly, her brother's countenance changed. Gon was any hint of relaxed good humor. In its place was a the stern authority of the Lord of Hawkforte.

"You haven't?" he inquired, and looked to Alex.

Who swiftly moved to make amends. There in th ancient hall of Hawkforte, where so many generations o lords and ladies had lived and loved, the proud Prince o Akora knelt, took his beloved's hand in his, and bid he be his wife. There she, heedless of her brother, who a any rate looked on kindly, sank to her knees beside th man she would cherish through all eternity and joyfull pledged her heart.

And in that moment, it was as though the great ha thronged with all those who had gone before and foun in the blessing of love life everlasting.

Much later, Royce walked alone in the gardens of hi ancestral home. The sun was setting, gilding every lea and blade of grass with its last gifts of the day. As h watched night seep over the land, he looked out towar the sea, following the silver trail of the risen moon. I the stillness of the moment, there rose from deep withi him the sense that he stood on the edge of somethin shadowy and undefined, yet momentous. Indeed, s powerful was the sensation that without thought, h raised a hand as though to seize it. The day had bee long and he was tired, and thus perhaps it was that as h stood there with hand outstretched, breathing in the fra grance of stone and sea, he thought, just thought, h caught the scent of lemons...

Drifting on the night air, mingling with the jasmin thyme and oleander to weave the fragrance she ha known all her life here in Akora, home and prison both

How she longed to leave it, how she would miss it when she did. Kassandra sighed and laid her head on folded arms, gazing out beyond the high windows of the palace to the sea turned silver by the risen moon. Moon that cast the ribbon of a road leading . . . where? Into which of all the futures lying just beyond the next breath, the next moment? For once, she could not see it, could only feel. In the feeling, she reached out her hand and for just an instant, touched another's.

about the author

JOSIE LITTON lives in New England where she is happily at work on a new trilogy of historical romances. She is also at home at WWW.JOSIELITTON.COM.

Read on for a preview of

Josie Litton's

KINGDOM OF
MOONLIGHT

✴

AVAILABLE SUMMER 2002
wherever Bantam Books are sold

ROYCE WALKED ALONE in the gardens of his ancestral home. The sun was setting, gilding every leaf and blade of grass with its last gifts of the day. As he watched night seep over the land, he looked out toward the sea, following the silver trail of the risen moon. In the stillness of the moment, there rose from deep within him the sense that he stood on the edge of something shadowy and undefined, yet momentous. Indeed, so powerful was the sensation that without thought, he raised a hand as though to seize it. The day had been long and he was tired, and thus perhaps it was that as he stood there with hand outstretched, breathing in the fragrance of stone and sea, he thought, just thought, he caught the scent of lemons . . .

Drifting on the night air, mingling with the jasmine, thyme, and oleander to weave the fragrance she had known all her life here in Akora, home and prison both. How she longed to leave it, how she would miss it when she did. Kassandra sighed and laid her head on folded arms, gazing out beyond the high windows of the palace to the sea turned *silver by the risen moon. The moon that cast the ribbon of a road leading... where? Into which all the futures lying just beyond the next breath, the next moment? For once, she could not see it, could only feel. In the feeling, she reached out her hand and for just an instant, touched another's.*

London
April 1812

THROUGH THE THIN SOLES of her silk slippers, she felt the thickness of the Persian rugs varying with the smoothness of the polished floors over which she passed as she made her way along the corridor from her bedroom to the stairs. The curving banister was slick and cool beneath her palm. The house smelled of lemon oil, dried roses, the lavender water used to scent the linens, and faintly of vinegar, for all the drains had been cleaned the day before, as they were weekly.

The dove-grey light of morning softened every edge, blurring color that would emerge only in the full glare of day to withdraw again into shadow when night came and the lamps were lit. One night she had been there, one glorious night since setting foot on the quay at Southwark. Her first glimpse of London seen from the great river had exposed the limits of her fantasies, paltry when compared to the stunning reality. So, too, the ride through the crowded streets, brimming with people, smells not entirely or even slightly pleasant, and a din so impressive that the keeners for the dead would fall silent with envy. Never had she imagined such a place for all that she had imagined a great deal, dreaming there in Ilius of the journey she longed to make.

Was making. She was here, glorious here, and the enormity of that had kept her wide-eyed and wakeful as, all around her, the house slept. Until she could bear it no longer, and having dressed herself, an awkward process for all that she had practiced before arriving, came tiptoeing down to pause in the hushed hall and...

...listen. She could hear the city, only faintly, to be sure, for the house was surrounded by generous lawns and gardens, and further sheltered by a high stone wall. But beyond the twittering of birds already darting after worms, the whisper of a breeze in the fragile spring leaves, and the occasional murmur of voices from the distant kitchen, she could just make out the creak of wagon wheels and the clop of hooves ringing on cobblestone streets. Delight jolted her. The sounds were proof that the city really did exist and she was really in it. She did not merely dream, following the silver ribbon of the moon over the sea, as she had on so many nights lingering at the palace windows when she should have been in bed. As she would be now but for the excitement that thrummed within her.

She laughed and turned, the jonquil yellow of her skirt belling out around her, twirling with arms flung wide to embrace the new day in so wondrous a place.

So Royce first saw her. Through the high windows near the front door, the sight shimmering behind the veil of the breeze-wafted muslin curtains. The Lord of Hawkforte stopped and stared.

Kassandra, Princess of Akora, the Fortress Kingdom beyond the Pillars of Hercules, daughter of the royal House of Atreides, bearer of a name out of bloody legend, dancing as though round the maypole in the giddy flush of fairest spring.

He knew her at once. Had he not been aware of her arrival, he would still have guessed her name for there was an air of the exotic in the tumble of ebony curls down her back and the sun-kissed blush of her skin. She bore a faint, highly feminized resemblance to his brother-in-law, understandably enough, as Alex was her own brother. They were both half-British through their father, but just then and despite the fashionable garb she wore, he thought her the embodiment of the mystery that had fascinated him since boyhood.

Akora. For a long time, men had called it a myth yet gone in search of it all the same. Those who returned did so disappointed. Others, perhaps cursed with better luck, were never seen again. Stories abounded: Akora was a fortress island, the dwelling place of fierce warriors who slew any foreigner unfortunate enough to near their shores; it was the last refuge and ultimate glory of the selfsame race that had stormed the walls of fabled Troy; it sheltered wealth and wisdom beyond calculation; it would emerge one day from the realms of legend to challenge the world.

For a shorter time, not even a thousand years, men had known it truly did exist but little else. Sheltered behind impregnable cliffs, guarded by warriors who were indeed among the fiercest on earth, Akora remained inviolate. Or nearly so. In the library at Hawkforte, Royce's ancestral home, was a collection of artifacts believed sent from Akora by a younger son who had stumbled across the place about the time of the First Crusade. It was even said that for some years thereafter contact had been maintained between the Fortress Kingdom and Royce's own ancestors.

Contact that had been renewed the previous year with the marriage of Alexandros, the Prince of Akora who was also Marquess of Boswick, and the Lady Joanna Hawkforte, herself the daughter of a house more ancient than any other in England. The union had thrilled the *ton,* which for months had seemed unable to talk of anything else. Had they known the true circumstances attending the wedding, they would have chattered even more. But only a select few suspected and even they could not be sure.

Such obscurity suited Royce perfectly. He preferred to

work in the shadows. Yet just then he stood revealed in sunlight, a figure of such masculine perfection that, catching sight of him, Kassandra stopped suddenly and stared over her shoulder, half-turned away, half-turning to him, suspended between one and the other.

Hawkforte. She knew him instantly though she had seen him only once. No, not true, seen him only once in person, and then only a glimpse. Elsewhere was another mater. Hawkforte yet not Hawkforte, not remotely as she recalled the man who had survived a captivity the previous year that would have killed most anyone else. He looked...like the sun, she decided, entrancing yet dangerous to gaze at directly. His hair was golden, untainted by powder, and thick, just brushing the collar of his morning coat. His features were not handsome precisely, but compelling, powerful and unrelenting. He was as tall as her brother, which was tall indeed, and he had the same broad sweep of shoulders and torso. He stood with the easy grace of a warrior, likely unaware of the perfect balance of his body. But he was aware in other ways...of her and, she saw just then, of them both caught in that moment.

She was a young, unmarried woman alone in the hall of a house not her own, confronted at an unfashionably early hour by the arrival of a man to whom she had never been introduced. She might reasonably withdraw and summon a servant to deal with him. Indeed, Royce expected her to do exactly that.

She turned fully toward him, regarding him through the muslin curtains. Her skirt still swung slightly with her exuberance. A faint smile touched her mouth. Without hesitation, she walked across the marble floor and opened the door to him.

He was a sensible man, though just then sense seemed to be deserting him. In the back of his mind, he made note not to expect the Princess Kassandra to do the expected.

"Good morning, Your Highness. My apologies fo disturbing you at such an hour. I am Lord Royc Hawkforte, Joanna's brother."

She offered her hand. He bent over it as she said, "Le us not stand on formality, my lord. After all, we are fam ily. Please call me Kassandra."

He straightened and she saw the surprise in his haze eyes. "Oh, dear," she said, "is that too forward? Should not have asked you to call me by my given name? It i just that we do not put so much store in ceremony o Akora."

"No, it's fine," he assured her. "And please call m Royce. For all that I spent several months on Akora—" h discreetly avoided mention of the unpleasant nature o that stay "—I know little of it, but I tend to find formal ity tiresome and am glad to know it is not so much th custom there."

He released her, but reluctantly, and promptl clasped both his hands behind him as though suspectin he might reach out for her again.

A pleasing female awareness stirred within Kas sandra. She knew what that signified, of course, for n young woman growing up in the sensual atmosphere o Akora could possibly not know. Yet she was startled a the same for no such awareness had ever come upon he before. It made her look at the Englishman warily.

Unless she was very much mistaken, the same su prised caution lingered in his eyes. Already they ha something in common.

"What amuses you?" he asked as she smiled.

She laughed, a little flustered, she who had neve been flustered in her life, and shook her head. "Nothing I am just very excited to be here."

"Joanna and Alex were both delighted when wor came that you would be allowed to visit."

"No more delighted than I was myself, I am certain. have dreamed of such a trip for years. My eldest brothe

Atreus, is a wise and good leader but he does tend to be quite protective. At any rate, it is very rare for anyone to leave Akora."

"So I understand. May I ask what persuaded the Vanax Atreus to allow you to come?"

"He has complete trust in Alex and Joanna, of course, and they are expecting their first child. It was only natural that I should wish to be with them at such a time. Besides, conditions seem to be calmer than they were a few months ago."

"They do seem that way," Royce agreed, but doubtfully.

Her eyebrows rose. "You have not come at such an hour with some dire news, have you? Has Napoleon suddenly launched a fleet toward England's shores? Are we about to be invaded? No, wait, I know! It is that fellow, what is his name, Byron? The one who wrote the poem of which everyone is speaking. He has foresworn poetry and vows never to write another line. Is that it?"

Royce shook his head in masculine befuddlement. Her speech was quicksilver, her mind seemingly the same. She challenged him to keep up with her.

"How can you possibly know about Byron? That poem of his was only published a few weeks ago and you have scarcely arrived."

"Ah, but Joanna sent me a copy with the clothes she so kindly arranged. I read it on the voyage here."

"I see, and what did you think of it?"

"He is being hailed as the poet of the age, is he not?"

"I suppose. At any rate, all society is agog. But you have not told me, what is your opinion of the work itself?"

"It is very . . . vivid."

"It is that."

"And romantic. People are saying it is romantic, are they not, and Byron the man as well?"

"People say all sorts of things. What do *you* think of it?"

"I think the poet rather taken with himself, if you must know. But as I am looking forward to going about in society, I shall probably refrain from announcing that to all and sundry."

"A diplomat," Royce said with a grin.

"Do I perceive you are no more enamored of Lord Byron than I?"

"In time, should he ever emerge from his absorption with himself, he might produce something worth reading."

"I shall not wait with bated breath. At any rate, it is good to know I am not alone in my view of him. But come, I am rude to keep you standing in the hall. The servants are awake, I heard them in the kitchens. Perhaps we can beg tea."

"A princess beg?"

"Beseech? Entreat? Courteously request? Is none of that the done thing?" She sighed, anticipating his answer. "I have so much to learn."

"No," Royce murmured, looking at the play of light over the fullness of her mouth. "I rather think you don't." All gallantry, he offered his arm.

They were seated in the morning room overlooking the gardens when Alex found them. Royce stood as his brother-in-law entered. "I hope you will forgive me for coming round so early but I thought we needed to talk."

Dressed casually in trousers and a white cambric shirt left loose at neck and cuffs, Alex looked relaxed and at ease but his eyes were as perceptive as ever. He missed nothing, as Kassandra reminded herself.

"Of course, Royce, you are always welcome. I see you have met Kassandra."

"We introduced ourselves," she said blithely, "no doubt a dreadful breach of protocol but somehow we've survived. How is Joanna?"

"Fine, or so she claims, and I have to admit, she looks it. She is awake. I'm sure she would welcome your company."

That was rather pointed but she supposed it meant Royce's early arrival really did signify something of importance. Much as she would have liked to linger, Kassandra was far too schooled in the ways of men to do other than nod demurely. She stood, smoothing her skirt. "I will take tea with her and we will chatter about all sorts of suitably female matters, nothing too serious or substantial, of course, for that would tax our brains."

Alex put an arm around her shoulders, kissed her cheek lightly, and said, "Behave yourself, scamp." He led her to the door. She stopped, glancing back over her shoulder at Royce, who still stood watching her.

"Very nice to meet you, Lord Hawkforte."

Her effort at propriety made him grin despite himself. But she knew even before the door closed behind her that his amusement was likely to be fleeting. Something was wrong in this England to which she had come. Alex and Royce both might be intent on keeping such knowledge from her, no doubt for the best of male motives, but they would not succeed. She would discover it, and probably sooner rather than later. After all, to do otherwise would betray her purpose in being there. Her own purpose, to be sure, and no one else's, but one she intended to see to completion no matter what the risk or difficulty.

That, too, was of importance.

JOANNA WAS SITTING UP in bed when Kassandra entered. Her sister-in-law did indeed look very fit despite the advanced state of her pregnancy. Her hair, of a shade akin to honey, was in its usual wild disarray but slightly tamed by silk ribbons that matched her lacy bedgown. She was leafing through a silver basket filled with invitations.

"Oh, lord, Lady Melbourne already," Joanna said. She held up the envelope, peering at it warily. "You were barely off the dock yesterday when she sent this round. Whatever it is, you may have no choice but to go."

"Why would I wish not to?" Kassandra asked as she sat down beside the bed.

"Lady Melbourne is known as 'the Spider'. She is said to despise anyone's happiness and to take no greater pleasure than in destroying it. Yet for all that, she is a power to be reckoned with. If you refuse her now, she will pursue you relentlessly. Perhaps better to just go and be done with it."

"Oh, lord..."

"Exactly. Well, how are you today? Did you sleep?"

"Not a wink," Kassandra admitted, her natural good cheer returning. "It is all far too wonderful for that. I met Royce just now."

"Royce? He has called already?" Joanna made to rise but Kassandra stopped her.

"Don't bother, he and Alex want to talk alone. I was sent up here."

"The gall. Never mind, we'll amuse ourselves and find out why he's come later. Ring for Mulridge, will you? Oh, here she is."

The tall, black-garbed woman who entered with a tray gazed down the sharp beak of her nose at Kassandra and nodded. "Princess, you rise early."

"I hope I did not disturb anyone?"

"Not at all. Early rising is a virtue. Here, my lady, I've brought your tea and another cup for the Princess."

Joanna sat up farther and peered at the tray. "You've brought warm scones, as well. Bless you, Mulridge."

Mulridge sniffed and withdrew but not without a pleased look. Having buttered one of the scones, Joanna handed it to Kassandra. "Be kind and do not let me eat alone. I swear, these days I am hungry every hour."

"But that is to the good. In these last weeks, the baby must gain sufficient weight to be strong when she is born."

About to bite into her scone, Joanna looked at her sister-in-law instead. "She?"

Kassandra bought herself a moment as she chewed and swallowed. "Did I say she?"

"Don't toy...oh, no, do. I do not truly want to know...I think."

Another would have been hard-pressed to take her meaning but Kassandra understood perfectly. "Joanna," she said softly, "you know that I do not always see."

"I know, of course I do and I would never ask. It is only that—" Her fingers plucked at the sheet of fine Holland linen fringed with lace. "My mother bore two children safely but she lost her first at birth."

"I did not know that." After a moment, Kassandra added, "Does Alex?"

"No, and I have no thought to tell him. He worries enough as it is."

"But Elena says you are very fit. She assured me of that yesterday."

Alex had summoned the renowned Akoran healer almost as soon as he learned of Joanna's pregnancy. Kassandra had hoped to travel with her but Atreus had withheld his permission, concerned by civil unrest in England. The Vanax had not allowed his sister to depart until it appeared the situation had calmed.

"Elena is wonderful," Joanna said. "I felt terribly guilty about her having to leave Akora but she told me she always wanted to travel and is delighted to be here. So is her niece, Brianna, who accompanied her. Elena also says my pregnancy is completely normal, I am the picture of health and all will be well."

"Yet still Alex worries . . . as do you."

Joanna touched her belly lightly. "The child moves. I feel his"—she looked at Kassandra—"or her strength and eagerness. To come so close to knowing the world yet be snatched away—"

Kassandra covered her sister-in-law's hand with her

own. In truth, she had seen, but only faintly, months before, when Joanna and Alex visited Akora with the news that they were to be blessed with a child. Then she had gone into the temple beneath the palace to pray and meditate. There the pathways of possible futures opened to her vision as they had for her namesake long ago in doomed Troy. She never knew what she would see: good or evil, horror or joy. Often, the experience left her drained and sick. But on that occasion, what she had sought proved gentle yet elusive. She had gleaned only enough to bring the birth gift as yet unpacked.

Now, her hand on Joanna's and both theirs resting near the child, Kassandra needed almost no effort at all. Scarcely had she begun to reach out than she knew, simply and utterly knew. Joanna's fears, though understandable, were misplaced.

"You are not your mother," she said softly. "The tragedy of a first babe lost will not be yours."

Joanna blinked back quick tears of relief. "Thank you, Kassandra, with all my heart, thank you." She laughed a little shakily. "Oh, my, I did not realize how deeply that fear had taken hold of me until you rooted it out."

That which was called her gift, and which as often seemed a curse, did not allow for many such moments of unfettered joy. Kassandra laughed and hugged her sister of the spirit. The two women chatted a little longer, sipping tea and eating scones, before Joanna rose to dress.

"We have given the men long enough," she declared.

Together, they went down to the morning room but Alex and Royce were no longer there. They had gone out to the stables where the women found them in conversation with a short, shaggy-haired fellow whose black brows thick as caterpillars were drawn tightly together.

"Good morning, Bolkum," Joanna said. "Lovely day." She smiled at her husband and her brother. "Going riding?"

Bolkum cleared his throat and glanced away.

"Not at the moment," Alex replied, with a quick glance at his brother-in-law.

"Just having a chat with Bolkum here," Royce said.

"What about?"

She asked with such cheerful innocence, Kassandra thought, that they could hardly refuse to reply. Yet they did try.

"Nothing in particular," Alex said.

"The weather," Royce ventured. "Warmer than expected."

Joanna shrugged. "I'll ask Mulridge. She'll know."

Stroking his beard, Bolkum said, "Best see to...uh... what we were discussing." He nodded to the women and departed, vanishing round a corner of the stable.

Joanna waited, still smiling. Kassandra looked at Royce and found him looking back. Time passed. Off in the distance, stable boys called out to each other.

"For heaven's sake," Alex muttered. "I suppose there's no point trying to keep anything from you, even for your own benefit."

"None at all," Joanna agreed.

"You know," Alex said, "that I have asked you to leave London. You could choose our estate at Boswick, which you have given every indication of enjoying, or, if you prefer, go to Hawkforte. It matters not to me whether our child is born at one or the other so long as you are comfortable and safe."

"And you know," she replied, "that I have said I will do so gladly provided you accompany me."

"Which I cannot do yet, given the situation." Alex turned to his sister. "Now that Kassandra is here, I hoped you would be more inclined to do what anyone with an ounce of sense—" He broke off, visibly fighting for patience. "That is to say, what I'm certain you realize is best for you."

Kassandra pressed her lips together tightly. Having

attained London at last, she was loath to leave it. Yet she had to admit the sight of her brother cast in the role of a harried husband unable to compel his wife's obedience was so diverting that it almost made up for the threat of being sent to rusticate in the countryside. Although she loved Alex dearly and thought him among the best of men, she knew he had once been prey to the typical arrogance of the male, which had led him to believe that women and marriage were vastly simpler than he had since discovered.

His wife went to him and placed a hand gently on his arm. "Our child and I will be safe wherever you are. Now will you tell me what has happened?"